BLACK BIRD

GREG ENSLEN

Third Edition

GYPSY
PUBLICATIONS

Published in 2019, by Gypsy Publications
Troy, OH 45373, U.S.A.
www.GypsyPublications.com

Third Edition

This book was originally published by iUniverse, Inc.
A second printing was produced by Lulu Press.

Enslen, Greg
Black Bird / by Greg Enslen
ISBN 978-1-938768-89-7 (paperback)

Edited by Diana Ceres
Cover Design by Pamela Schwartz
Revised Cover by Nikky Hopkins and Greg Enslen

For more information, please visit the author's
website at www.GregEnslen.com

DEDICATION

The first and second editions of this book were dedicated to several people, so for this new, third edition, I will repeat some of those here and add a couple of new ones.

This book is dedicated to:

My wife Samantha, for supporting my life-long obsession with writing and storytelling. She's always listening to me prattle on—at length—about my various ideas and plots and schemes related to my books and screenplays. She also pushed me to get this book published in 2003, and for that, I thank her.

My beautiful kids: my son **Alexander Bailey**, and my two beautiful daughters, **Annabelle Willow** and **Catherine Cordelia**, who were born since the original version of this book was released in 2003.

My sister, Pam Schwartz, for producing the cover for the second edition and for many of my other books. Thank you—it looks great!

The hilarious cast and crew of WJFK's **"Don and Mike Show,"** out of Washington D.C., who have kept me laughing and entertained for years. They made many long D.C.-area commutes and slow days at work more bearable with their constant funny stories, inventiveness, and amazing impressions. I was saddened when the crew closed shop. UPDATE: Alas, the "Don and Mike Show" is no more, but I'm listening to and enjoying the hilarious Mike O'Meara and Robb Spewak (that's "Robb" with two "b"s!) again! They're back with the "Mike O'Meara Show" podcast and Bonus Show, and they've added a new partner, Oscar Santana. They keep me laughing all day long with great impressions, Robb's "audio vault," and countless kooky stories about their lives. Say "hi" to Charly for me!

Neil Peart, Geddy Lee, and Alex Lifeson, the illustrious members of the timeless band Rush, for producing a masterful collection of albums over the decades of some of the greatest rock and roll ever recorded. Their cerebral material goes a lot deeper than "Tom

Sawyer"—their amazing studio albums and live recordings have inspired, motivated, and captivated me for as long as I can remember.

And most of all, my parents, **Al and Delores Enslen**, for their unflagging support and hours of reading and re-reading drafts of this book. Their suggestions and comments always make my books better, more exciting, and more interesting. Thank you for your invaluable help in getting this bad boy out the door. Again!

— Greg

NOTES ON THE THIRD EDITION

This book was originally published in 2003, but ever since it came out, I've wanted a chance to go back and make a few tweaks to the original. There have always been a few scenes I wanted to change, a few things that I wanted to remove, and a few aspects of the overarching story that I thought could benefit from more attention and more explanation.

In 2010, on the occasion of the publishing of my second book, *The Ghost of Blackwood Lane*, it occurred to me that an updated edition would not be that difficult to produce—in fact, with advances in publishing in the intervening years, it would allow me to release a version of this book that would cost the reader significantly less than the original paperback, which retailed for $26.99. I produced a second edition of this book in 2010.

Now, with this third edition, I've gotten a chance to go back and produce the book I always wanted to. I've had it professionally edited, cleaning up a host of typos and cutting it down from over 191,000 words to just over 150,000. This was accomplished by editing out some extraneous scenes and duplicatory sections, making the story faster and tighter. Over my last three fiction titles, I've developed a more compact writing style, and now I'm applying some of those methodologies to this first book of mine.

I also took the opportunity to excise a number of particularly violent or distasteful parts from the original version that always bothered me. Stuff I wasn't happy with was removed and a few things were added, hopefully making for a better and faster read.

Please enjoy this completely rewritten edition of my first book, *Black Bird*. For those who read the other two editions, I hope this version lives up to them. Fingers crossed, it surpasses them.

BLACK BIRD

PROLOGUE:

BEFORE THE STORM

April 22, 1978

Jack Terrington ran blindly through the dark woods, out of breath and wheezing heavily. The ground was uneven, and he stumbled down a small grassy hill, barely ducking in time to avoid crashing into a low-hanging tree branch. Heavy rain pelted the soggy ground around him, making each step more dangerous than the last.

He could easily hear the labored breathing of the dogs approaching.

Jack reached the base of the small hill and splashed into a shallow, muddy creek. Turning, he ran upstream in the water for fifty yards or so before splashing out of the water and starting up the hill on the opposite bank.

That should stall them, Jack thought.

or at least slow them down a few minutes

Even though it was a tired trick, one overused in bad movies, he knew that it actually had some grounding in the world of non-fiction. Dogs, even trained bloodhounds, can lose the scent trail when it hits water. The water washed away the little particles they detected. That creek, and the rain, might mask the trail he left behind.

He ran, hitting the top of the second hill at a dead sprint, weaving his way down through a thick stand of trees. Above him, a half-dozen birds circled, dark against the swollen clouds.

Jack wanted to look back, to see if the dogs had made it to the creek yet, but he didn't have time. He could only hope he was heading due east, out of town. With the woods and all the twists and turns, he couldn't be sure. Blood from his cut forehead ran into his eyes. He angrily wiped it away with one arm of his green army coat.

The base of the hill led to a large, muddy field. It looked freshly plowed—his boots sloshed in the muck, kicking up mud and water as he ran. The short silver chains that looped beneath each of his boots usually clinked when he moved, but now the boots were silent, caked with mud.

He ran for his life.

Jack had managed to elude the deputies of this little town for several days. He'd avoided capture, but the sheriff here was smart. He'd put together the clues fast, much faster than Jack had thought possible.

And now, the little voice inside Jack's head—the same voice that often gave him ideas and suggestions—was wailing, shrilly screaming. The voice, his constant companion, told him to find a way out of this stupid little town.

Liberty, Virginia, was a quiet town about 50 miles southwest of Washington, D.C., nestled in the rolling foothills east of the Shenandoah Mountains. Highway 132, the main road through town, ran west, curving up into the foothills and mountains before reaching Shenandoah National Park. The road also ran east out of town through intermixed forests and farmland to the I-95, which ran north to Washington, D.C., and south to Richmond and points beyond.

Coming to Liberty had seemed like a good idea at the time. Like many of the other small towns he had visited, Jack had seen the town as just another wide spot in the road. Another town full of potential victims.

This was his ninth small town in less than three years. Usually he came and went like a ghost. In Jack's experience, it usually took these small-town cops at least a week to realize what was happening. But this time things had been different. Jack had never seen anyone catch on so quickly.

This Sheriff Beaumont, he was smart.

And now Jack was running.

He'd spent the last twelve hours holed up in a grimy shed behind an abandoned house on the eastern edge of town. The sheriff had formed several citizens' search parties, calling them posses like it was the wild west. Jack had guessed that Beaumont would assume he would head west, toward the safety of the Shenandoah Mountains and the expansive valley beyond. Guessing this, Jack went east, walking Highway 132 out to I-95 to catch a ride.

Getting a car of his own someday was high on his list of things to do. For now, Jack usually traveled by hitching from one place to the next, catching rides with motorists and truck drivers that frequented the expansive stretches of lonely blacktop. Not only was hitching rides an easy way to travel, but the people he caught rides with were usually just passing through the area. They had very short memories. And if something ever did get reported in the local media, the drivers were long gone.

But the plan to head east hadn't worked, either. Beaumont must have changed his mind, because a day later, as he started east, Jack heard that the search parties had been reassigned to the east, to search the fields and forests that separated the town from the interstate.

And now they searched, backed up by police. They had cars, radios, and snarling, braying dogs. Jack had his brain, his green duffel bag of clothes and some guns, and little else.

Jack rounded some trees, almost slipping again on the wet grass. He found a small clearing dotted with large puddles of rainwater and ducked under the branches of an evergreen tree, dropping his duffel bag and sitting down heavily on a mat of pine needles. He needed to rest, even if it was only for a moment. His head was spinning, and his breath was labored from running, but it was relatively dry under the tree, out of the pouring rain. He could relax.

He needed to think.

He couldn't hear the braying sounds of the dogs any more, and figured he had a scant few minutes to collect his thoughts. He needed to at least try to plan his next move.

Jack leaned back against the tree trunk, its bark moist from the rain. His heart slowed its pounding in his chest. Should he hitch a ride north to D.C.? South to Richmond? Should he maybe double back and try to slip past the search parties? It had been nerve-wracking, crossing the County Line Bridge. He'd sprinted across the bridge that arched over a wide river, hoping against hope that no police cars or other vehicles would suddenly appear from either direction. Should he gamble with another crossing, this time in the opposite direction?

No, he wanted out. Jack wanted nothing more than to leave this town and never return.

Jack relaxed under the tree, happy to be out of the rain for a moment to consider his options. He didn't realize how tired he was, or Jack Terrington would have caught himself nodding off.

———

The bloodhounds had something.

Deputy Jes Brown started to call it in, but then they reached the muddy creek and the deputy knew the scent was lost. He knew that most dogs could smell the minute particles that came off any person's body, and bloodhounds were the best breed in the business at it. But Brown also knew that tracking only worked if those particles fell on a solid surface, like the ground or a street. A moving stream did a very good job of erasing a trail.

Brown cursed under his breath and shook his head. This plan was stupid. He reached around to the back of his sizable belt for his radio and clicked it, still breathing heavy from the chase.

A momentary pause, and then, "Beaumont here."

"Yeah, Chief. Brown here."

"Go ahead."

"We had him there for a while, a fresh trail, but we just hit a creek and the dogs lost the scent." Deputy Brown could see the dogs now, sniffing around on both banks and rutting in the low bushes, dragging their handlers. Men breathed clouds of steam in the cold, wet air. Behind them, a group of twenty other volunteers, recruited for the search, waded across the shallow creek.

Brown didn't have much faith in the volunteers, or the dogs. Or in the sheriff's dumb-ass plan to trap the Killer near the interstate. Of course, Brown kept that to himself. No need to cause any trouble—or jeopardize his career. Brown rarely agreed with his boss—or his boss's methods—but the townspeople seemed to like him, and Jes knew enough about small-town politics to stay quiet.

Beaumont wanted these dogs and the volunteers to make lots of noise, flush the guy out. His ragged voice came back. "Well, keep trying. Cross the creek and have the handlers take the dogs up and down the opposite bank until they pick up the scent again."

Deputy Brown could hear the labored breathing of Sheriff Beaumont over the radio. After taking a bullet, it was amazing the guy was walking around.

"Jes, you got that?"

"Yeah, Chief. Out." Brown replied, shaking his head and wishing for nothing more than pie and coffee. The sheriff was a rank amateur—even the few classes Deputy Brown had taken at the academy down in Richmond had taught him better. But if they did catch the Killer, Brown wanted to be right there to get some of the credit.

Deputy Brown hooked his radio back onto the loop on his belt and stood in the heavy rain for a few moments longer, just watching the dogs rummaging around. Whatever the boss wanted, he would get. Noise, and lots of it.

The memories of the past four weeks washed over him like a comfortable wave.

Jack had chosen the little town of Liberty, Virginia, at random, as he did each town in turn. He'd gotten the approximate location from a map bought at an Exxon station while hitching through northern Pennsylvania three weeks earlier.

When he first arrived in Liberty, it looked like a harmless, modern-day Mayberry. He'd half-expected to see Andy and Barney strolling down the street headed to that diner they always went to.

The town consisted of three dozen thin, crisscrossing streets with rustic, small-town names like Oak and Maple and Dale. There was a small downtown section with quaint businesses and offices clustered around a grassy town square, three or four stoplights, and one McDonald's, the lone sign of modern encroachment. Didn't these people know it was 1978? This place looked like it was still trapped somewhere back in the '50s.

Jack had drifted quietly into town and begun his search. He found what he needed quickly and satisfied his urge. After, he relaxed and waited. You'd think the disappearance of a local resident or two would set off alarm bells all over town. But in Jack's experience, it didn't work that way. The police were used to dealing with petty crimes. When a real case came along, it usually took them days—or weeks—to realize something was happening. Longer still to grasp its importance or start piecing together the clues.

Most of the time, Jack could do as he liked for a week or so. By the time anyone had a clue something was happening, he had already satisfied his urge and moved on to the next small town. And, of course, Jack never made it too easy for them.

He liked what he did. He planned to keep doing it for as long as he could.

But Liberty was different. Within mere hours of the first disappearance, Sheriff Beaumont had immediately begun working to find an explanation. When the missing boy, thirteen, was found dumped behind a tool shed on the south end of town, his throat cut, Beaumont had mobilized his entire police force with one task: question any new people in town.

Jack had given the name "Jasper Fines" to anyone in town that had gotten curious enough to ask him. That lie, like so many others, had come naturally to his lips.

When a second person disappeared a few days later, a thirty-eight-year-old city councilman, a family man and respected member of the local business community, the citizens of Liberty grew vocal. They demanded Beaumont spare no time or expense in hunting for "The Killer." Whoever the murderer was, they had been elevated to the level of legend. When the councilman's body was found a day later, dumped in a shallow drainage ditch near the town's water treatment station, the town had gone crazy. Sheriff Beaumont wrote columns in the paper and made announcements on the radio, promising to end the violence.

Looking back, Jack should have left then.

But Jack wanted to take one more before he left. Maybe it was pride, or something else, but he wanted to prove to himself that he could kill when and where he wanted and not get caught.

Jack had packed up his things and left the hotel he'd stayed in, drifting around town, searching, but no one was out. Beaumont had ordered a dusk-to-dawn curfew, and people were instructed to come out at night only in pairs and only when absolutely necessary.

Two nights later, Jack had staked out the parking lot of a supermarket, tired and hungry. The town was shut down tight, but he'd figured people would need food.

He had no idea it was a setup.

He'd watched for an hour before making his move, choosing a short female as she came out of the supermarket. He concealed himself in the shadows. As she walked by, he grabbed her roughly and pulled her down behind a metallic trash dumpster. One of the trashcan lids slid off and clanged loudly to the pavement. A sudden stench of rotten food and old grease erupted around them. But from the moment he grabbed her, Jack knew something was wrong. Her clothes felt too thick, even in April with rain in the air.

Jack threw her down and straddled her, but she was much stronger than she appeared and bucked him off. As she did, the woman groped into her ratty jacket and pulled out a gun.

Amused, he slapped it from her hand, but by then he could hear footsteps approaching. He punched her hard. Jack felt her nose snap under the blow, and blood gushed down her face.

Jack growled and leapt up from the deep shadows behind the dumpster. Several deputies raced toward him, including the now too-familiar face of Sheriff William T. Beaumont. They were coming from every direction, cutting off all his escape routes except one. Jack ducked around the front of the Food Town supermarket and dashed through the automatic doors, upsetting a woman's cart of groceries as he went in.

Dashing around the checkout counters and surprising several employees and shoppers, he ran around a display of canned peas, knocking them over, and sprinted for the back of the supermarket. Jack knew that most supermarkets had loading doors in the back for deliveries. A few moments later, in the frozen food section, Jack found the doors marked EMPLOYEES ONLY and dove through them.

Beaumont and the others burst into the store, ordering the civilians outside. As the frightened civilians streamed out, the deputies fanned out. Each of them took an aisle, slowly searching, guns drawn.

He had his entire complement of deputies with him, but most were nervous and angry; one of their own had been hurt outside, and now she was with them, refusing Beaumont's orders to go to the hospital and have her broken nose tended to. They each searched their aisles carefully, but each came up empty.

A few short, silent minutes later, they met at the back of the store. Beaumont saw the two heavy metal doors, still swinging slightly. He stopped his deputies with his outstretched arms. He glanced around and motioned to two of them. "You and you," he hissed. "Go outside and around back. Secure any outside doors, and DON'T let him past you. Lethal force is authorized."

The deputies scurried off. Beaumont and others slowly made their way into the storage area of the supermarket, guns drawn. It was a vast, dark area, much darker than the public areas. The entire space seemed crammed to capacity with stacks of large cardboard boxes. A thousand places to hide, a thousand shadows to watch out for.

The deputies fanned out and searched the storeroom, this time even more warily, moving slowly toward the large loading doors in the rear. The doors stood open, and the other two deputies waited on the raised concrete platform outside, their breath steaming in the cold night air.

Their search revealed nothing.

Beaumont was not pleased. He stepped out through the back doors onto the shipping platform, striped with yellow and black paint. This was where delivery drivers backed their trucks up to the rear of the supermarket.

"Are you sure nobody went out past you?" he turned, asking one of the two deputies. The other looked down at the pavement, suddenly finding the concrete and weeds around his boots very interesting.

The deputy Beaumont had addressed swallowed hard. "Very sure, sir. Nobody came out of there."

Beaumont looked around for a moment and then looked past the nervous deputies, seemingly almost through them, and then stepped quickly toward them. One of the deputies flinched and stepped out of the sheriff's way.

Beaumont pointed at the field of grass and scrub behind the grocery. "Maybe he got out before you guys got here. If he did..."

His voice trailed off, as he looked past the field to a group of small houses. The sheriff was completely unaware that he was standing ankle-deep in a good-sized puddle of rainwater.

He turned to his deputies. "Two of you, stay here. The rest of you, come on!" He leapt down from the raised concrete platform and took off at a dead run. The deputies hurried to catch up, chasing their sheriff across the soggy field.

Inside the supermarket, Jack waited another minute before crawling out of the large cardboard box he'd been hiding in. His legs had cramped from the odd position. As he climbed out, he almost fell, catching himself on a stack of boxes. A carton of canned pineapples tipped over and fell loudly to the concrete, spilling its contents. Cans of fruit rolled down the aisle and hit boxes and cartons. He froze in his tracks, but when he didn't hear anyone coming to investigate, he carefully stepped over the scattered cans and moved a few steps to a place where he could see outside.

Two deputies stood just outside the loading doors on the raised platform, guns drawn, one on either side of the doors. They were looking out across the field.

Jack knew the loading doors were his only way out. If he stepped out into the civilian part of the supermarket, he'd be seen.

The sheriff and his other deputies were headed across the field. Maybe he could...

He went back and picked up one of the cans of pineapples and, trying to judge distances in the darkness of the storage area, carefully heaved it across the room. It clattered against something on the far side of the room.

One of the deputies turned his head and peeked inside, listening for a few seconds. After he heard nothing more, he turned back to his partner.

"What do you think that was?"

The other blinked. "Nothing."

Jack gritted his teeth, felt around for another can, and heaved it in the same direction.

The second deputy heard it this time and looked at the first, nodding his head. "Go."

The first deputy cocked his revolver and headed in. Jack watched as the deputy checked each aisle. Jack waited until the deputy passed him, then crept up behind him and hit him in the back of the head with another can. The deputy crumpled to the ground, his gun clattering loudly to the concrete.

"Winslade?" The other deputy glanced inside, trying to see his partner. "What was that?"

Jack grabbed the fallen gun and crouched behind a case of root beer, watching the other deputy approaching.

Beaumont turned sharply as he heard the second POP from behind him, echoing loudly across the soggy field. Deputy Norma Jenkins also heard it.

"What was that?" she asked Beaumont, her face bloodied and her nose rudely plugged with tissue. Her heart pounded in her chest like an animal wanting to get out. At least she'd gotten a good look at Jasper Fines. She hoped it was worth it.

Beaumont's face seemed to flicker, like a TV changing channels. His expression shifted quickly from hopefulness to surprise. And fear.

"Gunshots. Back at the Food Town. Round up the men." Before he even got the last words out, he took off sprinting across the field, but a voice in Norma's head told her that it wouldn't really matter. No matter how fast he ran, it wouldn't be fast enough.

Jack grabbed the second revolver from the hand of the other fallen deputy and dove out the loading doors, rolling off the concrete ramp and running at full speed away from the sheriff and his deputies.

He knew he had only seconds to get to cover. An eighth of a mile, maybe, and he would be in a residential neighborhood next to the supermarket. He could even see lights in several of the windows. Jack had a hunch, or maybe it was some kind of dark killer instinct, that told him that all or most of the Liberty Sheriff's Department was in this field right now with him. If he could make it away, he would be free.

As he sprinted for the market, Beaumont saw a darkened figure bolt out of the loading doors. Even at this distance, Beaumont knew it had to be him.

"Stop!" Beaumont shouted, but the figure ignored him.

Beaumont leveled both guns and fired four times, twice per sidearm. Even though he was running at top speed, he saw the shots bring up sprays of water and mud on either side of the fleeing figure.

The suspect stopped in his tracks and turned in Beaumont's direction. Beaumont clearly saw glints of light off the twin barrels of the revolvers in the Killer's hands. Beaumont suddenly knew that both of his deputies were down.

The Killer raised the guns and pointed, firing four quick shots, twice from each gun like a gunslinger in an old western, alternating just as Beaumont had. The first three went wide and useless, but the fourth struck Beaumont squarely in one uniformed leg just above the knee, taking him down.

As he fell to the mud, agony coursing through his leg, Beaumont saw a smile dawn on the Killer's face before turning to run away, disappearing into the dark.

———————

That had been a week ago, a long week of desperate hiding, of sweat-soaked, shivering nights holed up in drafty barns. Chased by Beaumont and his deputies and their mangy, stupid dogs.

Dogs. Braying, howling.

Jack sat upright, dazed for a moment.

How could he doze off in the middle of running? There he was, lying on the wet ground, just waiting for them to come and find him. Cursing, he jumped up, grabbed his green duffel bag and raced out of the clearing, heading east toward the highway.

stupid stupid stupid

The dogs were not close yet, not as close as he'd initially thought. The dogs were making a lot of noise, almost too much. He wondered as he ran why their handlers weren't keeping them quiet. If they hadn't been so loud, they would have caught him in that clearing.

Jack smiled as he ran. That made sense. And that meant that up ahead, probably where the interstate and Highway 132 met up, Sheriff Beaumont was waiting for him.

Jack just had to keep his cool, keep his head about him, keep on thinking straight and not get stupid. He knew the interstate could take him anywhere. If he could get past Beaumont and his men, Jack could catch a ride out of this godforsaken place.

Liberty.

The name of this stupid little town was seared into his memory. He wondered if he would ever forget this place.

Jack rounded another thick group of trees and saw the ground sloping up sharply, rain running down it in a hundred rivulets. He climbed the embankment, hearing a car pass by, the sound loud and hollow and dead in the rainy night. He could hear the tires splashing water.

He waited until the car was gone and climbed to the top. It had to be the interstate—the road was a six-lane, three lanes in each direction, stretching off both ways into the gloomy darkness, separated by a patch of grass and gravel.

He looked up and saw no vehicles in either direction.

Jack dared not stop a car—it was far too easy to mistake a police car for a regular one. Besides, he was looking for a truck. Truckers were less likely to be concerned about the local authorities and their problems. Like Jack, they were just passing through.

Never looking back.

Hitching his green bag higher on his shoulder, Jack jogged across the wet pavement.

He was about ten steps out onto the road when red and blue lights splashed the trees around him. To his left, a police car rounded the curve about a mile to the north, racing toward him.

It was coming very fast.

Jack hesitated for a moment that felt like an eternity. He was exposed. Jump back over the steep embankment he had just climbed and roll to the bottom? Or try to make it to the other side?

He ran, sprinting across the wet road, his boots slapping at the rainy surface as the car sped closer. They sounded so loud, the chains jingling crazily. He felt twenty feet tall in the approaching headlights.

Jack had just reached the grassy median and started across it when his foot caught on something in the median, sending him sprawling. His bag went flying. Jack landed with a hard THUD on the muddy grass of the median, the wind knocked from him. He lay gasping for air, the rain spattering to the ground around him.

Jack thought about getting up to run.

stay down

He lifted his head and saw the police car racing toward him. He stayed down, glued to the ground, willing the deputies to ignore the dark shape he made on the median. He was just a tire, or a dead animal. He was nothing.

The car came closer. Jack buried his face in the mud, ignoring the disgusting squishing sound, and laid as flat as he could.

The police car, its lights flashing and spinning lazily, raced past him, but did not stop. He couldn't see it, but he heard its passage. When it was gone, he looked up, seeing the twin red taillights, like two red eyes, as they disappeared into the distance.

Lucky. Again.

He would've never made it all the way across the road without being spotted. A lucky fall, sending him to the ground. Just like his lucky realization that he was being driven instead of chased.

Jack stood and wiped mud and water from his face and clothes. He retrieved his duffel bag, hearing the guns clatter inside. He headed across the northbound lanes of traffic, reaching the far side of the road without any more problems.

Scrambling down the opposite embankment and back into the woods, he turned south. His mind was made up now—he should head north and get away from this trouble, but he had to end it all, here, tonight. The sheriff needed to pay, or he would hound him forever, sending out APBs and manhunts and announcing Jack's presence to the world. And Jack wanted to stay unknown for a long, long time.

Jack skirted the tree line that edged the highway, working his way south, following the patrol car. Chances were good it was headed for a roadblock of some sort.

Hopefully the sheriff would be there, waiting for him.

———————

Sheriff Beaumont sat in the back seat of his cruiser, thinking and playing a flashlight over the map of Liberty and the surrounding area that was spread out across his lap. His mind was a million miles away. Actually, only twenty miles away—he was thinking about his young wife and the little child in her belly. His wife Grace was so beautiful, basking in her pregnant glow. Beaumont's joy at the baby's impending arrival was rivaled only by his pride in his wife—the pregnancy had been an unexpected, and long overdue, surprise.

Grace Beaumont was not supposed to be able to have children.

Her doctors were not so overjoyed. Grace was not as strong as they wanted, and the delivery, sometime in mid-September, would be difficult for her.

He'd resisted going to the dance/mixer where he and Grace had met, but now he wondered what would have happened if he'd never gone? Grace had accepted his awkward request to dance, and, barely a year later, they were married. She'd taken some convincing—she hated his job and hated the idea of being a policeman's wife. But now, five years later, they were expecting a child. It was amazing how a baby can change one's opinions about life.

When the doctors had informed them only a couple of days ago that they would be having a boy, he and Grace decided on the name of David Jonathan, a tribute to ancestors on both sides of their families.

Beaumont had seen the nervousness in her eyes, though, when they settled on a name. She knew of the dangers of her pregnancy—the doctors with their cautionary words about how her anatomy would make a natural birth extremely painful and dangerous. Somehow, giving the baby boy a name had made the fear clearer, more defined, yet easier to manage.

But even knowing that he would be a father soon couldn't help him shake the notion that it a very bad idea to be having a baby, especially now. What if he couldn't stop the Killer? Was it right to bring his son into a world populated with such sick people?

Of course, he hadn't told Grace any of this. She was very happy about the baby.

Whoever he was, this guy was crafty, resourceful, smart—three dangerous attributes in any criminal. And the guy was a sicko. Beaumont had been there. He'd seen the dead little boy, his arms sprawled out like he was trying to hug the ground, trying to find someone in that dark field to help him. Beaumont saw what this "Jasper Fines" character had done to that little boy, things that were beyond words. One of the boy's toes had been missing.

And last night, Beaumont had a horrible dream—Beaumont had been wandering through the same dark field. He found the body of a little boy, but this time, in the dream, Beaumont reached down and turned the body over and it was the face of his son. The eyes were glazed over and dead, but as Beaumont watched with growing horror, his dead son's hand drifted up from the soggy ground and pointed a dirty finger at him.

His unborn son was blaming him for everything that had gone wrong in Liberty.

Beaumont had been pushing himself too hard for weeks and was running out of energy. He was tired, and last night's dream hadn't helped. His leg hurt like hell, but Beaumont knew this whole thing had to end tonight. One way or another. He knew that he could chase this monster out of his town, if luck and careful planning were on Beaumont's side.

Beaumont looked back down at his map, tearing his thoughts away from his family.

I-95 ran north to D.C. and south to Richmond, and he had roadblocks set up ten miles apart, five miles north and south of the junction with Highway 132. If Beaumont knew anything about criminals, he knew that he would probably try to hitch a ride, and then they could catch the guy.

"The guy," he said out loud. They didn't even know this joker's name, for Christ's sake! He, the "Killer," had given his name as "Jasper Fines," but that had been an alias. A quick call to the state police confirmed that. Most sheriff's offices didn't rely on the state police for much help, but Beaumont had found them indispensable on many occasions.

Two of his citizens, butchered. Two of his deputies in the hospital, one with a fractured skull, the other shot twice and very lucky to be alive. And Beaumont himself, laid up in the back seat of his cruiser. The bullet had gone straight through, and now his leg was encased in a pale gray cast that felt as heavy as a tree trunk.

And not even a real name to hang it all on!

Deputy Jenkins had given a description of the guy to their sketch artist, but that was all they had. Copies of the sketch now adorned every signpost and telephone pole in Liberty. So far it had turned up nothing.

If this guy doubled back to the west or kept heading east when he reached the road instead of hitching north or south, they'd never catch him...

No, that wasn't the way to think. Even if Beaumont lost him, at least the monster would be gone, and this town could go back to being normal. Bake sales, teenage pregnancies, and the occasional theft. Nothing he and his men couldn't handle.

This plan, to drive him out of the woods and into the roadblocks, it had to work. Then they would catch him and arrest him, and Beaumont could drive home, take his wife into his arms, and gingerly rest his hand on her growing stomach.

Deputy Jenkins leaned her head into his car, the white bandage across her broken nose looking large in the pale moonlight. The rain had slowed, and it looked like the clouds were starting to break up. A thin glow of moonlight reflected off the puddles on the pavement.

"Deputy Brown's calling in again, sir." Her voice was odd, clipped. The tone reminded Beaumont of someone with a really bad head cold.

"Good." He nodded and awkwardly folded the map before painfully adjusting his leg to reach over the front seat and grab the radio handset. "Deputy Brown? What have you got for me, son?" His voice sounded hopeful, almost upbeat.

A voice crackled back over the receiver, tinny and distant. "Nothing here yet, sir. We crossed the creek and picked up another trail, but it turned out to be nothing. We're back at the creek, trying again."

Beaumont thought for a moment. "Forget the creek. Fan your men out in a north-south line and head in this direction. That'll drive him to us."

"Roger that, sir." Brown replied. "Whatever you say. You all set up?"

Beaumont smiled. He knew that Deputy Brown didn't like this plan very much, but Brown would just have to deal with it. "Yeah, half the cars are here, and the rest at the other roadblock. We're checking all the cars and trucks. If he thumbs a ride, we'll get him." He didn't like justifying himself or his plan to anybody, but Jes Brown was a good deputy, even if he was headstrong and cocky. A few more years of close supervision and the big man might turn out to be a decent cop.

Beaumont signed off and painfully climbed out of the back of his cruiser, trying not to bang the gray cast into anything. He was taking a gamble, having his entire force here at the roadblock or beating the bushes with dogs. It was a Saturday night, but Liberty was on its own— he hoped the curfew would keep people home. He crossed his fingers no one decided to knock over a convenience store tonight.

He hobbled awkwardly up behind Jenkins and the other deputies. She was studying another map laid out on the hood of a patrol car, and the others were just finishing checking a southbound van.

Here, the six lanes, three northbound and three southbound, were separated by a flat, grassy median. Beaumont saw several dark birds he couldn't identify in the darkness, rutting around in the short grass. They looked like crows or ravens. Funny how you never see birds at night— he guessed they were almost invisible against a night sky.

Other than their winged visitors, it had been a quiet night.

"Are we set up?" The others turned around and assumed a more respectful stance.

"Yes, sir," Deputy Jenkins answered in her nasally voice. "Hollins, Jordan, and two cars are set up here, about ten miles north," she said, indicating the positions on the map. "And we're here. A little spread out to cover all the bases. We don't have as many men as I would like," she said. Jenkins seemed lost in her own thoughts for a moment as she looked around at the other deputies, but when she glanced up and saw the look on Beaumont's face, she added a clipped, "Sir."

Beaumont chuckled softly and rubbed his face with one hand. "It's okay, Jenkins. I know we're short-handed, but it's a small department. And we have those three staties joining us Monday."

"We need them. We don't have enough—"

Beaumont nodded. "I know how much you want this guy. Believe me, so do the rest of us." He thought for a moment. "How many do we have here?"

"Five, sir. Including you and me."

Beaumont nodded. "Good." He looked around for a moment and then continued. "He should be here within the next hour, if he shows at all."

———

Jack was working his way through the trees by the side of the road when he spotted the lights. They spun lazily atop three cruisers, splashing the night and the trees with their bright lights. The cars were positioned to form a roadblock on the southern side, and the three northbound lanes were marked with roadside flares, hissing and spitting their sparks onto the asphalt

As he watched, Jack saw a southbound van stopped and searched thoroughly by several of Beaumont's deputies. He was suddenly glad he hadn't tried to steal a car.

As he watched from the trees, Jack saw Sheriff Beaumont climb out of the last car. The sheriff, one leg in a cast, hobbled over to the group of deputies.

Good, Jack thought. He smiled as he worked his way closer,

concealing himself behind the stands of trees and bushes until he was directly opposite the squad cars.

Sheriff Beaumont turned and started to hobble slowly back to his car. Deputy Jenkins called after him and came up behind him.

"Brown is on the horn, sir."

"Again? Thanks." He turned and grimaced, reaching inside his squad car to pull out the handset. He held it up to his mouth and thumbed the talk button.

"Beaumont here."

Jack was almost even with Beaumont's car. He was forty or fifty feet from the sheriff. Jack slowly crouched, one of his knees popping, and set his green duffel bag on the ground, rummaging blindly inside, feeling. He pulled both revolvers out, one in each hand, and flipped them both open to make sure they were fully loaded, trying to be quiet. He emptied more shells out of a box in the bag and pocketed them, just in case.

Even in the darkness he could see the scar on his left palm, and for a moment, he wondered why he was doing this. He remembered the day he'd gotten that scar. It had all starting with that bike ride.

The scar had started it all. The voice, the urge...

Jack pushed the thoughts from his mind, shouldered his green duffel bag, and stood, waiting for the right moment.

"Brown here, sir. We've found his trail. He's heading northeast, straight for the highway. Unless I miss my guess, he should be coming out onto the road about a half mile north of you."

Beaumont smiled—he could hear the disbelief in Deputy Brown's voice. The plan had worked. Fines was all but captured.

"Good work, son," Beaumont replied, nodding. "When he hits the road, he'll have to go one way or the other, and then we'll get him." His mind was already planning what to do next: Beaumont should probably call the men at the other roadblock and tell them what was happening, and then he should have dispatch contact his wife to let her know that he was okay...

There was a long silence. Beaumont began to think that Brown had shut off his radio without signing off, maybe not hearing the sheriff's last comment. But after a second, Brown replied with a small laugh.

"Well, I hope so, sir."

Jes Brown's chuckle came over the radio, as clear as if the big deputy were standing right there on the wet pavement next to Beaumont. The sound made the hairs on the back of Beaumont's neck stand up.

Deputy Brown continued. "I'm getting real tired of tellin' all the boys and their dogs to make so much noise. It was starting to give me a headache."

Beaumont's stomach tightened. "What?"

"Well," Brown continued, "we've been making a whole lot of noise here...a lot more than we need to. The dogs have really been whooping it up. We're supposed to be driving him to you, right?"

The handset suddenly felt heavy in Beaumont's hand. He grimaced as the realization struck him like a bolt of lightning from a cloudless sky.

"You can't do that," Beaumont said frantically. "He'll know what you're doing! He'll figure out you're driving him, and he'll—"

The first shot caught Beaumont squarely in the chest. It jerked him around rudely and knocked him down behind the open door of his squad car.

The other officers spun at the sudden sound and futilely reached for their sidearms, but Jack quickly dropped three of them as he strode up the hill to the roadway. Surprise, utter surprise, was his ally. He marched up the hill, guns firing, taking out the other two before pausing. The man crossed the northbound lanes, his green bag slung over his shoulder, forgotten. He looked just like the hero from one of those old westerns, except this hero was dressed in a dusty green army jacket, his boots clinking in the night.

This hero looked like a demon.

The deputies fell behind their cars or down the opposite embankment. Some of them tried to return fire, but Jack, buoyed by his good luck, seemed unstoppable. After a few short seconds of gunfire, a deep silence descended, cloaking the dark road, broken only by Jack's solid, echoing footsteps.

Wounded officers lay on the ground, groaning weakly.

Jack slowly walked over to them each in turn and kicked their guns away while reloading his own. One deputy was the dark-haired woman with the large white bandage covering her nose. She was curled up, grasping her bleeding leg.

Jack pointed his gun in her face.

Her eyes went wide, her voice trapped in her throat. He smiled, recognizing her from the supermarket alley, and he held the gun in her

face for a long, agonizing moment before he suddenly shouted, "BANG!"
She jumped.

Jack smiled and walked away, forgetting her. He crossed to Beaumont,
the chains on his boots jingling merrily, and stood over him. Where was
his bulletproof vest? Any fool should know to wear one of those new-
fangled things.

not so tough now

Beaumont groaned weakly and moved one arm, tentatively, toward
the gaping red hole in his chest. Jack, surprised, stepped back and raised
his gun, but it was clear that the sheriff wasn't a threat to anyone any
more.

"Having a bad day, Sheriff?" Jack smiled, the expression reflected in
the tone in his voice. "You should have left me alone."

Something shiny on the front of Beaumont's bloodied uniform caught
Jack's eye. He stooped casually over the fallen sheriff and picked it off,
wiping it clean on Beaumont's shirt. Standing straight, Jack held it up to
the sparse light to regard it more carefully.

The sheriff's five-pointed star read LIBERTY SHERIFF'S
DEPARTMENT. Jack pinned it to his own dusty coat and smiled. The
badge looked good, as if it had always belonged there.

Beaumont opened one eye, locking on the fuzzy image of a man
standing over him, a man wearing his sheriff's badge. It was him, the
Killer, the man from the sketch. Some part of his mind noticed that the
sketch hadn't gotten the man's eyes right—they were wilder. Crazier.

Beaumont's clouded, fading mind was racing, thinking about his
family and trying to answer distress calls screaming from everywhere in
his ruined body. Beaumont knew he couldn't help his family, couldn't
help his little boy. The thoughts raced through his mind, the regret and
the anger. Everything hurt so much.

"Goodnight, sheriff."

For a moment, Beaumont's mind swam in and out of focus. Behind
the Killer, Beaumont saw a huge black bird standing on the roof
of Beaumont's squad car. Through the deafening static of pain and
emotion, he tried to ignore the man standing over him, pointing the gun.
Beaumont shut him out, concentrating on the black bird. Beaumont
stared at its small, sharp eyes. The bird stared back. Beaumont shivered,
feeling an odd connection to something so free—

The gunshot echoed loudly, coldly in the still night.

Deputy Jenkins lay motionless, until she heard the Killer climb into the sheriff's patrol car, start it up, and drive away. Jenkins was hit in the leg and had gone down in the first volley of shots. She saw Beaumont fall, toppling over like a clothing store mannequin.

She'd done nothing, even as the Killer walked over and pretended to shoot her. And she did nothing as the Killer walked over and shot Sheriff Beaumont directly in the face.

Something moved in her stomach, an angry roiling of acids. It felt like a coiled serpent, newly born. A restless entity created by guilt and pain and anger.

Norma Jenkins crawled painfully over to Beaumont, lying by himself in the middle of the road, his car gone.

He lay motionless, face up, his eyes wide and blank and pointless. She saw a quickly spreading pool of what looked like rain surrounding his head. It was too dark to be water.

She tried to lift his head with her hands, praying for some sign of life in his vacant eyes, but she suddenly realized that not all of his head was there. She knew he was dead, just as surely as she knew that her name was Norma Jenkins. It was at that moment that she realized how much she admired him, respected him, almost like a father.

The newly-born snake twisted again in her gut.

She glanced up at the highway. The retreating taillights of the patrol car pierced the night, casting gloom like a pair of red eyes. Eyes of a demon, reflected in the damp surface of the road, mocking her and her useless anguish.

On the median, the small clutch of birds, including the large black bird, turned and flapped into the night sky. They seemed to follow the demon eyes into the darkness. And Deputy Norma Jenkins, sitting in the middle of a dark, rainy highway, cradling the head of her fallen hero, began to cry.

Jack Terrington's murderous trek had begun five years earlier, soon after he dropped out of high school in 1973. He had never been a good student, and thoughts of finishing high school or attending college seemed irrelevant to him. He'd remained in Maine for over a year after dropping out, working as an auto mechanic. But soon he decided to leave for good—the memories were just too painful for him to stay.

He had no family, no real friends, no reason to stay, and the scar reminded him every day that it was all his fault.

Jack left his hometown and drifted around Maine, working odd jobs and killing and moving on. Eventually he left Maine and, over the years, traced a rough circle around the Continental United States.

In those early years, he traveled slowly south, mostly by hitchhiking or, on rare occasions, by hotwiring a car. He had discovered his rare talent at a young age and had indulged it, and that meant he had to stay mobile.

As he traveled, he killed when he could, savoring the hunt. Satisfying the urge.

But after the incident in Liberty, Jack felt a sudden and undeniable urge to move west. He felt the urge to kill more often, as if the narrow escape in Liberty had awakened something even more terrible inside him. The voice in his head became more insistent, more commanding, and came with more frequency.

As the eighties approached, he drifted through most of the Midwestern states, killing as he went. He—and death—visited Knoxville, Cleveland, Chicago, St. Louis, and a host of smaller towns in between. He moved on whenever the heat grew, or people started asking too many questions.

He became very good at covering his tracks. Jack purchased a vehicle and various weapons under assumed names in a dozen different states. He moved constantly, like a missionary of evil.

And as he amassed more victims, his contempt for them grew.

He began to see his victims as something less than human. Jack felt no pity or compassion for them, even as he took their lives. He began to wonder if maybe he had somehow become something more. Something like a god.

He'd read about the theory of evolution—Darwin theorized that mankind was still evolving and would, in some murky future, appear very different than the mankind of today. What if Jack was that next step in human evolution? Did his power make him something more than human? He felt nothing for these huddled squalid masses, moving through them and cutting them down like a gardener with a black scythe, weeding out the sick and the weak.

Maybe that's what he was—Darwin's Gardener, an Angel of Death. Moving through the world and pruning out those who were frail or useless. Maybe he was a crucial part of evolution, weeding out the weak to breed a better, stronger mankind. A mankind more like himself. And wouldn't the next generation appear almost godlike to this one? If he wasn't a god, why did he possess this power to take and take and never get caught? He was good at it. Very good.

Jack Terrington eventually made it to the Seattle, Washington, area in the early eighties, coming to the city like a hurricane that first darkens the horizon and then overwhelms anything in its path.

And he killed.

Jack stayed for a while, eluding the police and their task force for several long, terrible years, years that would never pass from the memory of those who had lived in the area, those who lived through it. He used those years to learn a great many things, teaching himself the finer parts of the black art of killing, and he learned something else about himself. He learned that the greatest pleasure he could obtain was from inflicting pain on others. He could feed off their fear. He learned how to cultivate that fear, to nurture it, to help it grow and bloom and expand.

In those years, he began to keep his victims alive longer, toying with them, teasing them with their own mortality.

He tortured, he frightened, he degraded. He learned what methods worked best on different people. He even took on helpers, training them in Jack's dark methods. And during that terrible time, Jack's talent for the dealing of death grew. As did his ego.

Finally, someone gave Jack and his associates' activities a name: the Green River Killer, based on a small river near the location of some of their first dump sites. Between Jack and his apprentices, the body count multiplied.

But soon, Jack began to tire of the Seattle area. Maybe the hunt had grown too easy, or maybe it was the fact that his helpers were doing most of the work now. Jack's urges settled into a quiet pattern, telling him to move on. The insistent voice commanded him to find a new hunting ground. And he'd learned over time to listen to that voice.

Jack left Seattle to his apprentices and drifted down the coast to California. While the murders continued in Seattle, Jack spent several happy years in Los Angeles, a town that seemed to have been invented just for him. Millions of angry, distant, helpless souls. His time in LA was one of joyous release, taking and taking and never even coming close to getting caught. The people of Los Angeles seemed to take anything and everything in stride, even horrifying and repulsive deaths in their midst. Few people even seemed to take notice of his work.

Jack Terrington killed nearly 40 people in Los Angeles in just over five years, and only fourteen of those ever even made it into the papers. Evidently, crimes in Los Angeles had to be particularly gruesome to be noticed.

He got restless again and moved on in 1994, moving east, looping back toward the East Coast. Arizona. Texas. The Deep South, which he found to be anything but deep. The sheriffs in the sleepy small towns were not as stupid as he'd imagined (and hoped), and he was forced to curtail his habits, relocating often. He didn't like it.

Soon, a comfortable new thought drifted into his mind in those lean years after Los Angeles: retirement. He couldn't stop killing any more than he could stop breathing—it was a compulsion. It was almost like a fever that roared through his mind, *demanding* that he take his next one, no matter what the consequences. Sometimes he tried to fight it, but he had long since given up on the idea of defeating his instinct—and part of him, most of him, didn't want to fight it.

He liked what he did.

He couldn't stop, but he could try and find a place that would allow him to continue his work without fear of punishment. Someplace like Los Angeles, where he could take as few as possible, only when the urge became unbearable, and never be noticed. He was getting older, and Jack liked the idea of returning to LA. He had not known how good he'd had it until he'd left.

As he drifted across the country, Jack decided that Florida would be his last killing ground. He would wrap up his "tour" and return to California and settle down for good.

But another memory also drifted through the back of his mind, a memory that had driven him for many years. A near defeat at the hands of a most intelligent opponent. The knowledge that it had taken a bizarre combination of good timing and coincidence and pure dumb luck for Jack to avoid capture. A memory of running through rainy woods, chased by dogs.

A memory, clear and undeniable, of being afraid. How long had it been since he had felt fear? He dealt it out often enough, but it had been years...

he was smarter than you

His ego rebelled, trying to convince him that he hadn't been truly afraid then, or ever. Nobody scared Jack any more, he knew that. Nobody. But the memory still plagued him, upsetting him in his dreams and, to a lesser degree, in his waking moments. It reminded him, every time Jack started to feel good about himself, that he had once been beaten, badly, and it hadn't been his skill or brains that had gotten him out.

He had just tripped and fallen.

he was better than you

Jack had been running across the wet pavement and tripped and landed face down in the mud. It had saved him. Every time his ego tried to swell and sing his praises, his memory reminded him of his failure, and of Liberty, Virginia. And Sheriff William T. Beaumont.

Lucky, his mind told him. He beat you, fair and square. You got away because of an accident.

you were just lucky

Part One:

A Coalescing Formation

Chapter 1
Saturday, September 10, 1996

David Beaumont was in his bedroom, a junky room with clothes and books and trash and old food, all fighting for space on the floor around his bed. He had been dreaming, afloat on the ocean and trying to save his girlfriend and others from a tidal wave. The phone was ringing next to his bed.

He moaned and reached for it, already knowing who it was. He slapped away a few magazines and picked up the phone handset next to his bed, knocking a half-empty bottle of warm beer off the bedside table. The bottle fell onto a pile of dirty clothes and rolled away. A glance at the clock told him it was already 4:20 p.m.

He swung his legs around and sat up. "Yeah?"

"Where the hell are you? You were supposed to be here twenty minutes ago."

It was Mel Rivers, his boss at the store. David was usually five or ten minutes late, but Mel sounded like he might burst.

"Sorry," David answered. "I ain't feeling too well. Can somebody else cover for me?" David noticed out of the corner of his eye that the bottle of old beer was chugging out onto a stack of papers on the floor. With one bare foot he kicked the bottle away toward the open closet.

Mel sighed, loud enough for David to hear.

"No, David, no one can cover for you, just like nobody could cover for you last week, remember? I got tickets to Depeche Mode in D.C., and I shoulda already left—I'm gonna be late as it is. Mike is still in Florida, and Bethany ain't trained enough yet to close the store by herself, especially not on a Saturday night. Get your butt in here, or you'll have all the time in the world to get better."

David shook his head and pinched the bridge of his nose, right between his eyes, with his thumb and forefinger.

"I got it. Just let me change, and I'll be right in."

"Well, don't take too long. Its 4:22 now, and I'm leaving at 4:45, whether you're here or not. And if anything gets screwed up, it'll be your ass." David got the earpiece of the phone away from his head in time to avoid being deafened by Mel slammed his phone down.

He hung up the phone and slid out of the bed, already regretting the day.

He shook his head, the remnants of a strange dream fading. He'd been on the ocean, on a raft with Bethany. And a tidal wave of water had been approaching. Weirdly, the wave was filled with floating people.

David stood and stumbled to the closet to pick out some clothes. Everything was dirty, so he stooped and picked a shirt from the pile of dirty clothes. He also grabbed the bottle of beer. It was warm and flat, but he drained the bottle anyway, trying to chase the odd, salty taste from his mouth.

Jack Terrington used the serrated tip of his trusty old knife to carefully slit the pale skin open.

Slowly, he began pulling it away from the tenuous connections to the tissues beneath. The skin came away cleanly, easily. Blood seemed to seep from everywhere inside the wound, and Jack held it away from himself to avoid getting any if it on him.

He knew how difficult it was to get bloodstains out of clothes.

Jack looked around for a stick or a piece of wood big enough, spotting one across the clearing. He retrieved the stick, and soon afterward, when he'd used the knife to sharpen the stick enough, the rabbit was spitted over the fire, cooking.

Jack Terrington had parked his van in a wooded area near the beach, and he could hear the slow rumble of the waves beyond the trees. He was just off the road a little west of Carrabelle, a small town on the gulf coast of Florida south of Tallahassee. Jack was making dinner. He had become quite adept at catching and cooking his own meals after nearly twenty years on the road, and he was particularly proud of himself tonight. He rarely caught a rabbit, and it was a special treat. Properly cooked, the meat would be juicy and tender.

Well, he hadn't spent twenty years on the road, not exactly. More like twenty years of wandering, sometimes aimlessly, sometimes full of purpose. His was a life of drifting, like a wave on the ocean, a life absent of family or friends or a steady job or a permanent place to live.

His scar had seen to that.

His residence consisted solely of the large, dusty white van parked behind him, its twin rear windows covered with a pair of unfriendly black curtains, its interior customized to suit his purposes. He had no address, no credit cards, and maybe one of the only people in the country without a credit rating. No responsibilities to anything or anyone but himself. He imagined himself to be something like a modern-day hobo, wandering, endlessly in search of something.

He got up when he saw that the rabbit was beginning to blacken, ignoring the open doors of the van and the bound and gagged woman struggling inside. Jack removed the rabbit from the fire and gingerly began to eat, carefully holding it by the stick it was spitted on. The meat was very hot and tasted good, smoky and tender.

When he was finished, he burned the bones from the rabbit along with the girl's clothes, and then kicked the fire out with one of his dusty rattlesnake-skin boots, the short chains jingling as he kicked sand over the flames. He kept her Florida Seminoles sweatshirt as a souvenir but burned everything else.

After taking one more careful glance around the clearing to make sure he'd left no evidence, he took a long breath of the salty ocean air, climbed into his creaky white van, and drove off, heading east.

The road was a pleasant one that hugged the quiet coastline, weaving in and out of large stands of trees and an occasional small town. It was easy to find a quiet clearing on a rural road like this. A hundred miles west on the two-lane road, and he would've been back in Pensacola, the biggest city on Florida's gulf coast. He'd come from that direction, passing through New Orleans and Mobile, working his way east. Now, he planned to head up to Tallahassee and over to Jacksonville before heading south onto the Florida peninsula.

Florida was one of the few places in the country he'd never visited, and he was looking forward to one more long stretch of indulging his habit before he retired to Los Angeles.

He glanced into the back of the van to check on her. The girl was still there, tied up on the floor, her arms and legs bound together in front of her with pieces of rope. She was completely naked. She looked ragged, dead, but she stared back at him with cold, humorless eyes. Three days on the cold vinyl floor in the back of his van, and she had yet to be broken.

This one was tough.

He'd beaten her. He'd stripped her naked and gagged her and tied her to the rough bark of a tree and left her there all night last night. He had abused her in every possible way he could think of, and yet she had stubbornly refused to give him the satisfaction. He wanted to break her. When they finally begged for their lives, he knew they were beaten. She would cry out; eventually, she had to.

they always did

Tonight, he would break her, just as he had broken all the others before her. He would find a nice, quiet, out-of-the-way place in the woods south of Tallahassee, and he would take her out into the woods and break her. He wasn't exactly sure how, but he knew that eventually he would. He'd kill her too—that was a given. But the important thing was to break her will, to break her spirit. Make her beg for her life before he took it from her.

At his latest count, he'd killed at least 194 men, women, and children.

At least that was what the bottles in the racks of his van told him, the last time he'd taken the trouble to count his trophies. To those people, he was the Angel of Death, the Reaper, something that came with the silence of a chill wind, a predator of man, seeking out and destroying those who crossed his path. He took them off, usually one by one but sometimes by the pair or even in small groups. He ended their pitiful lives, making room for the stronger, like himself.

Jack noticed out of the corner of his eye that a car was behind him as he passed the city limits, but he thought nothing of it. He drove into the small town of Carrabelle, the town dark for the night, and Jack saw that the only lights on were the ones at a gas station. As he passed the gas and convenience store, it reminded him of the 7-Eleven where he picked up the girl, convincing her to climb into his van with his charming smile and a pleading request for directions.

He passed slowly out of town, thinking about what he would do to her and didn't notice the car that continued to follow him.

cut her

Yeah, Jack thought. He could take her into the woods and tie her to a tree and cut her, carefully and slowly, in a dozen places, maybe a hundred places, until she called out. If that didn't work, he would think of something else. It took power to break a person's will, and Jack knew that he exuded power, and menace, and control.

the battery

If nothing else worked, there was always the van's battery. It had worked wonders on a few of his stronger victims, the stubborn ones, in the past. Just the thought of uncoiling the blue jumper cables made a smile steal across his rugged face.

Blue and red lights splashed in his side mirror, catching him dreaming.

POLICE LIGHTS, his mind screamed at him. He hated police lights, always had. His mind raced. Pull over? He might have to shoot a cop or two if he couldn't talk his way free. They might want to inspect the inside of the van, something Jack could never allow.

A messy business, killing cops. You had to be extra careful in getting rid of the bodies.

or else you could face a posse

Posse? No, they didn't send out "posses" to hunt down killers. They set up an organized search pattern, working outward in concentric circles. Outrun them? No chance. He couldn't tell for sure, but it looked like they were driving a late-model Ford Taurus. His van was strong and sturdy, and he maintained it well, but a race car it would never be. They would catch and overtake him in thirty seconds, sixty at the most.

The police cruiser was now less than three or four car-lengths back, the lights still flashing brightly in the night, the siren wailing like an injured animal.

Jack shrugged and eased the van slowly over to the shoulder. It was useless to run, and now he had to handle it. He didn't like it, but it couldn't be helped. He reached around behind the driver's seat, feeling for one of his guns, and out of the corner of his eye, he saw the girl, straining to see out of one of the curtained rear windows. The thin rope around her neck was stretched taut to where it was tied to the sidewall of the van. Her hands, lashed together, were reaching for one of the black curtains.

"Sit down, pig!" he hissed.

She cursed at him, her voice muffled by the gag, and then went back to trying to see out of the window. When he was finished with these cops, he would have to teach her some respect—she was one of the most willful people he had ever met. He needed to fix that. Before he ended her.

The van rolled to a stop on the gravel shoulder, and the police car stopped two car lengths behind it, the flashing lights staying on.

A patrolman emerged, slipping his nightstick into his belt. There were no other cars in sight. The policeman's boots crunched on the loose gravel as he approached. The only other sound was the quiet rumble of the gulf, a hundred yards to the south.

Jack strained to see if he could catch a glimpse of the policeman's partner, if he had one, but Jack saw no one else. He relaxed his left elbow on the window frame, eased the gun slowly around his chest, and cocked the hammer back, tucking the barrel into the corner formed by his left elbow.

The policeman approached and stood in Jack's open window. He looked quite young, his youthful face cautious under the curve of his black policeman's hat. His gold police shield reminded Jack of Sheriff Beaumont's six-pointed star.

"Good evening, sir. We're conducting random sobriety checks tonight. As you probably know, most traffic fatalities are caused by drunk driving on Friday and Saturday nights." He went through the short speech as if he had repeated the same tired litany countless times. The policeman's careful eyes roamed all over Jack and the van as he talked. "Could you please step out of the van?"

"Thank you, officer, for your kind attention in protecting our streets from inebriated drivers, but I can assure you that I have had nothing whatsoever to drink tonight." Jack was projecting his most congenial smile, and he was sure that, combined with the flowery language, the cop would be helpless to resist. Besides, he didn't sound drunk at all—maybe this problem would just get back in his car and go away.

The officer smiled back.

"I'm sure that's true, sir, but I still need you to step out of the van." The officer's eyes met Jack's and held them for a moment. "You and your passenger."

Jack swallowed, his hand tightening on the gun.

"Passenger?"

The officer seemed genuinely amused at Jack's response.

"Yes sir. There is someone in the back of your van. I can hear them moving around." He leaned forward, as if to look in the window. "Now, if they are drunk, there's nothing to worry—"

Jack jerked up on the door handle and kicked the door open savagely, catching the cop's face squarely with the metal doorframe. The cop staggered backward, his hands drifting up toward his bloodied face, and turned and fell heavily, right in the middle of the westbound lane of the road.

Jack hopped down quickly from the open door and strode over to where the cop lay, face down.

"Having a bad night?" he asked, his smile genuine. He worked the revolver in his hand, spinning the chamber and letting it snap to a stop. The course of action was now decided, and there was nothing anybody could do about it now. Jack looked down at the gun and saw the faint markings of the faded Liberty Sheriff's Department symbol on the butt of the revolver. It was a very old gun. "Where's your partner?"

The cop rolled over on the asphalt and looked up at Jack. His nose was shattered and several of his front teeth were broken. Blood, shiny and black in the glare of the police car's headlights, covered most of his face except for the eyes, which darted back and forth between Jack's face and the barrel of Jack's gun, watching it move and sway in Jacks' hands like a cobra, waiting to strike.

"Ain' god no pardner," he answered from his ruined mouth. Brackish blood bubbled from one corner of it, dribbling onto his chin.

Jack's head tilted back as he laughed, a strangely hollow noise that echoed on the deserted highway. He saw a dark bird float down from the sky and land with a quiet thud on the roof of the police cruiser. It turned and looked at Jack.

"'Ain't got no partner?' Oh well. Next time, maybe they won't send you out into this mean old nasty world all by your little lonesome?" He looked back at the cop, expecting a fearful look on the cop's face, but Jack was surprised to see that the cop wasn't even looking at him.

He was looking behind Jack.

Jack turned and saw the naked girl climbing down from the open driver's door of the van. Her skin was pale and ghostly in the glow of the brightening horizon and the glare of the police car's headlights. Her hands were still tied together, but her feet had somehow come free of their bindings and, even after three endless days of excruciating physical abuse, she somehow still managed to scamper down and run quickly away from the van, toward the cop car.

radio radio she's gonna call someone

Jack leapt after her, his gun coming up. She ran, barefoot on the rough gravel, straight to the driver's door of the patrol car, scaring the black bird away. She stopped and started to pull up on the door handle and that was when she saw him coming for her.

She screamed.

The defiance! Didn't she know he could snuff her out at any moment? The only thing she hadn't done was beg for mercy. So, why was he running at her now?

He stopped and fired just as she got the driver's door open, and the window shattered next to her. Shards of glass cut her bare skin from neck to knees, painting dozens of thin ribbons of blood across her. She let go of the door handle and fell to the sandy road beside the car, falling between the car and the yellow strip that signaled the edge of the blacktop.

He walked over, kicking the door closed and looking down at her closely. Here, without the benefit of the cars' headlights, he could only see that she lay on her side, crawling and bleeding profusely from a hundred shallow cuts. He didn't have time for this, or to break her. Jack shook his head and raised the gun and shot her in the back. She stopped moving.

The cop was busy trying to crawl away, the sand from the nearby beach gritting under his knees and hands. He had almost made it to the center yellow line when Jack returned. He kicked the cop once solidly in the ribs.

"Hey. Turn over."

The cop stopped crawling and flopped over to look up at Jack.

hurry up

"Hey, man, you don' have do do dis," the cop muttered through his broken mouth. "Dey'll jus hund you down. You can' get away wid killing a cop." The words slurred from his mouth like a career drunk.

Liberty, Virginia, popped back into Jack's mind, that night by the highway. Striding confidently up that rain-slicked hill, his bag banging against his side. Wearing the same boots as tonight. Firing, dropping the police one by one. He had felt immortal, godlike.

this is taking way too long what if a car comes

Jack smiled. "Can't kill a cop? Done it before, my friend. More times than I can count." Jack's eyes drifted down to the revolver he was holding, and he looked at the faded markings on it for a long moment before pointing it at the cop.

The cop stared cross-eyed at the barrel. "You bastard," the cop hissed.

"Yeah." Jack answered and fired, killing him.

"Huh?"

David Beaumont sat up, suddenly awake. He shook his head, dazed.

Bethany, his ex-girlfriend, was standing over him, looking at him oddly. Her long dark hair was almost touching him. She was beautiful, better than he'd ever deserved.

"Are you okay, David? I came back to tell you that the last customer just left. You looked asleep. What's wrong?" There was genuine concern in her eyes, deep and blue.

He looked up at her and for a moment their eyes connected, and he felt a sudden pang of regret. He'd broken up with her three weeks ago. At the time it had seemed like the smart thing to do—he was leaving town soon, moving away—but now he was starting to wonder.

David Beaumont shook his head. "I'm fine."

He turned his back on her and began setting up the paperwork on the counter, ignoring her other attempts at conversation. She finally gave up and left the back room.

The big clock said it was 10:10 p.m., and he had drifted off while adding up and matching the nightly figures. He worked at Big Video and More, a large video and music store, and his boss, Mel, was religiously meticulous about the nightly figures. Everything had to match exactly, down to the penny, every night, or someone would be written up, usually the manager in charge.

David was an assistant manager for the store and third in charge. He usually closed the store two or three nights a week, including Saturday nights. He was already on Mel's shit list for being 40 minutes late, so David knew ahead of time that everything would have to match, and the store would have to look perfect, even if the whole crew had to stay until midnight.

Bethany also worked at Big Video—she was in line for a management position. A few months ago, David had begun training her in all the jobs he did, and she had picked up quickly. So far, Mel had neglected to promote her to manager trainee, the lowest level of the store's management structure.

One reason he had broken up with her three weeks ago was the fact that at Big Video employees and managers were not supposed to date. It was one of the first rules in the photocopied handbook that every new Big Video employee was given on their first day at the store. David had even fired someone for the same offense last year. David and Bethany had gone to great lengths to hide the fact that they were dating, and the relationship amazingly had lasted almost ten months, a record for David. But he had gotten very tired of hiding the fact that they were dating, and for that reason, among many others, he had broken it off.

He'd regretted it an hour later.

Actually, it was only a convenient excuse. His real reason was much bigger.

David finished counting down the fourth cash drawer and checked the total he had written down with the register report to make sure it matched. It did. He moved over to the calculator and ran a strip total of all the checks and credit card charges taken in for the day. At the same time, he instructed the store PC on the back counter to run the nightly totals report.

The back room of Big Video was huge, and one of the walls of the back room was taken up by a three-foot-wide wooden counter that ran for thirty feet along the wall. Stacked along this counter were various bundles of paperwork, movies, CDs, and other merchandise waiting to go out onto the sales floor. At the far end of the counter, away from the door out to the main sales floor, there sat the large PC and an industrial-grade printer.

A hole had been cut in the counter under the printer to feed paper up into it, and several boxes of computer paper were stacked underneath the counter. If a person was curious enough to crawl under the counter and look up, they would see a hodgepodge of names and signatures and little jokes, drawings, and dedications, all written in a dozen colors of ink. Everyone that had ever worked at Big Video had, at one time or another, crawled under the counter and scrawled their own dedication to history. It was like a wooden yearbook, filled with graffiti.

The printer finished pushing out the nightly report, and David tore it off. Checks, cash, credit card charges, redeemed store coupons, and other various bits of paperwork had been separated out into piles, and on top of each one was the adding-machine strips he'd run. He compared the totals on each, and they all matched the final totals from the master printout.

Nodding, he gathered up all the paperwork except for the cash and stuffed it into a large manila envelope, filling out the front of the envelope with the date and totals. He left the envelope on the counter, unsealed, next to the cash, and began straightening up the back room. Mel was opening the store in the morning, and David wanted everything shipshape. When he was done, he leaned out the door to the main sales floor and called the other employees back to clock out and go home.

Franklin was a part-time employee and a high school senior, a big guy who favored tight black shirts that showed off his muscled chest and wide shoulders. He always seemed to have places to go and things to do. Tonight, he had a girl to see, so he sprinted to the back room.

"Lights?" Franklin asked, running over to the fuse box that controlled the lighting on the main sales floor and putting his hand over the four switches.

"Not yet," David answered. "Double-count the cash, okay?"

Franklin frowned, grabbing the stack of money and rapidly counting it. He checked the total against what David had written on the small pink envelope marked "Saturday."

"Yup, it matches," he said, stuffing the bills and the few coins into the pink envelope. He sealed it, initialing it. It took less than a minute. David always got Franklin to double-count the cash envelope when he could—the guy didn't mess around.

"Lights now?" Franklin asked, expectantly.

"Yeah," David answered, smiling. David added the cash to the big manila envelope and sealed it.

Franklin flipped the rows of switches and moved to the computer, clocking out. He went over to the break area—part of the back room was taken up with a small microwave, a hot and cold-water dispenser, a refrigerator, and several chairs. Franklin grabbed his backpack and car keys and ran past David, headed for the front doors.

Lisa and Bethany came into the back room. Lisa Stevens, another employee, played soccer at CEVA, or Central Virginia Community College, the school that David had attended for one semester last summer before dropping out. Lisa walked past David without a word and clocked out and left the back room.

Bethany came up to David after she clocked out, carrying her purse, a simple white one that David had bought her for her birthday several months ago. Back in happier times.

"Are you okay, David? I'm very worried about you."

"I'm fine."

He turned and walked over and grabbed his stuff, clocking out last and exiting the system. The dream image leapt into his mind again, both of them on that wooden raft with the huge tidal wave full of people towering over them. He felt a sudden, overpowering urge to take her into his arms to protect her. He needed to ask for her forgiveness, beg her to take him back.

He fought the urge and turned to leave.

"One more thing," she said.

"Bethany, I don't want to talk about it..." David started, but she swept past him and grabbed a computer data-tape cartridge from the shelving above the main terminal and slipped it into a slot on the front of computer. Thank God she'd remembered—Mel would have been furious.

She turned and walked past him, not saying a thing. After a moment, he followed—he really didn't want to walk out with her.

David walked slowly up the aisles, checking the rows and shelves of CDs and movies and advertising displays on either side of him as he walked toward the front of the store. It was on him to make sure the place was spotless.

Bethany was standing by the alarm panel, waiting, her face blank and expressionless. Lisa was talking to Franklin, who looked like a greyhound straining in his slip, waiting to be released to roam the countryside.

Franklin turned as he saw David coming.

"Backup tape in?"

David glanced at Bethany. "Yeah."

All the computers in the store were directed by the main terminal, and the main computer ran a nightly backup, recording a log of all the days' transactions onto the tape cartridge. David had forgotten to put it in twice in the past two years, and he had gotten written up on both occasions. Mel probably would not have tolerated another screwup. But telling Bethany "thank you" would involve talking to her.

David saw one row of movies in the Drama section that didn't look straight, and when he got to the front doors, he pointed over and asked Lisa to fix them.

David turned to Franklin. "Hot date?"

Franklin smiled. "Yeah, Chrissie Smalls—she's a junior, cheerleader. Very cute. We're driving into D.C., Georgetown, to go to a new club, some place called Liquid. Great name for a club, huh?" He adjusted his backpack and watched impatiently as Lisa straightened the videos.

David shook his head. "Yeah, great name. But it's almost 10:30. Even leaving right now, you won't get there until midnight. Then you've got to find the place."

Franklin smiled. "I drive fast, man."

Lisa rejoined them, nodding simply to David, anger in her eyes. She and Bethany were close friends. Lisa probably hated him now. That would explain the cold shoulder he'd been getting from Lisa for the past couple of weeks. Oh well, it couldn't be helped. David was leaving soon, and it was all for the best.

David turned and motioned to Bethany.

She turned to the wall and, as everyone stood very still, she tapped a four-digit code onto the small panel set into the wall behind the main sales counter.

"Okay," she said, and then hurried around the counter. David unlocked the door and let everyone else out. They had 30 seconds to get out and lock up before the motion detectors set off an alarm.

David pulled his keys out from the inside lock and put them in the outside lock, leaving them hanging in the door. Bethany came out and locked the door behind her, tossing the keys to David. They had done this little locking-up dance so many times, it was almost second nature. But usually she smiled.

David yelled after Franklin, who was already jogging away across the parking lot.

"Don't you ever sleep?"

Franklin yelled over his shoulder. "Yeah, I sleep. Just not on the weekends!"

Lisa said goodnight—to Bethany only—and then started toward her little red Toyota Tercel.

The night was warm. Even the late-afternoon rain had done little to cool the air. It had been a warm September here in Liberty and all along the Eastern Seaboard.

David and Bethany stood outside the doors of the darkened store and waited. Thirty seconds later, an abbreviated alarm sounded, three quick chirps that echoed across the rain-puddled blacktop. The security system was active. In the morning, Mel would have the same thirty seconds to unlock the door, enter the store, and enter the code, or an alarm would sound.

As soon as the alarm signaled, David nodded at Bethany and turned, starting toward his rusty Mazda 323. The rain had completely stopped, but a thin mist hung in the air. He looked up and saw that Bethany's little red Dodge Colt was parked only two spaces over from his car. After a moment, he heard her footsteps following, matching his, and then she was walking beside him.

"I don't think Lisa likes you very much," Bethany began. He could almost hear her thinking, trying to come up with something to say, something to talk about.

"I've never liked her either."

His tone was short, clipped, as he nervously toyed with the keys in his hand. He didn't want to talk to her, not after what he'd done to her. It was for the best anyway—he would be leaving soon, as soon as he got his money, and he didn't want to hurt her any more. If they were still dating, happy together, the decision to stay or leave would be that much harder.

For now, he just wanted to get in his car and go home to his junky apartment and forget it. Why should he be happy? He could never be happy here in Liberty, no matter who he was dating. He wished he'd never even asked Bethany out in the first place.

They were almost to their cars. She touched him on the arm. He turned around and she was staring at him.

"David, I love you."

He hesitated for a moment and then kept walking, saying nothing.

"Did you hear me, David?" She hurried to catch up, and when he glanced at her again, there were tears in her eyes. "Breaking up was a mistake. Don't you care how I feel?"

He stopped at his car and turned, putting the key in the door.

"I heard you, Bethany." He pulled the door open and stepped around it, putting it between them. "But the thing is, I don't care. You might love me, but I don't love you."

He was lying, and she probably knew it, but he had to say something to hurt her. She needed to move on with her life. He looked at her crying, and it tore him up inside more than he would ever admit. David decided that if he was going to end their relationship once and for all, this would be the perfect moment. He spoke up, his voice only cracking a little.

"Just get over it, Bethany. I did."

He got into his car and drove away, leaving her standing there, sobbing alone in the middle of a dark, rain-puddled parking lot.

Jack drove east. As the road curved northward, he continued to watch behind him. It was just past 1:00 a.m. He drove slowly and methodically, putting as much mileage as possible between him and the bodies lying on the road.

195 and 196, he calculated.

He knew that, in most cases, cops were required to report in on their car radios at regular intervals, and that if they failed to check in, alarms would be raised. Jack was also sure that in Florida, as in most other states, it was customary for policemen to call in their latest location, or 10-20, any time they were preparing to leave their cars, even for something as simple as pulling over a car for a Saturday night sobriety check.

Cops were probably all over the scene by now.

Not that it mattered much. The two bodies wouldn't have anything interesting to say, except to a forensic pathologist. It had been a dark, deserted, lonely stretch of road, with no witnesses. The gun that he had used to kill them had been in his possession for many years. It was impossible for them to match up the bullet and a serial number without the actual weapon, and it was lying safely on the passenger seat next to him.

A word drifted up from the depths of his murky brain.

videotape

He had seen a thing on *60 Minutes* about how some patrol cars had recently been outfitted with ceiling-mounted video cameras, taping routine traffic stops and the like. They used the film from one of those cameras to catch a pair of cop killers in Virginia a few years back, and ever since that incident, the cameras had become very popular, acting as a sort of insurance policy for the police.

Had the patrol car had one? Jack hadn't even thought to look.

The license plates on Jack's van were 100% valid, so if there had been a video camera in the cop's car, all they would get would be an alias. Still, he should change the plates the next time he stopped. He had a stack of them in the back.

They probably had a description of his van, either from the videotape or from the driver of that car that had approached as Jack fled. How could he have been so stupid? He began to beat his fist on the dashboard of the van, hard. He really hadn't had time to check the police car; he hadn't stayed at the scene long enough.

After he shot the cop, Jack had removed the cop's gun from its holster, careful not to touch anything that could leave a fingerprint. He tucked the new gun down into his belt as the cop took his last gasping, ragged breaths.

Jack also took the gold badge—he always kept the badges.

Jack had walked to his van and opened the back. The van had been refurbished on the inside to suit his needs. Directly behind the van's driver and passenger seats was a small kitchen and dinette area, with a microwave, a small refrigerator, a pop-out stove, and a little porta-potty that slid back out of the way under the sink. A small table and benches lined both sides of the van, and above these seats, sturdy wooden racks held his big glass jars.

The last six feet of the van, where a bed had been before Jack had begun his modifications, was bare floor completely covered with slick linoleum. On either side of this flat area, a row of thick metal loops and hooks ran above a series of locked cabinets that contained the tools and implements he'd spent years collecting.

The back of the van was two windowed doors, and built into the hollow areas of the back doors were two more locked cabinets. The hinged lids folded down into place, creating small work surfaces for his tools.

Jack opened the left panel and folded down the brownish-red shelf, stained by the blood of scores of dead. Inside the cabinet, a series of hooks held objects, some shiny and pointy and deadly serious, others blunt and menacing. The cabinet also contained a small rolled-up kit of sharp tools and tweezers and pliers.

gotta move

He pulled out a pair of wire cutters and walked back over to the cop's prone body. The cop looked dead, his blood seeping in a dozen directions away from the body. Jack knelt beside the cop and lifted up the cop's right hand.

He had to have proof.

Jack cut off the cop's right thumb.

He held it up to the light, then stood and walked over to the girl. The dark bird had returned, sitting silently on the roof of the police cruiser, watching him.

The girl lay half in shadow, her legs illuminated by the glow of the patrol car's headlights. Blood ran down her back from the hole in her shoulder. The face was turned away in the darkness, an arm curled around her head. Too bad—he would've enjoyed seeing the dead eyes, but there wasn't time.

He kneeled by her left foot, put his hand on her cold leg to steady it, and cut away the small toe.

Jack stood and walked back to the van, ignoring the bird. It seemed unperturbed by his presence. After hanging the wire cutters back on their hook, he climbed up into the back of the van. He stepped carefully over the vinyl area, still slick from the girl's blood and sweat. He would have to clean that up before he could sleep in his regular place.

He stepped around the table and pulled open the refrigerator. From the freezer, he pulled out a blue ice tray. The tray held several other small objects, pink and frosted with a rime of ice crystals, all collected in the last few weeks. Jack shook the ice tray slightly and smiled, watching the fingers and toes jiggle in their little individual compartments.

what if a car comes

He dropped the girl's toe and cop's thumb into empty spots. The thumb barely fit. Jack shook the tray once more, just for fun, and then put it back in the freezer to keep them fresh until he had a chance to cure them.

Hopping down from the van again, he reached into the open cabinet and pulled out a very large knife and a pair of gloves. Jack walked back over to the cop, looking both ways on the darkened highway. No cars or approaching lights.

this is taking too long

Kneeling over the body, he got to work. He tried to hurry.

When he was done, he stood, smiling, and starting over to the girl. What he'd done to the cop would put the fear of God into anyone who tried to follow him. They'd see what he'd done to their brethren and—

A pair of headlights crested the distant hill, coming from the direction of Carrabelle.

run run

The vehicle was still a mile away, but Jack bolted for the van, figuring as he went. A minute, maybe two, before the car got here. There was no way that the car wouldn't stop—hell, the cop was lying right on the yellow line in the middle of the road. And the patrol car's lights were still on, lighting the whole area.

He pitched the bloody knife into the back of the van and slammed the doors. He ran around the front and jumped into the drivers' seat, starting the van and punching the gas pedal all in one smooth motion. He left the van's headlights off; he could pick out the road in the pale moonlight.

Jack drove, watching in his side mirror. The headlights of the vehicle slowed as they reached the scene and stopped, joining the other glowing set of headlights.

Jack had watched, but the headlights had not followed.

And now, three hours later, he was still glancing at his side mirror. His palms stuck to the steering wheel. He had forgotten and driven the first few minutes with his rubber gloves on. He'd removed them, but now the wheel was tacky with the cop's blood.

TOO CLOSE. The words repeated over and over in his head like some kind of psychotic chant.

if the girl had gotten away

Had the person in the vehicle gotten a good description of Jack's van? They must have seen his van pulling away, glowing dull white. It hadn't been that far. And the cop might have called it in. Two witnesses.

yes officer it was a big van white or yellow going east

"STOP!" he shouted into the empty van, making himself jump. He was driving himself crazy.

Even if they did see him pull away, all they could've seen was a white van. Nothing distinctive about that, right? "What kind of white van was it?" the cop asks the witness, but she just stands there dazed. "I don't know what kind of van, officer. I came up on the scene, and I was so concerned about that poor policeman, I didn't really pay that good of attention to the van as it drove away." The obligatory tears, as the cop comforts the innocent who discovered the grisly scene.

There had to be dozens of white vans in this county alone. And as soon as he could get across the border into Mississippi, the heat would be off. It would take the Florida State Police time to coordinate with the Mississippi authorities, and by then, Jack Terrington would be well on his way back to California, back to where he could finally stop running.

He glanced again into the side mirror. Nothing.

Cops were regimental. They loved an organized search pattern. They would start at the crime scene and move out in concentric circles, checking everything before moving on. He needed to put as much distance between him and those bodies.

That had been close, though. Closer to getting caught than he had come in a long time. Of course, they had no way of knowing this, but if the Florida State Police did manage to collar him, the contents of his van would close the book on a great number of unsolved cases nationwide, including three near Florida State University. He was a wandering predator, taking what he wanted when he wanted it, and he didn't apologize for it. But he wasn't stupid, either.

Take this van, he thought. Everything about it and his ownership of it was completely legal and aboveboard. The van was registered under an alias of his with the California DMV, registered there when he'd come down from Seattle. He'd bought the van fifteen years ago in Ohio, paying cash. Every March, he settled in a small town for two or three weeks, long enough to establish an address and mail off the registration card to Ohio. He had a stack of the forms in his glove compartment. He mailed in one of the cards with his money order, covering another year's registration and the plates on the van. He would get a job at some restaurant, washing dishes, and after a week or two, he would receive his new registration card and tax sticker. And then he left town, usually the next day.

And he was never stupid enough to kill in these towns.

It sounded like a lot of trouble, but when you got pulled over by some redneck cop in Oklahoma, you'd better have a valid license and registration, or you could end up in some dusty backroom jail somewhere, and they would impound your car.

Wouldn't the cops get a surprise if they searched Jack's van?

His driver's licenses were all fakes, though; he'd destroyed his real license years ago when he discovered the fake ones were just as good. He now carried a fake California driver's license, mostly because nobody east of Vegas knew what a real one was supposed to look like. He had a whole collection in one of the cabinets in back. Four other identities, one from New York State, for when he was on the West Coast. $160 to a college kid in Seattle who had run a sideline of making fake IDs, or at least he had up until the point he met Jack. The kid made him a license, taking Jack's picture with a ratty old Polaroid. Jack had taken the licenses with a smile—and the negatives, the unused photos, and the kid's life.

No, Jack was definitely not stupid. Not by a long shot. As long as Jack understood the methods and madness behind what he was doing, and as long as he carefully concealed his tracks and gave no hints of suspicion, Jack was confident he could go on killing for as long as he wanted. Over the years, he had developed a dark talent that kept him from getting caught. His was an instinct, able to lift his nose and sniff at the proverbial winds, spotting trouble before it approached.

lucky

Oh, sure, he'd been in some tight spots before. But situations like tonight only served to keep him sharp, testing and practicing the skills and methods of avoiding capture. If these types of situations didn't come along occasionally, Jack would be in danger of becoming lazy, greedy, soft. They wouldn't catch him if he stayed honed, sharp as his knife.

He had never been truly frightened, truly scared, not since the town of Liberty. Beaumont and his deputies had tracked him, pursued him. So many years had passed, and he could still recall every detail about that last night in Liberty—the soft sounds of the rain on the trees, the cop cars sitting at the roadblock at odd angles, their lights spinning dizzily, nauseating, reflected off the wet pavement.

How it had felt to be chased, to be hunted. Walking up the hill, feeling like a god. Standing over the body of the fallen sheriff, in a pool of his own blood, moaning. Jack killing him, taking the car, watching the scene retreating behind him in the rearview mirror: the cop cars and the birds and the woman deputy, kneeling over her fallen boss.

He would never forget it.

Jack had kept Beaumont's car for less than an hour—he'd turned on the lights and siren and pulled someone over. He had killed them and taken their car, leaving the patrol car by the side of the road.

Driving and remembering, Jack reached over and grabbed the gun, holding it up to the light of the fading moon. LIBERTY SHERIFF'S DEPARTMENT, it read, the letters faded from use and time. The images in Jack's head seemed dreamlike and unreal, but this cold hunk of steel in his hand proved that it was all true.

Beaumont had been a clever SOB, but he hadn't been clever enough. And he'd died on that road. He'd paid the price of crossing Jack.

What if they could face off today? Would Jack win again? Jack had just been starting out. His career as a predator was in its infancy. He had been green, predictable.

you just got lucky

Yeah, Jack had lucked out back there in Liberty. Coincidence, timing, pure dumb luck. Had Beaumont been smarter? It was hard to say.

lucky

Jack had run like a scared child and tripped in the rain. Falling down had saved his bacon.

Jack signaled and changed lanes to pass the car he had quickly come up on. He was about halfway around the car when he noticed the blue and red bubble of lights, dim, on top.

Images raced through his mind. Cop looks over. Sees the white van. Realizes the van is passing him, exceeding the speed limit. Remembers what came over the radio just ten minutes ago. Something clicks inside his dull mind: WHITE VAN.

Jack backed off and slid back into the space behind the cop car, mostly out of reflex.

Stupid, stupid! That only attracts attention! Now the cop is thinking, why didn't he just pass me? He was already halfway around.

Jack knew that it seemed suspicious, but he couldn't pass the cop, not out here in the middle of nowhere. He had gotten just a glimpse of two cops in the car and killing again tonight was out of the question. No more dead cops.

beaumont dead on the pavement

Beaumont, Beaumont, Beaumont! If he hadn't been so busy thinking about that stupid sheriff, he wouldn't have been so distracted and tried to pass this cop car.

The old man wouldn't leave Jack alone.

Jack slowed off on the gas and allowed the cop car to pull away slowly, but not enough to attract any attention. Soon the car was a half-mile ahead and Jack could relax.

He remembered what he'd been thinking. But had Beaumont really beaten Jack? Beaumont's face floated in and out of Jack's awareness, calling him. Calling as he had in that field behind the supermarket. Calling from the grave.

Jack drove on, deep in thought. He'd forgotten the dried blood that caked the steering wheel and made his hands tacky. He'd forgotten the racks of jars and bottles in the back that held the proof of his travels. His mind was far away, in a wet and rainy forest filled with the sounds of dogs.

When the van reached a crossroads—one way led back west into Mississippi, the other north into Georgia and Virginia and points beyond—Jack was too busy thinking to notice. The van drifted onto the on-ramp going north. When Jack realized he'd turned north, the decision seemed like the right one.

Liberty was this way.

Tropical Storm (TS) Mandy churned slowly across the Atlantic, heading for the US Virgin Islands and the Bahamas beyond.

Until 2:00 a.m. early Sunday morning, the circular collection of wind and clouds was known simply as Tropical Depression 24. When the winds picked up and strengthened, as predicted, the US National Weather Service upgraded it to an official tropical storm. Being the thirteenth such storm in a season of active tropical weather, which ran from June 1 through the end of November, the storm gained a name starting with the 13th letter of the alphabet.

The tempestuous currents and wind patterns of the southern Atlantic had only spawned two major hurricanes during the four months of the official 1996 hurricane season, but scientists and meteorologists were already writing papers and commenting on the active season. Lots of storms, but few of them serious; in fact, it was the first year in a long time when a major hurricane had not caused property damage or any fatalities in the Continental United States.

Some people saw that as a good thing. Others, like Tracker Randy Kovacs, felt that it was only a harbinger of things to come.

He had spent many years studying and tracking hurricanes, cyclones, and typhoons, and he had grown to feel that the storms came and went in cycles. A cycle marked by only small storms meant things could be worse in the future. Maybe not this year, but next season or maybe the season after. In Randy's experience, it all evened out.

Kovacs sat at his Power Mac terminal in the National Hurricane Center (NHC), an underground concrete bunker operated by the National Weather Service (NWS) in Coral Gables, Florida, just north of Miami. Kovacs was studying the latest satellite photos from GEOSat 4, the newest of the GEOSat satellites. It gave the clearest, most accurate views of the Southern Atlantic. Careful study of these satellite images, along with reams of atmospheric data compiled by weather balloons and the high-flying Maverick and Cessna planes, would help Randy and other hurricane experts try and determine where TS Mandy would go.

A secure land line also connected the NWS computers with the National Climatic Data Center in Houston, a huge complex of buildings full of scientists and meteorologists who compiled data on weather patterns all over the world. But Randy was only interested in wind and rain patterns in the western Caribbean right now.

It was funny how these storms got personified, Randy thought. When it was a number, no one really cared. But as soon as a name was tacked on, a storm seemed to take on a life of its own.

Randy and the other Trackers were the best in the business at trying to guess where and when the storms would go. They invariably spoke about the hurricanes as if they were actual people, often equating them with temperamental females. The storms would "think," or "walk," or "sprint," depending on what else was going on around them. "She's thinking about heading over Florida" or "she's feeding off the warm water in the Gulf of Mexico." Something like that.

And really, even with all the information and hard data that the computers processed, all that Randy and the other Trackers could do was give an educated guess as to where the storms were headed.

Sometimes the storms tricked them or echoed other storms from the past. Hurricane Enid in 1993 had refused to come ashore despite all the best models and guesses, which predicted the storm should make landfall near Charleston, South Carolina. She'd coasted along, a hundred miles offshore, and finally sputtered out of existence somewhere near Greenland.

Other storms were ferocious, spiteful, and angry. The concept of alternating male and female names, instituted back in 1987, was still viewed with grudging acceptance. Most of the scientists and trackers were men, and it was far easier to think of the massive, deadly storms as feminine, feisty and unpredictable.

But the storms with male names could be equally deadly. Three years ago, Hurricane Max roared into Miami, far outpacing what the scientists predicted its top possible speed could be over the open stretch of water between Florida and Cuba. Max hit land twelve hours early, surprising the city and tearing up the city. Max flattened two large warehouses in Miami and causing extensive property damage up and down the coast. Max ended up with a death toll of sixty-three—twenty-four were killed in Vero Beach when a bingo parlor ceiling collapsed on a group of senior citizens seeking shelter from the storm.

The NWS had learned their lesson. Now warnings were offered for the next forty-eight hours instead of the next twenty-four. Many coastal

Florida cities and towns had multiplied in size, and now it took longer than twenty-four hours to evacuate the inhabitants inland. The big wigs at the NWS in D.C. had decreed the forty-eight-hour warnings, and the NHC staff complied, even though the accuracy of such long-range predictions was iffy at best.

To Kovacs, Tropical Storm Mandy looked harmless, nothing more than a collection of false-color images swirling on his computer screen. The colors denoted different wind speeds and precipitation amounts, all moving in jumbled unison around the dark blue of the calm eye. The swirling pattern of clouds didn't look like it was coalescing quickly enough to be dangerous, at least not in the next twelve hours.

Of course, you never knew for sure. It was big for a mid-season storm. Mandy's arms extended out for a couple hundred miles—it was the largest storm they'd seen in months. Most likely, she would coalesce and reduce size before making land. Kovacs wrote up a little note on a Post-it—the entire center was fueled by those little yellow slips of paper—and stuck it on the picture before throwing it in his boss's inbox.

CHAPTER 2
Sunday, September 11

David Beaumont shared a small apartment on the north side of Liberty with a quiet guy named Bernie Wilkins, a friend from high school. The area of town was known for tracts of low-rent housing and a stretch of bars that seemed to attract drunken fights on Friday and Saturday nights. David didn't particularly like where he lived, but that would all be changing soon.

Bernie wasn't a bad guy to live with, but he was even messier than David, and David was certainly not nitpicky about keeping the place spotless. Several weeks often passed before someone tidied up. More likely than not, the sink was full of dirty dishes and old beer bottles.

On Sunday morning, September 11, the sun rose and hung in the sky for several hours before David came out of his sad-looking building and looked up into the glare of the bright blue sky. By 10:30 a.m., the temperature was already up around the 80-degree mark, or at least that was what the bank sign across the street from his building said. The day had all the earmarks of another scorcher, just another in a long string of them. If David heard the term "Indian summer" one more time, he thought he might kill somebody.

He walked across the street and climbed into his Mazda, starting it up. David listened for a moment to the awful, rickety, metallic clatter. It came from beneath the dented blue hood decorated with a small but ever-growing patch of reddish rust by the windshield wipers.

The engine sounded like it was being tortured. Bernie was supposed to have fixed that annoying rattle last week, but here it was, back again. David tried to roll both windows down, but the passenger window only went halfway down before grinding to a halt, catching on something inside. David shook his head and popped the gearshift into DRIVE, pulling away from the trash-filled gutter and heading south toward a better part of town.

The stereo worked just fine. David popped in a CD from his favorite band, Rush. Today it was *"Hold Your Fire,"* one of his favorites. There were several excellent songs on this one, but his favorite was *"Time Stand Still,"* one about how life seems to speed by in a blur, unless people make a point of noticing things. It had a cameo by Aimee Mann, the lead singer from 'Til Tuesday.

For David, listening to Rush was more need than habit. Other people talked about their favorite bands, like Aerosmith or Green Day, and David had given them all a try, playing their CDs at work from the play list, but none of them had ever come close. Rush had a way of playing together that made them sound like one unit, like one person, intent on crafting the best sounding, most well-constructed music ever recorded. He knew he could count on an argument whenever he announced his favorite band, but look how long they had been around! Rush had put out something like 16 studio albums since 1968, each good and new and different in its own way. It was a musical and recording heritage that could never be taken away from them.

As much as he liked them, he had yet to buy every CD they had put out. He enjoyed getting their new ones as soon as they came out, but he only bought their catalog titles one at a time, and then only occasionally. Every new song by them was like a precious gem, whether it was new, or just new to him.

David drove across town, trying to calm his nerves. He tried to make time to visit his aunt every Sunday morning—she had taken him in and raised him after his mother had died in the delivery room. She was the only family he had. He didn't think of her as his mother, of course, but sometimes, when other people would talk about their mothers and pass along cute stories about them, his thoughts would turn to Gloria. He'd remember the shouting matches and the thrown bottles.

His aunt had only one real interest, one far more compelling than her nephew or his life. She didn't seem to care about what was going on his life, no more than she cared about anything else that went on in the world that swirled around her. Gloria was content with her hobby, which consisted of trying to empty every bottle of vodka she could get her hands on. She got drunk every night, but on Fridays and Saturdays she really went for the record books. Most Sunday mornings, she was usually still too hung over from the night before to be good company.

She'd raised him, but now she was too far gone to care, especially after the turbulent period in his life when he had turned sixteen and moved out. He knew that he visited her out of love, and out of regret for the missing parents he had never known. But he also visited her out of some sense of commitment, almost as if she was now the child and he was the parent.

He also hoped the clouds in her mind would part, even for a moment, and she would tell him something about his dad. He knew a lot about his mother, but David's father was a mystery. He hoped in vain that maybe his drunken aunt would give him a little more insight into his father's life. He didn't want to hate his father, but sometimes the hatred went so deep, it was hard to get past.

Of course, he'd heard the "Story" too many times—everyone in Liberty had. His father had been the Hero, had saved the town. Hero with a capital "H," just like the Killer had a capital "K." His father's last night on Earth, the dogs chasing Jasper Fines, the epic gunfight out on the interstate. The Killer driving away, Norma Jenkins holding Sheriff Beaumont. "The Story" had grown into legend in this town.

David hated it.

David wove his car through the streets of Liberty and pulled up in front of his aunt's squat, little two-story house. He climbed out and was almost all the way up the stained driveway before the Mazda's engine finally sputtered to a stop.

The yard around the house was disheveled and unattractive, the heat of the past weeks scorching the grass a shade of yellow that reminded David of bile. The yard that he used to mow weekly was now attended to irregularly by a neighbor. Apparently, the neighbor had found better things to do than seed and water the lawn of the sister-in-law of the town's most famous legend.

David walked up the cracked sidewalk and rang the doorbell, already regretting the visit. He had other stuff to do. But it was probably only a few more times. Soon, he could take his money and climb into his car and drive away forever. Away from the Story. A distracted part of his mind noticed how worn the house looked. The shutters on either side of the large living room window were cracked and broken.

Nothing happened for a few minutes, and David leaned over and rang the bell again and again, holding the button in for a long time. Finally, he heard movement from inside, the crystal sound of the clinking of a bottle, and then the door unlocked, and his Aunt Gloria was looking at him, bleary eyed.

"Hi." He tried to smile but nothing came.

She held the door open with her tilted head, as if holding it open with her hands was too much work. She looked at him for a long moment and then recognition dawned in her eyes.

"Oh, hi, David. Come to see me?"

"Yeah." He saw in one hand a tumbler full of ice and clear liquid. The Great God Vodka, her one and only savior, on earth as it is in heaven. Give us this day our daily bottle. Bottles. "It's Sunday. Time for my visit."

Gloria seemed genuinely surprised, her eyebrows going up.

"Is it Sunday, already?"

She tittered, a high, squeaky laugh that David had always hated, a laugh that she usually reserved for those extra-special times when she was particularly plastered. "Time fries when you're having fun," she said, pulling the door open a little and waving the glass in his direction. There was no point in correcting her. She smiled at him for another long, awkward moment, and when it finally dawned on her that he wasn't going to laugh, she turned and shuffled back inside, heading down the dark hallway. Her hair was a mess, and the clothes she was wearing looked like they'd gone unwashed for weeks.

He pushed the door open and followed, making his way between piles of clothes, books, and mail. Not unlike his own apartment, he thought with a half-smile. Maybe his aunt and he had more in common than he thought.

She walked in front of him with short, shuffling steps, almost like a waddle. Every time she lurched forward, liquid lapped over the rim of her glass and splashed onto the wooden floor. The bottom of her dirty housecoat trailed, streaking the spill into long lines of moisture that followed her out of the foyer and into the living room.

The house smelled. Actually, it was worse than just a smell. It stank of old liquor and old clothes and dusty furniture, but underneath those smells, another odor pervaded every corner, every surface of the house's interior. It smelled of loss, of regret, of years wasted away.

To David it was the smell of death, mute and unstoppable.

She staggered to the ragged, brown couch in the living room and flopped down with a loud grunt. Somehow, she avoided spilling more of her drink or knocking her shin against the low glass coffee table that squatted in front of the couch. She looked at him, her eyes just thin slits against the morning light, even though most of the shades were closed.

"What brings you out to see me? Is it Sunday, already?" she asked, oblivious. Her words slurred together like boats jamming into a narrow harbor.

"Yeah, Gloria. It's Sunday," he began. "Er...don't you think it's a little early for that?" He nodded at the half-empty glass in her hand.

"Ha!" she blurted out, startling him. "Only fifteen and already telling me what to do?"

He rolled his eyes. She didn't even remember how old he was. How many brain cells did she have left? They said in Health class that each drink you took killed off like a thousand. If that was true, Gloria was running on empty.

"Aunt Gloria, I turn eighteen soon. Tomorrow, in fact."

He doubted she even remembered the importance of the date, but he needed to warn her. Things were going to start happening soon, things that were out of her control—

"Really, honey? I'm so happy for you!" And then, to his horror, she began to sing the birthday song to him, her voice broken and off-key. He sat and patiently waited for her to finish. It was like something from a bad movie, sitting in the gloom, watching his drunk aunt sing to him. David wanted nothing more than to get up and run. Instead, he sat and waited. She stopped half-way through, losing her train of thought. Finally, painfully, she finished.

"Thank you," he said when she was done. "It's a big day for me. Do you know why?"

She looked at him, and he could almost hear her alcohol-clouded mind working on the problem, chugging along, trying to figure it out. But it was too early, or there was too much booze, or both.

"It's your birthday, and..."

David waited, finally filling the long silence that followed her words.

"It's my eighteenth birthday. I start getting my money tomorrow."

She was silent, probably thinking back. His father and mother had set up a will that left David most of what money they had, but he could not start receiving it until he turned eighteen. In the years between their deaths and his upcoming birthday, the money had grown substantially, mostly thanks to Abe Foreman, the family lawyer. Now, David was scheduled to receive ten yearly payments of nearly $25,000. She had been provided money, too, from the will to help in the raising of young David. It had bought this house and supplied her with enough means to avoid work for the rest of her life.

He had waited a long time for his first payment, and the freedom it would grant him. Freedom to leave. She had to know the significance of it, but if she did, it didn't register on her face.

He looked around the living room and up the wide stairs. At the top was a banister overlooking the living room and a hallway leading to the bedrooms on the second floor. He could just see the door to his old room. It had been a long time since he had been up there.

David turned back to her, and she was looking up at the banister too. "You remember what I always talked about doing with my first check, don't you?"

She nodded, turning to him, and he was surprised to see her eyes had seemed to clear a little. "Yeah, you always hated this town. You're leaving, aren't you? That's why you came here today, to say good-bye and leave me here to rot away."

"Gloria, I'm not leaving," he said. "Not yet. I came over today to visit, not to say good-bye."

David wondered if he would get up the nerve to leave. He wanted to, hating this town and its past. But would he go through with it? "I still think you're drinking too early."

She cut him off, her mood whiplashing to a defensive, angry posture, "I'm a grown woman, and I can do what I want, when I want!"

"Auntie!" he shouted, a little more forcefully than he had to, his hands up in front of him. He hated calling her that—it made him feel ten years old, but it seemed like the only thing that would get her attention. It broke through the fog like nothing else he'd found. "I didn't come over here to argue with you, okay? I'm not trying to live your life for you, or anything," he answered slowly, carefully, trying to keep his voice down. He didn't like to get upset. "It's just that I want to see you take care of yourself, that's all. I mean, who would I have to bother on Sunday mornings if you weren't around?"

That got a weak smile out of her.

"I'm sorry, honey. I know you mean well." She seemed to drop out of the conversation for a moment, thinking, and then she started again. "Abe Foreman was here last night for a while, reminding me of how bad I am with money. I didn't mean to yell at you, it's just..." She seemed to be suddenly on the verge of tears, even though seconds ago she'd been smiling. Her sudden seriousness troubled him.

"What did Abe say?"

She rolled her eyes and set down her drink on the glass coffee table so quickly, some it splashed out over the lip and onto her pallid, thin-looking hand. "Oh, the same old shit. Money, money, money, blah, blah, blah." She turned introspective again for a moment. "He said they might take the house away," she said, her voice low with emotion.

"What?" As far as he knew, her financial situation was fine. Mr. Foreman had taken over the finances and done a whiz-bang job, investing some of the money. He thought Abe had used the rest to pay off the house years ago. "I thought the house was paid for. What did he say?"

She shook her head.

"I guess I should have been paying more attention to the bills," she said, waving one hand at a wicker basket of papers on the kitchen counter. It was overflowing with what looked like at least three months' worth of paperwork. If he had known she was forgetting to pay her bills again, he would've checked in with Abe sooner.

He watched as her face worked. She was having trouble remembering what Abe said.

"Um, the power company contacted him. To shut off the power. And the city people called him, said I was behind on the taxes. I swear, Davy, I didn't mean to forget." She was quiet for a moment, looking down at the nearly empty glass of vodka on the table in front of her like it was her only friend in the world. "Sometimes I forget."

After a few seconds, she continued. "Abe said I should sell the house, and I don't want to do that, Davy!" she said, reaching over to the chair across from the couch and taking his hand in hers, almost pleading with him.

She looked around lovingly at the dingy, dusty furnishings, not seeing them for what they were but probably seeing them as they used to be, years ago. One golden wedge of light came in through the shade pulled over the window and fought its way through the dusty air to paint a yellow triangle on the carpet at her feet. "I just can't bear to think about selling." She was very close to tears. "It's all I have left to remember your parents by. They let me live here with them for a while before..."

David looked up sharply. They never talked about his parents. His aunt hated Sheriff William Beaumont—he had taken her beloved sister away. He'd gotten her pregnant and then abandoned her to bleed to death in the delivery room. Gloria must have been more drunk than she had first appeared to him, or she was really scared. As he watched, she fought the tears, and the tears won, coming in long, hitching gasps.

"They were so happy, you know. For a while," she said through the tears. "They had everything, and then it all went away. He was good to her, good for her. They had me over here for dinner the night they moved in. They were so happy. That was a year or so before they found out they would be having you. And your mother, she was so strong. She just wasn't strong enough. And losing your father, that just took too much out of her..."

David glanced up at the mantle and the picture in the frame. His parents, on their honeymoon, one of the few artifacts of his parents his aunt allowed in her home. There were other pictures of his mom, of course, with Gloria, but that was the only photo of his father in the entire house. He'd spent a long time staring at that photo, hating it.

David moved over and held her, something he had not done in years. They rarely hugged. David could not remember the last time he had held her for longer than a second. Now, her head was tucked into the space by his shoulder, and she cried, long and hard, her chest hitching.

The tears finally slowed, and then he pulled away, straightening her up and looking into her eyes.

"Auntie, don't worry. I'll go talk to Abe, and we'll get this whole mess fixed, okay?"

She smiled back at him. For a second, she looked like the mother figure he'd never had.

"Thanks, David. You're a good boy. So much like your father," she said, holding his face between her hands for a moment before turning and curling up on the couch.

He covered her with a dusty, flowery afghan that he had gotten her for Christmas several years before. He looked at her for a moment and saw the steady rise and fall of her chest, and then he let himself out, taking with him two large paper bags full of empty bottles from her kitchen and pantry. He thought about taking some of the full ones as well, but she'd just buy more.

Outside, he got into his car, put the bottles in the passenger seat, and, with a long glance back at the house, drove away.

Jack Terrington got most of the way to Brunswick, Georgia, on Sunday morning, before he came to his senses and decided to turn around.

He had spent most of the morning thinking about Liberty, Virginia. After a night parked in a gas station parking lot, arguing with himself and dozing, he'd gotten a late start. He passed through Jacksonville around noon. Heading toward Liberty had felt like the right thing to do, but now he wondered. Thoughts of anger alternated with memories of exultation and happiness at the idea of visiting his past and putting his ghosts to rest. Ghosts that haunted him during the day, ghosts that kept him awake at night.

He was convinced he had to go back to Liberty and kill again and not get caught. Then he could forget all about that place.

But why go back at all? It was a monumentally stupid idea.

He'd asked himself that same question over and over, ever since he'd crossed the border from Florida into Georgia, following I-95 north. Why was he going? Beaumont was dead, rotting in his grave. The memories that haunted Jack were probably never going to go away, even if he returned to kill in Beaumont's town and retired to Los Angeles. Nothing could ever change what happened on that rainy interstate so many years ago, and even if Jack could've somehow changed it, he wouldn't have. Beaumont had been good, but Jack had beaten him, fair and square.

So why go back at all? What could he possibly hope to prove by returning?

you got lucky

Because it was the site of his only defeat and Jack knew it. He hated to admit it, even to himself, but Beaumont had beaten him. After all these years, he realized that Beaumont was somehow still chasing him. A ghostly figure from Jack's past, pursuing him, driving him.

But he didn't need to go back to put his ghosts to rest. He only needed to recognize them and then put them out of his mind.

Jack decided to forget the whole nonsensical notion. He was retiring, going west, back to Los Angeles. Jack nodded and smiled.

It would feel good to let it go.

He signaled and left the roadway at the next exit, taking the turn into the seaside burg of Brunswick, Georgia. It looked like any other typical little roadside town, fast food places and hotels grouped expectantly along the access road, paralleling the highway. Sprouting around these buildings were tall, gaudy signs, advertising other hotels and restaurants that evidently couldn't afford the expensive real estate near the freeway.

He found a Burger King and parked the van, heading inside for a quick bite. After he ate, he'd continue north to Savannah and then take I-16 west toward Atlanta and points beyond. No more worrying about the past, no more thinking about ghosts.

Crossing the parking lot, the sky darkened above him. He craned his neck and saw a passing flock of dozens of birds, a ragtag group of different species. They flew over the restaurant and settled in a field beyond. He watched them for a long moment, wondering if it was normal for different kinds of birds to fly together.

Finally, Jack headed inside, ordering and sitting down. The meal was not memorable, but the myriad thoughts that raced through his mind were. The idea of returning to Liberty picked at him, but it seemed like a horrible idea. He needed to drop it, leave Beaumont and that stupid town behind.

He finished the chicken sandwich and fries and headed back up to the counter to order a chocolate milkshake for the road. Jack was distracted, already thinking about how nice Los Angeles was and how much he had enjoyed living there. Tourist season was over and fall was coming. Maybe he could get another little place in Manhattan Beach and...

He looked up and saw Sheriff Beaumont.

The man was older and heavier, but there he was. Standing right there. Jack could reach out and touch him. The face was longer, probably from years of hard living, and wrinkled with age, but other than that, Beaumont looked exactly like Jack remembered.

"Can I help you?" a voice came from behind him, but Jack didn't pay any attention. He was far too busy staring at ex-Sheriff William T. Beaumont, who was apparently alive and now worked at a Burger King. The man had traded in his sheriff's uniform for the same ridiculous brown and orange uniform worn by the other employees.

Ignoring Jack's stare, Beaumont shuffled past. The old man wore a name tag, pinned in the exact location where the man had worn his sheriff's star back in 1978. That same star was now in Jack's pocket. It was worn and faded around the edges. For Jack, the star was a talisman.

"Sir, can I help you?" the insistent voice called again. He turned angrily and saw a teenage girl behind the counter looking at him, a hand hovering expectantly over the register keypad.

Jack scowled and turned away and saw the man was gone. He pushed away from the counter, bumping into someone behind him, and ran to the dining area, looking.

Beaumont was nearly to the restrooms, and Jack noticed he was pushing a mop and bucket on wheels.

A scraggly-looking family made up of an obese mother and three children walked in front of Jack, as he stood there looking at Beaumont. Each, even the youngest one, carried their own brown trays loaded down with food and soda, and Jack noticed out of the corner of his eye that even the youngest was already pudgy around the waist. The mother was like a huge moving blob, her purse swinging with each step, beating out an odd slapping rhythm as it banged against one meaty thigh.

Jack batted the last of the fat children aside and made his way toward the back of the store, intent on catching Beaumont before he could disappear again. The fat kid fell and dropped his tray, sending food and dessert and soda splattering to the tiled floor. The kid on the ground started wailing. The mother set her tray of food on the nearest plastic table and jostled over to her boy, scooping him up and cradling him to her ample bosom.

"Hey, you!" she yelled after Jack. "What do you think you're doing, knocking over my boy! Come back here and apologize, and you'd better buy him some more food!" Her voice was thin and shrill, like it was having trouble getting all the way out of her.

Jack stopped and turned and stared at her. The fat lady shut up so fast, he actually heard her teeth pop together with a little snap.

Jack turned. The old man was slowly setting down his broom and dustpan next to the sign marked "Restrooms." Jack grabbed one of his arms and spun him around.

The old man standing in front of Jack looked nothing like Beaumont.

The hair, the face, the build were all wrong. This man was far too heavy, even accounting for the difference in years. His chin was weak and unimpressive. His eyes were empty, vacant. The man stared back at Jack's face for ten seconds, then the dull eyes slowly drifted down to Jack's hand, still roughly clenching the old man's arm.

Jack was speechless. He let go of the man's arm and found his voice.

"Sorry. Thought you were somebody else."

The old man nodded slowly in Jack's general direction, mumbling something under his breath, and then he turned around, moving toward the bathrooms again. One of his hands drifted mindlessly up and rubbed the place where Jack had grabbed him.

Jack shook his head and sat down at an empty table and took out the sheriff's star, clenching it tightly in his fist.

ghost ghost he's a ghost

His mind was playing tricks on him. Jack had genuinely thought it was Beaumont, but the old cleaning man looked nothing like him. Same general build, maybe, and same height, but was that enough to start imagining things? His hand uncurled from around the metal star. The rounded points of the star had managed to draw blood, beading on his fingers. The scar was there, too, whiter than normal today. Jack's mind wandered back to that day on his bike.

grab it grab it see how it feels

The images flashed through his mind until he shook his head to make them stop.

He felt eyes on him and glanced up. The fat woman's children were staring at him, especially the one who looked lonely without a tray of food.

The mom snapped at the kids. "Don't look at the bad man."

Jack could hear her talking about him, and he didn't like it. Not one bit. He didn't like being fooled by an old man, and he didn't like being spoken about like he was a monster. If anyone was a monster, it was Free Willy and her litter of fat kids.

right now

Suddenly, the urge bloomed inside of him, white hot and angry. He needed to kill. Somebody, anybody, it didn't matter.

He stood and walked for the exit—as fast as it was growing, the urge would soon be very difficult to control. He had to get to his van and do some serious thinking. And he had to get away from people, and fast. Had Jack's mind finally deserted him, happy to wander off on its own and ponder whatever it wanted to, leaving him high and dry and looking like a fool in front of a dozen witnesses in a fast-food restaurant?

Maybe the only answer *was* to return to Liberty, if only to convince himself that he could kill there and get away with it.

As crazy as it sounded, the idea appealed to him even more now. He couldn't kill Beaumont again, that was obvious. But he could take some of those the sheriff had protected. Kill again in the man's precious town, bring it to its knees. Face the demons that haunted him and defeat them. And then forget them.

He popped his shades on and stepped outside into the September sunlight, streaming down in thin ribbons from a cloudy, gray sky. When he got back to the freeway, it wasn't even a question.

Jack headed north.

Tropical Storm Mandy slammed into the eastern Bahamas with enough gusto to make the *NBC Sunday Evening News,* the last story before the first commercial break. Though technically not a hurricane yet—its sustained winds were still in the high sixties—the storm was a big one, the cloud pattern and central mass already much larger than a typical tropical storm.

The Trackers in the underground National Hurricane Center had estimated that, with such a large, decentralized circular mass, the storm would be weaker than most. They were wrong.

Mandy, at double the width of most tropical storms, loomed huge on his computer screen. Randy Kovacs staring at it intently, puzzling out the details, trying to understand the whirling patterns of color. It would almost certainly be upgraded to a hurricane in the next few hours.

The center was full of activity tonight, much busier than the night before or any other night so far in the month of September—they were staffing up for a potentially serious situation.

Kovacs wondered if this would be the first big storm of the season. The 1965 season had also started out relatively mild until a huge storm, Betsy, coalesced off the Cayman Islands. It eventually slammed into Mobile, Alabama, killing almost a hundred people. The storm was an estimated Category 4. A Category 5 storm was the worst, one that came along only once in a decade.

Other Trackers sat at their terminals, crunching data, their fingers flying around their keyboards, as they accessed information from historic data banks and up-to-date observations, running innumerable computer models and estimations about the storm and its track. They were trying to predict the future path of the storm by examining wind patterns and currents, storm fronts, water temperatures and salinity, and a half-dozen other variables.

Estimating the storm track was one of the most difficult things they did at the center, and many people counted on their information. The National Weather Service, the Weather Channel, CNN, and other news sources all relied on them to get their estimates out as quickly—and accurately—as possible. And federal and state agencies were waiting for information so they could issue warnings and evacuations, close beaches and bridges, and inform local and state police authorities.

But Randy wasn't plotting the track—his job was to estimate the maximum strength.

Randy pulled up all the information he could find, culling data from a dozen different sources, and dumped it all into a strength estimation program he and others had developed. It was the best model they had, but still, it was only accurate about 28% of the time. The computer processed the data, thinking it over. Randy watched the computer work through several hundred permutations, flashing them on the screen, as it made assumptions about variables and calculated the potential outcomes.

Finally, the computer was finished. It projected forty-six different strength scenarios, displaying a table of results. Twenty of the scenarios had the storm losing strength after staying on its present track, crossing the Bahamas and over mainland Florida before passing into the Gulf of Mexico and dying out. Fifteen of them had the storm staying at about the same strength, currently just under a Category 1. The other scenarios had it growing in strength, but none of them had it growing bigger than a Category 3. Still nothing to sneeze at.

Randy hit the PRINT button and walked over, waiting by the printer. The full-color printer took a minute to produce the hard copy, and then he went to find his boss, handing her the sheet.

She glanced at the data. "What do you think?" she asked him, handing the paper back.

He shook his head. "I don't think it'll get any bigger, but then you never know. Edouard was this level for a while, and then it grew to a Category 4, and we still don't know why," Randy answered, glancing up at the TV. "The models didn't show it getting any bigger, but you know that it depends on how long it tracks over warm water. It'll feed on that. Ed and the others should finish their track estimates before I run the data again on max strength." He used the word "it" to describe the storm, because he was supposed to—the higher-ups frowned on the politically incorrect.

She nodded. "That sounds good. Anything else I need to know?"

His boss was new, down from the National Weather Services' Severe Storm Center in Kansas. She was smart enough to understand that she might need help on this one. She had never been here on staff when they had a big one. Randy had, and she knew it, so she asked for his opinion.

"No, not really. We've got those fly-throughs out of Nassau and Kemp's Bay planned in the next half-hour. Those, combined with the San Salvador balloon data, should give us a better idea."

He glanced into the center's main control room—it looked like mission control for a space shuttle launch. Big screens flashed maps and data in front of rows of technicians and scientists hunched over their computers. He nodded at the large, computerized weather map of the Continental United States. "There's that large high-pressure mass sitting over the Eastern Seaboard that's been causing warmer-than-normal temperatures from New York to North Carolina. And another one over Texas and the Western Gulf. If Mandy goes very far north, the coastal air mass should steer her out, keeping her from making deep landfall. And if she crosses Florida and heads into the Gulf, she should hit that high-pressure mass and sputter out in the open water, before she even gets close to Texas. Or she...I mean it could turn north and go between them."

She followed his eyes and nodded.

"Then they'd get heavy rain along those lines, if the storm bumps up against either of the warm air masses."

She was a good meteorologist, despite what some of the guys said. Randy knew she was excellent at precipitation patterns. And she was smart enough to let others lead on the stuff she wasn't strong in.

"Yeah," he said, nodding. "Mandy will have trouble turning inland with that air mass there, assuming it stays. But they'll get severe weather along the line where the two systems meet." He thought about it for another moment, then continued. "Not enough to put out a warning. Yet."

They both stared at the full-color computer weather map in the other room, each alone with their thoughts, before he excused himself and went back to his desk.

The data from the track estimations came through a few minutes later from the team, and Randy took their possible storm tracks and fed them into his computer model, and then he sat back, waiting for the results. The storm was coming, and no one in the room was sure where it would go, or how strong it would be when it got there.

All they could do was crunch the numbers and make an educated guess.

CHAPTER 3
Monday, September 12

"And this here, this will be where you work. At least until we can find you a bigger office."

Agent Jeff Collings was talking to her, but she wasn't paying him, or his long, appreciative looks at her legs, much attention. She was too busy staring at—or into—her new office.

Closer to a closet, Julie thought.

The room measured no more than twelve feet on a side, and the small, used desk and computer terminal seemed to take up most of the usable space. There was no window—that was really too much to ask for, she reminded herself—and the room smelled musty and hot, as if it hadn't been used in years. Plastic wrap covered the computer monitor and keyboard. A dead plant sulked on a table in the corner.

"Well, it's not much, but it's a start," she said, trying to be optimistic. "Where's the nearest bathroom?"

Collings seemed to fidget uselessly. "Well, this east wing of the whole fifth floor is pretty much out of commission, but the floor above has plenty of offices and people—and bathrooms." He smiled in a way that he probably thought was charming. To Julie, it looked like he was trying to imagine what color bra she had on.

He looked up at the door and smiled again, this time to himself. "Oh, and we'll get rid of that, too," he said, pointing.

She looked up. Great. The sign holder on the door still held a corroded, yellowing sign, designating the room's previous use, "Maintenance."

After he had finally left—he'd looked like he was trying to get up the nerve to ask her out—Agent Julie Noble began to unpack the small satchel of things she'd brought with her: three boxes of pencils and two boxes of good pens, all made in America and often difficult to find; a stapler; a small framed picture of her with her little dog, Mr. Smith; her calculator, the same old one that she'd used all the way through high school and college; her appointment book; a Far Side calendar to hang on the bare walls; and a coffee mug that read, "If I were any smarter, I'd be a threat to national security," an all-too recent gift from her sister upon Julie's graduation from the Academy.

Julie sat back and surveyed her domain.

Not much to look at, but it was her first day, she thought. Eleven weeks out of the academy, and she was one of the only two or three graduates in her class to land a job at headquarters here in Washington, D.C. Sure, she was working deep inside the bowels of the vast complex, hiking distance from the offices of power and influence, but at least she was in the building.

I guess all those hours of homework and extra study paid off, she thought. Tina, her academy roommate, had spent most of the year out partying with her friends. Julie had politely declined their invitations, which eventually had stopped coming. Tina had still managed to graduate in the top half of the class and had been offered an exciting and challenging position in the Nashville office.

Julie suddenly remembered something else she had forgotten. She dug in her satchel and pulled out one more item, a nicely engraved nameplate, the other graduation gift from her sister. She set it on the desk in front of her, facing the door.

"Julie Noble—Special Agent. FBI."

———

"Well, her credentials are great, for someone right out of the academy." Mike Wallace, Deputy Director of Personnel, laid her file down on his supervisor's expansive and impeccably maintained desk.

"She graduated at the top of her class at the academy?" Director of Personnel Paynod asked, reaching for the file.

"Yes, several points ahead of her next closest competitor," Wallace answered.

"Does she have any particular interests?" Paynod asked.

Mike had scanned her file earlier and was thoroughly familiar with it.

"Well, she seems to be a whiz at computers."

Paynod laughed.

"Aren't they all, nowadays? All we seem to get these days are computer nerds or martial arts experts."

Wallace smiled. "But true computer experts are rare, sir—her scores were very high. And she concentrated more on the human side of technology. She cataloged and computerized all the academy's training courses, and then she transferred them into the centralized computer network. Now any of the trainees can instantly access the training files via the network without having to leave their dorm rooms. They can just pull the files up on their personal computers. And multiple students can access the same files at the same time."

Director Paynod's eyebrows arched upward slightly, which was about the most emotion Paynod ever showed.

"Well, I like that a lot," Paynod said. "I remember lugging those stupid case files from the Central Library all the way across campus to my dorm room."

Mike nodded, agreeing. "Or showing up and finding out someone else had already checked out the one file you needed to complete your report. That happened to me more than once."

Director Paynod smiled and kept reading, and Mike sat back in his chair to give him a moment. Students of the FBI Academy studied the cases and files from actual investigations and reports that had been submitted by the FBI agents that had worked the original cases. The cadets were challenged to come to their own conclusions about the case. Second-guessing the original agent was something of a student requirement.

Mike sat patiently, waiting. One of the first things he'd learned about his boss was to keep your mouth shut while he was thinking.

Finally, Paynod sat up straight.

"How is the new computer coming?"

Mike's brain changed gears smoothly. He had guessed that this would be the approach Paynod would take, and he was prepared. And there was only one new computer system coming to the FBI that deserved a title of its own.

"Well, the peripherals and subsystems were installed over the last three weeks. The main unit is scheduled to be installed by the Cray technicians on Thursday," Mike answered.

Paynod nodded. "Where is the Team now?"

"They are just finishing up in Europe. That Paris thing, remember?"

The Team, the FBI's first group of dedicated computer experts, had been sent to Paris to help the French government tighten security on their internal computer network. Evidently, the French had some problems with on-site staff getting into their fledgling computer network and skulking around in their national security files. They called it "hacking," whatever that meant. Whether it had been a kid playing on his personal computer at home or a more serious matter, Mike did not know, and frankly, he didn't really care. The loaning of the team to the Frenchies had been purely a sign of good will between two powerful allies. The FBI had enough problems to deal with without getting involved in the internal security of other countries.

"Attach her to the Team and brief her on testing the Cray. I want her up to speed by the time the rest of the Team returns. If they're delayed, she'll need to cover any local issues." Director Paynod handed her thin file back to Mike. "And keep me informed of her progress. Set up an informal meeting here on..." He glanced at his appointment book, open on one corner of his huge desk. "...Friday afternoon."

"Yes, sir." He's like a boulder, Mike thought. Just sits there most of the time, but when he gets moving, you'd better dive out of the way. "Anything special you'd like her to do on the Team?"

"No, just find her a place that she's comfortable with." Mike could tell the director's mind had already moved on to the next topic. Mike nodded and stood and was most of the way to the door when Paynod added another instruction.

"Oh, and keep Collings and the single boys away from her for a while," Paynod said with a laugh. "She doesn't need the distractions."

Abe Foreman's office was smallish but neat. It was decorated with the obligatory framed diplomas and citations, along with a dozen framed pictures of himself with some of the more prominent businessmen and politicians in the town of Liberty and Anne County. In the middle of the wall was his favorite photo, holding a place of reverence. The small framed color photo showed a smiling and obviously very happy Abe Foreman shaking hands with then-President Ronald Reagan.

David wasn't looking at the pictures or admiring the framed proof of Mr. Foreman's extensive education. The boy was obviously trying to keep his cool.

"And...?" David asked pointedly, his voice having risen an octave or two in last five minutes.

Abe Foreman relaxed as far back in his chair as he could. He knew that the Beaumont boy was a pushover, but Abe wondered if there was any of his father's notoriously short temper lurking underneath that detached and cool exterior. Abe didn't think so. Evidently, David was one of those people that liked to keep everything inside. He would not have made a great sheriff, in Abe Foreman's opinion. Not able to stand up for himself.

David looked at him expectantly, but Abe just couldn't help but keep him waiting for a few more seconds. It was just so much fun to bait the kid.

"Okay, David," Abe began. "I know that you want the story, so here it is, as straight as I can tell it to you. I talked to your aunt the other night and suggested that she sell the house and move into someplace smaller. That's it."

"Why? Is she out of money? I thought you were..." David started, but then backed off. "I thought all of her money was safe."

Abe searched this young man's eyes for some clue as to what he was thinking or feeling, but there was nothing in his crystal green eyes that gave any hints. It looked as if he might be trying to get up a head of steam and get angry, and this pleased Abe. Abe liked to think of himself as a student of human nature, and David Beaumont was one of his favorite subjects. Whenever the kid tried to get angry or upset, something made him back off, keep it all inside. The boy always controlled his emotions. Abe wondered at the heaps of anger he must have locked away. Someday, it was all going to blow up. Abe just hoped he'd be there to see it.

David spoke up, interrupting Abe's thoughts. "She said she was behind on the taxes..."

Abe smiled and leaned forward, planting his elbows on the desk blotter. He loved to give people information they didn't have.

"She has more than forty-five thousand put away, in T-bills and other investments. Listen, David, your aunt is perfectly fine. She's behind on some bills, but I took care of them. The only reason I suggested that she move was that she is in that big house all by herself. I thought she might want to move into a smaller place."

He watched the kid's face and continued.

"Even though the house is paid for, she still spends a lot of money to heat it and cool it. There are probably rooms that she hasn't even been in in a long time. And when she forgets to send in the electric payments, or the property taxes, which is often, they get upset."

He was talking about the little three-bedroom row house like it was a mansion, but even that didn't seem to get any reaction from David. He just sat there, nodding along, driving Abe crazy. What was going on inside that head of his? Was he distracted? Abe continued, trying from another direction.

"All of the money from your father's will is safe and sound; don't worry."

David cringed visibly at the mention of his father. The boy always reacted that way. Was the Beaumont boy truly haunted by the memories of his dead father, like people thought? People said that the boy would rather run away than make peace with his father's legend. Everyone who lived in Liberty had heard the Story a dozen times. How many times had the kid heard it?

It was popular speculation around town that David would leave town as soon as he got his money, which was sitting in a clearly marked envelope on Abe's desk. And today was the boy's eighteenth birthday. The boy must be itching to ask for the money—his eyes had lingered on the envelope.

Abe wanted to get this business about the aunt out of the way first. And Abe wanted to see how long the kid would go before he asked.

Abe had also heard that David had just dumped his girlfriend, a cute little brunette he'd seen around. Cutting all the strings, preparing to leave. Abe could see it in the boy's eyes. He was concerned about making sure his aunt was taken care of.

But would the kid really leave? He looked weak, scared. Abe didn't think he had it in him.

"With Clinton in the White House, interest rates will continue to climb," Abe said. "Your Aunt will be getting even more of a return on her money. As will you, since most of the money in your account is also in T-bills, with some real estate thrown in."

The kid nodded, glancing at the envelope on the desk again.

Abe turned and opened a folder. "Your account contained a small portion of the property that the new mall was built on. That alone means that the cash payouts you'll get on your next ten birthdays will be handsome. $25,000 a year, and then a balloon payout on your 28th birthday of whatever is left. I'm happy to say I saw that opportunity coming and bought small lots of property for both you and your aunt— and myself and my investors. When the property was sold to the mall developers, we all made a sizable profit."

David didn't say anything, but Abe could tell he was itching to finish the discussion and get his money. The kid was deliciously fidgety. He probably wasn't asking any questions to avoid any delays.

Abe was pretty sure he would just go out and blow it—Abe didn't think the kid had the guts to do anything decisive, especially something as drastic as moving away.

Abe continued. "I think she would be happier in something smaller. Don't you?" Abe watched the boy think.

He nodded. "Yes, Mr. Foreman, you may be right. I don't like her living there all by herself."

Abe smiled. "There are all kinds of places where she could live, maybe even meet some new people, get out more often."

David nodded again. Maybe the kid was thinking it would get her off the sauce. Abe plunged ahead, inwardly delighted at how easy the kid was to manipulate.

"Combined with the proceeds from the sale of the house, she could easily afford one of those nice townhomes they are building out west of town." He paused for effect, thinking about the handsome percentage of the transaction fees and finder's fees he might earn. "I think she would be more likely to sell if you supported the idea. Then let me know, and I'll take care of everything."

"Okay, I'll talk to her about it," the boy said after a few moments' thought.

Abe stood up and smiled, thinking about a new BMW he was eyeing. "That would be great, David."

The boy looked at him for a moment and stood, his hands playing with his baseball cap, and it reminded Abe of a little kid getting ready to ask his parents for a favor, or maybe an advance on his allowance. After a minute, he spoke up.

"So, my money. That's the first payment?"

Abe nodded. "I bet you've been looking forward to this for a long time, haven't you?"

The boy nodded like a kid at the candy store.

Abe picked up the envelope and pulled out the check. It was made out to David—Abe knew that because he'd checked it earlier. But now he spent a moment verifying all the details, prolonging the boy's anticipation. The check was right here, and the kid could see it, but he couldn't have it until Abe was finished. Abe nodded and took out a pen, then reached over and jotted down the routing and check numbers at the bottom. He didn't need to, but it made the kid wait.

Finally, Abe nodded very gravely and turned and handed the check to the boy, who took it gingerly, as if it were made of glass. He held the check and read it, his eyes wide.

"Now, don't sign that until you get to the bank and are ready to deposit it," Abe said. "And don't spend it all in the next twenty-four hours. That's a lot of money, and you need to be careful with it. Your father would've wanted it that way." Abe waited, but the reference to David's father got no reaction this time—the kid was too absorbed in reading the numbers on the check.

The kid finally looked up at Abe, and it looked like he was going to cry. Abe almost laughed out loud! The boy was an emotional wreck and having this money would probably push him over the edge. It was going to end up frittered away, Abe was certain. And the kid was never going to leave. This first check would be spent before the bank had even cleared it. A new car, or a computer, or drugs. Whatever kids spent money on nowadays.

Looking into the kid's eyes, Abe was sure of it.

"Thank you, Mr. Foreman. I think I'll take it to the bank right now." The boy spoke to Abe, but his eyes never left the check. "I promise to speak to my aunt about what we talked about."

Abe nodded, even though the kid wasn't looking. The aunt's money was locked in her T-bill account, but this kid's investments were still under Abe's discretion. A little creative bookkeeping, and Abe could play the market with most of the kids' money. The kid would never check on the status of the principal—he would be far too concerned with spending his annual payout. Abe could play the market or take a trip.

He showed the kid out, already trying to decide what to do first. The commission Abe would make from the transfer of the aunt's house was chump change compared to the cash he could skim from the kid's account. Not the principal, of course, but interest and "future earnings" were malleable things, easily manipulated. Easily pocketed.

The first step would be to set up a dummy corporation in the kids' name, then move some of the account over to it "for tax purposes." Abe would control it, of course. There were unlimited options on how to use the money. Just the thought of it made Abe smile.

Her lunch was simple and straightforward, taken in the FBI cafeteria one floor up from her "office." The floor above hers, floor six, bustled with people and excitement, and Julie felt a pang of resentment for all of these busy people seated around her in the cafeteria, all chatting with friends and coworkers or busily working on important projects during their lunch breaks.

She felt like a school kid on a field trip to a bustling office. All she had brought with her was a sack lunch and a paperback book.

Julie finished up her sandwich and wrapped up the remains of her banana and drink box in the brown paper of her lunch sack, collected her purse and book, and started out of the cafeteria. She could feel the eyes of others on her, but maybe she was just imagining it. It was her first day, and she didn't know anybody. Just like back in school.

Her family moved around a lot when she was young. Her father had been a career Navy man, always out to sea on one of his "big boats," as her mother called them.

The only times her dad seemed to be around for extended periods was whenever they moved. He would appear, seemingly by magic, help them pack and move and unpack, get them settled into a new house and at new schools, and then be off again for six months or a year. In a sense, she hadn't really had a father, only a mysterious kind man who, on occasion, came to Julie's house and helped them move.

But she had gotten used to it—she'd grown up constantly being exposed to new things, new people. She was used to the new-school mentality, felt it had made her a better person. Or maybe she was just kidding herself. But the moves had made her good at making friends, and curious about the world around her. She was pretty sure she'd settle in here with no problems.

She left the cafeteria and started down the hall, looking for the particular stairwell that would take her back down to her floor. All this commotion, all these people. At least on her floor she could concentrate— if only she had something to concentrate on.

She found the right stairwell and was about to blindly push the door open, when it popped open as if on its own accord. She jumped back to avoid being hit, bumping against another person walking down the hall, their head buried in a report. The other person mumbled something and moved on down the hallway, already buried again in their papers.

A nicely dressed man emerged from the stairwell, looking apologetic. "Oh, I'm sorry, Miss Noble. I didn't mean to frighten you."

She smiled. "That's okay. I wasn't looking where I was going." She looked at him for a moment. "Do I know you?"

He extended his hand. "No, but I was just downstairs, looking for you. I am Mike Wallace, Deputy Director of Personnel. We need to discuss your future."

Mike Wallace's office was impressive—the man clearly had an interest in amateur interior decorating, and in Julie's opinion, he had a flair for it. Everything in the office had been done in an angular, modern style, even down to the hexagonal rug on the floor, knitted in an odd, abstract design. Nothing in the room seemed cold or inhuman, just modern. Sleek.

Wallace sat behind his desk, looking at her file. His desk was made completely of large sheets of smoky gray glass. Julie thought it was beautiful—and not standard issue. She would've guessed he paid for it himself.

She had been sitting in his office for over five minutes and, except for his initial offer of a chair, he had yet to say anything.

Julie shifted in her seat and straightened her skirt absently. She looked at the neo-abstract lithographs on the walls and realized that all of them in the room were related—variations on the same theme, using the same colors in subtly different ways. She spent a long time looking out of the line of windows at a group of trees outside, swaying gently over what looked like 10th Street in the early fall breeze. The leaves were just starting to change, and the colors looked strangely muted through the window's thick and smoky glass. Across the street, she could see the Old Post Office, her favorite downtown building. She admired the exterior and promised herself she would eat lunch there at least once a week. When she was done, she set about calculating her checking account balance as close as she could and wondered if the car payment she had just sent in had cleared yet.

"Am I making you nervous?" Wallace asked her, the ghost of a grin on his face. He didn't look up.

She looked at him. "Not particularly, sir."

Wallace looked up at her. "Well, it says here that you are very good with computers."

The question hung in the air for several seconds as Julie tried to decide whether it was rhetorical or not.

"Yes, I'm pretty good with them."

Wallace sat back in his odd, angular chair that looked as if it had been stolen from the set of some science fiction movie and regarded her for a moment.

"Miss Noble, you'll have to do better than that. If I didn't know any better, I would think you're not confident about your abilities. Now, let's try again, shall we?" He placed an elbow on each side of her open file and asked again.

This time she came back without a moments' hesitation.

"Yes, sir, I'm very good with computers. At the academy, I helped set up a Local Area Network, or LAN, that services all the computer terminals on the campus. The LAN connects all of the PCs in the individual dorm rooms. We, that is, Dr. Morrison from Computer Sciences and I, set up a mid-line electronic mail system that linked all the campus PCs together by 24,000 BPS modems, allowing anyone with access to a computer to instantly send and receive information to any other linked terminal on campus. This required the addition of several miles of new telephone wire. The system was so successful that the academy officials approached us with a second project."

She took a breath and continued.

"We started converting all of the historic case files and case records and storing them in a large multi-access CD-ROM system with a 40-millisecond respond time, all controlled by two Compaq 4876 mainframe servers that regulated access to the information and handled and maintained the security of the files. This system allows end users to download three pages of text per second using a 12,000 BPS modem, or eight pages of text per second using a 24,000 BPS modem. We set up and completed a CD-ROM system and hooked it into the LAN to allow campus-wide access. Then we constructed a message center, and, using a commercially purchased gateway, we connected..."

Mike was holding up one of his hands.

"Okay, okay. You've convinced me that you know what you're

talking about." He was smiling at what seemed to be some inner, private joke. "It's difficult when you get to be my age to cut through all the jargon, but it sounds like you made the academy's training case files remotely accessible, and that's good. Now, my second question. Do you like working with computers?"

Julie thought about this before answering. Yes, she liked working with computers, and she knew this was her strong suit. But she joined the FBI to become a field agent, to get out there into the real world and try to help in the best way she could. Sitting behind a computer for the next twenty or thirty years at FBI Headquarters was not her idea of field work. But she got the feeling there might not be any other choice, at least not right now. She just hoped the next words she said didn't dictate the rest of her career.

"Yes, sir, I do like working with computers. But I think computers should be used as any other tool, just like a pencil or a calculator. They should help you get to where you want to go and maybe even get you there a little faster, but they shouldn't be studied just for the sake of studying them." Her face flushed a little, perhaps slightly embarrassed for expressing her opinion so candidly. "It's just that I don't want to be stuck behind a computer for the rest of my career," she continued.

Mike nodded and steepled his fingers, an expression that instantly reminded Julie of her father. When he was around, he used to watch the news with his hands up in front of him, steepled in the same thoughtful manner.

Mike nodded. Then he spun around in his odd chair and reached into an open file cabinet behind his desk, pulling out a manila folder that was bordered and sealed with bright blue tape. He studied it once more, as if having second thoughts, and then spun back around and handed the file over to Julie. She took it carefully, keeping it flat like a waitress trying to keep from spilling a tray of drinks. She saw the blue SECRET tape first and then the title:

PROJECT 546DF: WILDFIRE

"We have an exciting new project starting up next week, and we think you will make a valuable addition," Wallace said, nodding at the file. "Are you familiar with the Team?"

She nodded. Everyone knew about the FBI's newly-formed group of computer experts. She'd never dreamed—

"Good. We're attaching you to them for now. Take that and read it carefully. Then spend the rest of the day writing down your opinions and comments on the possible uses and benefits of such a system. A wish list, so to speak. There is also a timetable included, describing when each part of the new system will be online."

He looked up at the wildly modernistic clock hanging on the gray wall behind Julie, which read 1:08. "Let's see you back here tomorrow at 9:00 a.m. with some ideas, okay?"

Julie nodded, and then finally found her tongue.

"Yes, sir. 9:00. Thank you, sir." She got up and reached for his hand.

"Oh, and don't take that file home," he said as he shook her hand.

"Yes, sir," she said, smiling, and left his office.

Julie managed to get almost all the way back to her office before she broke the blue tape seal on the folder and began looking through it.

Project Wildfire was a fancy name for a new Cray Mark IV supercomputer being installed for use at FBI Headquarters. The computer was years ahead of anything she had heard of, but the advances made in this unit followed logically from what she knew of the present generation. Companies all over the world would have salivated over the mere prospect of using it. This unit was the only one of its kind in the world, a prototype, and the FBI had been challenged by the Cray Corporation to construct programs sophisticated enough to make full use of the computer's advanced abilities.

Eventually, the rest of the FBI would be able to use the Cray Mark IV, but for now, preliminary testing would be carried out by the eleven members of the Computer Response Team. She'd heard all about the Team, back at the academy, but she would never have dared dream of being made a part of it. Julie did not see her name on the printed Team roster, so she assumed hers would make it twelve.

The main thrust of the test project would be to construct a massive database to hold the files on all known crimes in the Continental United States. It sounded like an incredible undertaking, and something that had never been attempted before, but Julie knew it would not be as difficult as it sounded on paper. She knew the country's master lists and files on crimes had been computerized for many years. The new twist on this project would be that all of the files would be stored inside one master data bank, instead of spread out in a dozen room-sized mainframes scattered across the country.

This mass storage would create advances in two separate areas. First, access to the files would be increased and access times would be reduced. Second, the structure of the database would hopefully allow, for the first time, a comparison of multiple files from all over the country.

One of the most successful methods of police investigation is the discerning of subtle patterns in a series of crimes. Sometimes it was something as simple as a common tire track or a type of rope that could be the key to cracking a case, or a whole string of cases.

Julie remembered reading about a case several years ago that involved a series of unsolved disappearances from several neighboring towns. Because the police officers of these towns were seldom in communication with one another, the pattern went undetected for years. Finally, a waitress at a local roadside restaurant happened to mention the latest disappearance to a highway patrolman who stopped off for coffee.

It was discovered that all the cases, some of them five counties over, had one distinct, unpublished fact in common. In each case, the killer had been wearing a red baseball cap. In hindsight, the answer had been simple, but it had taken a lucky fluke to put it all together. And the FBI was apparently hoping that this powerful new machine would be a high-tech answer to that lucky fluke.

David got into his car and started back to his apartment. He got about halfway there when he realized that he didn't want to go home. There was nothing at his apartment for him, and the news that he needed to pass along to his aunt could wait—she was most likely passed out, anyway. David turned the car west, toward the mountains.

Let Abe Foreman handle the details, David thought. He seemed more than willing to step in and help Aunt Gloria find a new place to live. He'd even offered to oversee the selling of the house and deposit the proceeds for her. The guy was probably angling for some commission or something.

And the check in his pocket—it could wait to be deposited. The money was his now. The years of waiting were over. Now, more than anything, it was time to figure out what he was going to do next.

His aunt was slowly drinking herself to death. It was not difficult to imagine attending her funeral soon. Some of the things Abe said were very true. She had drunk a lot of the money away, back when she'd first started receiving the payments on David's eighth birthday. Abe had apparently seen what was happening and locked her out of most of the funds.

But without the house and all its memories of his parents hanging over her, David's aunt might be able to get on with living the rest of her life instead of focusing on the past. Just the thought of his aunt out and about, no longer shackled to the altar of the great god vodka, brought a smile to his face. To see her enjoying life and meeting new people would be great. It would be one less thing on his mind.

As he drove, David thought about the condition of the house yesterday morning and how it had smelled like death and decay. And even though the man was probably right, David never really liked Mr. Foreman. Every time David talked to him, he felt like he was being examined, like a bug under a microscope.

He drove past the restaurant where he and Bethany went on their first date, and that was all it took to flood his mind with memories and thoughts of her. But she wasn't in his life any more, and that was a good thing, even if it had been his most successful relationship ever. They would go places together, spend quiet evenings with a pizza from Tony's and a rented movie, and sometimes they would sleep together. And sometimes they wouldn't. Either way, David had been happy.

But the timing had been all wrong. And they had plenty of fights. The longer they went out, the more they fought. "David, why don't you go back to school and study architecture? You always say that you always wanted to be an architect..."

"David, do you want to work at a video store for the rest of your life? There's no future..."

"David, why don't you and your aunt talk very much? I think if you talked more, spent more time together. In my family, we always..."

It always seemed to come down to the same things. She wanted more from him than he could give her. She wanted him to have more, to BE more. Him constantly talking about leaving hadn't helped. Bethany had said she was only trying to urge him to improve himself, to go back to college. But then he would think about how good it would feel to just pack up and leave town and never look back.

He hated Liberty.

He hated the way the past lay over the town like a thick blanket, choking everyone. He hated hearing about his father and the Killer. The Story had long ago stopped amusing David, if it ever had. He had the sneaking suspicion that he would never, could never amount to anything as long as he stayed in Liberty, trapped in the shadow of his father. He could live to be ninety and people would still be comparing him to Sheriff Beaumont.

David had imagined leaving for so long. But now that he had the money, could he do it? Would he actually leave?

Getting away would be good for him. The Story only reminded him of how unfair life had been to him. He wanted to blame someone, and more often than not, he ended up blaming those around him, those closest to him, including his girlfriends. But most of all, underneath what felt like a swirling whirlpool of pain and sorrow and anger, he felt like he'd been abandoned.

David passed a sign that marked the western city limits of Liberty.

Already, the road was starting to twist its way upwards into the Shenandoah foothills. Several housing developments and subdivisions, including the one Abe Foreman suggested, were scattered about the hills overlooking the town. The rocky slope of the foothills jutted into the sky in places, affording lovely views of the town, spread out like a blanket in the valley below. He often drove up here, enjoying the view but wishing he could just keep driving west and never turn back.

The road continued upward, switching back and forth on itself as it wound into Shenandoah National Park and its myriad recreational facilities, camping areas, and hiking trails. David was in the right lane, his blue Mazda chugging slowly up the long incline. The other cars going this way easily blew past him, honking as they accelerated smoothly around him. The turns became more pronounced, switchbacks working their way up the steep hillside. On one particularly sharp turn, he tried to take it too fast, and his glove compartment popped open. A sheaf of papers and bills and sundries spilled out onto the passenger floorboard.

Bethany had been good for him, though. She'd encouraged him to take a summer semester of classes at the local community college. Drafting and architecture had always fascinated him. He loved the way buildings looked as they stood tall against the sky, and he dreamed of designing them. He remembered several years ago when he had been fascinated by the plans for the mall—they hung on the wall outside Abe Foreman's office for months. He'd spent long hours alone in that hallway, studying the colorful plans. He probably knew the inside of that mall better than anyone around.

He'd decided to further that useless pipe dream by taking classes in architecture and drafting, along with classes in English and psychology.

But even the classes he liked failed to grab and hold his attention. He dropped out after that summer semester, after getting a C- in psychology, doing well only in architecture. The professor told David he possessed some real talent in the field, but David was sure that was just something he told everyone to keep his enrollment up. David failed English, and that's when he'd decided college just wasn't for him. Failing at your native language wasn't a good sign. After dropping out of college, David realized that nothing in Liberty would ever change for him.

David saw the turnout he was looking for and slowed. A car behind him changed lanes and roared around him, and David looked away when the car passed, in case the guy was shouting at him or flipping him off. It was easier to ignore if you didn't see it.

He pulled across the oncoming lane and rolled to a stop in the paved turnout, edged by some short trees and a three-foot wall of stone, high enough to warn of the drop-off on the other side.

He had driven all the way to the top. From here, he could see west, looking out over the rolling expanse of the Shenandoah Valley. It lay before him like a sweeping green blanket, crisscrossed with roads and interrupted regularly with square swatches of different colors, different crops, as seen from high above. From up here, it looked like a patchwork quilt.

He came up here whenever he needed to be alone. And he'd come here more often over the past few months, thinking a lot about Bethany and his birthday and the money.

David had the turnout to himself. He got out and walked over to the edge, sitting on the stone wall, dangling his feet over the side. It was a five-foot drop to the ground on the other side of the stone wall, but then the ground sloped away quickly, disappearing into a thick stand of trees.

David Beaumont looked to the west. The valley spread out before him. In a few hours, the sun would dip behind another shallow range of mountains on the far side of the valley. He had sat up here many times and watched the sun disappear in the West.

It was impossible for him to stay long enough to see that same sight today—he needed to get to the bank before 5 p.m. The check felt like a heavy, hot stone in his pocket.

He took it out and looked at it, staring at the numbers. Now that it was real, now that it happened, it seemed like a dream.

$24,502.

He glanced up at the mountains on the far side of the valley. West. Everything looked better in that direction. The sky even looked bluer, richer.

He found himself thinking about Brian Church for the first time in months. Brian and David had been good friends in high school up until Brian and his family moved to somewhere in Los Angeles. Brian kept in touch, and never failed to invite David out for a visit—or something even more permanent.

"It's so nice here," the letters always said. "The weather is great ten months out of the year, the beaches are close, and the women are all beautiful. Seriously. You should really come and see LA and Long Beach, bud. You would love it." Brian was working for a power company in Long Beach and had even offered to get David a job there.

The idea held great appeal for him. David just wanted to be somewhere else, someplace where nobody knew about him or his family. Someplace where no one had heard the Story. Or even knew that the Story existed.

But could he really do it? Could David really just pack up all of his things in his car and leave? Could he call Brian out of the blue and take him up on his offer? Was it genuine?

The thing with Bethany was finished, and that had seemed like the best shot David would ever get at happiness in this town. Maybe falling in love or being truly happy just wasn't in the cards for David.

Or maybe just here in Liberty.

He had a dead-end job and a boss that hated him. Working with Bethany was starting to drive him nuts. One of these days, she was going to bat her eyelashes at him, and they would get back together. And inside of a week, they'd be fighting about him moving, or she'd be back to riding him about something, "David, go back to college. David, go find a better job. David, go talk to your aunt and straighten her out—it's like you're the parent and she's the kid!"

His aunt. Things were starting to get really bad in that department, too. One of the old timers in town once confided in him that she must've started drinking heavily as soon as she got home from her sister's funeral, and she just never stopped. David wondered if she would even miss him.

He heard a rough squawk from off to his left, and he turned to see a large black bird perched on the rough stone wall twenty feet down from him. It was a crow, he thought, or maybe a big raven. It seemed huge, sitting so close. The bird was looking at him, first with one eye and then with the other, its head bobbing back and forth.

"Hey, bird."

It looked at him for a long second, and then the black bird hopped carefully up to the edge of the stone wall and kicked off, fluttering up into the blue sky. It flew slowly, tracing a long, lazy circle in the clear air above the roadside turnout, and after a minute or two, it squawked again and alighted on the stone wall, closer to him this time.

David thought about the check. With that kind of money and his car, he could coast on that for a while in California. And he would be getting more money, annually, whether or not he stayed here. All Abe needed was an account where he could send the checks. The truth was, Liberty held nothing for him any more.

"You'll love it out here."

He could actually hear Brian's voice as he said the words, pulling him like a magnet with their powerful simplicity.

David suddenly remembered Brian's last letter was probably one of those pieces of paper that tumbled out of his broken glove compartment when he had tried to take that one corner too fast.

He stood up and was startled to see that the black bird had gotten within three feet of him while he was daydreaming. David jumped back, and the bird leapt into the air and flapped over, settling casually on the blue hood of David's Mazda.

Great. The claws looked sharp—the bird was probably going to scratch the paint. Of course, the car was a piece of shit, so it didn't really matter. David shook his head and walked over to his car, keeping one wary eye on the bird. He noticed the blacks and greens and subtle dark grays that made up the bird's appearance as he fished out his keys and unlocked the passenger door.

He climbed in, straddling the mess of papers and closed the door behind him. The bird preened itself on his hood, ignoring David completely. It looked huge through the window, sitting on the hood only a few feet away. It seemed to be favoring one leg, like it was injured or something.

The floorboard of the Mazda was covered with papers. Some had fallen from the glove box when it popped open, but the rest were permanent residents. Piles and piles of stuff, useful and useless, all mingled together in a hodgepodge that was always frightening-looking enough to discourage David from ever cleaning it up. His aunt didn't have a monopoly on living like a slob.

He started digging. He knew that the letter was rubber-banded to a short stack of letters from other friends from out of state, letters that he was notoriously bad about answering. He'd lost more than his fair share of friends for reasons like that. He found his April MasterCard bill, unpaid, but since it was now September, it didn't really matter, although it did explain why, lately, he seemed to be perpetually one payment behind every time.

He found tapes and movies that he had forgotten he'd bought, still in their little plastic bags. He found old food, some he could identify and one package that he didn't dare open. He tossed them into the backseat that constituted his trashcan. He also found a five-dollar bill and a small bag of older movies that he'd been planning to sell at that ever-elusive garage sale he'd always planned on having but never seemed to get around to.

Here they were.

He pulled out a loose stack of different-sized envelopes and letters, all rubber-banded together. He rummaged through the pile until he found it and pulled the letter and its envelope free.

David climbed out of the car and walked back over to the stone wall.

The envelope read "Brian Church, 3031 Haversham Lane, Long Beach, CA, 90231." When he pulled the actual letter out, he saw it was only a few lines long, the classic symptoms of someone who hasn't heard from a friend in a long time but can't quite seem to give up hope that someday the delinquent friend would write back. It was anybody's guess how long Brian would continue to send these short little letters, before he finally decides to chuck the whole thing and give up.

Or maybe he thought David really would take him up on his invitation when he hit eighteen.

Hey Davey-Boy,

It's been a while since I heard from you. How've you been? I'd love to hear all about things. Did you ever ask that Bethany girl out? Last time you wrote, you were thinking about it, but that was almost a year ago. Things are good here. Sheela and I are talking about getting married. I told you about her—I met her at Fashions, a little club on the Redondo Beach Pier, remember?

The job at the warehouse is fine—I can get you on anytime. And Sheela says she knows some cute single girls where she works. Or there's the psychic she goes to a lot, Meredith Black, who might be able to find you a girl. Right?

Hey, come out and see me sometime, okay? I know it probably won't ever happen, but a guy can keep his hopes up, right? You'd love it out here.

Well, gotta go. Write me back sometime you big jerk.

The bottom of the letter was signed "Your Friend Brian" and Brian had listed his address again, just to be sure. And his home phone number.

David folded up the letter and stuffed it into his pocket, his mind working. Could he really go? For the first time in his life, he was really and truly considering leaving Liberty.

"SQUAWK!"

The black bird was looking at him again, now back on the stone wall and working its head back and forth again. The bird was probably only hungry, but to David it looked like it was nodding at him, its dingy yellow beak pointing right at him.

"What?" David felt giddy, as if some weight had been lifted from his shoulders. He could do it. He could really do it—for once in his life, he could do something for himself, something that might make him happy.

"What do you think, bird? West, into the sunset? Like a cowboy?"

The black bird squawked again, louder this time, and leapt into the air. It circled the turnout once, twice, as it had done before, and then it waggled its wings and took off out over the trees and the valley, straight as an arrow.

Due west.

David smiled and patted the letter in his pocket as he walked back to his car. He took one more look at the odd bird as it flew west into the setting sun, nodded to himself, and then he climbed into his Mazda and headed home.

Norma Jenkins was famous in the town of Liberty, Virginia. Just not in a good way. She was a critical part of the Story about the Killer and Beaumont. No one, no matter how hurried they were to tell the whole thing, ever left her out. She was crucial to the ending, and important to making sure the story ended on the saddest note possible.

Everyone in town knew Norma. She was the last person to see Beaumont alive. The Story always ended with her, sitting with him, as the Killer drove away in Beaumont's vehicle. Around town, Norma was famous. She hated it.

And, of course, everyone knew what came after. Everyone knew she had quit the sheriff's department only a couple months after that terrible rainy night. The speculation was obvious and not very inventive: she had admired and respected the man. Some said she had loved him. It wasn't true, but she did take his death very hard, no matter what people thought of their relationship.

After leaving the force, she'd tried other jobs before landing behind the big flat wheel of a yellow school bus. Norma was a good driver, albeit a little strict on her helpless passengers. She was an ex-cop, and the kids didn't like her much, and that suited Norma just fine. She didn't like them either. She made them sit down and behave themselves. There was no yelling, no eating, no drinking, no throwing anything on Norma's bus. No one was allowed to stand up or change seats while the bus was in motion. Period.

Any foul-ups and Norma would make the kid come up and sit in the seat directly behind hers, and then the kid would have to stay there for the rest of the bus ride. Everyone else was allowed to get off at their stops or at the school, depending on which route Norma was on, morning or afternoon, but the kid who acted up was not. That kid was made to return to wherever he or she had been picked up. Norma Jenkins was known to retrace, on occasion, her entire morning bus route, dropping off kids all along the way, and each of them—and their parents—were then responsible for finding his or her own way to school or be absent.

Most of the parents of these kids were upset when they found out they had to take time off from work and bring their little "angels" in to school, or to go to the school and bring them home in the afternoon. But they were angrier at their kids after they contacted Norma and found out what their particular "darling" had done to warrant being punished.

Norma rarely had trouble on her bus.

One popular rumor with the students was that she was a little crazy. She'd been driving a school bus for something like ten years, and the kids figured that that would drive anyone crazy. Behind her back—but never to her face—they made fun of her crooked nose. But when they were standing at the bus stop and saw her yellow #3 bus pull up to the curb to pick them up, they quickly shelved any ideas they might have had about being rowdy.

Monday afternoon, Norma finished up with the last kids on her morning route and returned to the high school, parking next to the other four buses that serviced the Liberty School District. Her car, an old Dodge Duster, was parked in a small lot behind the bus maintenance shed, and she got into the car and drove home. Some of the other bus drivers were there in the parking area also, chatting, but she didn't speak to any of them, and they didn't speak to her. After a quick trip to the grocery store—not the Food Town, a place she avoided—she headed home.

Norma lived by herself in a smallish one-bedroom house on the southern end of town. She hadn't consciously chosen to live on the opposite side of town from Mrs. Grace Beaumont, William's widow, or the Beaumont boy, but the distance had not been lost on her. In the many years since, she had chosen to avoid the Beaumont's and Gloria, Grace's sister, as much as possible.

Just the sight of them brought up too many bad memories for her.

Norma kept the rage inside until she'd finished her grocery shopping and made it to the door of her house, but then she couldn't hold it in any longer. She wasn't far inside the door before she dropped her purse and set her bag of groceries down and staggered into the living room, crying. The bag fell over and food spilled onto the floor.

It wasn't too often that she got into one of her crying jags, but sometimes something would happen to trigger one.

Today, it was the new kid in town. He obviously hadn't yet heard about Norma from the other kids. He'd climbed on her bus and proceeded to ask her a question.

"Hey, lady? What happened to your nose?"

Norma had ignored the little brat. One of the other kids grabbed the boy roughly and pulled him away from Norma, whispering to him. Norma heard the kid tell the new boy he must never, EVER ask Miss Jenkins about her crooked nose.

A few minutes later, she felt a little better. She got up from the couch and went to the kitchen. The bread and apples from the fallen bag were fine, but two of the eggs had broken and oozed out of the bag onto the rug in the foyer. She cleaned them up, put the remaining groceries away, and then changed into an old gray sweat suit.

Beaumont had always told her that she was like a boy trapped inside a girl's body. He didn't mean it in any bad way—he'd said it because she was more aggressive and more fitness-oriented than many of the other deputies. On her way back to the living room, she caught a quick flash of her reflection, and she could see what he meant. It wasn't that she was unattractive. She just carried herself like a tomboy. And the crooked nose certainly didn't help.

She looked closer at her face in the mirror. It was, in her opinion, attractive, or at least it had been up until the point where Jasper Fines had given her a jagged souvenir to remember him by. But she was still attractive. She had dated men, off and on, over the years. A few times it had grown quite serious until she threw on the brakes and ended it.

Norma was certain, deep down, that she didn't deserve to be happy. Gloria wasn't happy either, drinking her life away. Grace was dead. The Beaumont kid, David, was miserable, trapped in town and constantly being compared to his father. And Sheriff William T. Beaumont certainly wasn't happy anymore.

The thing that tore her up inside the most was the nagging guilt. She should have done something that dark night. She should have gotten up and helped Beaumont before that madman killed him. Maybe it would've gotten her killed, too, but at least it would've been a good way to check out. Go out in a blaze of glory, not cowering like a scared child. She realized that night, holding Beaumont after he died, that she was never cut out to be a cop.

She made herself yet another bland and tasteless dinner. Norma's doctors had warned her long ago to avoid spicy foods or anything that might aggravate her two gastric ulcers. Even though she had followed the doctor's orders to the letter, they never healed. They were a pair of close companions that she was sure, after so many years of gnawing and tearing at her insides, would never leave her.

She ate her bland macaroni and cheese and watched *Wheel of Fortune*, chasing her meal down with several Tums, popping them like candy. She felt like putting in a movie, but she didn't know what to watch. She liked action movies and suspense-filled dramas the best, ones with lots of guns and shooting and car chases. But every time she watched a thrilling movie, the twisting pain in her gut flared up. Instead, Norma put on *City Slickers* and sat back to lose herself in the light-hearted comedy.

———————

David was in his apartment, the phone in his hand, ringing.

He had gone by and talked to his aunt on his way home. After an hour, he finally got her to at least consider moving to a smaller place. The whole time he was there, all he could think about was getting to the bank before they close, then going home and making this phone call. He'd left his aunt's house and raced to the bank, then back to the apartment. And now he stood with the phone tucked into the crook between his ear and shoulder, his keys still in the door.

It felt as if he were at a crossroads. Whatever words he heard next would change the direction of his life forever. But change was what he wanted. It felt good, doing something. And the money was deposited, and he had a nice wad of twenties in his pocket to get started—

A woman's voice answered. "Hello?"

"Hi, is Brian there?" he asked, tentative but trying to sound like he knew what he was doing. Who says people can't change overnight? David felt like he was changing with each passing moment.

"Ah, no, he's not here right now," she said, sounding sleepy. "He's at work. Do you want to...uh, like, leave a message or something?"

Damn, he thought, almost saying it out loud. It's like deciding to buy a car and getting to the dealership and picking it out and then finding out that you didn't have enough money to pay for it. He collected his thoughts.

"Uh, yeah. My name's David. Beaumont. I knew Brian back in—"

"David?" she interrupted. "Did you say David?"

"Yeah," he said, confused. "David. Brian and I have been writing back and forth for a couple of years, and he—"

"I know, I know!" she shouted, her voice high and tinny like a radio with no bass, exactly the voice a mouse would use if it could talk. "He's told me all about you! You were friends in high school, right? We were just talking about you the other day. Weird, huh?" She talked so rapidly that it was impossible to get a word in until she stopped to take a breath.

"Yeah, we went to high school together," he answered quickly. He hated being interrupted, especially by someone he didn't even know.

"That's great! Oh, my name's Sheela, but people call me Crystal. I'm Brian's girlfriend...what am I saying? I'm his fiancé! How could I have forgotten a thing like that? Sometimes I still call him my boyfriend, even though we've been engaged for 34 days, and I guess he probably still calls me his girlfriend sometimes, but hey—why complain, right?"

David wasn't sure if he was supposed to answer or if she had just stopped long enough to take another breath, but he dove into the opening anyway.

"Yeah, congratulations. Listen, when will Brian be back? I'm thinking about coming out to visit, and I wanted to know about—"

"Oh, he would just *love* that," she interrupted again. "He always complains that no one from Virginia ever comes out to see him, and here you are on the phone, wanting to come out and see him! Isn't that great? He would just love to have you come out—he could show you around and introduce you to his friends. Maybe even get you a job at the power company, if you want. Hey, are you single? I know some great girls out here. They are all looking for a nice guy."

David was getting a serious headache. It was the tinny voice, and the rush of words.

"Yeah, that sounds great. Listen, when will he be in? I really want to talk to him before I get in my car and start driving. Does he get home from work soon?"

"Oh, no," she said. "He's up in Santa Cruz till next weekend, installing some power lines. They had a fire. I miss him so much! They lost some lines in that fire last week, and he and some of the other guys from the company went up to install new ones. You're gonna drive out? Oh, wow, that's great. When I drove here from Texas, it was a long trip, and you'll be coming even further, won't you? Wow, that's a lot of driving. Those long road trips can sure get awful dull, don't you think? Better make sure you've got plenty of good tunes to listen to. That part from Arizona to Nevada, that part was a real..."

David half-tuned her out; it wasn't like he was going to miss anything important. Brian was gone for a while, but David wanted to get going soon. Could he trust this motor mouth Crystal, or Sheela, or whatever her name was, that Brian wanted David to come out? Between her and the letters, David was pretty sure that Brian wouldn't toss him out on his can if he showed up to visit.

He really wanted to talk to Brian first...the old David wouldn't leave without confirming things, but it felt so good to be moving forward, to be making changes...

"...because in Texas they don't have no laws against open containers, so we used to just drive around looking for parties and getting drunk at the same time. When I got here, I couldn't believe that you could get arrested for..."

"Crystal?" he interrupted. "I've got to go now. Are you sure Brian won't mind if I come out? I feel like I should talk to him first."

She didn't seem to be offended at all that he had cut her off. "You don't need to. I'm sure. Come on out. I'll have him call if he checks in, but we've got plenty of room here for you to crash. If you decide to stay longer, there's an empty apartment in this building. Believe me, he'd love it. We'd love it."

It was the first coherent thing she'd said. He didn't press his luck.

"Okay, I will. I'll be leaving next Monday, the nineteenth," he sputtered, glancing up at the wall calendar in the kitchen and making it up on the spot. He needed to pick a date, before she started talking again and the whole plan collapsed. "Tell Brian the next time you talk to him. I should be in LA by the twenty-fifth or twenty-sixth, assuming it takes a week to get there."

"Great!" she said, and her voice moved even higher up in tone. Now it sounded like a mouse on helium. "Oh, you'll just love it here. Have you ever been out here before? I loved it when I first moved here, and there is so much to do. You're gonna love it, especially—"

David smiled and interrupted again. He was getting better at it. "That sounds good, Crystal. And have him call me before the nineteenth, if he can. Thanks."

She started to talk again, saying something about the weather and a hurricane in Florida, but he hung up. It was so empowering, just taking charge and doing what he wanted. Like breaking up with Bethany—it had been painful, but now it was clearly the right thing to do. He could move on, get out of this town. And she could move on, find someone else.

His mind slid away from that train of thought. He didn't like thinking about Bethany with someone else. But they would all be better off—Bethany, his aunt, the people at work—if he were gone.

David retrieved his keys from the front door and went to his room, standing in the middle of the mess with his hands on his hips.

He was doing it.

He'd secured an invitation and found a place to stay. After he took care of the money, he could start getting ready to leave. There wasn't much to pack, just his clothes and his movies and books. There wasn't a lot he wanted with him. The rest could get stored at his aunt's house. Bernie might be pissed if David bailed in the middle of the month, but he had already paid his rent. Maybe he'd pay for next month too, just to be nice. He could afford it. He hated having people mad at him—and now, money wasn't a problem. Maybe Bernie would finish fixing David's car—he really needed it to be running well before he drove it cross-country. He'd leave Bernie a note.

First, David needed to make a list. He grabbed a pad of paper and started scribbling: pack, Bernie car repair (pay him), purge clothes, get more cash and travelers checks for the trip, quit job (!), check the weather. Crystal had mentioned the hurricane in Florida—he wasn't sure, but he didn't think it was predicted to get anywhere near Liberty.

David dug through a drawer and started organizing the clothes he wanted to keep. And in his mind, he started planning what to say to his aunt, to Mel, to Bethany.

After that, he was as good as gone.

———

The National Weather Service issued a hurricane warning for the area of Miami and southern Florida at 5:00 p.m. on Monday night, warning of high surf and drenching rains over the next twenty-four hours. The storm was pushing water ahead of it, with reports of spotty beach flooding all the way north to Cape Canaveral.

Hurricane Mandy was now a Category 1 storm with sustained winds of 77 miles per hour. It was churning in the Caribbean between Cuba and Miami, centered over Nassau and moving very slowly west, picking up strength. The storm was already one of the largest on record in terms of size, with cloud bands reaching out for two hundred miles in every direction from the central eye. This meant that even though the storm was still hours from making official landfall, clouds and smaller storms already battered the southern half of Florida, drenching the state with moisture it didn't need. Florida was still recovering from the last tropical storm that had dumped nine inches of rain only two weeks earlier.

The storm was not expected to make landfall anywhere near Miami. Instead, it was predicted to turn north and head up the coast. BEACH CLOSED signs went up for a hundred miles north of Miami within hours of the announcement. Those experienced with past hurricane warnings made their decisions, and many people packed up a few important things and left the low-lying areas, heading inland or in the direction of St. Petersburg and the Gulf Coast.

But, as usual, many long-time Florida residents dismissed the warnings as doomsday thinking. They hunkered down and planned their parties, while others took the warnings seriously and got out of Mandy's way.

CHAPTER 4
Tuesday, September 13

Jack Terrington, driving with a particular destination in mind for perhaps the first time in his life, drove north.

He spent Monday night in a hotel, trying to get the urge under control. It was difficult, harder than it had ever been before. He didn't want to kill anyone, at least until he got to Liberty. He didn't need any more heat chasing him, complicating the situation. Hopefully he would be able to quell the urge until he could let loose in Liberty.

Tuesday morning, he checked out of his hotel south of Savannah and headed north. The guys on the TV said something about a hurricane moving toward Miami, and Jack thought it best to stay ahead of it, just in case it decided to turn north.

He'd learned the hard way, a long time ago, about being trapped by the weather. Once, he was stuck in a Wyoming town for almost three weeks by a huge snowstorm, and his urge almost drove him insane over those twenty horrible, frozen days. He'd killed on his way out of town, fleeing the scene in a panic. He'd learned to never let nature trap him in one place for too long.

He passed another sign that said northbound I-95, and it brought back the memories again, that night on the highway. He'd traveled all over the United States, making one huge looping circle, before heading back to the town that haunted him.

Jack reached into his shirt pocket and took out Beaumont's star. He studied it, driving by instinct. The edges were dull, and the five points had lost most of their sharpness, but the letters were still clear, easy to read. He curled his fingers around it and squeezed, hard, until he felt the familiar, dulled points jab into his flesh. Blood oozed out between his clenched fingers.

Jack uncurled his hand. The bloody holes looked like stigmata. He set the star on the dashboard of the van. The wounds would not scar. And even if they did, they would look nothing like the palm of his left hand. He'd gotten that scar a long time ago, back when he'd lost an argument with a barbed-wire fence.

The scar had caused so many things to go wrong...

Jack had been young and still living in Salem, Maine with his mother and her latest boyfriend. It was summer, and he'd taken to riding his bicycle all over town. Jack was a precocious kid, always in the way, and on some level, maybe he was acting out to grasp and hold the tenuous and short-lived attention of his mother. She was mostly concerned with her own pleasures. Jack had grown accustomed to the endless new "uncles" that paraded through his mothers' bedroom, and the sounds that issued from it. He preferred the freedom of the outdoors.

But she took good care of Jack. She loved him as best she could, even though she must have recognized early on that Jack was a different sort of child, a loner. He was much more content off by himself.

Salem was a small farming community in southern Maine. Its only claim to fame was the annual Harvest Festival in September. The festival often attracted crowds from all over Maine, Vermont, New Hampshire, and even from as far away as upstate New York. The entire town anticipated the festival for several months. It was the only time the town swelled above its normal population of 3,500.

Young Jack Terrington rode his pride and joy, a used red and white Huffy, all over town, exploring the countryside. Jack was a troublemaker, plain and simple.

On the last day of August of 1966, only weeks before the Harvest Festival, Jack was off on one of his adventures, the kind that all little boys invented for themselves to pass the time and prove their worth as explorers. Jack had been riding his bike out on Seven Hills Road, north of town. Seven Hills was a long country road that was lined on both sides by huge, flat fields of crops baking in the late afternoon sun. The road was paved, an oddity for a county road that ran through long stretches of farmland. It also had only five hills along it; no one was sure how the road had gotten its name.

Somewhere between the third and fourth hill, the fields on the left side of the road swung much closer to the road, butting right up against the gravel shoulder. The wooden posts of the fence held a chain-link fence topped by three nasty-looking strands of barbed wire, each studded with wicked points of the rusty metal. The wooden posts stood at twenty-foot intervals like stolid wooden soldiers, holding up a defensive line against unknown invaders.

Jack swung his bike over onto the wrong side of the road to get a closer look at the wire. It fascinated him, sparkling in the sun.

He had killed a cat or three by tying them to barbed wire fences, watching how they reacted. They'd torn their own feet off trying to get free, and he'd loved the sounds they made. There had been so much blood.

Even then, he had enjoyed killing.

It started with animals, teasing them into their final moments, fascinated by the mechanics of death. Young Jack searched for the terror that filled the animals' eyes. He'd killed birds, mostly, dozens of them. He loved catching them and tying them to things: trees or fences or to the back of his bike. He loved watching them try to fly away and only manage to beat themselves to death against the ground. He'd tie them together and watch them kill each other, or tie a rock to their feet and throw it into the river. They would flap against the current, and the rock would sink and slowly pull them under. One bird had chewed off its own leg to get free.

But today, Jack was fascinated with the wire fence. It whizzed past him at a dizzying speed. He was probably riding along at no more than ten miles an hour, but to him, seeing the wire and the studded barbs and the wooden posts rush past him was exhilarating. But he grew bored quickly and swerved back out onto the main part of the road.

Young Jack pedaled faster, trying to pick up momentum to conquer what looked to be a long, grueling hill. His legs pumped up and down like little pistons wrapped in blue-striped socks. The bike tilted back and forth as he pedaled fiercely. His legs burned.

The incline finally leveled off, and he crested the hill, tired. He coasted to a stop, braking with his shoes. The road sloped down for a while and then leveled off. On either side of the road were more fields of yellow and green butting up against the road. The road was a thin gray streak in a vast plain of greens and yellows and browns. An occasional tree dotted the area, rare and precious. Waves of heat rose off the road, distorting it and making it dance in the harsh August sunlight.

After a rest, he started down the hill, still heading away from town. He pedaled faster, picking up speed. The fence was on his left, right next to the shoulder. He moved over and carefully edged his bike off the paved road and onto the hard-packed gravel of the shoulder. Jack wanted to see how close he could ride to the fence.

The naked spurs of the barbed-wire fence were close. The wooden posts raced past him, making a WHOOSH—WHOOSH—WHOOSH sound. As he flew past each of them, they sounded like the wings of some giant bird. It was a thrill to do something so dangerous. One jerk of the handlebars, and he would crash to his death.

Suddenly, Jack felt an urge, much like the urge he felt to kill animals. Jack reached out and touched the fence.

He dragged his fingers along the chain-link well below the barbed wire, his fingers reverberating against the thin metal wires. His hand wasn't pressed hard against the fence, but it was still beating against the metal incredibly fast, so fast that he couldn't even see it. He could feel the hard WHOOMP as each wooden post passed under his hand.

The barbed wire was passing along at about shoulder level, jagged and angry. Each of the barbed points seemed to reflect the sun above, flashing light into his eyes, taunting him, teasing him to

(*touch us, touch us*, a strange, raspy voice said in his mind)

reach out and touch them.

Young Jack took his hand away. He raised his left hand and held it just above the top strand of barbed wire, his hand pointed, flat like an airplane. He was careful to pull his hand up before the tops of each post or else he would've smacked into one of them. But the hand always returned to its dangerous position just above the wire.

Jack felt giddy. It was a thrill, his hand near the barbed wire, but then suddenly it wasn't enough. He wanted to do something *really* exciting.

He grabbed the handlebars of his bike with both sweaty hands and steered for a little while, trying to steel up his courage. Jack saw the road was starting to level out just below him, stretching out for a while before sloping upward again. He could just make out the fuzzy image of a car in the distance, its lines and colors wavering from the heat coming up off the road.

Jack swallowed and then closed his eyes for a second to get up his courage. Then he took his left hand off its handlebar and lifted it up

it won't hurt not one little bit, the voice said

and grabbed the strand of barbed-wire fence as it rushed by.

Instantly, the palm and the skin on the insides of his fingers and thumb were shredded away. The skin came off in long, jagged pieces, snagging on the barbs. Blood shot out from his palm and fingers, painting the top strand of wire red.

He couldn't let go.

The skin was gone from the inside of his hand in an instant. The barbs slashed at his muscles and tendons. Blood splashed all the way up his arm, past the elbow.

Still he could not let go. It all happened so quickly that he felt nothing except an odd moving pressure on his palm. Just as the pain was moving in like a hurricane, roaring and unstoppable, his still-clenched fist slammed into the next wooden post, and he was knocked away from the fence.

The bike swerved into the road and tipped over, spilling Jack onto the hot pavement. He rolled and skidded before he came to a stop in the middle of the road.

Jack's hand was on fire.

It felt like someone had dipped his entire arm in gasoline and set it ablaze. The pain came in waves that crashed against him like an incoming tide. Heat and fire and pain seemed to drip from his clenched fist and run down his elbow, his arm, all the way down into his feet.

Jack screamed, louder than he'd ever screamed before.

He opened his eyes and looked at his clenched hand. The back of his fist was uncut, but blood drenched it, painting it red. The web of skin that stretched between his thumb and forefinger was gone, evaporated as if by magic. Tattered strips of skin and muscle hung from the ball of his fist. The wire had torn it loose but had not had time to take it.

He tried to uncurl his fist. For a long, painful moment, his hand would not take orders from his brain. It was as if his hand were disgusted with his brain and rebelled. Finally, his fingers began to slowly, painfully uncurl.

bones white bones

He could see the bones of his fingers, naked and white and shiny in the late summer light. The skin was gone, the muscles exposed. Only the tips of his fingers, above the last knuckle, and heel of his hand still had skin on them.

Jack only had a moment to look at what was left of the palm of his hand before blood welled up and began pulsating out. The blood was coming in waves, pumped by his heart up his arm and out into the sunlight.

It was so beautiful. Even through his pain, the sight of all that blood amazed him.

He shook his head to clear a sleepy feeling that had suddenly gripped him and clenched his hand together again. The sudden force with which he squeezed spattered blood on his face and neck. He only had time to notice the hot blood on his face before the world around him wavered and went black.

Jack found out later what had happened. The couple in the car had found him and bundled him up, racing him to the hospital. The staff and doctors at the hospital called his mother right away, needing her permission before they could operate. She gave her consent over the phone before hanging up and climbing into her car for the twenty-minute drive up to Bangor General.

He had no idea what his mother was thinking as she raced to the hospital. In the years since, he had spent a lot of time imagining. He thought her mind would have been filled with horrible images of his injury. She'd probably been hurrying, distracted.

She probably never even heard the train or noticed the lights at the crossing. If she did see it at the last second, his mother might have screamed, screeching like a drowning bird. The police said the train dragged her car for almost a half mile before it fell off to one side and finally tumbled to a rest. The coroner had difficulty finding enough of Miss Terrington to make a positive identification. And of course, everyone thought it was all little Jack's fault. He could see it in their eyes.

The surgery to repair his hand was successful, amazingly. Little Jack had been very lucky not to lose his hand, or bleed to death. The quick response of the medical team and his mother's timely permission allowed the doctors to stop the bleeding and begin the delicate reattachment of his hand muscles. The new skin for the graft came from his legs and back, and the palm was completely reconstructed, resulting in the large scar that he would carry for the rest of his life. The hospital covered all the costs, in view of what happened to Jack's mother. Apparently, the hospital wrote it off, chalking the whole cost up to advancing the state-of-the-art in reconstructive surgery.

By the time his hand was bandaged, little Jack had heard about his mother. He said nothing as the days passed, filled with more surgeries and skin grafting sessions. Jack lapsed into a long period of silence that the hospital staff could not break. The mother's boyfriend had conveniently left town, and one of Jack's mother's coworkers had arranged for the funeral services. It was a closed casket ceremony, with few attendees.

After a few months, Jack seemed to come back to himself. He was examined by a county child welfare specialist and deemed physically and mentally healthy. He moved through foster homes, never staying with one family for long. There were too many complaints, too many "missing" pets. Jack developed a taste for the profane, feeding his fascination with death. And, as soon as he was old enough, Jack disappeared.

———

The young woman awoke on the leaf-strewn floor of a dark forest. Brooding trees surrounded her, stretching up into a black canopy of leaves that blotted out the sky. She rolled over, ignoring a sharp pain from her shoulder. She was in a small clearing, trees blocking her view in all directions except one. A dark trail led off into the darkness.

She sat up, confused. Her head spun for a moment, and she looked down. She was wearing a long silky dress.

What am I doing in my wedding dress?

After a moment of deep concentration, she remembered her name was Sally. Why had that been so difficult to remember? Of course her name was Sally, and she was in a forest because...she drew a blank. The huge trees stood like silent guards around her, mute in their indifference.

Sally wasn't sure what to do. Part of her—most of her, really—wanted to lie back down on the cold ground and go to sleep.

Tommy.

His name sprang into her clouded mind like a spooked deer. Tommy was her fiancé, her best friend. She and Tommy were to be married in a month.

This was the dress she'd bought.

She stood and brushed leaves and dirt from the dress, taking in her appearance again. The dress was beautiful, ethereal, glowing in the gloom.

On the ground was her bridal bouquet. It looked out of place on the muddy ground. She stooped and reaching for it, and her shoulder screamed in pain. Sally ignored the pain and cradled the bouquet. The scent of the flowers washed over her as a low, soothing sound drifted over the clearing. To her confused mind, it sounded like a voice.

Movement drew her eyes. A low fog rolled into the clearing from all directions, cloaking the leaves and ground around her. Only the trail was clear. The fog rolled around her ankles, cold. She felt an overpowering urge to lie down. Somehow, she knew it would end the pain in her shoulder. End her confusion. But she sensed that doing so, she would never see Tommy again.

She loved him. And there was something she needed to tell him.

She waded through the fog, moving toward the trail that led away from the clearing. Several times, her feet caught on unknown obstructions. She kicked away what felt like branches that grabbed at her dress, ripping it in places. She kept her balance, struggling across the clearing. She moved down the dark trail, leaving the fog behind.

David was not enjoying himself.

His boss at Big Video and More, Mel Rivers, surprised him. He'd figured Mel would jump for joy when David quit.

"So that's it?" Mel asked. "You're going where?"

David looked down at the water-stained counter where he'd spent so many hours over the past two years, counting money or fixing broken movies or putting together displays or promotional materials. The wooden counter always smelled strange, woody and moist.

"Yeah, Mel," David said, not looking at his boss. "I guess I just finally realized that there's nothing left for me in Liberty. I want to get on with my life."

He wanted to say more, to explain about how his father and his aunt and his girlfriend and his job made him feel trapped, but he couldn't. Mel had been good to him, and he didn't need to hear more about David's troubles.

There wasn't a lot to say. Mel had that look on his face that meant he was too mad to speak, so David thanked Mel and reminded him when his last shift would be before he left.

Walking out onto the sales floor, David felt immediate relief. His future was elsewhere, not here with the Story constantly hanging over him.

———

Mel Rivers stood by the windows and watched the kid leave the Big Video and More parking lot in his beat-up old Mazda. Mel had never really understood David, but it didn't mean that Mel wouldn't miss him when he was gone. The kid was undependable, hard-headed, irrational. Some of the things that boy did were infuriating. But, on several occasions, Mel had been pleasantly surprised.

Last year, David had expressed an interest in decorating the store to compete in the annual Pack-It contest, a sales competition held across all retail Pack-It locations. Big Video carried the entire Pack-It line of soft-sided storage and carrying cases for CDs and cassettes, and the contest tracked sales improvement over a two-month period.

Normally, little retailers like Big Video and More could never compete with total sales against the bigger retailers like Kmart or Blockbuster. They just didn't do the volume. But a contest based on the percentage of increase in sales was one they could actually have a chance at winning.

David was in charge of ordering and inventorying the accessories carried by Big Video. He'd read about the promotion in a monthly sales flyer and asked if he could spearhead the event, nationally titled as "Pack-It's Explosion of Savings!" Mel hadn't planned on even entering the contest, seeing it as just more work.

And the sales were just not there. Or so Mel had thought. But when David had wanted a go at it, Mel agreed. "Okay, go for it," he'd said at the time. "You run it, but I want some graphs or something showing our Pack-It sales figures for the last year. And you'll need to come up with daily and weekly sales goals, okay?"

Mel had half-expected David to balk, but the kid had only nodded and walked away.

The next day, when Mel came in, he'd completely forgotten the conversation. But it was hard to miss the two large, hand-drawn posters in the back room.

The first chart showed past Pack-It! sales and the projected sales needed to have a chance at winning. According to the chart, David meant to triple their sales. Impossible, Mel thought.

The second chart listed every employee of Big Video and More—including Mel—on a grid of squares with dates along the top. David would track sales by employee, promising to reward those people with the highest sales. Along the bottom were spaces for daily, weekly, and monthly goals and sales totals. The bottom of the chart outlined the rules for the in-store sales contest. Beneath the rules was another interesting line, written in a script that was bigger than any other on the chart: "Prizes to be announced!"

David was a slacker, late every other shift. Mel had come close to firing him half a dozen times. Why was he so fired up about this?

David had come into the back room and saw Mel standing there, staring at his charts. Mel turned to him.

"Prizes? You're buying prizes to give away?"

David smiled and pulled a piece of paper out of his pocket.

"I've been on the phone with some local retailers, wrangling promotional coupons or gift certificates. So far, I've got some from Subway and the arcade up the street. I was hoping to get you to donate some promotional CDs and movies," David said.

Again, Mel was more impressed than he would've admitted. "Yeah, I can do that. I'll call corporate, see if they have anything lying around."

David smiled. "Thank you."

"Oh, and you can add a $100 and a $50 gift certificate from our store, too."

"Really?"

"Yeah," Mel said, smiling. "Now, tell me how to you plan to triple our sales."

David walked over to the chart and started explaining his sales projections to Mel. Anyone walking in on them might've mistaken them for two serious businessmen, charting out the explosive growth of a big company.

Two days later, Mel came in and found a third piece of poster board next to others, this one detailing eight different prizes and the order in which they would be given out. They included Mel's store gift certificates, free food from Subway, movie tickets to the Multiplex theater out at the Liberty Place Mall, and car washes from the Exxon on the corner. The top prize was dinner for two at the Outback up in Woodbridge. How David had swung all that, Mel had no idea.

Mel also found a volcano in his store.

David had constructed a six-foot-tall volcano out of wood, chicken wire, and paper maché. He'd painted the sides with black and gray paint, streaking it with red dribbles of "lava" along the top and down the sides. Above, below, and all around the volcano, David had displayed the entire store inventory of Pack-It products, some of it appearing to be erupting out of the volcano. Above the volcano hung a huge, hand-printed sign with the contest's slogan, "Pack-It's Explosion of Savings!"

Damned impressive. Mel stood there and looked at it for a long time. No one had ever done anything like this before, not in his store or any other he'd visited. Hulking by the front door, the volcano certainly made an impression. David had stacked up a few of the carpet-covered wooden crates that they sometimes used for display purposes and then set the volcano atop them—the top of the volcano was at least nine feet above the carpet. He'd piled Pack-It cases around the base and attached to the sides of the volcano. It was sure to increase sales—even as Mel watched, four customers were examining the merchandise and two of them headed to the counter to make a purchase.

Mel reminded himself: David would need to order more Pack-It cases, and soon.

Big Video and More won second place in the national contest in the Improved Sales category. They were beaten only by a Blockbuster in Colorado Springs that had spent hundreds of dollars redecorating the entire store into a jungle-like atmosphere. They brought in real trees in pots and even had an employee in a rented monkey costume.

Hard to beat that, considering David had had no advertising or expense budget. He'd paid for all the supplies and construction materials out of his own pocket. But the store won a cash prize of $1,000, and Mel cheerfully gave it all to David, minus the money Mel had spent on the contest prizes and a pizza party for the entire store.

David had surprised Mel back then, and he surprised Mel again this afternoon.

Mel turned from his place by the door, starting back to the back room. He glanced over where the volcano stood last year—it was long gone, withering away up on the roof. After the contest, Mel had let David drag it up there, just in case there would be a second part of the sales contest. David had worked too hard on that volcano to force him take it home or to the dump. The paper maché and paint were long gone by now. The last time Mel had climbed the long ladder to the roof, the volcano had been reduced to a rough and weathered skeleton of two-by-fours and chicken wire.

Mel still had no idea how David had gotten that thing up there. He might be a shy, weak boy on the outside, but when that kid put his mind to something, he could work wonders. Mel would miss him, as strange as that was to admit.

The girl continued through the woods, glancing behind her often. No fog appeared on the trail, which wound in and out of the tall trees. She hadn't seen any animals or other people, and yet she got the distinct feeling she was being watched.

After a while, she stopped to rest on a large rock. Her right shoulder was hurting. She glanced around and unzipped the back of her dress, pulling the lacy bodice down. She was wearing a silky white bra underneath, and her skin was very pale and white.

There was a huge hole in her shoulder.

It wasn't ragged or bleeding, but three inches across. Sally could see through it, clearly seeing the rock she was sitting on through the hole. She suddenly felt nauseous. Strange things were happening to her—that much was obvious. People didn't just walk around with big holes in them. So why wasn't she bleeding?

Maybe she was dead. Maybe this was a dream. It would explain waking up in a strange place wearing a wedding dress. If she was dead, was this heaven? Hell? Was this all in her head? Would the trail lead somewhere, or would she just walk until she dropped from exhaustion?

Out of the corner of her eye, she caught a glimmer of movement. The churning mass of fog had reappeared, moving slowly down the trail toward her. Sally hopped up and moved on, jogging down the rough trail for several minutes until the path split in two. One way led back up, winding deep into dark forest. The other trail led down a slope, where the forest seemed to be thinning out. She took the downhill path because it seemed cheerier, and Sally soon got her first glimpse of sky, blue and lovely, above the trees.

Up ahead, the trees ended at the edge of the forest. She picked up the sides of her dress, now dirty and torn, and ran. Reaching the forest edge, she emerged from the trees. Beyond, a vast field of green grass spread out before her like a huge emerald blanket, sloping down away from her.

In the distance stood a huge mountain.

Hundreds of birds of all shapes and sizes flew against the blue sky, the only animals she had seen. The gray mountain was gigantic, casting a ragged shadow over the plain. A layer of snow that looked as light as powdered sugar coated the top third of the mountain.

Atop the mountain, she saw a white, square building. Ornate and ancient, with a flat roof and huge columns around the sides.

Sally sat down. This was all too much. Where was she?

Suddenly, inexplicably, she knew that she should climb the mountain. It was something she had to do. Maybe Tommy was in that building. That made her smile as another deep, voice-like rumble drifted over the world again.

She stood and started down the grassy slope. In the distance, the flocks of dark birds circled the base of the huge gray mountain.

Julie Noble was getting used to the idea of being busy in her closet-sized office.

She had plenty of material to read, with the files on Wildfire, all the documentation and supplementary material on the Cray and the Team, and all of the assorted paperwork related to her recent employment. She had no idea the government had so many things for her to sign! Retirement plans, health plans, more security clearance applications, and other assorted papers covered her small desk. Julie wanted to complete all her paperwork before plunging into the Wildfire project information. The blue file sat on one side of her desk, untouched since yesterday. Whenever she got tired or fed up with completing all her paperwork, she would glace at the WILDFIRE file and feel inspired to work faster.

As soon as she finished, she walked the paperwork up to personnel on the sixth floor and then returned to her office. In addition to the Wildfire file, she had found several other thick files on her desk this morning when she came in. The files covered the Computer Response Team, its component members, and some of the Team's past projects.

The Team was a group of computer hardware and software experts employed by the FBI to assist the government in matters related to computers and computer security. It sounded to Julie like an intentionally vague description.

The Team was made up of twelve people (including her) from diverse backgrounds. Most had been recruited from other branches of the government, but a few had come from the private sector. Surprisingly, three of the Team members had extensive criminal backgrounds. They were employed by the FBI as part of their "rehabilitation" within the federal court system. One of them was even on parole.

The Team leader was an enigmatic man by the name of Peter Turner, and his background as listed was sketchy and ambiguous. Mr. Turner had worked in technology while attached to the State Department. Evidently, he'd been involved in several incidents before being recruited by the FBI.

But the interesting backgrounds of some of the Team members failed to compare with the descriptions of some of the operations the Team had carried out since its formation six years ago.

One file recounted the Team's involvement in Saudi Arabia during Operation Desert Storm in 1991. The Team had been flown in with some of the first troops and had set up operations in a warehouse on the outskirts of Hafar al Batin, a small town in Saudi Arabia about 40 miles south of the border with Iraq. Using sophisticated computer equipment, radar and parabolic dish systems, satellite uplinks, and other "unspecified equipment," the Team had done more in three weeks to bring Iraq to its proverbial knees than all of the diplomatic mumbo jumbo that preceded their arrival.

Years before the approaching threat of war, most of the Iraqi banks and financial institutions had been linked together with governmental observation posts by a telephone-line-based communications system. This network, primitive by US standards but still state-of-the-art for the Middle East, allowed the Iraqi government to monitor all financial transactions going on throughout the entire network.

Before the US invasion, the Team established a clandestine satellite uplink into the network and soon began toying with the Iraqi's financial system, posing as banks and other financial institutions that were already hardwired into the system.

One day, the information created and infused by the Team would appear to be originating from the First Baghdad Bank, and the next day the Team would masquerade as the official Treasury of Iraq's branch involved with currency exchange. By hiding under assumed names, the Team carried out weeks and weeks of clandestine financial espionage and terrorism. They transferred huge amounts of electronic funds to off-shore accounts controlled by America. They tied up computer access time for actual institutions attempting to do their own legitimate business. Automated systems within the Team's warehouse would uplink to the satellites at regular intervals and carry out thousands of small dummy transactions to confuse the system or siphon off money into American accounts.

These actions against the financial infrastructure of the Iraqi economy came close to throwing the entire country into a frenzy, an occurrence that was kept out of the local papers. Had the Team been allowed another six or eight weeks of uninterrupted financial sabotage, the actual US military invasion with troops and planes might have been unnecessary.

But the Iraqis somehow got wind of hackers in their computer network and shut the network down, going back to the even more primitive method of transacting all their financial business by telephone instruction and messenger service. The Iraqis were forced to scramble to obtain enough funds to continue arming up for the approaching conflict.

The Team members received a special private citation from then-president George Bush for their actions involving the clandestine financial operations in Desert Storm. In a speech presented at a private Rose Garden ceremony, President Bush spoke eloquently, estimating that the members of the Team, by their actions, had shortened the length of the war by several months—and saved countless American lives.

Julie was amazed. She had heard nothing, not even at the academy, of any computer espionage or sabotage on the part of the United States prior or during Desert Storm. She suddenly understood the depth of her naiveté. As a member of the Team, she would probably have her eyes opened very soon to all kinds of new things.

Other files outlined other past Team missions, often working under the auspices of some type of "computer consultant" cover. Financial, military, scientific, and humanitarian institutions and causes were most often the targets of the Team's missions. Some of the countries the Team had visited in recent years were supposed to be our allies, or so she had thought. England, France, Russia, Japan.

Many of the Team projects were stateside. In some cases, fraud or espionage was detected by companies or other branches of government and reported to the FBI, and the Team was brought in to find ways to combat it.

The secure landline phone on her desk rang loudly, startling her.

"Hello?"

There was a momentary clicking sound and then the connection was made. "Miss Nolan, I presume?"

She sat up a little straighter in her chair and set aside the last of the Team files.

"Yes?"

"This is Pete, Peter Turner," the man said. The voice was staticky and hollow, an overseas call. "I'm the Team leader. Mike tells me you're going to be joining us. I just wanted to call and officially introduce myself and welcome you to the Team."

"Thank you, sir," she answered, instinctively raising her voice, as if speaking louder would carry her voice farther through the bad phone line. "I'm looking forward to meeting the rest of the Team and to working with them and you." She glanced down at the cases spread all over her little desk. "I've been reading through some of your case files—they are very interesting."

"Yes," Turner said with a chuckle. "We get into some situations."

Turner paused long enough for Julie to begin thinking they might have been somehow disconnected, and then he continued.

"Wallace tells me that you are very good. I hope we get a chance to see that in action soon. Actually, I called to tell you that the plans have changed. That's something you'll have to get used to."

She nodded. "I understand."

"We're not going to be finished here as anticipated. Another week, maybe two. After that, some of the Team will be going on to another location, but the rest are heading home to D.C. It looks like you'll be meeting us in stages."

"Yes, sir," Julie replied, unsure of exactly what she was supposed to say.

"I assume you've read up on Wildfire?"

"Yes, sir. It looks quite exciting. I've never worked with that large of a mainframe before, and I've certainly never worked with a Cray."

"Good, good," he answered. "Wallace told me that the main unit is supposed to be delivered on Friday. Is that still right?"

"Yes," Julie answered, looking at her notes. "The power subsystems and peripherals are already installed. The main unit should be delivered on Friday the sixteenth."

"Ah, yeah," Turner said, sounding disappointed. "That's what I thought. I was hoping we'd be back in time. You're gonna be on your own with the Cray for a week or two. Can you handle it?"

She sat up a little straighter. "What do you mean?"

"Well, the Frenchies have no concept of network security. We should have been out of here weeks ago," he said. "I need you to represent the Team when they install the Cray and do whatever else Paynod asks to test it. Okay?"

She swallowed, her throat dry. "Ah, yes, sir."

Turner laughed, and even though the laugh was wavering and electronic and static-filled by the overseas connection, it still made her feel a lot better. "Don't worry. The computer hardware techs will oversee the installation procedure. The techies are already briefed on what to do. I just want a representative of the Team to be there, keeping an eye on things."

She relaxed a little. "I can do that."

"Good," Turner answered. "Talk to Wallace—we're supposed to do some basic testing as part of taking delivery. They're loading in all that state and local data..." There was a momentary pause. "Okay, just a sec," Turner said to someone else. After a second, he came back on. "I've gotta go. Oversee the installation and thank the Cray people, okay?"

"Yes, sir," Julie answered. "Things will be fine here. Nice talking to you," Julie said, trying hard not to sound like she was kissing up to him.

"Okay, talk to you soon," he said.

"Good-bye, sir," she replied, and hung up.

Sounded like a nice guy, except for the part where he had practically dumped the whole Wildfire project into her lap.

Julie already knew about the initial testing. She wasn't even sure why she was nervous. Maybe she just wanted to make a good first impression.

After the Cray was set up and the memory loaded, it would contain information on every crime carried out in the United States in the past fifty years. Julie was supposed to come up with some initial tests for the data, and she'd already scribbled some ideas.

David Beaumont sat in his Mazda for a long time, staring at his aunt's front door. He really didn't want to go in the house. To occupy his mind, David wrote a list of the things he needed to say to her, but they all boiled down to the same words:

"Aunt Gloria, I'm moving to California."

Everything that came before or after was just garnish. If he could just go in there and tell her, the rest would be easy. But he couldn't get over the feeling that he was abandoning her.

Abe said he'd take care of the move, take care of getting her set up in the new place. David had been by to see the apartment complex earlier in the day. The place was nice, with perfectly landscaped lawns. The apartments—they called them "bungalows" at this place, like they were some kind of log cabin up in the mountains—were nice. David saw several other groups of people in their fifties and sixties wandering around the complex. Maybe his aunt would meet some people, make a few new friends.

He'd had a busy day, crossing things off his lists. The car had been oiled and lubed and checked for problems, both by the guy at Jiffy Lube and by Bernie. The apartment was mostly packed up, with his stuff in boxes or bagged up for Goodwill. A few boxes sat in the back of the car, waiting to go into storage in his aunt's house, if she would have them. He'd have her send them along once he got settled.

He'd also emptied his bank account. David had stashed the money and traveler's checks in a cigar box that now rested comfortably under the driver's seat of his car. The money would get him across the country and let him start a new life in California.

The biggest item left on the list was right there at the top. He'd skipped over it all day, eager to get the easier things done first:

- TELL AUNT GLORIA

David sighed and finally climbed out, his knees popping from too much time sitting in the car. The streetlights were starting to come on. He couldn't put this off any longer.

David banged the door for several minutes before she answered, rubbing the sleep from her eyes and saying good morning. He didn't have the heart to tell her it was just past 8:00 p.m. Was she heading to bed early, or still in bed from the night before? He didn't know and realized that he didn't care. Soon, these were the kinds of things he wouldn't have to worry about.

"Hi, Aunt Gloria." He smiled, but his stomach was a tight fist in his gut, queasy and sick. She nodded, and he went inside.

On the ratty couch, the conversation moved in fits and starts, starting with pleasantries and quickly moving to the real reason he was here. That's when the shouting started.

"You're leaving me?!"

"I'm not leaving you," David said. He knew she would try to guilt him into staying. "I'm just going away for a while." The lie came to him easily, hanging in the air between them.

She shook her head and grabbed a tumbler full of clear liquid from the counter.

"Bull."

"I'm going to visit Brian," he said, not caring if she bought it or not. It was just easier than being straight up. "I just need some time to get away—I've never even been out of Liberty for more than a week."

Gloria started crying, and he hated himself. First came the guilt, then the tears. She had a whole arsenal of ways to persuade him to change his mind. But he'd planned for this. He was a tree in a storm—he just had to hold on. Too many other things were already in motion to back out now.

The conversation ranged for a while longer, but once he'd gotten it all out, David felt a lot better, a lot calmer. His aunt tried every argument, but he stood his ground.

An hour later, he was carrying his boxes into her basement. She didn't help him carry his boxes, but she watched without complaining too much, and he took that as a win. When he finally left, she was smiling and crying a little at the same time. To David, she looked more awake, more alive, than he'd seen in a long time.

The boy was sitting at her bedside again. He was half asleep but still managed to hold one of her hands.

The night nurse walked in and paused. It was heartbreaking, what had happened to this girl. It was good that she had someone looking out for her.

Finally, the nurse opened her mouth, telling him visiting hours were over. It took him a moment to register that someone was talking to him. He looked up, his eyes bleary and red from tears and lack of sleep. The nurse, stolid and used to the cycle of loss and death that accompany the normal workings of any hospital, felt her stomach do a queasy little slide as the boy looked up. She suddenly realized how much pain the boy was in.

"Ten more minutes," she smiled. "But if anyone asks, I already told you to leave." She tried to grin at the joke, but somehow it just didn't feel right.

Tommy nodded his grateful thanks and turned back to his fiancé, squeezing her hand and talking to her again.

"It's going to be okay. The doctors say you should come out soon. When you do, I'll be right here. We'll make it through this, you'll see, and then we'll get married. We've already paid for everything. You don't want to let all those people down, right?"

The nurse didn't say anything. It probably made him feel better to talk to the poor girl in the coma; it would just be cruel to point out she was unlikely to hear him. Or anything else.

The nurse moved away, but her eyes must have been playing tricks on her. It was late, and she was tired. But for a moment, it looked like the girl in the coma was trying to smile.

CHAPTER 5
Wednesday, September 14

Jack was taking his time moving up the coast. He kept one ear on the storm reports. The only thing pushing him was the urge. It was a thirst that never went away.

On Wednesday afternoon, he was meandering through coastal South Carolina, passing through a dozen small towns along the water after exiting the interstate. He wasn't really sure why he got off the highway. It just seemed like the right thing to do at the time. If the cops or anyone was looking for him, that's where they'd be.

He'd learned to trust his instincts long ago. The traffic on the highway just seemed too sparse, and it made him feel like the white van, likely still wanted in Florida, was sticking out like a sore thumb. But getting off the freeway greatly slowed his progress—he didn't think he would make it to Liberty before the weekend.

Not that it mattered. Beaumont was dead, and a few days wouldn't matter. Job #1 was to get there, safe and sound, without any more entanglements with the cops.

But the urge was growing stronger by the hour, so strong now he could hardly contain it. It pounded in his head like a relentless migraine. It would back off, sometimes, but it was always there, lurking

very hungry

in the back of his head.

Jack looked at his haggard, unshaven reflection in the rearview mirror and could feel the eager blood pumping through him, stronger with each passing hour. Hot blood, craving action and gratification, like an animal that needed feeding, but was never truly satiated.

Jack shook his head and stared at the road, concentrating on his surroundings. He was working hard to ignore the urge, on some level Jack was hunting again. As much as Jack liked to tell himself he could stop killing any time he wanted to, that was a lie. His killing was now an integral part of him, a dark and cobwebbed corner full of anger and hatred. The instinct was not just a facet of his mind—it had become the driving force behind everything he did. He would follow that instinct wherever it led him, no questions asked.

Tuesday night he slept in his van parked on the gravel shoulder of a country road. His dreams were dark and angry, full of killing and death and destruction, the kind of dreams that he experienced only when fully in the throes of the urge.

Wednesday, the van rolled north and into Clearwater in the late afternoon. He needed a break—Jack was tired of looking in his mirrors every few minutes since he'd left Florida. No cops had shown any interest in him, but he knew he'd screwed up. That killing on the road in Florida had been way too public, too sloppy. He hadn't been thinking straight, and now he was running, lying low. Liberty still called him like a lighthouse on a raging sea, so Jack drove, ignoring the urge.

Sometimes it began as a background murmur, a quiet buzzing that slowly grew louder, increasing maddeningly in urgency, until it became a wailing call, unbearable in intensity. When that happened, Jack felt as if his head were going to split down the middle. Only after a killing would the buzzing back off, if only for a while.

Other times, he would be driving along, and the urge would spring upon him, full blown and undeniable, a voice that could not be denied or ignored or reasoned with.

Jack hoped that maybe all that killing back in Florida had driven the urge underground for a while. The Florida killings had already made a splash in the national papers. The speculation pointed toward a tourist murder, much like those that plagued the lower half of Florida. Even though the incident involved a policeman and a student from nearby Florida State University (FSU), the police theorized that the killer or killers had mistaken Sally Townsend, the FSU student, for a visiting out-of-towner. The papers further speculated that the policeman had interrupted the killers and there had been some type of struggle for the cop's gun, which was not found at the scene. Several "unusual" marks had been found on the policeman's body, indicating some type of struggle.

Unusual marks, to say the least. The wording had made Jack smile— marks, indeed. Jack had kept the gun as a memento, a reminder of his exploits, just like the contents of his jars.

The urge surged through him again when he thought about the jars and his trophies.

time it was time

He didn't dare stop. Dinner in this town was out of the question. Too many people around, too many potential victims. He needed to get away from people. Even the simple act of driving felt like a Herculean chore. It was almost too much to control. He ignored the pain and rummaged through his cluttered glove compartment, digging for aspirin or alcohol.

we should feed

Jack made it almost all the way out of town before the dam of resolve in his mind broke, and the urge flooded his mind, overwhelming his defenses and inundating his conscious. When he rounded a corner a couple miles north of Clearwater, and he saw the hitchhiker

there you go that's good

standing by the side of the road dressed in old jeans and a plaid shirt, one thumb out, Jack did not even hesitate. He slowed the van and pulled it over to the shoulder.

It was not a conscious decision. Long ago, he'd lost the battle to control his own mind.

The lines on his dark, tanned face made the young man appear much older at first glance. He was wearing a dusty pair of old jeans with one knee worn away to nothing, an old checkered flannel shirt that stood open. The bottoms of his jeans hung over a tattered pair of old tennis shoes that looked like they had walked all the way around the world. Over his shoulder the boy had slung an old green duffel bag, decorated in several places with water stains. The bag beat a tympanic rhythm against the boy's thigh, as he loped slowly over to the idling van. His face appeared in the open passenger window.

"Goin' north?"

Jack was pleased to see that the boy was probably only eighteen or nineteen at most, not the twenty-seven or twenty-eight that Jack had first thought. Jack was weary, and he didn't want to pick up anyone that might have the slightest chance of overpowering him. Jack was no slouch in a fight, but he was tired.

that's good he's perfect

Jack also had learned not to underestimate people, like he'd done with Beaumont all those years back. If you weren't careful, people could have a nasty way of surprising you.

"Yeah," Jack said, his lips curling up on the ends to approximate a smile. "Goin' north."

The kid thanked him and climbed in, and the van pulled smoothly away.

He drove, winding through the stands of trees that lined each side of the road, crowding it. Jack tried to relax, but it was useless. A fine sheen of sweat had sprung up, glistening, on his upper lip. His hands were constantly gripping the steering wheel. The urge was here, and he couldn't do anything about it.

now now gotta do it now don't make me wait

Well, there was one thing he could do.

The kid was a talker, but Jack really wasn't in the mood for conversation. He kept glancing at the side mirrors and no part of his mind noticed the beauty of the darkening blue sky that arched over the road or the tall, wisteria-draped live oaks on either side of the road. He was far too busy looking for other cars.

shut up kid

There were none.

As they rounded another corner, Jack saw the road ahead was clear. He shifted his feet and suddenly reached over and grabbed the back of the kid's head, pushing forward. At the same time, he kicked out violently with both feet, stomping on the brake.

The nose of the van dipped as it slammed to a halt. The forward momentum, aided by Jack's hand guiding it, threw the kid's head into the metal and plastic hardness of the dashboard. Jack's seat belt caught him with a jerk.

The kid died instantly.

Jack pulled the kid's body back up into a sitting position. The kid's head lolled lifelessly on his neck. His eyes were glazed and obscured by the shattered forehead. Blood flowed freely down his face to drip off the point of his chin.

better much better

He relaxed, putting the van back in gear and started it up again, checking his mirrors, his eyes now searching for a side road to pull off onto.

The kid's eyes bothered Jack, so he grabbed the head and turned it away.

He crossed a river and a turnoff came up shortly thereafter. Jack turned off, and the road wound back into the woods and came out into a parking area that bordered on a large picnic area. The picnic tables and covered shelter did not appear to have been used in a long time.

Perfect.

He got out and opened the passenger side door and grabbed the kid's body, lowering it to the muddy ground. Jack did not notice the birds as they began to collect in the trees around him, a flock of different species, settling onto the high branches of the live oaks and pines around the rest area.

Jack was just finished getting the kid down when he heard water moving nearby and realized a large, wide river flowed just past the recreation area, leading away from the highway, flowing toward the ocean.

Ten minutes later, he was done with number 197.

Over the years, he'd gotten good at killing and disposing of people— he was a regular Angel of Death. But every time he killed someone, the victim was new and a little bit different.

This time it was a fake leg.

The young man's plastic and metal leg moved and flexed just like a real leg, only it had been painted a sickly flesh tone that did a poor job of simulating a real skin color. The ball and socket joints of the knee and ankle were made of gleaming, shiny metal, well-oiled and carefully maintained. Several belts and buckles held the prosthetic piece in place.

Jack had only planned to stun the kid when he grabbed his head and bashed it against the headboard. But the blow had killed him instantly. Jack had wanted to knock him out and drag him into the dark woods and work on him for a while before he killed him. He needed an outlet, somewhere to express his anger at this whole Beaumont thing.

Killing the kid slowly would've relaxed him, helped him focus.

After Jack was finished, he dressed the kid back in his old, dingy clothes, trying to get everything back in the right place. While he'd been working, Jack was also turning a question over and over in his mind. Should he keep the leg? It would make a great souvenir, one of his best. It would not fit into any of the glass jars, obviously, but he was sure he could find some place of importance to display it. Maybe mount it on the wall over the jars, for future "guests" to see.

a prize

But would a body missing a leg draw more attention to itself than any other dead body? Not that the body was ever going to be found. Jack pulled out his maps and saw that the river that passed by this recreation area moved quickly to the coast. It was very likely that the body would be carried out to sea. But, just to be sure, Jack frayed the ends of the straps that held the leg and ripped off most of the empty pant leg, leaving belts and buckles hanging from the ragged opening. Hopefully, it would convince anybody that the leg had been lost to the river. Jack would keep the leg, hang it on a hook in the back of his van. The kid certainly didn't need it any more.

Jack laid out a plastic tarp next to the body and rolled it onto the tarp. Tired from driving all day and with too many things competing for attention in his mind, he dragged the body with its one missing pant leg over to the edge. He didn't notice the tracks he left, or the boot prints. He didn't notice the long gouge the dragged body dug into the mud.

He also didn't notice the flock of birds that sat perched in the trees around the parking area. They had quietly watched him as he worked on the boy earlier, and now they watched silently as Jack wrapped the kid in the plastic tarp. As he dragged the dark shape across the mud, several of the birds stepped off their branches and flapped away into the sky.

The river here flowed fast and deep, black in the growing dark. Jack dragged the plastic over the rocks to an outcropping, dismayed to hear the plastic snag and tear in several places.

no matter the body will float right out to sea

Directly below the outcropping of rock, the river moved silently.

"One express ticket to the Atlantic coming right up, sir," Jack told the dark shape.

No one was going to find the kid. Even if they did, Jack would be in Liberty by then. And no one would ever catch him, because he was the greatest killer that had ever lived.

Jack tugged and pulled and finally managed to maneuver the body over to the edge. Jack leaned over and grabbed one edge of the plastic and tugged up on it, hard. The body rolled off the tarp and over the edge, spinning lazily before it splashed into the dark water. Jack smiled and watched the dark shape move quickly away with the current.

He walked back over to the van, relieved. All the stress was gone now. He balled up the ripped tarp and tossed it into the open doors before closing them. He was happy now, relaxed and calm.

Tracker Randy Kovacs watched the storm as it made landfall.

The storm was huge, the colored bands of clouds on his false-image computer representation superimposed across Florida. Storms always looked bigger when they made landfall, as Mandy did at 10:32 p.m. Wednesday night. It was a full ten hours later than expected.

The center's trackers and scientists were baffled by the seemingly random speed course, but Randy knew what was happening. She had hung out in the Caribbean for a few extra hours, sucking up as much energy as she could before marching on to Miami. She was moving so slowly because she was picking up power and strength. Even as protected as they were inside the underground concrete bunker of the National Hurricane Center, Randy could hear the wind and rain howling outside.

Mandy had roared ashore near Pompano Beach, north of Miami. CNN carried it live on one of the big screens in the control room, the typical scenes of wind-lashed trees and uprooted plants, videos of boarded-up buildings and the inevitable people who stayed behind to brave the storm. "Ride it out," they always said. These were the first people to call 911 when they got in trouble. Randy always wondered about their sanity, but wasn't he one of them now, staying and "riding it out" when all the numbers shouted at him to get out?

But Randy was needed here. Mandy was easily the biggest storm of the year. People needed to be warned, needed to know where Mandy would go next. The best track they had now took Mandy straight across Florida and into the Gulf, back over warm water.

Where she went after that was anybody's guess. Most of the tracks predicted she would turn northwest toward New Orleans. Watches had been issued from Apalachicola in the Florida panhandle to Galveston on the Texas Gulf Coast. But a big high-pressure front, stalled over Texas and extending out from the coast for a hundred miles, would block the hurricane. When and if Mandy bumped into that, she would probably head north along the front. But knowing this storm, she might just take up residence in the gulf and spin herself out, dying down to a tropical storm and then dissipating completely.

Randy didn't believe it. For some reason, he felt there was a lot more to this storm.

He leaned forward and punched up more weather charts and wind pattern graphs of the southern United States, trying to guess where Mandy would go.

CHAPTER 6
Thursday, September 15

David was finishing up his packing, listening to *Presto* as he piled items into boxes before he went in for his noon shift on Thursday. It was one of Rush's better CDs, introspective and almost sad, all about magic and illusion. His favorite song was "The Pass," about making the best with what you've got in life, facing your problems, then doing something about them.

That was what David was trying to do—get on with his life. If he was lucky, he'd never have to hear the Story about his father and the Killer ever again. Rush also had a new CD out, *Test for Echo*. He wanted to pick up a copy before he took off for California. He'd heard it was good but different, something Rush was good at. They were always mixing it up.

David was leaving behind almost everything he had, fitting it all into boxes that he'd be storing at his aunt's house. She would move them along with her stuff into her new place.

His roommate Bernie had taken the news well and declined David's offer to pay ahead for October's rent. David didn't see how Bernie could find another roommate so quickly, but Bernie was a very laid-back individual. Or maybe he wanted the place to himself for a while.

David planned to work his last two shifts, Thursday afternoon and Saturday night, and then he would leave Sunday morning, the eighteenth. He'd spent a couple of hours doing the calculations, which put him into Los Angeles six days later, arriving on Saturday morning the twenty-fourth. He could push himself and get there a lot faster, but he wanted to see some of the sites. He wasn't in any particular hurry to get to LA. The route would take him south through Richmond and then west, through West Virginia and up into Ohio and Illinois and Missouri, where he wanted to see the Gateway Arch. He'd always thought it sounded like an architectural miracle. It reminded him of those days when he wanted to be an architect.

After St. Louis, David would go through Kansas and Nebraska, then up into Colorado to see the mountains. The route sounded more interesting than going south through the desert. After passing through

Colorado and Utah, he'd cross Nevada and come into California at Lake Tahoe, supposedly a beautiful sight. From there, he'd cross California at Sacramento and hit the coast at San Francisco, home of the Golden Gate Bridge, that pyramid building, and several other interesting buildings and landmarks.

He still hadn't told Bethany he was leaving.

David didn't even know when he would get up the courage to do it. It wasn't fair, not telling her, but if he didn't do it soon, she would find out from someone else. That would be worse.

David looked around his room and nodded. Everything was boxed up except for his personal effects and day-to-day items. He'd donated the bed and his other furniture to Bernie, telling him to either sell or trash it all. David didn't need any of it.

The rest was going with him in the car, bags and suitcases. He would live out of them for the next few weeks, at least until he got to Long Beach and rented a place. He was already looking forward to picking out and decorating a place of his own in a town where they never had snow or sleet. A place where nobody knew him. He wanted a place where he could start over, a place where he could make his own stories.

After what seemed like endless hours of walking, the young woman in the wedding dress reached the base of the snow-capped mountain. The sun hung motionless in the sky, unmoving. Above, the ever-present birds floated on distant winds.

Sally stopped twice along the way to rest, and there was no sign of the fog coming out of the entrance to the forest. Thirst and hunger never came, even though she'd been expecting them. How could she be walking all this distance and not even need any water?

Her death theory was starting to look more possible.

As she approached the mountain, Sally could see areas where the rock leveled off and sloped into gentle grassy areas before it resumed its harsh angle upward. There were paths up the mountain. Above the sharp tree line, the mountain continued upward for a short distance before the patches of gray and brown rock were blanketed with glistening snow.

At some point, she'd realized she was wearing a strange pair of dusty cowboy boots she didn't recognize. The design on the boots was very distinctive: rattlesnake skin and leather strips in alternating rows. A short silver metal chain looped beneath each boot, attached on either side. The metal chains jingled when she moved.

Whether she was dreaming or dead, Sally did not know. The boots, the dress, the forest: they could all be in her head. She shook her head and started climbing—she had to get to the top. It had something to do with seeing Tommy. She had to tell him something important.

————

Thursday morning, Julie was waiting with her coffee when they arrived with the Cray.

The Mark 4 supercomputer, the only one of its kind in the world, was delivered to the FBI loading dock in a Brink's armored truck, accompanied by armed security guards. The Brink's security people swung the truck doors open, revealing a metal shape covered with heavy blankets to discourage shifting during transport. Two Cray Corporation trucks arrived as well, bringing the specially-built Cray platform, along with technicians and equipment.

The Cray was unlike anything else she had ever seen before. While the earlier versions of the Cray looked boxy and utilitarian, this unit was rounded off at the top, looking futuristic and streamlined.

The room where the Cray would be installed had been specially built; the computer generated so much heat, the Cray room and its contents had to be kept at a constant—and chilly—forty degrees. Technicians and staff of the FBI computer room would have limited access to the unit, using a separate room, the Input/Output or I/O room, next to the Cray room. The I/O room had been outfitted with a row of video screens and computer keyboards, all hooked into the batch processing systems of the Cray. An insulated window separated the rooms, and along the opposite wall stood a long row of workstations, hard drives, and printers.

Julie followed as the equipment was wheeled to a freight elevator and delivered to the main computer lab. The Cray techs and the FBI computer engineers worked in concert to install the main unit, connecting a virtual forest of cables, couplings, power cords, air ducts, and other connections. The entire process took over four hours.

While she waited, Julie wandered the computer lab, a repurposed conference room outfitted with tables and cubicles of bulky desktop computers and monitors. The equipment was a mishmash of new and old. This division—and the Team itself—were clearly a work in progress. A recently installed LAN sat in one corner, designed to service computer terminals throughout the building. Secure landlines also connected the network to several offsite location.

Over the past few years, the FBI had brought in technicians and programmers to assist in certain areas where computing power could make a difference. The workstations were grouped together by function and separated off from the other areas by head-high partitions. Hanging signs above each area designated its function.

The sign above the largest section read "Fingerprints," where fingerprints were scanned into the computers and compared with all of the other registered fingerprints on file. Another area was marked "Travel," and Julie had learned that this area was responsible for tracking the locations of several classifications of people: US officials, upper-level government employees; military members; visiting foreign dignitaries and staff; known criminal leaders in the United States and abroad; and a half-dozen other specific groups of people.

Some of the signs she did not understand: "Cold," "Friendly," and even one sign that read, oddly enough, "Dead."

"Fascinating, huh?"

Julie turned around and saw a balding, short man who reminded her immediately of Santa Claus. "What?"

"It's fascinating, isn't it? I've worked here for years, ever since they brought in the old Wang's back in '83."

She glanced around. "I didn't know they had a computer department that far back."

He nodded, smiling. "We did. Not here—the computers were scattered throughout the building. Everything was consolidated here last year when they decided we needed a LAN," he said, pointing at the bulky server unit in the corner. "Makes things a lot faster. No more sneaker net, running floppy disks around the building. The name's McIvey, by the way. Shawn McIvey."

"Julie Noble, new arrival. I'm supposed to be here representing the Team, but so far all I've done is stand around and drink coffee and watch other people work. I'm staying out of their way."

At the mention of the Team, she saw Shawn's brow darken. A subtle change in his body language told her the Team wasn't high on his list of favorite things.

"Yup, everyone's been excited about the Cray install. So, you're part of the Team, huh?" he asked pointedly.

"Yes, but don't hold it against me, okay? I haven't even met anybody else yet. I get the impression that you're not too fond of them. Us."

"It's not that I don't like them, it's just that they do some mysterious stuff. And the rest of the staff gets stepped on every time the Team needs extra equipment."

He looked around and motioned his head toward a petitioned-off area on one side of the large room.

She followed his gaze and saw a sign she hadn't noticed before. It hung above a door into a partitioned-off area. Above the door hung a small sign: "Section 8—Team."

"Is that where the Team works?" she asked. "I've been here before and didn't know they had a dedicated lab."

McIvey smiled. "There's probably a lot about the Team you don't know."

"What do you do here?"

"I work over there," he said, pointing at the "Dead" sign.

She nodded. "I was wondering what that meant. Keeping track of 'dead' people seems like a pretty simple job," she said, grinning. "Don't they usually stay in one place?"

Shawn smiled. "That's not exactly what we do." He walked away, and she followed. "If you're cleared to be on the Team, you're cleared to know what we do." They arrived at his workstation under the sign and he tapped at his terminal, bringing up a detailed map of the United States. The map was sprinkled with what appeared to be hundreds of little dots, most of them red, but others were different colors.

"We track the locations and movements of people who are publicly, officially dead," he said. "Most are in the bureau's Witness Relocation Program. Those are in red. For example," he said, typing on the computer until only two red lights were glowing in Sacramento. To Julie, the glowing dots looked like eyes.

"Who are they?"

"That's a father and son into protective custody. They were moved to Sacramento by the FBI. Witnesses in a mafia-related case, if I remember correctly."

He tapped at the screen again, and all the dots reappeared. "The others represent people who are in hiding. Most of them have faked their own deaths for one reason or another, but we track who we can here. Most of the ones that faked their own deaths are involved in some type of criminal activity. We track them, wait for them to slip up, then pass the information along to field offices."

From somewhere else in the large room, a voice was raised, calling out her name. "Oh, that's me," Julie said. "Thank you, Mr. McIvey. Very interesting."

"The name is Shawn, Miss. Not 'Mr. McIvey.' Nobody calls me that, except the girls at the credit union upstairs."

"Okay, call me Julie."

Walking back to the installation in progress, she saw one of the Cray Corporation techs motioning her over.

"Hi, Agent Nolan? I'm Chris Hanson, liaison between the Cray Corporation and the bureau. I was told you should be here when they power it up."

"Thanks, Chris. Nice to meet you. Just call me Julie, okay? I'm not really sure what it is that I'm supposed to be doing here, except representing the Team."

Chris smiled. "That's okay. Once the installation is over, you can get started."

She looked at him. "Started?"

"Testing. Testing the system. You ready?"

She nodded. "Yup."

They walked over to the I/O room and looked in on the Cray through the window. The Cray technicians were finishing up the connections. She'd read that two separate power lines fed into the machine, buffered by a series of surge suppressors and voltage regulators. These ensured that the flow of power into the unit was clean and uninterrupted. A third power line connected to a huge battery backup system that was specially designed for use with the Cray. This line would power the main unit and its input/output systems for up to twenty-four hours in case the main and secondary power lines failed.

One of the techs nodded through the window, and Hanson gave them a thumbs-up. Someone flipped a switch somewhere and the front of the Cray powered on, a bank of red lights flashing and blinking. Hanson walked Julie through the basic power-up and log-on functions on one of the terminals in the I/O room. She chose a password and logged on, setting up a personal account and setting aside some of the unit's massive 100 terabyte hard drive space for herself.

"You'll need to set up accounts for the rest of the Team," Hanson said.

Julie nodded and began exploring the programs and operation system. Hanson, after glancing at his watch several more times, finally excused himself and left her alone to play. And she quickly got lost—the machine was faster than anything else she'd ever seen.

Sally climbed the mountain. Birds circled above and screeched. The sun never moved against the blue sky.

After what felt like hours, she found a boulder and sat. She was exhausted, and her shoulder had started aching. This whole exercise seemed pointless. As far as she could tell, she wasn't getting any closer to the top of the mountain or the familiar white building.

Maybe she should just wait for the fog to come for her. She'd seen it, pooling around the base of the mountain. The grassy plain and the forests beyond were gone, covered in gray.

She heard a voice. Not the one from before, shapeless and unrecognizable. This was a man, yelling, somewhere nearby. His voice was deep and powerful, and she was instantly overjoyed. Someone else was here! Her exhaustion faded in her excitement.

Sally stood, wavering, and began making her way up the mountain again, moving toward the voice. She rounded a rocky outcropping and was afforded a view of the opposite side of the mountain. Here the ground was flat before sloping upward sharply.

A man in a weird, white dress was struggling to push a round boulder up the sharp incline. The man was huge, and she realized with a start that he was wearing a toga, like something out of a bad Hercules movie. He pushed, his muscles straining, and the huge rock rolled slowly, grudging upward. As she watched, he strained, and screamed, pushing. He turned around and spread his arms and pushed the rock with his back, the muscles on his neck standing out like thick brown ropes. But she saw that he could never get the rock all the way up. He was near the top now, but the slope was nearly vertical. He'd have to literally carry the rock on his back up the last five or six feet of the slope. How he was even keeping his footing was a mystery.

And then he howled. It was the same scream she had heard before, but now she was much closer and the ground around her feet rumbled as he yelled in rage and frustration. The howl was like that of a huge, trapped animal. It sent shivers up Sally's spine—no matter what the guy looked like, nothing human could make that noise.

Suddenly, the man stepped aside and deftly allowed the rock to roll off of his back. The boulder dropped away and rolled smoothly down a well-worn path, coming to rest near Sally.

The man just stood there. He held his head in his hands, and then looked up and began examining the very top of the slope. He kicked at the rim of dirt and rock, trying to dig a path, but the dirt would not move. Sally did not understand this. He could carry a thousand-pound rock on his wide back, but he could not dig in the dirt.

And then he saw her.

Sally walked over to inspect the massive boulder, running her hands over it. It was impossibly smooth, like it had spent an eternity at the bottom of a rushing river. From here, she could also see the deep, smooth groove that ran all the way up to the top. It was obvious the groove had been carved over time by the man and his rock.

Something else clicked in the back of her mind.

"WHO are you?" The man bellowed. He towered over her like a statue in a museum, sweaty and panting and clenching his fists.

"My name is Sally, and I'm...not really sure what I'm doing here.

I woke up in the forest, and I crossed the plain, and now I'm trying to climb this mountain," she said.

The giant man listened to her intently, then nodded and sat, the ground shaking.

She sat as well, smoothing out her dress. It felt good to sit. "I'm trying to get to the building," she said, pointing at the distant structure. "But you're the first person I've seen here," she said. Trying to remember the last person she had seen only brought on a jumbled image of a silhouette, pointing something shiny at her.

The man nodded. "I, too, have seen the temple on high. It stands strong and proud as a testimony to the gods. I have spent many a long hour gazing upon its beauty." He grew quiet for a moment, thinking, his eyes glazing over with inner searching. "I will enter Zeus's temple when I complete my task."

"Zeus's temple?"

"Zeus was most kind in choosing this place for his temple. It gives me hope. As soon as I am strong enough, I will complete my task. Only after I have proven my strength will I be worthy of entering the temple."

Sally could see truth in his eyes.

"Why?" she asked. "Why must you push the rock up the hill?"

The man seemed confused by her simple question, a question that she assumed he must have asked himself a million times.

"Because I must," he answered. "Soon, Zeus will know that I am worthy. He charged me with this task long ago."

Suddenly she remembered. She leapt to her feet, pointing at the rock. "Wait a minute, I know this story!" she said. "Dr. Macintyre, Greek Mythology, ninth grade. You're that guy that rolls the rock up the hill for all eternity. Oh, what was the name?" She tried to remember. Her face worked as her mind struggled to recall. And, for once, her mind did not rebel against her. "Sisyphus! That's your name. And Zeus charged you with an impossible task."

"How do you know of me?" he said quietly. "I have not met you."

In that moment, she knew this was all a dream. The man, the rock, the mountain, the fog, the dress. Everything she had seen since awakening. On some level, it made her feel better. But why had her mind constructed this particular scene? His task was hopeless. Was hers?

"Dr. Macintyre said that the legend was a parable, a representation of the ancient Greek methodology that once a task is begun, it should be completed, whatever the cost."

Was her brain trying to tell her to keep going? Sisyphus had never given up. Did this dream mean she should continue as well? Suddenly, she felt calm. In control.

She looked at him. "I will help you."

He stood and backed away. "You? You are going to help me push the rock?" he laughed. "I could break you in half with one hand. It would do better for you to ride on the rock, as much help as you would be!"

She understood, accepting his anger from inside the shell of her newfound calm, unfettered by his shouting. Power seemed to surge through her, and the exhaustion and doubt fell away. She held one of his huge hands. It was wrinkled and scarred.

"You can do this," she said. Somehow, she divided off a tiny fraction of her new power and passed it to him, channeling it through her hands. "Servant of Zeus, you are worthy," she said, her voice reverberating with a power she did not understand. "Know that and complete your task."

Her hands dropped away. The man shook his head as she turned and started back up the mountain. She made it to the next outcropping and turned to watch.

The man rolled the rock forward, up and up, building momentum. He pushed it as far as he could and then turned around to lift with his legs. The momentum of the rock carried it upward. The veins on his forehead stood out, and the rock moved upward. He pushed, and after a few moments, the boulder crested the lip and came to a rest on top of the hill.

Sisyphus stopped and placed his hands on the rock to steady it, smiling. He glanced up at her, and she nodded her approval before turning away, heading up the mountain.

————

East of Clearwater, South Carolina, the Columbus River wove in and out of thick stands of trees on either side. The river was wider here than farther upstream and flowed slowly toward the ocean.

In the growing darkness, the river carried its passenger farther downstream. The body of the young man with one leg bobbed in the water, occasionally becoming entangled for a moment in the underbrush and weeds that grew out from the riverbanks. Several birds, some of different species, swooped down out of the sky.

The body sunk almost immediately upon entering the river, but after three or four hours, the natural buoyancy in the body overcame its weight, and the head and chest broke the dark surface.

The body gazed at the moonless sky with unseeing eyes.

CHAPTER 7
Friday, September 16

The Cray supercomputer was amazing.

Just in sheer computing speed, it easily outdistanced any other computer Julie had heard of by a factor of five. Poring over the technical manuals she had borrowed, she began to grasp how powerful this new breed of computer could be. And they wanted her to program it!

Technically, Chris Hanson and the FBI techies would be doing the actual input of her initial test run, and then she would write up a progress and implementation report on it.

Hanson was down in the computer lab, spending the day uploading the files from every major crime committed in the United States in the past 30 years. Just storing it all in one machine was a breakthrough. But manipulating that data? There were too many possibilities to calculate.

Julie finally closed the manuals and sat back, thinking. What to do? The list of ideas she had worked up was okay, but it seemed a shame to waste the incredible computing power of this machine on the simplistic searches she'd come up with. She would have today and the weekend to come up with something before programming began on Monday. And she had to find a better use for it. Others later would use the machine to its fullest potential—why shouldn't she?

Randy Kovacs sat behind his computer, staring at his screen. It seemed like this was all he had been doing for the past week.

Wednesday afternoon, he'd surveyed the damage done to his apartment complex. The damage was minor—missing shingles and uprooted palm trees. That night, he did not sleep well, his dreams full of visions of huge storms moving across the face of the planet, each with a mind of its own, and each intent on a single purpose—to scrape the Earth clean. The storms flattened everything in their paths, killing people, destroying homes and businesses, ripping away topsoil and washing everything into the hungry ocean.

The dreams kept him awake that night, and Thursday night, too.

Now, Friday afternoon, he was back in the office, tracking Mandy. It had become a storm like no other. Just when the trackers thought they had a fix on her, she would juke one way or the other, seemingly moving just to throw them off track.

Mandy had stopped in the gulf, pulling up and spinning lazily halfway between Florida and Texas, due south of New Orleans. After crossing Florida once, now she was sitting still, drinking the warm, shallow water of the gulf. The trackers and other meteorologists were not happy to see this—a storm grew in strength the longer it remained over warm, open water. Mandy had come up against the high-pressure air bubble parked over the Texas coast. Even though the longest arms of clouds dropped rain on the coast from Florida to Texas, the central mass of the storm began spinning faster. It picked up strength and power again, increasing to a Category 2 storm only hours after she slowed to a stop.

There were a few possible track scenarios that put Mandy overpowering the warm front and pushing into Texas anyway, but those calculations seemed to be wrong. As powerful as Mandy was, the warm air mass over Texas stopped the storm from moving any farther west.

Now, Mandy looked like she would be heading back toward Florida. She was slowly drifting east at under three miles per hour, barely moving. High altitude fly-throughs had gathered wind speed and directional measurements. The computer models now put the storm on an easterly track back toward northern Florida and southern Georgia.

After that, she might die out. Or she could turn, moving up the coast and hammering the eastern seaboard with hurricane-force winds and huge amounts of rain. The models were all over the place, but if she turned north, rain and floods would follow as the precipitation fell, collected, and raced back to the sea. Roads and bridges would be washed out all up and down the eastern seaboard, just as they had been in the Miami area only a few days before.

Randy thought about it for another minute or two, then took his concerns to his boss. She listened and agreed with him.

"I see what you're saying," she said. "And if Mandy crosses Florida and turns north, we could be in for a very bad week. If she makes landfall again and hasn't lost any strength, I think it would be a good idea to issue a general hurricane watch. The Carolinas, Virginia coast—maybe all the way up to New York."

Randy nodded and headed back to his cubicle, writing it all down before he forgot her instructions. The storm was a bad one, one of the worst he'd ever seen, but its sheer unpredictability was the most frightening part. And if the Trackers at the center couldn't estimate where it would go or warn people in time, how many people would die?

Norma Jenkins sat alone in her home, watching TV. *The X-Files* was on, and it was the only exciting show she ever allowed herself to watch. There were other shows on TV that she liked, like *ER* and *Star Trek Deep Space Nine*, but *The X-Files* was her favorite. Sometimes the show was so suspenseful that her stomach reacted, churning and angry.

She wished she could be like other people. It was Friday night, and everyone else was out doing something exciting. There was a county fair going on over in Fredericksburg, only a few miles south on I-95. People were having fun, enjoying rides and eating cotton candy. But just the thought set her stomach on edge.

Her two ulcers were getting worse, according to the doctors. Medicines and operations hadn't cured them. When she asked what they could do next, the doctors grew quiet before reminding her to "take it easy" and "avoid stress and excitement." The fact that they had no new ideas troubled her. It was as if her doctor had given up on the idea of ever curing Norma of her demons, as she called them.

This episode of *The X-Files* was one of her favorites. It was about Flukeman, a crazy looking fish guy that lived in the swamps and sewers under New York City. During the commercial breaks, Fox News kept showing updates on Hurricane Mandy. It had damaged Miami, gone out into the Gulf of Mexico, and now it looked like it was moving back toward Florida. The cop part of her wondered what they would do to help people. Evacuations, probably. Boarding up windows. Watching for looters. Watching for criminals.

Her stomach turned over at the thought of it. Sometimes, Norma still longed for the life of law enforcement. She still loved to read mystery and detective novels, and movies about courtrooms and juries and trials and long-lost evidence always thrilled her. Sometimes, she wondered what her life would have been like if she had stayed in law enforcement.

It was impossible after everything that had happened, of course, but what would it have been like? She had been pretty good at it. Even now, sometimes her friend in the Liberty Sheriff's Department would contact Norma to get her opinion on a case or a piece of evidence. It made Norma feel as if her life still meant something to someone.

The X-Files went to commercial, and Norma got up and padded into the kitchen to grab another Pepsi. She usually didn't drink carbonated beverages—another vice sacrificed—but tonight she was making an exception. The Pepsi went well with the popcorn, and she'd be going to bed soon.

She resigned herself to the fact that if anything exciting was ever going to happen in her life, she would either have to watch it on the "magic box" or read about it in some novel.

Exciting things didn't usually happen in Liberty. And, if they did, Norma would be under doctor's orders to stay away.

CHAPTER 8
Saturday, September 17

As the sun began to peek over the horizon, a new day dawned on the wide, slow-moving Cooper River. The body, missing one leg, drifted quietly, occasionally snagging on underwater growth that grew close to the surface. As it slowly approached the huge Charleston Municipal Bridge, the river narrowed, and the body drifted near the northern bank. Here, the river was less than ten feet deep, and the plants and tendrils reached toward the sun. Plants grasped at the body as it moved. Sometimes they caught it for a long moment before the current would win and push the body on toward the ocean.

A few miles away, a man's alarm clock sounded noisily in the growing light of dawn.

The man's hand drifted from his sleeping wife's waist and flopped down on the alarm, silencing it. The man rolled over and sat up, holding his face in his hands. A glance at the alarm clock told him that it was indeed 3:50 in the morning, and there were only two possible reasons for someone to be up that early: either someone had died, or someone was going fishing.

The man stood and tottered once back toward the bed, threatening to topple like a tree. He caught himself and quietly moved off toward the bathroom, trying to not wake his wife.

The body finally came to rest in the shallow waters less than a half-mile from the ocean. A large bridge spanned the wide river here, and the body got caught in some of the underwater growth near the base of one of the bridge's massive supports. One of the buckles became wedged in between rusty pieces of metal, and the body came to a halt, floating on the dark surface, as the rare car raced by on the bridge high above.

The fisherman yawned in the darkness and finished his coffee as he climbed down from his red Dodge truck and grabbed his gear out of the back. He started down the hill toward the river. The Charleston Municipal Bridge arched above him, its shape a black patch against the dark sky. He liked to fish the areas around the base of the bridge, where lots of low-hanging branches and weeds formed a perfect screen for fish to hide in. After a few minutes, he finally managed to make his way down to the bank of the river. To his right, streaks of light began to paint the far horizon.

The first thing he always noticed about the river in the morning was how incredibly peaceful it was. Tranquil, to the point of making him smile and thank God that he was alive.

Reaching the riverbank, he looked around, curiously sniffing at the air. Usually the new morning was reflected in the heady, pleasant scents of the river, but this morning he also caught the distinct odor of dead fish. Probably one had washed up onto the shore.

He shook it off and reached for his equipment. He wasn't going to let a little thing like that bother him.

The fisherman took his time laying out all of the equipment he'd collected over the years. Many lures, the most important part of any fisherman's tackle, had been lost to a zillion branches or underwater weeds or broken lines, but some had managed to stick around and survive his years of torture and abuse. Those colorful lures now rested in the top tray of his tackle box, surrounded by several shiny, pointed hooks, some different-colored sinkers and floaters, and a pair of pliers. He set about threading his pole, hooking on a red-and-white sinker and a hook, and then topped it off with a lure, one of his favorites. This one, a King Zinger, had been with him for years.

He stepped over to the muddy riverbank and tossed the lure out into the water with practiced ease, using a sidearm motion. It plopped down into the water, making only the slightest splash on the slow-moving surface. He allowed it to drift for a moment and then tipped the wooden pole up toward him and began slowly reeling the line back in, already comfortably relaxed by the reassuring motion.

The fisherman settled down into his rhythm: cast out into the water, let it float for a couple of minutes, then reel it in. Occasionally, from upstream, he'd hear the sounds of birds, screeching near the shore. Cast, float, reel. It was relaxing and monotonous and somehow lovely, a feeling that his wife never seemed to understand.

Maybe it was a hunter instinct in males, being out in the wilderness and catching his own food. Maybe he was crazy, but fishing always seemed to tap into some primal instinct.

The fisherman reeled in his lure again, probably for the fiftieth time this morning, but this time the lure caught on something in the water. At first, he thought it was a fish, but as he tugged a little harder, he realized the lure was caught on something much heavier. The thin silver line bobbed and weaved as he tugged, but it still drew a line as straight as a laser into the water.

Whatever it was caught on, the line wasn't coming free. Probably rocks on the bottom. He released some of the tension, letting the line slacken, before trying to reel it in again.

The fisherman snugged his pole into a crevice between two rocks and turned to grab his waders, pulling them on. He was suddenly glad he'd brought them down from the truck; usually he didn't. Too much hassle. From the tackle box he grabbed the wire-cutters, slipped them into one of the pockets of his shirt, and stepped carefully out into the water, gauging the depth and the speed of the current.

He wasn't about to lose one of his best lures.

The bottom was silty and clear of rocks. He used his hands to follow the line into the water, determined to not lose one of his favorite lures. The line appeared to be caught on something on the bottom, something large and dark and greenish. He bent over the mysterious object, spread his legs wide to get better traction on the muddy bottom, and began exploring the greenish object with his probing, curious hands.

His shirt front was instantly soaked as he strained to feel around the object, a moss-covered rock. The lure was there, too, caught on the rock just deep enough to make this difficult. His face was only an inch above the water's surface. He struggled with straining fingers and slipped, losing his footing and falling forward into the water.

He popped up instantly like a whale breaching, cursing loudly. He'd managed to grab the lure and the line and pull them free as he fell, but now he was completely soaked. He pulled the line up and looked at the lure hanging there, shaking his head and smiling despite his anger. He didn't have a dry change of clothes down here or up in the truck (he'd never needed one before) and now it looked like his relaxing day of fishing was over.

He shook his head and waded back toward the beach. He went slowly, not wanting to fall again. The fisherman was ten feet from shore when he heard more birds screeching loudly nearby. He glanced upstream, past where he could see before, and saw several more birds. They flapped and dipped from the sky, screeching and circling something in the water. It looked like a log, caught among the tall weeds just upriver from his favorite fishing spot.

A bird landed on the log. It squawked loudly at the fisherman and flapped away as he moved closer.

And then he saw the hand.

It was floating, palm up, fingers curled up. To his mind it looked like a dark, alien flower, floating on the brackish water.

Last day of work, David Beaumont thought nervously. It was weird, going in to work for the last time. 10:00 a.m. to 6:00 p.m. and then he was done. There were other jobs that he'd quit or been fired from, but he'd never had a job where he knew days ahead of time that he would be leaving.

His car was gassed and packed and ready, and he was nearly done with his to-do list. David was planning on leaving Liberty first thing tomorrow morning.

David parked right up front, up where the customers parked. Mel always told them to park away from the doors, saving the close spots for the customers, but David didn't think that Mel would mind this one time. He wanted the car where he could see it—nearly everything he owned was in it. David brought his cigar box of cash and traveler's checks inside, but the rest of his stuff was in the car.

His shift started at 10:00 a.m., but the store didn't open until 11:00 a.m. Two other employees were waiting at the front door when he arrived, including a new trainee. After David let them in, he sent them to straighten empty movie boxes, always messy after the busy Friday night.

When the store was prepped and ready to open, David did some shopping. It was the last day for his employee discount, and he took advantage of it by picking out eight CDs, including the new Rush, and a new CD holder. Choosing the Pack-it CD case made him remember the volcano he'd built. The store had come in second nationwide in that sales contest. He'd done a few good things in his life, a few things he could be proud of. That volcano had been one of them. The look on Mel's face when he came in that day had been worth all the work.

Behind the front counter, there was a CD and cassette system that played music through wall-mounted speakers. There was also a button for switching over to the video player audio output, in case they wanted to play a movie with sound. Video monitors were also mounted around the VHS rental section of the store. But the CD player was much more popular with the employees. There were always nightly discussions and arguments about which CD or tape would play next, or who would get "next pick" from the drawer full of tapes and CDs above the stereo system.

Mel ran the drawer, known as the play list, and technically only he could add things to it, but there were still the inevitable requests by the employees to open new things and listen to them. Over the years, several employees had been canned for opening too many pieces of product so they could hear them on the store's system. David thought Mel should just make them buy the CDs and tapes they opened or, better yet, make them buy something really bad that never sold.

Being his last day, David didn't think anyone would mind him playing his favorite music, or trying out the CDs he was buying, interspersed with his favorite movies playing over the speakers.

Just before 11:00 a.m., two more employees came in. One was Lisa Stevens, Bethany's best friend. She didn't say anything to David, or even acknowledge him when he held the door open for her. David didn't worry—everyone was entitled to their opinion. And David would have been the first person to admit he could have handled the breakup with Bethany better. It was no wonder Lisa Stevens was mad at him.

She and the other employee came in and hurriedly counted in their cash drawers as David prepared to open the store. The employees needed to verify there was a hundred dollars' worth of currency in the drawers that David had set up earlier, signing off on it. If the drawers came up short at the end of their shifts, they would be responsible for making up the difference out of their own pockets. If it happened too often, it was grounds for termination.

There was often a small group of people waiting outside when he opened. What did they want? Was buying CDs or renting videos so important that people would stand on a beautiful Saturday morning? As far as David could remember, he'd never stood outside of a store waiting for it to open, unless he was waiting in line for tickets.

It turned out a few of the people were waiting to buy tickets. The Washington Capitals were releasing a bunch of dates this morning. David went out early and had them line up against the wall outside the doors.

He checked the Ticketmaster menu after he booted up the system—the tickets wouldn't go on sale until 11:30. After letting the regular customers inside, he went back out and walked the hockey fans through the standard ticket procedures: Know exactly how many you want. Have your money out when he punched up the number of seats they requested. *Yes,* they were automatically the best available. Did anyone in line want tickets in a specific section? No? Good, because they would have to wait until all the other customers who wanted "best available" had bought theirs. Ticket sales went so quickly, there was never time to pick out specific seats or sections. Everyone always just wanted the "best" seats.

David talked to the first eight customers in line, jotting down how many tickets each of them wanted before heading back inside. Today's ticket sale did not involve all of the game dates for the entire season; the Capitals sold their tickets in two-month blocks, and today's tickets would be for next January and February of next year, 1997.

The tickets would be an easy sale, one he could easily handle by himself. Sometimes, the lines were so huge, it required they bring in extra employees just to control the crowds. Once, they had so many people line up, Mel kept the store closed for an extra hour, only allowing ticket buyers in, who were quickly escorted out after they purchased their tickets.

The sale brought in something like $30,000 in ticket sales that day. David remembered seeing all that cash in the back room, never having seen that much money all at once before. And when he glanced at Mel looking at the money, David wondered what was going through his mind. It almost looked like the big guy wanted to throw all of it in a bag, toss the keys to David, and bail.

Back inside, David made sure the other employees were set up and ready to go, then went back to picking out his purchases.

By 11:30, there were close to twenty people in line for tickets, so David got Lisa to take the money while he printed out the tickets. He could've done it all himself, but the extra time it would've taken would have made his customer's seats worse. He worked the Ticketmaster terminal, punching in the codes to get the best available, printed them out, and handed them to Lisa. She directed the customers around the counter and took their money, confirmed the ticket dates and locations, and sent them on their way. Never once during the twenty minutes did she say anything to David other than answer his direct questions.

David thought it was petty but let it go. In his head, he was already gone.

The next few hours were fun. David spent his last few hours as a Big Video employee finishing up a few projects around the store. He had Lisa ring up all of his purchases and took them out to his car. He played all his favorite movies, popping in *Die Hard*, *The Empire Strikes Back*, and *Back to the Future*, careful to run it up past the bad parts. There was a quick boob shot early on in *Die Hard* that you had to watch out for and skip. It came right after the terrorists broke up the party in the Nakatomi building. No way you could broadcast that in the store! He watched for the scene, zipping past it and hoping no one was looking at the screens for that split second.

David didn't bother with the sound. He knew all of these movies so well, he didn't need to hear them broadcast over the store's speakers.

All in all, it was a dream day at work. As if sensing his laid-back attitude, none of the employees gave him any hassles, and Lisa stayed away from him. It was perfect until Bethany came in.

He wasn't even sure it was her at first. She looked so tired and run-down that, for a moment, he thought it was someone else. Bethany walked past Lisa, nodding to her, and walked right over to him. He knew what she was doing. This was her last try.

"Hi, David."

He wanted to disappear, to pretend he didn't speak English, but it was useless.

"Hi, Bethany."

He had no idea what to say. She probably knew he was leaving—everyone else knew—but he hadn't had the courage to tell her himself. And now she was in here to make her case one last time.

She nodded and already her eyes were glistening up. Was she going to cry right here in front of everyone?

"Can we go in the back room?"

David nodded. If they stayed out here the scene might not get ugly, but he didn't want her to make a fool of herself in front of all of these people. He followed her to the backroom and closed the door behind them. She sat at the counter on one of the tall barstools. This wasn't how he'd planned it. He hadn't planned anything, content to just run out the clock and avoid her until he left. Very mature.

"Does Brian even know that you're coming?"

He'd mentioned it around the store, so Lisa had probably heard and passed it along.

"Yeah, I called him a few days ago. He wasn't there, but I talked to his girlfriend. She told me that he would be thrilled to see me."

"Don't you think you should've talked to him before you quit, before you left..." she started to ask, but stopped. It was clear she disapproved of this plan to just bail and head for California.

David started to answer her unspoken question, but then stopped. He didn't need to justify his actions to her or to anybody.

"I was going to call you tonight and tell you I was leaving. I thought it would be the best way to do things." He didn't say that putting off telling her to the last minute was the easiest thing on him. Or that getting all packed and ready to go before telling her minimized the chances that she could talk him out of it.

She started crying.

"I just wanted you to know..." he started, wanting desperately to lean over and hug her once more, a good-bye hug, but he didn't think he could handle it.

She looked up and held his gaze for a moment. She was struggling, starting and then stopping again before even getting half a word out, and David knew that she had something she wanted to say.

Should he tell her the words wouldn't matter?

"David...oh, god...I, I guess I just wanted to tell you to take care of yourself, okay? I guess...I guess I'll always love you, and I always thought that if we ever got a chance to really talk about it, we'd get back together..." She wasn't looking up at him. She was far too busy methodically tearing apart a Kleenex, shredding it into long, fuzzy strips that drifted down to the countertop. "I guess that's...that's never going to happen now."

David didn't want to be mean, but he also knew himself. The slightest backslide on his part might cause his resolve to waiver.

"No, Bethany. That's not going to happen—not now, not ever," he said, his voice cold and mechanical. "We're just not right for each other. Someday you'll see that."

Did she believe him? At this point, he didn't really care.

He turned and left the back room and wandered around the sales floor, straightening boxes and ignoring Doc Brown and Marty McFly on the TV monitors above the sales floor. After a while, she came out, crying. The others would see, but he didn't care. She headed right out the door, not even stopping to talk to Lisa.

But when she got to the door, she stopped and turned around and looked at him, and the hurt on her face broke his heart.

———

Hurricane Mandy headed east, roaring back onto the peninsula of Florida late Saturday night. Beaches were closed and seaside towns evacuated. Mandy continued on her deadly path, making a rare second landfall just after 2:00 a.m. on Sunday, September 18.

Tracker Kovacs and the others nervously watched the satellite pictures and the incoming flight data from the high-altitude Maverick planes flying through the storm. Usually, when a storm passed over land, it weakened. But Mandy had crossed Florida already once, then traversed the Gulf and was back for a second hit. The eye was over a hundred miles wide, and she was growing in strength again, a strong Category 3 verging on 4. Whole new computer programs were being hastily written to estimate her track, strength, and speed.

So far, they weren't having much luck.

The latest estimates put Mandy crossing Florida again and moving back into the Atlantic, then turning north on Monday, moving up the coast. But her speed was so achingly slow. If she continued at this same pace, it would take her a week to get to New York, a lifetime for a hurricane. Would she last that long, or sputter out over the Carolinas? Or would she die out over the open water?

Randy had no way to answer these or the dozen other questions his supervisor posed at their midnight staff meeting. Their computer programs were based on certain criteria, and this stormed seemed to be simply ignoring the norm. If they couldn't get a handle on it soon, cities and towns all up and down the Eastern Seaboard could be slammed by the biggest storm of the year, with little or no warning from the National Hurricane Center.

PART TWO:

TRACKING THE APPROACH

CHAPTER 9
Sunday, September 18

David was leaving Liberty for good.

It was nearly 10:00 a.m. on Sunday morning, and he was also barely holding it together.

His aunt, when she wasn't out and out sloshed, had often told him that he was too emotional for a boy. In his aunt's scheme of things, boys were supposed to be solid slabs of mute beef, marching through life and never looking back.

David hadn't cried in front of her since his sixth birthday and the party with the clown. His aunt had decided to throw him a surprise party in the grand tradition of kid's birthday parties. Balloons and presents and neighborhood kids spinning each other around and attempting to pin a small strip of paper with a painted-on tail onto a colorful poster of a donkey hung on a tree.

Oh, and there had been a clown.

Young David had never liked clowns, and his aunt knew this. She'd decided the only way he was going to get over his silly, childish fear of clowns was to face that fear head-on. She arranged for one to show up at his party—and neglected to tell David ahead of time.

The party started well. David was just finishing up another futile attempt to pin the tail on the donkey, managing only to pin the little tail to the tree a foot south of the donkey's behind. David pulled off the blindfold while the other kids clapped. He was still dizzy from the spinning and all of the excitement and laughed along with the others.

"BOO!" the clown screamed, jumping out from the crowd and grabbing David, who shrieked like a frightened woman. He bolted from the clown's grasp, backing into a small table and sending gifts and cameras and party favors flying. Everything crashed to the ground, accompanied by the sharps sounds of breakage.

David started crying.

His aunt was mortified, embarrassed beyond words. The other mothers looked at her with expressions of obvious distaste, probably wondering how she could have raised such a crybaby. It was the looks from the other mothers more than anything that caused her to race forward. She grabbed David up and swept him up under her arm like a football, carrying him into the house. She spanked him hard, repeatedly, taking out her frustration on David. The sound of the worn Ping-Pong paddle, her favorite tool for his frequent spankings, was loud enough for everyone to hear outside.

A few minutes later, she took him back outside, and he'd walked over to the clown, gingerly shaking his hand before turning to announce, in a very shaky voice, that it was time to open the presents.

David had learned his lesson, and he never cried around his aunt. He'd learned how to keep his emotions in check, to keep his feelings inside. But now David was struggling to not cry.

He was at her house, but all of the furniture had either been sold off or already moved over to the new townhouse. Abe was moving fast— David didn't even know they'd already picked out a new place. All that was left here at the house where he'd grown up were stacks and stacks of brown cardboard boxes. He saw a box or two whose markings included his name, and two were marked "William." His father? Aunt Gloria had stuff from his father?

He had no idea that his aunt had kept any of his father's things. He poked through one of the boxes out of curiosity while he was waiting for her to come down from her bedroom, but the box was just full of clothes. He held a shirt up to his face, wondering if it smelled like his father, but it only smelled like old clothes.

The other box contained old case files and paperwork, each with William T. Beaumont's name scrawled on the green covers. He flipped through the files, fascinated. Had this stuff been in the house all along? David found himself wishing for a month to examine every item in detail to get some type of insight into his father's true nature. Maybe he should take the box with him, look through it on the road?

No, he thought, shaking his head. I'm moving on. It doesn't matter.

He put the box down, turning away as his aunt came downstairs.

"I didn't know you have boxes of my father's things."

Gloria nodded. "Yup, found them in the basement. I'd forgotten. Do you...are you taking them?"

"No, I don't have room," David lied.

She looked at him for a moment and dropped it.

They walked out onto the porch and commenced their good-byes. David worked hard to keep his tears back. It felt like he should stay to make sure she got settled into the new place. Things were looking up for her. Wasn't that what he wanted?

"Gotta go, okay?" he said, shaking his head. "You sure you're going to be okay with the move and all?" he asked.

She dabbed at her eyes with the dishrag she'd been carrying and nodded. "Yeah, if I need help I'll call Abe or somebody. I'll be just fine. You drive careful and call me as soon as you get there, okay?"

As she finished, Gloria stepped forward and hugged him. For a flickering moment, he felt total love for her. When she let him go, he smiled and kissed her on the cheek. Her hugs were always like that, fleeting.

David turned to his car and saw that Bethany's Honda had pulled into the driveway behind it, blocking him in. She was getting out. How had he not heard her?

This was the last thing he needed. David felt emotional enough with leaving his aunt, the only family he'd ever known. Now here came the only girl he'd ever really loved. What was this, the last scene in some tearjerker movie? Were they both going to work on him? Would the music swell and the movie end with him deciding to stay? The idea of just driving away, going over the lawn if he had to, appealed to him.

"Morning, Miss Thatcher. How are you?" Bethany asked his aunt before turning to him. She was carrying something.

"Well, my little boy is leaving me," Gloria said, who was now crying.

Bethany handed him a thick red binder wrapped in a bow. He took it and started to open it, but she put one hand on top of it.

"Read it on the road." She looked up at him and leaned closer, kissing his cheek softly. "It's to remind you of us. So you don't forget." She looked into his eyes for a moment, then walked back to her car and got in without saying another word. He wasn't sure what to do, or what to say. He watched her car as she drove away.

"I think she really loves you, David," his aunt said. "You should think twice about leaving her."

He looked at his aunt. "I have thought twice, Gloria. I've thought about it a thousand times. She's better off without me. Everyone is."

He tucked the binder under his arm and hugged Gloria once more. He needed to leave, to get on the road before he changed his mind.

David took one last look at the old house. She followed him down the driveway.

"Tires?" she asked.

He smiled.

"Just aired them up yesterday. The guy at the shop said they're good for at least 30,000 more miles before I have to start worrying. They'll be fine."

She turned and saw him looking at her. "I just want you to be careful, and safe, okay?" The tears were close again, and he knew it. "Nothing wrong with me wanting the best for my only family, right?"

"Of course not."

He went around the driver's side and opened the door to get in when she came around and hugged him again, longer this time.

"You'll be careful, right?" she asked, pulling away. For a moment, she seemed as sober as a nun. The clarity in her eyes was something to behold.

"Of course, I'll be careful. And I'll call you when I get there. Same number?"

She nodded. "I'll be back and forth a lot." She glanced back up at the house. "Lots of stuff to move, you know."

"Yeah, I know." He kissed her on the cheek and climbed in, making a show of putting on his seat belt.

"Oh, cut that out," she said, her smile matching his. "You take care of yourself, okay?"

"I will," he said as he started the car up. David slowly backed it out of the driveway and put the Mazda into drive. It wheezed once before catching and popping into gear. She stood in the middle of the driveway, waving. As he slowly pulled away, he waved back until she was out of sight.

David Beaumont remained in Liberty for a half-hour longer as he topped off the gas and picked up a Big Gulp and some candy at the 7-Eleven. The tears never came. And they wouldn't, as far as he was concerned. He would miss his aunt, and he would miss Bethany, he was sure, but this decision was right.

He headed east, out of town. It felt good. It felt right.

He was almost to the County Line Bridge when he decided to get out his big folding map of Virginia, the one he'd highlighted. The route would take him down to Richmond and beyond.

David took his eyes off the road for just a moment to find the map, and therefore didn't see the old white van pass him going in the other direction. He didn't see the driver, a thin man with piercing eyes that never left the roadway before him.

David certainly didn't see the steely smile that darkened the man's face as the van crossed the bridge.

Jack drifted quietly back into Liberty, Virginia, largely unnoticed.

Everyone who Jack came into contact within those first few hours was under the age of thirty. To a person, they'd probably all head of him, heard of the Killer and the legend that had grown up around him. But none of them knew who they were looking at. They had no clue as to the significance of this bearded, leather-jacketed ghost from their town's past.

The people that might have remembered his last visit were older and busy doing things other than wiping down the counters at McDonald's or working the pumps at the Exxon station, and this was the main reason why, when Jack Terrington returned to Liberty on that Sunday afternoon, nobody recognized him.

The wind picked up and swirled fallen leaves in the gutters as Jack drove the old streets, remembering. The quickening wind mirrored the excitement in his mind. Liberty had grown over the intervening years, but it still held that simple, small-town feel. The town had added a good-sized mall that Jack passed on his way into town. Other than that, little had changed, as far as he could recall.

———————

Lisa Stevens was tired.

Her Sunday 10:00 a.m. to 6:00 p.m. shift was almost up, and all she wanted to do was go home and crash. She hadn't spoken to her best friend Bethany today, but David, her boyfriend, had left this morning. Lisa knew Bethany would be in bad shape over it.

Why Bethany should be sad was beyond Lisa's understanding—she'd never liked David, and had told Bethany as much. Bethany was gorgeous, with the kind of looks that most girls would kill for. For some reason, she had been dating this brooding, quiet guy with the famous father.

And worse, now she'd been dumped. If it had been Lisa getting dumped, she would've punched his lights out. Lisa Steven's father taught her at a very young age how to take care of herself around boys, and now she was something of a tomboy.

So, although she was tired, Lisa was heading over to Bethany's later for a girls' night out of pizza and movies. Hopefully, there would be no mention of boys at all.

Lisa hopped up off the sales floor where she'd been sitting and began stacking the large green and white computer printouts back into the right order. She'd been taking inventory of the New Age CDs, but she wasn't going to stay and finish it. She'd learned early on to look out for herself. If Big Mel (as just about everybody called him behind his sizable back) wanted the New Age CDs finished, he could either pay her overtime or get somebody else to do it. Or, heaven forbid, he might even peel himself out of his very sturdy chair in the back room and get out on the sales floor and do it himself.

Nah, it would never happen, she thought. Not unless you left a trail of M&M's leading over to it.

She clipped the stack of printouts and the pen onto the clipboard, and then walked to the backroom, hanging it with the other "inventory" clipboards. Big Mel was in his office, partitioned from the rest of the back room with a thin wall and a weak-looking door. He was on the phone, talking in a low voice. Maybe he was talking to a prospective date. Just the idea sent chills up Lisa's spine.

Lisa collected her schoolbooks and her purse from the break area and stood by the door into Mel's office, waiting to be recognized. It usually didn't take long for most people to recognize Lisa Stevens.

"Hold on a sec, okay?" Mel said, and then held one pale hand over the mouthpiece of the phone, turning to Lisa. She could feel his eyes on her and wondered why she'd picked today to wear her tightest skirt.

"Ready to go?" he said, staring at her legs.

She adjusted her books, trying to avoid looking at him.

"Yeah. I almost finished the New Age CDs. It's on the hook," she said, gesturing at the row of clipboards.

"Great. Have a good night," Mel said with a smile. She could see the curiosity in his eyes, wondering what—or who—she was doing tonight.

Well, sorry to disappoint you, fat boy. This evening will be boring. Just sitting around with a sobbing girl crying over her loser of an ex-boyfriend.

Mel looked like he was trying to think of something else to say to continue the conversation, but she took advantage of the pause and scooted away. She left the backroom and said good-bye to the other employees and left.

Outside, the weather was strange. It felt like a new season had begun. A cold wind rushed past her, pushing fallen leaves around the parking lot in swirling patterns. To the south, a storm front was moving in, a long line of dark clouds hugged the horizon.

As she headed for her car, she caught the faint whiff of approaching rain. She popped the door open, dumping her bag into the back seat. Starting the car, she flipped the heater on for the first time in months.

A flash of light caught her eyes. Her crystal soccer ball, a treasured keepsake, dangled from her rearview mirror, throwing off reflected slivers of the fading sunlight in all directions. She reached up and tapped one side of the ball, sending it spinning. She watched it turn as the car warmed. When her arms and legs began to warm, she put the car in drive and pulled away. Waiting to pull out into traffic, she popped a tape into her stereo and cracked a window.

Finally seeing an opening in front of a filthy white van, she darted into the opening, cutting the other driver off. She didn't have time to wait—she needed to get to the supermarket and then home to change before heading over to Bethany's.

————————

Jack Terrington had been cruising through town, sightseeing, when the driver of a little red car darted into traffic in front of him, cutting him off. Her long blonde hair, moving in the breeze of her open window, caught his attention.

He started to honk but hesitated. Jack felt an urge stir within him, sudden and ominous.

Instead of getting mad, he followed the red Toyota Tercel, watching the young woman beat her hands on the dashboard to music he couldn't hear. She swerved, barely missing a car, and then turned abruptly, without signaling, into the parking lot for a grocery store. He slowed and followed her. Jack realized with a start it was the Food Town, the same one where he'd been ambushed so many years ago.

The girl pulled into a parking space close but stayed in the car. She thrashed around, beating the dashboard, singing and drumming. He parked nearby and watched as she finished up with a flourish. She grabbed her wallet and climbed out.

His breath caught in his throat. She was beautiful, with long, flowing blonde hair that seemed to float and bounce under its own power. She had the long, thin legs of an athlete. Jack Terrington rarely chose his victims for their physical appearance, but he had the same sexual urges as any other man, he assumed.

Jack took only a second to make up his mind.

He reached around behind his seat and found his jimmy, then climbed down from his van and walked over to the passenger door of her car. Glancing around, he deftly slipped the jimmy down between the window and the rubber sealant, jerking it up quickly up inside the door to unlock it. Here he was, the Angel of Death, breaking into cars.

He only climbed halfway into the tiny car, keeping the door open while he searched her car for something to steal. There was the usual accumulation of junk: papers, napkins, change. A satchel in the passenger seat, college textbooks spilling out. The entire back seat seemed taken up by exercise clothes and a mesh bag stuffed with dirty soccer balls.

A crystal globe caught his eyes. The shiny, ball-shaped piece of crystal hung from the rearview mirror by a thin strand of fine chain. It spun slowly, throwing off sparks and rainbows.

"Bethany?"

Lisa was using a pay phone outside the entrance to the Food Town. Her back was to her car, or she might have seen her crystal soccer ball bobbing.

"Hey. Where are you?" Bethany asked. "I got movies, and I was just getting ready to call Domino's."

"I'm at the Food Town," Lisa said, glanced down at her plastic sacks. "Got salad stuff and ice cream. Go ahead and call. I'll be there in twenty minutes or so; I want to run home and change first."

"Good. Pepperoni and sausage, right?" Bethany asked.

"Sounds perfect. Be there in a flash."

Jack saw her coming and climbed out, pocketing the two things he'd taken. He scooted away, not looking back until he got to his van.

She was jingling her keys, her blonde hair bouncing as she carried two plastic bags of groceries. Jack watched her climb in and put the groceries in the passenger seat. She started up the car, and he waited.

It only took a moment.

She sat, looking at the radio. She leaned forward, fiddling with the stereo. The girl glanced around the interior of her car, confused.

He could almost read her mind: *What happened to my tape?*

He smiled and popped her tape into his own stereo, rolling down his windows. It was by R.E.M., a band he'd heard of. Jack cranked up the stereo.

Jack wasn't a fan, but he knew someone who was.

He was looking right at her when her head came up. She rolled her window down and listened, looking around. She spotted Jack, three rows away, listening to the music and beating his hands energetically on the steering wheel.

He waved at her.

She glanced away in an almost demure fashion, but then looked around again. He could feel thick waves of curiosity coming off of her.

Jack gave her a big smile and pulled away, exiting the parking lot and heading east on Main, back out of town, in the direction of the interstate and the new mall. Her red Tercel fell in behind him, several cars back, almost as if she were trying to tail him without his knowing. He smiled; over the years, Jack had been followed by drivers far more experienced then her.

He turned down the music and slowed to let her catch up.

Highway 132 was Main Street for most of the way through Liberty, and Lisa Stevens had driven every inch of it a hundred times. The white van was four car lengths in front of her, heading east out of town.

Of course, the tape might not have been hers. Or she might've taken it out and dropped it in the lot and he found it. But she didn't think so. The weird guy with the crazy eyes somehow knew it was hers. He'd played it loud, looking right at her.

It was one of her favorites. Lisa resolved to get her tape back, even if she had to use her famous center kick on this creep.

Trailing him, she studied his van in case she had to make a police report. It was your typical dirty white van, longer than normal, as if it had been lengthened. There were a pair of square windows in the back doors, each covered by small, black curtains. She memorized his California license plate number. This guy had come a long way.

She had no idea what else to do, and her impatience finally got the better of her. She accelerated, moving around the van and up next to it. She wanted another look at the creep.

Lisa could hear R.E.M. coming from the van's open windows. The driver glanced over and smiled at her, then raised one fist up to her. She thought he was going to wave again, but he opened his hand. Her crystal globe appeared, falling six inches before catching on the short silver chain that the man had looped around his palm.

She glanced at the rearview—her globe was gone. She hadn't even noticed.

He had been in her car.

When she looked back, the van had pulled away, rapidly accelerating. She dropped in behind him but couldn't match his speed. They were heading in the direction of the mall and the County Line Bridge beyond.

Something in her gut told her this was a bad idea. No one knew where she was. She was already late, and Bethany would be worried. If Lisa was smart, she'd find a pay phone and call the sheriff's office.

But Lisa felt violated, angry. She was getting her stuff back from this weirdo, no matter what. Her parents had her bought the soccer-shaped crystal to celebrate Lisa making the varsity team in high school.

The van was faster than it looked. When it pulled off onto a side road four or five miles later, she was still well behind him. He turned on side streets and led her through a small subdivision, heading into the woods south of the mall.

It was getting darker. She followed him deeper into the woods, her stomach tightening. This all felt wrong.

He was trying to lose her, but it wouldn't work—she knew the roads and streets of Liberty like the back of her hand. The mall was close, just to the north. If she needed help, it was there.

Minutes later, she rounded a sharp corner and found the van. It was stopped by the side of the road, the driver's door standing wide open. She pulled in behind it and sat in her idling car for several minutes, watching the van and the road and the trees around it. There was no movement.

She shut off her engine and opened her door slowly. Lisa Stevens felt a sudden ball of fear in her stomach.

The first thing she noticed was just how quiet it was.

She could hear the slow ticking of her car's engine as it cooled under the hood—the red paint looking dull and bloody in the gathering dark. Other than the engine and the exaggerated, hurried sound of her own breathing, the silence was ominous. No sounds of animals, rustling their way through the underbrush. No sounds from the Liberty Place Mall or Highway 132.

She realized with a start that she was much deeper into the woods south of the mall than she had previously thought.

Soldier on, she told herself. Get your stuff and get gone. He was probably in the woods, taking a leak.

She swallowed her fear and walked toward the van.

The driver's door stood open. As she stepped around to take a look inside, her stomach in her throat, she saw a sparkle of reflected light standing out in the relative gloom of the van's interior. Her crystal globe hung from the rearview mirror.

Lisa glanced around and leaned farther in the door, looking inside the van. There was not much light, but she could see all the way to the curtained windows at the back. There was a table just behind the passenger seat, and wooden cabinets lining both walls.

Where was her tape?

———

Jack watched the beautiful, long-legged girl climb up into the doorway of his van, stretching to peek inside. Her tight dark skirt rode up deliciously. After a moment, she climbed up and disappeared inside his van.

He stepped quietly out of the trees, moving toward the van. He had the tape in his hand, ready to go, and got out his keys. Jack had a plan.

————

Lisa Stevens slid between the two front seats. Her tape hadn't been in the old stereo or on the console between the two front seats, but she'd grabbed her crystal globe from around the rearview mirror and now held it in one fist like a weapon.

To her right was a small refrigerator and sink, like a miniature, built-in kitchen. Across from those, instead of the usual sliding door, there was a small dinette with a wooden table and two seats. The top of the table was scarred, gouged like an old cutting board. Mysterious streaks stained the flat, pitted surface.

Past the kitchenette and table, four or five feet of low wooden doors, cabinets lined each side of the van. Above the cabinets were two rows of large glass jars, one row on each side, secured by wooden slats that prevented the jars from tipping over or sliding off the cabinet tops.

There was something inside the dusty glass jars.

Lots of little somethings. Each jar was topped with a seal, like the ones people used on jars of preserves. She stepped closer. The first jar was over half full, the objects inside familiar. Dozens of them, roughly an inch long, ranging in color from pink near the top to a blackened gray near the bottom. Lisa leaned closer to the jar, brushing the dust away. She saw a small, whitish square on the top object, and it took her mind a few seconds to recognize it for what it was. The final clue was her own hand, resting on the glass jar next to it.

The shape was a fingernail. All of the shapes in this jar had fingernails...

She jumped back, gasping, one hand to her mouth.

There were at least forty or fifty fingers in the jar.

She looked around at the other jars. Now, with more opened eyes, she saw the contents for what they really were. Fingers, toes, other things she couldn't identify. Eyes floated in a green solution in one jar. Another jar held larger, floppy objects that looked like thick leaves, stacked atop each other like gray pancakes. The edge of one held three shiny gold dots that looked like earrings.

Ears. The flat shapes were ears.

Oh God no. Oh Jesus—

Lisa put her hand to her mouth, feeling the gorge rise up from her stomach. She turned to run, and music blared suddenly from every direction, blasting from speakers. Lisa screamed and clapped her hands to her ears, dropping to her knees.

She looked up at the front of the van and saw him. He stood

between the pair of seats, grinning like the Joker. The guy was holding something. The music was pounding in her ears, her tape at maximum volume. How could he stand the noise? She focused on his hands, which held something that sparked in the dark. He moved it slowly around, watching her stare at it, numb with terror. He flipped it on, a blue spark running across the object. A Taser. When he finally stepped toward her and jabbed her with the two sharp points of the stun gun, she didn't even try to move away.

Bethany was getting worried.

The pizza from Domino's was getting cold. So far, no sign of Lisa. Hadn't she said twenty, thirty minutes at the most? Bethany had hung up from talking to Lisa and immediately called, putting in their order. It had taken a half hour for the pizza to arrive, and now it had been here for at least that long.

Where was she?

She glanced at the clock that hung on the wall of the paneled downstairs family room, and it read 7:24. Lisa had been off at 6:00 and had called at around 6:20.

Should she call Lisa's house again? Lisa said she was going to stop off to change clothes. Bethany had already called twice. No answer, but that didn't mean anything. Lisa's parents were probably out.

Bethany knew that Lisa had been looking forward to coming over. Bethany had the house to herself—her parents were out of town on a cruise. Funny how things worked out—months ago, when she'd heard her parents were going to be out of town for three weeks in September on an Alaskan cruise, the first thing she'd thought of was David. She loved the idea of having David stay over for several nights; she'd been looking forward to the things they could do with all of that privacy.

But now David was gone, on his way to California.

And here she was, sitting in this big house all by herself, only a pair of cold pizzas and some rented movies to keep her company. She'd gotten them from work after she'd given the binder to David. She'd wanted to talk to him, to say something, but she hadn't known what to say—or even how to say it—and she decided to just let the binder speak for itself. She hoped he would read it, but she didn't know if it would matter.

Lisa went to school with Bethany at the local community college, just like the majority of last year's high school seniors. A few of the smarter kids had managed to lasso a scholarship and escape town, but most of the freshmen were the same faces she had seen every day at high school. Bethany and Lisa shared two classes, psychology and human studies. And they worked together, so they'd become close friends. Lisa was helping Bethany through the breakup, suggesting they get together tonight. It just didn't make any sense for Lisa to stand her up.

Bethany reached over and picked up the phone and hit the redial button. No answer. Nobody home. Maybe Lisa had run into somebody she knew at the supermarket.

Bethany got up and heated up some pizza and popped in one of the scary movies she had gotten. She tried to put Lisa and her tardiness out of her mind for a while.

Maybe she'd met a nice guy. Probably already had him twisted around her finger.

Lisa Stevens could feel something, rough and hard, scraping her face. Lisa blinked and tried to turn her face, but her hands were caught on something. Another moment of struggling told her that her hands were tied together on the other side of whatever it was she had her arms wrapped around. She leaned backward a little and looked up. Branches. She was strapped to a tree.

She remembered the weird man and finding the white van. The door had been open, and she'd climbed inside, finding...jars? Jars of something. Things. Fingers. She'd turned to leave and the music—

A cold breeze moved through the trees around her. She felt cold wind, a breeze on her exposed skin.

Lisa realized she was naked.

She tried to look down at herself, a reflex action, but the ropes were too tight. All she could see was the flattened rise of her breasts, smashed rudely against the rough bark of the tree. Every movement made the bark claw at her naked skin. Her legs were bound as well, a rope below her knees.

"You really shouldn't move around a lot."

The voice came from behind her, along with the sound of a fire, cracking. She could smell the smoke now.

She heard someone stand up and walk over to her. It was him, his face lined with age. The beard was scraggly, gray in parts, and he wore a dusty leather jacket over a blue stained T-shirt that looked like it had seen a whole year of better days. But it was his eyes that drew her attention. They were gray and deep and insane.

They reminded her of a movie she'd seen once in high school. In history class, they'd shown a film reel from a World War II concentration camp. Chelmo, she remembered, somewhere in Poland. Nazi soldiers leading groups of Jews to their deaths. Members of the SS corralling helpless, naked women and children into a series of concrete rooms, the walls scored with the fingernail scratches of those who had already been put to death.

The leader, standing nearby, was sorting the prisoners into two groups. Some would be spared to work in horrible conditions in the camp. The others were to be exterminated immediately.

The man sorted with cold German efficiency, but it was the eyes that Lisa remembered. They never betrayed a single ounce of feeling, not a spark of emotion. The guy had even lit up one of those weird thin cigarettes as he ordered those people to their deaths.

Now, in the forest, this man's eyes were the same. They held the same blankness of expression, the same careless disregard for suffering and death. Or maybe they did care. Maybe they felt amusement.

Lisa felt all the hope and goodness and light in the world turn away from her, abandoning her to her fate. In an instant, she knew she would never leave this man's gaze alive.

Jack Terrington held her eyes for a long time, feeling her size him up. She watched him warily, as an injured animal might watch the hunter as he moves in to finish the kill. He needed to convince her of the power that he held over her. The terror that he craved so much would come soon enough.

Now the test.

He crossed the clearing, moving past the fire. He wanted to have her in every possible way, but that could wait. She would be his, but he wanted to have her mind first. He could see her trembling, probably a combination of her fear and the chill. With agonizing slowness, Jack curled up the ends of his lips to form the worst, most frightening grin he could muster. She screamed.

And it was beautiful.

Bethany was driving over to Lisa's house.

Her curiosity and her concern for Lisa had gotten the best of her, and she'd finally given up on *The Town that Dreaded Sundown* and donned her coat. Besides, the movie was far too scary to watch alone. She had called the Stevens' again before she left, but there was no answer.

Bethany parked in front of the Stevens' house and went up and knocked. No response. Lights were on in the house, but there was no way to know who left them on.

She debated about what to do and finally went back to her car and rummaged around in the glove box, finding paper and a pencil to write a note. She didn't want to frighten Lisa's parents, but they would be concerned if their girl was missing.

Bethany wrote a quick note, included her phone number, and walked back up to the front door. She didn't have any tape or anything to stick the note to the door, so she held the piece of paper and closed the screen door on it, hoping that would hold it.

She returned to the warmth of her car. Suddenly, Bethany missed David terribly. He would've known what to do in a situation like this. They had been a good couple, even with all the troubles. Had he really been that unhappy? Had she asked him too many times about his family, or his lack of ambition?

She didn't know what it was like to be the only offspring of the most famous person in town. She knew he wanted to leave town, to get out of Liberty and try and make a name for himself somewhere else. She just never thought he would actually go through with it. Maybe she underestimated him.

She looked at her watch. 8:52. Lisa had been off work for hours. Bethany put the car in reverse and backed out of the driveway. Maybe someone at the Food Town would remember. Lisa was a pretty girl, hard to forget.

A few minutes after Bethany pulled away, a strong breeze moved through the neighborhood and rattled the Stevens' screen door. The door opened slightly, just enough to allow Bethany's note to fall onto the welcome mat. The next breeze carried it off the porch and into the bushes near the front door.

Bethany had no luck at the Food Town. Bethany guessed Lisa had used one of the pay phones outside of the Food Town to call. Two of the checkout people remembered Lisa, but no one had seen her for hours. Lisa's car wasn't there, either. Bethany checked at Big Video, too, and even drove past the soccer fields where Lisa usually played, just in case they'd called a weird, impromptu practice and Lisa had forgotten to call.

Finally, Bethany went home.

She was hoping Lisa's red Tercel would be waiting in her driveway, and Lisa would be mad for standing her up. But the driveway was empty. Going back inside, Bethany felt the first pangs of panic in her stomach. Another call to Lisa's house, but no answer. She hung up but didn't put the phone down. She wanted to talk to David and started dialing his number from memory before she realized that he didn't live there anymore and hung up before his roommate could answer.

What now? She had been everywhere and there was no sign of Lisa.

She wished her parents were home. They would know what to do, right?

And then she knew what she needed to do, amazed that she hadn't thought of it earlier.

She hung up the phone, waiting a moment, and then dialed the number for the Liberty Sheriff's Department.

———

Several hours later, Lisa Stevens' parents returned from a performance of *Show Boat* at the Kennedy Center in D.C. They pulled into the garage and Lisa's father was momentarily concerned that their daughter's car was not around. Mrs. Stevens reminded her husband that Lisa had planned a girls' night out with her friend Bethany and had probably decided to stay over.

Neither of them saw the note fluttering in the bush next to the front door.

Neither of them, for reasons that would haunt them for the rest of their days, checked the answering machine and its blinking red light until late the next morning.

By the time they checked it, there were four messages. The first three messages were from Bethany, Lisa's best friend. She was looking for Lisa, who hadn't shown up. Each message grew more panicked than the last.

The final message was from the sheriff's office.

CHAPTER 10
Monday, September 19

Agent Julie Noble caught the Orange Line near her apartment in northern Virginia, taking the metro into town. The D.C. Metrorail was one of her favorite things about living in this area. The stations were beautiful and always crystal clean, and the trains always came on time, even in bad weather.

She'd grabbed a copy of *USA Today* on her way through the subway station, and she hung her purse and bag over one arm and began reading the front page. The biggest story was Hurricane Mandy: the storm's path had moved back over Florida again yesterday, making it a rare storm that made two landfalls. Now it was looking like the massive storm could be heading up the coast, threatening the eastern seaboard and maybe, possibly, making an incredibly-rare third landfall. The experts were saying that, if it didn't sputter out off the Carolina coast, Hurricane Mandy could make it all the way to the D.C. area by Thursday or Friday.

Page three held local stories from regions all over the United States, and one of them caught her attention. It was accompanied by a picture of policemen standing on the edge of a wide river, pointing upstream.

ONE-LEGGED YOUTH FOUND DROWNED
Charleston, SC (AP)—Authorities found the body of Kevin Neeson floating in the Columbus River yesterday, just north of Charleston, South Carolina. Neeson, 21, a resident of Thomasville, Georgia, suffered from cholera in early childhood and wore a specially designed prosthetic leg not found at the scene. Authorities say the leg most likely sank to the bottom of the river.

A local fisherman discovered the body early Saturday morning along the northern bank of the river, where it had become entangled in a large group of weeds and branches near the foot of the Charleston Municipal Bridge. The fisherman used a CB radio to report the body to the local police department. Police spokesman said homicide had not been ruled out as a possible cause of death due to several "unusual" wounds found on the body. The spokesman also reported the FBI would be involved in the investigation.

She'd nearly laughed at the bizarre headline before realizing it wasn't some sick joke. As she read the article, her eyes kept returning to the photo of the cops. Julie read several more articles before disembarking at the Old Post Office, the closest stop to the FBI Building. But even as she crossed Pennsylvania Avenue in the warming morning air, she couldn't get the story out of her head.

David woke up with a terrible crick in his neck.

He sat up in his car, rubbing idly at the sharp pain and looked around. The sun hadn't been up long, and it barely lit the surroundings. He was in the parking lot of a hotel on the southern side of Lexington, Virginia. David had only driven five hours yesterday before deciding to look for a room. Driving was a lot more tiring than he'd thought, and he'd decided to take it easy on the first day, stopping around 6:00 p.m.

Unfortunately, by the time he finished eating and started looking for a room, the few hotels in town were all booked up. There was some kind of convention in town, the desk clerks all told him, and the next good-sized town was Charleston, West Virginia, four hours away. He ended up sleeping in the lot of the last hotel he checked.

He rubbed his neck—he needed to remember that lying down in the front seat of a 1989 Mazda 323 and trying to get a full night's sleep were two mutually exclusive concepts.

He popped the door handle and climbed out, feeling his muscles and bones groan as he stretched. There was a chill in the air. Fall was here, and winter was fast approaching. But this winter would find David Beaumont in sunny Southern California, he reminded himself with a smile.

The decision felt right. It felt good to be on the road, chasing a dream.

David smiled and climbed back in, intent on grabbing some breakfast and hitting the road when his eyes caught something in the passenger seat. Among the empty cups and the map with scribbled directions, was the red binder Bethany had given him.

He opened it, flipping through it, seeing dozens of handwritten pages. She'd written him a long letter, forty pages at least, with pictures pasted inside as well. He could guess the gist of the whole thing: "Stay here, David, don't leave Liberty."

David tossed the binder in the back seat. He'd need to get a few more states away before he was ready to look at the binder.

Bethany was on hold again, the third time in the last half hour. Her call to the sheriff's station last night had been pointless—she'd left a message when some recorded voice had informed her that no one was available. She wondered what they would do with a real emergency— schedule a meeting? She was desperate to report that Lisa was gone.

Calling 911 hadn't helped either—they'd only taken a message.

Bethany couldn't get the picture out of her head of Lisa wandering along the side of some road, her car wrecked. Lisa holding one hand to her bloody head, dazed and unable to think straight. There were a lot of creepy back roads around Liberty. Bethany could see it all so clearly in her mind's eye.

Lisa was in trouble.

Bethany slammed the receiver down, cursing. No one was talking to her. These cops were useless.

She grabbed her car keys and left, leaving a note in her mailbox for Lisa in case she showed up. She had to get out and do something—the phone wasn't helping.

A few minutes later, Bethany pulled up in front of the Stevens' house, but Lisa's little red Tercel still wasn't there. Neither was her parent's car. Bethany got out and tried the doorbell, but no one answered. She found the note she'd written—it had fallen out and gotten stuck in a nearby bush. She wedged it back into the doorjamb.

Her parents had probably stayed overnight in D.C., and if they weren't here, that meant it was up to Bethany to report Lisa's disappearance.

Bethany put her Honda into drive and headed for the sheriff's office.

―――――――

"Did you hear something?" Mrs. Stevens asked her sleeping husband, her voice groggy from the night before. It wasn't often they went all the way into D.C. for entertainment, and last night they had really painted the town. They had dinner on the open terrace atop the Hotel Washington, with its spectacular view of the city from the restaurant's choice location. The wine had flowed liberally, and then they'd walked the six blocks to the Kennedy Center.

Her husband gave a noncommittal response into his pillow and rolled away from her.

Mrs. Stevens listened for more sounds, but there were none and she laid back down to sleep. The postman or whoever it was could come back. Her head hurt too much to worry about it.

Downstairs, the lights on the answering machine blinked silently.

Everyone knew Sheriff Jes Brown was an opportunist. And while he was certainly well known around Liberty, few people seemed to like— or respect—him.

Most of the time, Jes Brown carried himself with an almost regal air, as if he were lord and master of this small town. He treated the citizens of Liberty like his subjects, and his considerable size was matched only by his outsized opinion of himself. As a sheriff, he was far more concerned with politics and befriending wealthy citizens than with tracking down criminals or keeping the peace.

His connection to the Story helped, as his fame preceded him. And sometimes Brown just went ahead and took all the credit, blaming Beaumont for messing up the collar and getting himself killed.

Over the years, there had been a few attempts to vote him out of office. The more disgruntled citizens, unimpressed by his less-than-stellar performance record, would rally behind another candidate. But Sheriff Brown knew exactly which people in town to keep close. He looked out for them and their interests, and when election time came around, they looked out for his.

Several years back, a councilman's teenage son had been picked up on a marijuana possession charge by one of Brown's deputies. A possession charge could bring up to six years in jail, along with the added bonus of destroying the councilman's career. The councilman had begged and pleaded with the sheriff to overlook the "childhood prank," and the Sheriff had only smiled, making the torture last as long as he could before offering a deal to keep the kid out of jail. Brown was adept at working out these sorts of "deals," and the drug charges went away. The Simons kid did a three-day stint in the sheriff's little backroom cell instead of a long stretch in the Prince William County Juvenile Detention Center up in Dumfries. The next year, to the surprise of exactly zero people in town, the councilman openly supported Brown's reelection campaign.

The rest of the town, the people with no power, were not as pleased with Brown's tenure. Crime was up in every part of town, and Liberty had become a new staging area for drugs finding their way up I-95 to D.C. and points north. The town itself had taken on an air of foreboding, as if this lackluster sheriff and his self-serving policies would someday doom Liberty. "Grin and bear it" was all the citizens could do—the only way Brown would leave the sheriff's office would be through promotion to the state police position. Or maybe he'd get killed on the job.

Bethany pulled into the expansive parking lot in front of the station and went inside. The sheriff's office was a beautiful building, smoked green glass and shiny black metal, a blemish of modern architecture among the quaint, historic stone buildings of Liberty's downtown.

The building was only a couple of years old, built to replace the old stone sheriff's office that Jes Brown hadn't liked. He'd convinced the city council of the need for a new, modern-looking building. The objections of several brave citizens fell on deaf ears. The city council, the same people that paid Sheriff Brown's salary, voted 6-1 to approve the new, garish building. Coincidentally, the one councilperson who'd voted "no" was forced from office several months later, disgraced after a lengthy and rancorous—and completely illegal—criminal investigation into her personal life. Nothing came from the investigation, but enough dirt surfaced about her personal life to destroy her career in city politics. Sheriff Brown had paid her back.

Bethany walked into the lobby, an expansive room with glass and metal stripes reflecting off of the wide, tiled floor that led up to the desk of the main reception. The place looked more museum than sheriff's office.

A large deputy stood behind the counter and glanced up when she came in. There were chairs and couches scattered around the reception area, and on a table in the center was a plastic machine that dispensed numbers. Bethany took the next little tab of paper—"36"—and sat. The display above the reception desk read "31," so Bethany decided to write down what had happened to give as a statement.

Beyond the reception desk, the rest of the squad room was filled with desks manned by a few other deputies. It was the cleanest sheriff's office she'd ever seen—it looked nothing like the squad rooms she'd seen in movies or on *NYPD Blue*. A casual observer would think that no crime at all had ever occurred in this town.

On the back wall were pictures of Sheriff Jes Brown with all the important people in town. Two doors led off from the main squad room, one leading to Sheriff Brown's office, the other leading back to the short-term incarceration cells and a deputy's locker room.

Bethany had plenty of time to finish writing everything down before the deputy called her number.

"I've got thirty-six," she said when called, handing the little number to the deputy who waved her into a chair.

"Okay, what can I help you with?" he asked, a completely uninterested look on his face.

"My friend is missing."

His expression remained the same. "How long?"

"Well, she called me last night, because she was supposed to come over, but she never..." Bethany stopped when the deputy put his hand up. He pulled up a clipboard, attached a form to it, and handed it to her along with a pen. "Fill this out and bring it back up to me."

She was momentarily speechless, and then she found her tongue.

"I've been waiting for twenty minutes. I'm worried about my missing friend, and you want me to fill out a form?"

Bethany struggled to keep her voice under control.

The deputy smiled as if he was enjoying himself for what might've been the first time all day. "Then a few more minutes won't really matter." He called "thirty-seven."

Bethany walked back over to her seat, feeling numb. She was trying to report a missing person. Why was he being so rude? She copied her responses onto the form as fast as she could and took the clipboard back up, standing behind the person seated at the man's desk, waiting. After a few moments of conversation, he looked up, taking the clipboard from her. "Have a seat, and I'll be with you in a moment."

"No," she said, her arms crossed.

The deputy, his attention already drifting back to number thirty-seven, looked back at Bethany, suddenly interested. "What?"

"No, I'm not sitting back down. My friend is missing, and I want you to do something about it."

The deputy smiled patronizingly.

"Well, little girl, you're not the only person with problems in this town. I'll speak to you in a few minutes," he said, his voice slowly climbing in volume until he finished in a commanding tone. Evidently, he was used to people doing what they were told.

Bethany shook her head, the sudden fire in her belly.

"I don't CARE if other people have problems," she shouted. "My friend could be out there right now, dead or dying by the side of the road. YOU ARE GOING TO LISTEN TO ME!"

Her heart pounded in her chest. She knew she shouldn't be yelling, but at this point she didn't really care. She just wanted someone to listen to her. If shouting at this stupid man was what it took, then that was what she would do.

In the chair next to the deputy's desk, an older gentleman, number thirty-seven, turned around and looked up at her. Other deputies looked around, unused to hearing shouting. In the back of the office, a door came open, and Sheriff Jes Brown popped his pudgy face out, looking like he'd just awakened.

The room was quiet for a moment, and then the deputy stood up and took her by the arm, leading her over to the water cooler. He sat her down in a chair.

"There's no need to shout. I'll look at your form, and then I'll come talk to you. Don't move from this seat."

She nodded, steaming, fighting back tears. Bethany watched the office return to normal. A few minutes later, the deputy finished with thirty-seven and looked at Bethany's clipboard, reviewing the form she'd filled out. He made a couple of phone calls, glancing over at Bethany, and then finally stood and walked over.

"Okay, I've reviewed your report. We'll call it out to our deputies and have them do a sweep of the town," the deputy said. "If that doesn't turn her up, we'll put out an APB on..." his eyes dropped, referring back to the clipboard. "er...Lisa Stevens. I called her parent's house and got the machine, so there's a squad car on the way over there now to speak to them. I also spoke to her place of employment. You're a coworker as well as her friend?"

Bethany nodded. She felt sick to her stomach.

"I also went to the Food Town last night," she said. "Two people saw her, but nobody remembered her leaving. And her parents were supposed to go to a show last night in D.C., but maybe they stayed over."

"Okay, we'll take it from here. You get some rest. And you can be reached at the number on the form?" He read back her parent's number.

She nodded. "Call me if you find anything. Please."

He nodded but didn't say anything else, then handed the clipboard to another deputy on the way back to his desk. She felt the tears coming and stood, hurrying out. As she passed the deputy's desk, he started to say something, and she paused. But he looked at the lobby and said "Thirty-eight."

Bethany walked through the doors. The air was cool outside, calming her stomach. First David left, and now Lisa was missing. And she felt lost, confused, unsure of what to do next.

There was no one she could call for help.

———

Jack awoke and sat up, stretching to work the kinks out of his back and shoulders. He always got a crick in his neck when he slept on the hard, vinyl-covered floor of his van.

As he sat up her arm fell off him.

He looked down at her on the floor of his van. She had made so much noise, but now she was quiet. She looked beautiful in the morning sun.

He opened the doors and climbed down, stretching. A light wind moved through the trees, stirring the leaves in the clearing where he'd parked. Jack could smell the woody, heady scent of the campfire he'd built. In the forest around him, dozens of birds chirped and squawked at the sunrise.

Jack smiled, remembering her screams.

He'd Tasered her, tied her to the tree. She had struggled, of course, but in the long and glorious hours before she expired, she had succumbed to his power. She had begged and pleaded and cried, all music to his ears. He'd been completely in control of her, especially at the end, when his hands had closed around her neck.

He looked down at her lying naked in the dappled sunlight. She was perfect, 198 now, nothing but a number. Her eyes seemed to take in the clearing and the fallen leaves and the trees beyond, black with scores of cawing, screeching birds. But the dead eyes saw nothing.

Jack smiled and leaned over and kissed her cold blue lips.

Driving away from the clearing, Jack took a detour through the large mall nearby. He'd passed it on the way into town and, as he drove the parking lot, realized it had been built where he'd spent one drenched and exhilarating evening chased through the woods by Sheriff Beaumont's incompetent deputies. Jack had traveled these stretches of concrete when they were open fields. He'd crossed the bridge beyond, then made his way through the rainy woods to the highway, emerging to gun the good sheriff down.

An hour later, Jack pulled up in front of the Motel 6 on Highway 132 and checked himself into a room. He grabbed his keys and the KFC he'd bought and headed up, eating before taking a shower and crashing for a nap. It wasn't even 1:00 p.m. yet, but he still had a lot of work to do. A rest would do him good. He'd taken 198 back to her little red car. She'd be found soon, and when she was, things should begin to happen very quickly in Liberty, Virginia.

Or maybe they wouldn't. His experience with cops was far ranging—sometimes, it took several kills before they caught on. Or, maybe as it had been the last time he'd been in this town, they would know something was wrong immediately.

Perhaps they would recognize his calling card for what it was—a ghost from the past.

As he ate, he pulled the Liberty phone book from the desk drawer. Jack flipped to the B's first, of course. Baner, Barabo, Bawers.

No Beaumont.

It was a long shot, but a man could hope. Jack assumed the old man was dead—he'd looked dead on the road that night—but there was always a chance he or his kin were still around. Jack was prepared to do a little detective work. It would be great to kill off Beaumont's family members—if there were any left—but maybe he'd managed to end the Beaumonts already.

Jack finished his meal and climbed into the shower, his first in almost two weeks. The hot water felt good against his skin, and Jack relished it. Big things were coming. He wanted to visit some of the old places from last time, but now that might have to wait. What to do first?

He'd planned on coming to town and observing a few days before making a kill. But, as it sometimes did, the urge had come over him.

Stepping from the shower and toweling himself off, he pondered what he would wear. It had been years since he had cause to consider his appearance. Most of his wardrobe, if one could use that term so loosely, consisted of several pairs of faded blue jeans and a collection of T-shirts, each festooned with different sayings and symbols. A few carried reminders of his travels or were souvenirs from his victims. Among the cleanest of his clothes was an FSU sweatshirt—"Go Seminoles!"—that had once belonged to Sally, the girl he'd killed down in Florida.

The cabinet behind the driver's seat in his van held three dressier shirts, unworn for many years, along with a jacket and a thick winter parka with a brownish stain on one of the arms. The parka had belonged to one of his victims from Seattle.

Above the cabinet was a large shoebox that contained his jewelry collection, consisting several dozen watches, a wad of gold jewelry, rings and bracelets and earrings, and a half-dozen faded police shields and stars. His victims, all remembered by their gold and silver. It was dangerous to keep these trinkets, but he enjoyed wearing trophies he could show off in public.

Few people ever saw his real trophies. People who saw his collection inevitably became part of it.

Getting dressed, Jack planned the rest of his day. He decided to start at the public library. He had research to do. He wanted to read everything he could in the town papers on what happened here eighteen years ago. How they had reacted to it, what Beaumont had done at the time. It would give Jack insight, certainly, but also allow him to relive those heady days. He wanted to read about how the town had reacted to his violence—it might give him insight into how they would react today.

And Jack wanted to know everything about Beaumont. Dates, times, locations, family members. Jack wanted to meet Beaumont's family, if he had any left, find them and find out what they knew, and then Jack would tell them what happened that night on the wet pavement. And after everyone close to Sheriff Beaumont was in the ground, Jack would be able to forget all about this stupid place.

Lunch was McDonald's again, a bag of cheeseburgers and fries and the super-sized Coke propped between his legs. David liked fast food just as much as the next person, but he had a sneaking suspicion that he would soon tire of the fare. A week or two of nothing but cheeseburgers and Cokes could ruin any craving.

Picking at the bag of fries, David found the on-ramp to I-64 westbound, taking him out of Charleston, West Virginia. Then he'd turn northwest in the direction of Dayton, Ohio, to catch I-70. He hoped to make it to Indiana tonight, if possible, but Richmond, a good-sized town on the border between Ohio and Indiana, would be far enough for his second day on the road. He had no idea it was so exhausting, sitting in a car all day and driving. Why was sitting and steering so tiring? It didn't make any sense.

Rush was keeping him company again today: *Hold Your Fire*, with great songs like "Turn the Page." It was an outstanding CD, one of their best. "Force Ten" was on here, a song about an approaching storm. The constant radio reports about Hurricane Mandy had reminded him just how much he enjoyed this half-forgotten song.

Music was strange. The circumstances in which you listen to a CD or tape might change, but the songs stayed the same. If he'd told himself six months ago that the next time he'd listen to this CD, he'd be in another state, David wouldn't have believed it.

"Can I help you?"

The voice, old and female and sounding eminently helpful, came from behind him. Jack instinctively began sizing her up, pondering ways to kill her, even as he turned around. As he'd guessed, she was an elderly woman, her ancient glasses dangling from around her neck from an ornate chain. She smelled old, like the pages of the books around her.

"I think I've got it." He was dressed nicely and seated at the library's only microfiche reader, going through the town's newspaper files from April of 1978. "I think I've finally gotten the hang of this machine."

She smiled at him and then leaned closer, squinting to read the title of the article currently displayed on Jack's screen. "Robert Nolan Found Murdered," the headline shouted in bold typeface.

"Oh, my goodness," she said quietly. "I remember when that dreadful thing happened," she said, one of her hands drifted aimlessly up to her throat, circling it in a gesture that Jack supposed was meant to be comforting. But it looked like she was strangling herself. After a moment of thought, she looked at him sharply. "Why are you looking at that, if you don't mind me asking?"

"I'm writing a book on serial killers. I think this boy might've been part of a string of killings on the eastern seaboard," he said, remembering not to smile. "Wasn't there another killing just a few days before?"

As soon as he said he was researching a book, the woman relaxed.

"Yes, that's right," she said, pulling over a chair. "A book, you say? There was another killing just two days before, a dreadful thing. Actually, two other murders."

"Two others?" Another person, dead? Jack had kept a clear count in his mind all these years, but he'd never known for sure how many deputies he'd managed to off that rainy night.

She nodded. "One of the little boys who helped out around here disappeared a few days before Councilman Nolan. Deputies found the boy the day before Roger disappeared. Horrible thing, those killings were. Drove this town to the brink of craziness."

Jack leaned forward, suppressing his glee.

"Thank God for Sheriff Beaumont," she said. "He was a very clever man, best sheriff we ever had."

Jack looked away, trying not to scowl at the mention of his name. Instead, he reached into his jacket and took out a notepad he'd brought. "Mind if I take notes?"

She shook her head. "No, that would be fine. As I said, Beaumont figured out the Killer was an outsider. He had search parties and fliers and instituted a curfew."

Jack took notes, relaxing into the tale that washed over him. Apparently, that final night on the highway—and Jack's showdown with Beaumont—had taken on the aura of legend. It was so strange to hear the tale told anew from a different perspective.

Jack had forgotten about the flyers. As she brought up articles on the microfiche reader and explained what took place, one of the flyers appeared, showing a much younger version of Jack. It was a surprise, seeing himself on the screen. He tensed, thinking he might be recognized, but the woman didn't even notice. She was just too caught up in telling her story.

The woman continued, using her long, aged finger to work the machine, punctuating her words with pictures. It was like having a walking, talking index of the history of Liberty and her people. It was much as he remembered it, although from the town's perspective, Beaumont saved them all by sacrificing himself like some religious martyr.

Some of the details he didn't know. The deputy in charge of the lines of dogs and deputies who'd driven him to the roadblock was now the sheriff. The woman deputy played a role in the story as well, surprising him. Jack had left her for dead on the road, but she was the last one to see Beaumont alive. She left the force soon after and now drives a school bus. Jack smiled—he would need to pay her a visit.

He was sure she would recognize him.

As the old lady went on, Jack got angrier. This town idolized Beaumont. If the sheriff had been all that clever, he wouldn't be dead! He had tuned out when she'd started talking about Beaumont's education—he didn't care.

"That's the same college that his son attended," the woman added casually.

Jack's head swam for a moment as he tuned back in to the conversation.

"Beaumont...had a son?" he asked cautiously, almost unwilling to believe the possibility.

"Oh, yes," she answered without hesitation. "Grace, Beaumont's wife, was pregnant when he died. She gave birth several months later, a little boy. Sadly, she died in childbirth. The boy was raised by her sister Gloria."

It suddenly felt very warm in the library. A son? Another Beaumont? He did the math, ignoring the woman. Beaumont died in '78, so the kid was seventeen? Eighteen?

Jack looked back at the old woman.

"Wow, I'll bet he'd be interesting to talk to," he said to the librarian, smiling. "I'd love to ask him what he thinks about his father, how growing up without parents affected him. It would be great for the book. Any chance I could get his address, maybe call on him?"

It was almost too much to ask for. Should he kill the kid right away, or make it more of a game? The possibilities...

She shook her head.

"He would be interesting to talk to, even though he never talked to or met his father. But I heard he was leaving. Moving to California."

Jack sat back. California? Where Jack was headed? What an odd coincidence. If he couldn't find him here, could he find him out there once Jack retired? California was a huge state...

"Are you listening?"

Jack looked up at the woman, confused. She was still talking, and he'd stopped paying attention again.

"I'm sorry," he said. "My mind wandered. Please continue."

She looked miffed. "You know, for a researcher, you're not a very good listener," she scowled. "If you want to learn more about young Mr.

Beaumont, you might want to pay better attention," she said, scolding him like an errant child.

Conflicting emotions raced through him. He'd killed a person just last night. Looking at this old woman in front of him, he knew he could simply reach up and snap her neck. The urge grew within him to

do it do it right here in the library

but he needed the information in her head.

"You're right, and I'm sorry. I was just thinking about such a missed opportunity. I want the book to be perfect, especially if it gets optioned for a film."

She sat back with a smile. "Wouldn't that be something? I was saying that he was leaving town, but I didn't know exactly when. He just turned eighteen, and he was heading out to California. You should visit his apartment, see if he's still there. I have the address. And I can put you in contact with Gloria Thatcher, Grace Beaumont's sister. Do you want the information?"

"Oh, yes, thank you." Jack said. He had questions for them, questions about Beaumont and the boy. So many questions.

"I'll be right back," she said, excusing herself.

He turned back to the microfiche machine and printed a stack of pages of information—Beaumont's obituary, the history of his career leading up to becoming sheriff, information about the new mall, and a detailed timeline about the history of Liberty, Virginia. While he worked, Jack watched the old lady converse with a pair of young and attractive female employees behind the circulation counter.

more to take more to enjoy

He ignored the voice. He had more important things to do right now. What if Jack could track the Beaumont boy down, and the sister, and add them to his collection? What if he ended Beaumont's family completely, wiping them off the face of the planet? That was true power, ending a bloodline.

As Jack was stacking up the printouts, the librarian returned and sat down. She had her glasses on, looking down at a sheet of paper before handing it over.

"Tina over there knows David's girlfriend," the old woman said. "Tina said David Beaumont left for Los Angeles yesterday, but she thinks he'll be back. Evidently most people think he's not serious about moving away. She gave me the address of where David had been living—he had a roommate, Bernie something," nodding at the sheet. "And Gloria lives across town. It's all on there."

"Interesting," Jack said, looking at the sheet with two addresses. "I would love a chance to talk to the Beaumont boy."

She nodded. "Such a pity you didn't get here a week sooner," she said. "So, tell me more about yourself? Why are you writing a book about serial killers?"

The woman was curious about Jack, never a good thing. He talked with her for a few more minutes, giving her a fake name and spinning a yarn about being down from D.C. to write a book proposal. He kept it short and finally managed to extricate himself from the conversation, thanking her for the information.

As he walked to the door, he didn't even look at the two young women behind the counter. He didn't need the temptation right now.

Jack needed to focus.

Outside, he could think. The weather was breezy and cool after the warm library. He walked and sat on a bench outside to collect his thoughts. It took him a second to realize that this was the very bench where the little boy, Roger Myers, had been sitting the last time Jack had been in Liberty. The little boy had been his first victim—he'd been sitting here when Jack first approached him and struck up a conversation. It had taken little effort to lure the kid away to a quieter location to make the kill—

focus

The Beaumont kid was gone, heading to California. Jack could either convince him to come back to Liberty or catch up with him once he got back out there. Either way, Jack was on his trail.

He looked around at the streets and buildings around the library and smiled. People were walking, chatting, riding bikes. It was a nice little town, completely unprepared for Jack's brand of mayhem.

It was good to be back.

Meteorologists and weather forecasters across the country scrambled, trying to stay one step ahead of Hurricane Mandy. Passing over Florida hadn't weakened it, and now she was back up to a Category 3.

At the National Hurricane Center in Coral Gables, forecasts and satellite pictures were being shared with news stations up and down the entire East Coast. The fact that the storm was moving so slowly made damage and storm intensity projections even more difficult. At any moment, the storm might just fizzle or turn out to sea. It was useless to announce any local advisories, because no one could pinpoint where Mandy was going, so a rare General Weather Alert was issued to all National Weather Service locations on the Eastern Seaboard for the next several days.

The high-pressure air mass that had been parked over the eastern United States for several days, affording the eastern states unseasonably warm temperatures, had shattered with the approach of Mandy. Where the outer bands of Mandy's rain and wind interacted with the other high- and low-pressure areas, severe storms battered towns and whole states. Flood watches and warnings were up all across Georgia and the Carolinas as Mandy churned toward shore. Across the country, meteorologists and weather forecasters crossed their fingers and studied their data, looking for any way to predict where the hurricane would go, hoping to warn people about it.

Or at least get them out of the way.

Hours later, Jack double-checked the address and slowed as he reached the house. 2716 Monroe Street, one in a long row of identical homes, this one shabbier than the rest.

Jack had had a busy afternoon. After his instructional visit to the library, he'd driven the streets of Liberty, searching, remembering.

The first address had taken him to a run-down part of town, where he'd visited the last place David Beaumont had called home. The roommate, Bernie, had let Jack in with a smile. The apartment had stunk of beer and marijuana, but the young man had told Jack everything he could remember about the Beaumont boy. It had taken some help from Jack to make the young man focus. Once the kid had found himself bound and gagged, he became very cooperative. And after Jack had killed him, Jack sat in the young man's living room and finished the boy's cold beer.

Turned out the librarian had been right—the Beaumont kid had left on Sunday morning. Bernie, the roommate, managed to find the address for where Beaumont was headed in California, and Jack had pocketed the letter—some friend of David's had invited him out to stay with him. Okay, that's fine, Jack thought. I'll look him up when I get out there.

Before leaving, Jack hung the young man from a pole in one closet, staging it to look like a suicide by hanging. Another twist for the cops to figure out.

Pulling up in front of Gloria Thatcher's home, Jack parked the van across the street and switched his headlights off. There were no curtains in any of the windows, giving him a clear view into the front of the house. Jack could see stacks of brown cardboard boxes piled around a scant grouping of furniture. It looked like she was moving as well.

A woman in her 50's strolled across one of the open windows. Jack instinctively scrunched down in his seat. The woman walked between the boxes, swinging a liquor bottle in one hand and a glass tumbler in the other. She was having an animated conversation with someone, but Jack couldn't see who. Maybe she was arguing with herself. She swayed and bumped into a short stack of boxes, upsetting them, and the top box tipped over and fell. She turned and stared at where the box had fallen, then raised the glass and toasted to the fallen box.

She was trashed. That would make Jack's job easier. Jack needed to talk to her, get more information, and then his plan was to either kill the old woman or kidnap her. Jack figured either would be enough to draw the Beaumont boy back to Liberty. The boy would come running, and then Jack and he would have a little game. A clever little game.

A pair of headlights splashed around the corner and came up the street toward the house, slowing and turning into the driveway. A tall, gray-haired man climbed out of his shiny Mercedes, stopping to wipe something off the hood before walking up the driveway to the front door and knocking. The woman pulled the door open, still gripping the glass and curling one arm around the bottle as if it were her good-luck charm. She said something to the man and staggered back inside, and he followed, closing the door behind him.

Jack watched, pulling on a pair of thin rubber gloves while he waited. Finally, the lights in the house went off and the front door opened again. The woman came out first, this time without her trusty bottle but wearing a thin coat against the chill. She managed to bang her shin good against the bumper of the man's car before making it around to the passenger door. The man followed, climbing in and starting up the car.

Jack expected them to drive away, but the overhead light came on and the woman opened her door. She leaned over and her shoulders heaved. Sitting back up, she wiped at her mouth and pulled the door closed. The man backed out of the driveway and headed east, disappearing around a corner.

Jack decided to let her go. He knew where she lived, and following her in public wouldn't do any good. He'd have more luck waiting and getting her when she got home. He and Gloria needed to have a long and productive discussion.

Quietly, Jack climbed out of the van and started for the darkened house.

"Getting an early start?" Abe asked as they drove away from her home. Gloria was smashed. Thank God she hadn't vomited in his new car—he'd only picked it up from the dealership yesterday.

She looked at him, her eyes bleary.

"I started yesserday, thank you very much," she said sharply. "With David gone...and the moving to a new place and all...I just got a little down. I needed a pick-me-up, I guess," she said.

"You need to be concentrating on getting moved," Abe said, watching the road. "I thought that was why we're going out tonight—to sign the townhouse papers. And to celebrate."

"I am celebrating."

Abe shook his head. Abe had trouble seeing how someone could give control of their life over to something like alcohol, but he saw it all the time. Booze, drugs, women, it was all the same. And ignoring your problems didn't solve them; it only put them off for a little while.

"Abe, I forgot my purse."

He looked over at her, glancing at her floorboard.

"You're kidding, right?"

It took a few seconds to register, as if the message had to wade through the mire of alcohol to get to the cognizant parts of her brain, and then she shook her head.

"No purse. I'm locked out."

"I have keys, remember?"

"I know. But I need my purse. Sorry."

Abe sighed as he turned the car around, heading back.

Jack only needed a minute to find a window that was not securely locked. It always amazed Jack how careless people could be. And carelessness got people killed.

Sliding one of the blades of his pocketknife between the window glass and the locking mechanism, he pushed the lock to the side and opened the window. Glancing around, Jack boosted himself inside.

It was too dark for Jack to see the large flock of dark birds sitting quietly on the tall wooden slats and gates of the back fence. The gathered throng silently watched Jack with many pairs of tiny black eyes. One large black bird watched Jack slip into the house before turning and leaping into the air, flying off on some unknown mission, disappearing into the night.

Nothing could have prepared him for the smell.

The interior of the house stank of the passage of years, of tattered wallpaper and threadbare carpets and faded paint on the walls. The musty, dusty smell penetrated everything.

Jack wandered the house, ignoring the smell. He had come in through a window in a back room and made his way into the kitchen. A stack of moving boxes stood in the middle of the floor, and Jack glanced through them—a set of old dishes, the pattern faded and the edges chipped. Other boxes held pantry items and kitchen utensils.

He moved on into the dining room and foyer, each with their own collection of boxes, some sealed tight, others still hanging open, the box flaps waiting for tape.

Passing into the living room, he saw a staircase leading up to a second floor. The living room held the stacks of boxes he'd seen from outside, including the box the woman had knocked over, along with a ratty couch and a dusty glass coffee table. A large fireplace took up one wall.

Above the fireplace was a mantle, and on it sat a small collection of things that had not yet been boxed. One was a picture of Sheriff Beaumont, his arm around a pregnant woman. Standing next to them was a much younger version of the stumbling, drunk woman who lived here.

beaumont

Jack felt a surge of excitement pass through his body as he looked at the old, fading photograph. Why did the dead man matter so much to him? The two women in the picture were obviously related. The sisters and Beaumont stood under a large tree.

Another frame held a photo of Beaumont and his wife. He was smiling and wearing what looked like a lifeguard ring, labeled "Sun Viking," around his neck. Beaumont had a fruity drink in one hand and his other around his wife's waist. Behind them stood a white railing and the open sea.

Jack turned the picture over and slid it out of its ornate gold frame.

Grace and Billy, Honeymoon, October 1975

Married in the winter of '75. The kid was born in September of 1978.

Jack pocketed the picture and moved around the knee-high glass coffee table and the couch it sat in front of, eyeing the box that the drunken woman had knocked over. It lay on its side on the carpeted floor, unopened. On the side of the box, written in a slanted, backward style with a large magic marker, were five words.

FILES OF WILLIAM BEAUMONT, SHERIFF

Jack's heart leapt into his throat. Beaumont's files and personal papers? Jack could taste the anticipation in his suddenly dry mouth. He was moving toward the box when a light splashed suddenly into the room. Headlights, a car pulling into the driveway. Had he been spotted? Glancing around, Jack headed for the stairs.

———————

"Did you see that?" Abe asked. As they were pulling into the driveway, Abe thought he saw movement inside the house.

"See what?" she asked, befuddled. She looked like she was going to puke again.

Abe glanced back up at the house, now well-lit by his headlights, but he saw nothing. He relaxed.

"Nothing, I guess."

They climbed from the car and he let her in with his set of keys. Abe had always kept an eye on her—she'd locked herself out more times than he could count.

Gloria scooted off to the hall restroom, evidently her first priority. Abe hoped it was just her bladder. He had a real problem with listening to people throw up—just the sound of it made him sick.

There was no sign of her purse, either in the foyer or in the kitchen. Abe walked through the house, searching. Nothing. He shook his head and called to Gloria but got no response. Maybe she had the fan running or something. Abe walked into the living room and up the stairs to find her purse.

———————

Jack hid like a scared rabbit, momentarily surprised. He'd planned on talking to the woman when she returned home. Jack hadn't expected her home so soon, and now she had company.

The urge came upon him. Circumstances and luck overpowered his plans. Here were more victims, served up to him. The man was expendable, and then Jack would have all night to spend with the woman. She'd answer all of his questions, and then he could decide what to do with her.

Jack got up from behind the bed and grabbed something from a tall dresser. He walked into the small bathroom and stood behind the door, waiting.

———————

At the top of the stairs, Abe glanced down the short hallway on his right toward the spare bedrooms, still a little spooked by his imagination.

No sounds came from anywhere in the house, and Abe relaxed. He walked left, down the balcony area that looked out over the living room, turning into Gloria's room and flipping on the lights. Her room was a mess, stacks and piles of things waiting to be packed, along with a few empty bottles of vodka thrown in for good measure. Her bathroom, off to the right, was a mess as well.

Abe shook his head and found her purse on a tall dresser near the door. He picked it up and checked the contents: keys, wallet, money.

He turned to head out of the room and stopped.

There was a man standing in the bathroom doorway.

The man was smiling at Abe. His eyes were beady, horrible. The man looked like a wild animal, as if the body he wore could barely contain all that was inside it.

A low, quiet sound escaped Abe's throat. He couldn't move as the man with the piercing eyes stepped closer. Abe suddenly questioned his superiority. He'd spent decades thinking he was better than most people, and now he couldn't even get his legs to move...

"Sorry, man," the man said. "Wrong place, wrong time."

The voice was low and powerful, and Abe realized that he had seen someone in the house. This realization didn't break the spell that the man's eyes held Abe in, and when the man stepped toward him, something moving in the man's hand, Abe didn't even move.

Jack smashed the heavy glass jar against the side of the man's head, catching the man's jacket before he could tumble loudly to the ground. Keeping him standing, Jack glanced down the stairs but heard no one coming to investigate.

The woman must be really trashed.

Blood welled from a dozen lacerations on the man's head as Jack walked him out of the bedroom and over to the balcony that overlooked the living room. Jack leaned him against the railing and took the purse out of the man's hands, then bent and grabbed the legs, lifting them over the balcony.

The man fell like a rag doll, hitting the glass coffee table ten feet below face first, shattering it. Large fragments of glass flew in every direction, littering the boxes and the couch and the old, threadbare carpet with long slivers of glass.

Gloria came out of the hall bathroom a few minutes later, leaving the fan on to clear out the smell. She'd thrown up again, and now she was looking for a bottle or glass to wash down the horrible taste in her mouth. This was all David's fault. If he hadn't abandoned her, she would have been fine. She'd be staying in this house, happy, instead of moving to a new place.

She walked unsteadily into the kitchen, finding an open bottle of vodka and taking a long pull on it. The door from the kitchen out to the garage was standing open, and it took her a moment to notice the cool draft. Had she left that open, or had Abe gone out there? He was probably looking for her purse.

Walking around the kitchen table, she glanced out into the garage but saw nothing except for her car. The overhead light was on. She reached around the doorjamb to flick it off, and closed the door, moving off toward the rest of the house.

Walking into the living room, she found Abe. He was lying in a pool of scarlet, blood slowly seeping from a hundred jagged wounds. It took her foggy mind a moment to realize what was going on. She stared at the pieces of glass all around the room, and she heard them crunch under her feet.

"Abe? Abe?"

What had happened? Was he bleeding? She looked slowly up at the balcony, then back down at Abe. His eyes were open, staring up at the fireplace mantel. Was he dead? Had he fallen? How could he be dead? He'd been fine only a few minutes before. Abe couldn't be—

"Gloria?"

She started and turned to find the source of the voice.

A strange man sat on the stairs that led up to her bedroom. A rugged, angry looking man, with intense eyes that seemed to be studying her, memorizing her.

"Who...who are you?"

Even through the fog of alcohol and shock, she could see the man smiling. And he had her purse in his lap, cradling it in his gloved hands.

"Hi, Gloria," the man said. "We need to talk. We haven't met, but I knew Sheriff Beaumont. A long time ago." His eyes never left hers. "Your friend here, he happened to be in the wrong place at the wrong time." The man pointed at Abe behind her. "He was number 200. Unless you want to be 201, tell me about David and Sheriff Beaumont. Slowly. Tell me everything."

It made no sense to her foggy mind. No sense at all.

Jack stood slowly, setting her purse to one side. He needed to scare her into telling him what he needed to know. And to do that, she needed to see that he was completely in control. He glanced at Abe's corpse and then back at her. She shivered a little, her arms crossed tightly. He knew he had her attention.

Jack moved to her, sitting her down in one of the ratty chairs. He stood over her and asked his questions, lying and telling her he might spare her life.

She told him everything.

He learned about the sheriff and everything that happened that rainy night and the months after, leading up to David's birth. Jack learned everything there was to know about David—his hopes, his fears. His dreams. When she had nothing left to offer, Jack took what he wanted from her mind and her body. And while she was busy dying, he relaxed on the couch in the living room and read through the box of files marked SHERIFF BEAUMONT. He studied the yellowed papers, learning things he'd never known, reading Beaumont's thoughts as written in his own handwriting.

Beaumont had been very clever.

Jack realized now, more than ever, that it had only been for a string of luck that Jack had gotten away. The information in these files was much more detailed than the story the old woman had told him this morning, but it didn't make him feel any better.

Jack also realized for the first time that Beaumont had actually won. The man had chased Jack out of town. Jack had been lucky to escape

lucky lucky just like i told you

and each page of notes only made it more clear. Beaumont had done everything right.

Jack thumbed through the files, occasionally smudging the pages with fresh blood. Jack was so intent on reading, he failed to notice his gloves were dappled with blood from the dead man at his feet. The room was sprinkled with tiny droplets of blood. One particularly large blob ran slowly down the side of a cardboard box, unseen.

One thick file covered "Jasper Fines," the fake name Jack had given so many years ago. The folder contained details Jack had forgotten he'd given. Taking a clue from the professional law enforcement officers at the state and federal level, Beaumont had sent a copy of the file to the FBI and requested a personality sketch be drawn up by the experts, something rarely done back in those days.

Some of the personality profile's suppositions sounded frighteningly familiar to Jack, too accurate for his taste. There were explanations of the killer's motivations, approximate descriptions of his physical and mental attributes, and an estimation of the killer's plans and future actions. They were all too close to the truth.

It also said Jack was a loner, probably cold and calculating, and had likely lost his mother at a young age.

Jack Terrington sat, reading the files with deep interest while he waited for Gloria to die. He'd decided to kill her—after their long talk, he didn't think she would be useful as bait. Her connection with David wasn't as strong as Jack had hoped. A convoluted kidnapping wouldn't serve any purpose. But her death would. And four deaths in two days in this little town? People would notice that. Someone would tell David Beaumont, and he'd race back to Liberty, Virginia.

And Jack would be waiting.

On Monday evening, the search for Lisa Stevens began in earnest.

Almost twelve hours had passed since she was originally reported missing, but the wheels in the sheriff's office were creaky and lacking in oil. The deputies sent to the Stevens' house had spoken to the parents, confirming that the girl had not come home last night. Her parents hadn't seen Lisa, and her car was missing. After that initial interaction with the sheriff's office, Lisa's mother had called in every hour or so since, frantic for updates. She'd been in tears, trying to explain to the deputy how sorry she was that she hadn't checked on her daughter or listened to the messages.

After hearing from the deputy that had interviewed the parents, Sheriff Jes Brown spent a few minutes discussing the situation with his deputies and then radioed out for a high-point search of the town. A missing person's report, usually filed after twenty-four hours, called for something known as a 'high-point' search, a quick investigation that involves contacting the missing person's family and friends and visiting work or school locations.

Lisa's description went out over the radio to each of the town's seven mobile units, and a picture of the missing girl was reproduced and shown around town. In 80% of cases where someone is reported missing, the high-point search usually finds them with friends or family. Only after a four- or five-hour phone and location search revealed no sign of the missing person would the investigation move up to the next level—the all-points bulletin, or APB. An APB is issued on a statewide basis, hence the reason that most jurisdictions conduct their own local search in the first twenty-four hours. No local police wanted to look like fools when their "missing" kid turned up at some friend's house playing Nintendo.

After an APB is issued, it is transmitted via fax statewide, and officers in hundreds of cities and towns across the state are shown the faxed pictures during their squad room briefings before they head out to begin their shifts. In this case, Sheriff Jes Brown wanted to keep the investigation under his control for as long as possible, so he delayed the state-wide APB and ordered volunteer searches be conducted around Liberty.

By 9:00 p.m. Monday night, no new information had come in to the sheriff's office, and no additional sightings were reported beyond what was already known about the girl's last confirmed location at the grocery store on Sunday night. Deputies at the sheriff's office began calling around to gather the groups of volunteers that usually assisted the department in their searches. Off-duty officers were also called in to assist and man the phones.

In less than thirty minutes, volunteers began gathering in the lobby of the station. Pictures and descriptions of Lisa Stevens were handed to them as they arrived, shaking the rain from their coats in the glass and steel lobby. A few of them knew the girl, and they nervously awaited their search assignments.

One of the last volunteers to arrive was the search coordinator. After hearing an assessment of the situation from the sheriff, he stepped over to a large map of the town on the wall in the lobby and began assigning volunteers to search areas. Some would be searching the local teen hangouts like bowling alleys and movie theaters and Liberty Place Mall, showing the girl's picture. Another group of volunteers were sent to search the neighborhood around the girl's home, working on the theory that she might've been out walking and gotten injured. Members of the sheriff's office would also be visiting the local hospital and clinics. Lastly, some of the volunteers were assigned large geographical search areas around town. These were vehicle-based searches for the girl's missing car—the theory was that if they could find the car, they would be a lot closer to finding the girl. Each volunteer or group of volunteers was also assigned a portable police radio to call in reports.

Simon Jeffers was one of these volunteers, and he was handed a map of the eastern side of town, the areas to the east and south of the Liberty Place Mall highlighted in green. Several subdivisions had sprung up in that area since the opening of the mall, and there were many twisty back roads behind the subdivisions and the mall. Simon saw the map he'd been handed was not clear enough to make out all of those little gravel and dirt roads he was expected to search, and he was glad he'd brought his own county map.

This wasn't his first search for a missing person in Liberty. Sheriff Brown relied heavily on his volunteers to help in these types of searches.

Simon Jeffers sold insurance by day and spent a few nights a week working for the town's volunteer fire department. He knew he was in for a long night, and he stopped by McDonald's for a large cup of coffee before heading toward his assigned search location near the mall.

The back roads behind the mall were confusing in their number and in their twisting, turning nature. After an hour of driving around, he realized he was doubling-back on himself. Simon started marking off the areas he'd already searched. He found a green highlighter in the glove compartment and started drawing on the page in his own book of maps.

He took his eyes off the dark, rain-puddled road and, consequently, nearly ran into the back of the little red Tercel as he came around a blind corner. The car had appeared suddenly, dark against the trees by the side of the road. He swerved to avoid it and stopped his truck.

It had to be her car.

Even in the darkness and the rain, he'd seen enough Toyota Tercels to recognize the general body shape. Bright red paint could look like a bloody maroon under thick, overhanging trees. He grabbed the police radio and started to call it in but then changed his mind. There was no need to alert anyone unless it really was her car. It could just be some kids out here making out.

Jeffers set the map aside, picked up the flashlight that he hadn't planned to use, and opened his door into the falling rain.

The first thing he noticed was the sound. The forest around him was alive with noises of insects and small animals, a monotonous chorus that hummed and chirped. He heard birds in the night, cawing and flapping in the dark. Even those sounds were nearly drowned out by the falling rain, slapping the muddy ground and leaves around his feet. The smell of decaying leaves was strong, accentuated by the rain.

He pulled his coat a little tighter around him and moved toward the car, careful to avoid the growing puddles of muddy rainwater.

The car sat with two wheels off the road, and the rain-slicked windows made it impossible to see inside. The car looked to be in good condition, eliminating the possibility of a car wreck or some type of accident. The tires looked fine—no flats, but then he could only see two of them.

Maybe engine trouble, or maybe the girl had just run out of gas and walked to get more. Simon hoped that wasn't the case—from the color pictures he'd seen, Lisa Stevens was a very pretty girl, and he knew that bad things could happen to pretty girls when they were alone in unfamiliar situations. He'd heard about it happening before, too many times.

A flash of lightning whitened the sky and trees above him for one electric moment, and Simon Jeffers saw a figure sitting in the driver's seat. Hurrying, he skirted the puddles. Ignoring the door handle, he swiped the raindrops from the driver's side window and flashed his light inside.

What he saw would forever haunt him.

Lisa Stevens was in the car, that much was certain. She was naked, her eyes were wide open and staring straight ahead. Her right arm was propped up on the steering wheel, fingers only inches away from the glass.

It took only a glance to see that she was dead.

He collected himself and reached up, trying the door handle, and swung the car door open.

A thick cloud of nauseating odor escaped the car, washing over Simon and sending him coughing and hacking to his knees. The smell was so bad—it was like meat left in the bottom of a trashcan for a week at the height of summer. Somehow, the stench from the interior of this tightly closed wheeled coffin was even worse.

Simon backed away from the car, almost tripping over his own feet. He stumbled back to his truck, trying to keep from puking again. Leaning over his truck, his lips inches from the hood, he repeated two words over and over to himself like a mantra, two words borne out of fear but serving to calm his mind—

"Oh shit, oh shit..."

After a few minutes he turned around, his heart slowed from its hectic pace, and he looked up into the darkness, the rain falling cold and wet on his upturned face.

He went slowly back to the car, just wishing this was over. He played the flashlight over the girl. It had to be her. The hair and general description were a match, and the car was right, too. She was completely naked, her left hand curled in her lap. The right index finger outstretched, as if pointing at something in front of the car.

Simon moved closer to look at her face, being very careful to not touch the body or the inside of the car in any way. Her eyes and mouth were wide open, her chin spattered with dried rivulets of what could only be blood, although in the glare of Simon's flashlight the blood was black and dull.

Solid objects peeked through the dried blood in her open mouth. It took Simon a moment to realize that they weren't her teeth. Her mouth had been wedged open with sticks.

It made her look like she was screaming. Screaming and pointing,

wide-eyed, at something. Like she'd literally been scared to death.
But her tongue. Where was her tongue?

"Sheriff's department. Search desk. Can I help you?"

Simon held the radio shakily, his other hand gripping the steering wheel. He was back in his truck, the heat on, the door closed and locked. He'd seen car wrecks and burn victims and shotgun suicides and murders that had left pieces of skull and brain dripping from the ceiling. He'd seen a lot of stuff, stuff he'd never forget. But nothing like this.

He was still staring at the Tercel when he realized that the dispatch officer had answered.

"Dispatch, this is Jeffers. Volunteer 21," Simon said, thumbing the radio. "I've located the missing girl and her car. Send units. All of them," he said, then gave directions to his location.

The dispatcher signed off. In town, Simon was sure sheriff units were scrambling to follow the directions he'd given.

When they arrived, he was waiting in his truck. He climbed out and stood in the rain, describing what he'd seen to the lead deputy, gesturing to the blood-red car and himself as he spoke. But Simon made no move toward the Tercel. When the deputies finished interviewing him and began their work, off-duty volunteer fireman Simon Jeffers turned in his radio, then climbed back into his truck and drove away, not looking back.

He'd seen enough.

CHAPTER 11
Tuesday, September 20

Jack was feeling great.

Yesterday had been good. He'd made a lot of progress, and last night, he'd set things in motion. To celebrate, he'd grabbed four bottles of Stoli from the woman's house, come back to the hotel and drunk until he passed out. The vodka was good, more expensive than the kind he normally got to drink.

He rarely got drunk, but sometimes Jack liked to splurge. And things were going very well so far in Liberty, better than he'd expected. Once the Beaumont kid heard about his aunt, he'd come running back. She was the only family the kid had ever known. He would return, and then they would meet someplace interesting. Maybe in the woods where Jack had been chased. Or that mall...

Wherever it happened, Jack would be waiting. And after the boy was dead, Jack would go out with a bang, making his mark on this town. Hold up a restaurant, or something at the mall. He wanted to make a big splash, kill a lot of people. And then he could be on his way, forgetting the ghosts of this town.

Today he could relax. Jack hadn't heard anything about the girl yet. The aunt and her friend might be found today, but most likely not until Thursday. Same with the dirty roommate. Jack had plenty of time to wander around town and talk to people before things got hairy.

For now, he was just going to relax here in bed and watch the free HBO. And drink.

———

Julie Noble sat in her lonely office in the FBI headquarters building, thinking. Her task to come up with a list of tests for the Cray had led to some interesting ideas, including one to search all unsolved murders that fit a particular pattern.

To be a good test, the search pattern would have to be specific and rare. It wouldn't do any good to search for all cases involving gunshot wounds. A list of 50,000 unsolved cases would be no help to anyone.

Julie wanted to create a very unique search, something that would only turn up a few dozen cases. She'd scratched the idea down along with all her others, but the specific search parameters had eluded her until she'd read that story in the paper on the Metro yesterday morning.

After reading about the boy and his missing leg, Julie went to the FBI library and did some reading. She learned that some killers liked to take portions of their victims as trophies or mementos. These murderers, usually drifters, moved around a lot, killing for years without being caught. In the vocabulary of serial killers, they were known as "collectors," a simple title for such a gruesome obsession. And a search of unsolved killings in which the victim was missing a body part could turn up a set of unsolved, related cases.

Today, she was presenting her list of ideas to Mike Wallace, the man who'd given her the assignment of testing the Cray. Some of the boys in the computer center had already run simple, one-field searches to make sure the Cray and its databases were up and running. Julie's search would be the first real test.

"You've got some interesting ideas here," Mike Wallace said, sitting back after reviewing them. He tapped her list on his desk. "Any in particular you want to do?"

She nodded. "The 'collector' search, sir."

He glanced down and read it again. "I saw that. Gruesome."

"Yes, but there should be a limited number of them," she said. "It's a subsection of the standard serial killer mindset."

Wallace shook his head. "Thank God those guys down in Behavioral Sciences have managed to put some of these maniacs away. You've read the research?"

"Spent most of this morning in the library."

"This boy's leg might've been lost in the water," Mike Wallace said, glancing at the article she'd attached to her list.

"Well, the boy was killed and part of him was missing. I don't know if he was the victim of a collector or not, but it gave me the idea about the search." She was silent for a moment, then continued. "And if this case did involve a collector, what better body part to take than a part no one would suspect?"

"Uh-huh," he answered skeptically. It was good to see her taking initiative, but the search was pointless, and he knew it. "I'm afraid this search won't result in anything actionable, Ms. Noble. There will probably be thousands of cases over the last 30 years that would fit the parameters of your search."

She nodded, not saying anything.

He looked up at her and frowned. Oh well, it was her time to waste. And it would give the Cray a good chance to show its stuff. Wasn't that the whole point of this exercise? And for her to get her feet wet before the Team returned from France.

Finally, he nodded and handed her the list back. "Go ahead. But unless you narrow the parameters, you're going to get too many returns. Try the 'extremities' one, but narrow it down. See what you get."

She stood. "If you don't mind, sir, I'd like to program the search engine myself. With supervision, of course. The language is a combination of XML and old Fortran."

"Okay, but make sure the Cray liaison is there."

Mike Wallace smiled, watching her leave. At least she was motivated.

Chris Hanson looked at Julie's paperwork and made a face.

"You want me to program it to search for what?" he asked sharply.

She nodded. They were standing outside the I/O room. "Mike Wallace approved it."

It never ceased to amaze Chris how the government worked. They seemed to be bent on spending as much money as possible to get the fewest results. Assigning some new employee to program the world's most powerful computer was just the latest example.

"I don't see how this would be a good use of the search function."

"It's not a waste of time."

Chris looked up at her—he could tell she was serious. He read through the *USA Today* article quickly while she talked.

"There are people out there who do that sort of thing," she continued. "And I'd like to program it in, if I may. I've been studying your programming language."

He finished the article with a shiver. He didn't even understand how someone could kill another person, yet it was something these FBI folks dealt with on a regular basis.

Chris looked up at her. "What makes you think anything will come back from this search? We could come up with nothing. Why don't you do something simple? I like your other ideas, like all the unsolved bank robberies where the getaway car was red. That seems simple, and a good test of the Cray's capabilities."

"I was going to go with something simple. But I read that article— look, can we just get started?" she asked, her hands on her hips.

Being a contractor, he was able to push the subject for a while, but that was it. The FBI was paying the contract, and he was here to oblige.

He could only shake his head and wonder where his tax dollars were spent.

"Okay, but I still think it's a waste of time."

She smiled and followed him into the I/O room, glancing through the thick, frosted windows at the Cray unit sitting on its raised vibration-proof pedestal.

Hanson sat at one of the workstations and tapped in his password to access the system. A series of commands accessed the FBI database they'd spent the last few days loading. He clicked on the SEARCH function and stood, allowing Julie to sit in his place. He walked her through the basic search parameters until she got it all typed in:

SEARCH>ALL UNSOLVED HOMICIDES
    FIND>FILE CONTAINS "FINGER"
AND
    FIND>FILE CONTAINS "TOE"
AND
    FIND>FILE CONTAINS "MISSING"
AND
    FIND>REMOVE FILES CONTAINING "ANIMAL"
AND
    FIND>WORDSPACE 15 OR LESS

"Now what?" she asked over her shoulder.

"Hit ENTER."

She did. After a few seconds, a series of numbers flashed up on the screen. "Results: 41 minutes."

"It'll take just under an hour to search. I'll bring you the printout when it's generated."

She thanked him and left, heading to her office. He shook his head—it felt good to be working on the Cray for real, even if it was for pointless make-work.

Bethany barely had the strength to stand.

No one could take her place at Big Video at the last minute, so she had to go in to work. Even though she was in charge of the store, she spent the day in the back room at the long wooden counter, sobbing.

None of the employees bothered her. They were all in a similar state of shock.

The deputies had arrived a little after 11:00 a.m. and given Bethany the news. Lisa had been found dead in her car in the woods out by the mall. The deputies had come to tell her in private, because she had made the initial report. Upon arriving, however, they decided to inform the entire crew—they'd all known and worked with Lisa and would find out soon enough.

One deputy had shooed the two customers out—"official business," he'd told them—and the other informed the crew that Lisa was deceased. They could give out no details, but the news was enough to send Bethany into the back room crying and the rest of the crew into a full day of silent introspection.

The deputies left a few minutes later, and the store reopened. As the customers drifted back in, the employees went back to their jobs, their minds filled with their own experiences and memories of Lisa Stevens. Someone put on a CD of very somber classical music, and no one complained. It just seemed right.

Bethany sat at the wooden counter in the back room, crying and flipping aimlessly through a cover-less copy of *Rolling Stone*. She'd taken the magazine from a stack in the break area. It was missing its cover because it had been torn off and returned to the company for credit. A cover-less magazine could not legally be sold, and therefore could be trashed or taken home by the employees. It saved a lot on postage, but it was kind of a scam, she thought.

But the legality of her reading material did not concern her today. She glanced at the phone by the door and wanted, more than anything else in the world, to talk to David. She needed to get her questions and her grief out. She stared at the beige handset, willing him to call, but the phone just hung there on the wall. David wasn't going to call her, not now, not ever.

Bethany was on her own.

Jeffers was terrified.

Liberty, Virginia, didn't have a press corps. Simon Jeffers knew that most of these men and women with their microphones and their shoulder-mounted cameras had to be from out of town. He saw colorful logos from Fredericksburg, Richmond, and even the D.C. television stations, along with print reporters from a score of other smaller towns in the area. The press had assembled in the sheriff's station for a noon press conference—the sheriff was going to take questions about the Lisa Stevens case.

Sheriff Jes Brown would come out of his office any moment now and officially begin the press conference. Then Brown would introduce Jeffers, who'd be expected to stand up there in front of all of these people and their lights and cameras and talk about finding the girl.

Jeffers fidgeted behind the elevated podium, anxious for this to be over. Sheriff Brown had insisted he be there, but Jeffers only wanted to be anywhere else. He hated speaking in front of people, hated the way their eyes laid on him, expectantly, like they were waiting for his pounding heart to burst out of his chest.

What would he say when they asked him questions? Brown had told him what he could and couldn't talk about. What if they asked him something he wasn't supposed to comment on? Would they know? Of course, they'd know. These people were used to questioning politicians and actors and experienced public leaders.

The door to Brown's office suddenly opened, and the man waddled out, followed by several deputies and Councilman Simons. The sheriff's office had no official press conference facilities, so a raised platform and podium area, where Jeffers now stood, had been set up on one side of the lobby. It was sunny outside, and the light streamed in through the large windows.

Sheriff Brown crossed the room and climbed carefully up to the platform, raising his big hands to quiet the members of the press.

Brown savored the moment. The unfortunate death of the girl had created a great deal of publicity, and the sheriff dragged out the silence, enjoying the anticipation.

"As you all know, the body of a missing girl was found early this morning," he finally said, nodding over at Simon Jeffers. "As of right now, we have no suspects, and there have been no new developments in the case."

He spoke slowly, carefully, making sure he appeared on as many TV stations as possible, and for that, the TV folks needed shock and awe. Excitement. And Brown could deliver.

"I can tell you that every member of this office is dedicated to solving this horrible crime as quickly as possible. I have already taken the initiative to invite the state police to assist, and a member of the state police, Lieutenant Blake, will be arriving within hours to join my investigation."

He smiled even as he spoke the words. It was a fine line to walk—calling in outside help made them look weak, but if he played it right, it might be his ticket to a job with the Staties. Brown was certain he and his men were perfectly capable of solving this murder, and Sheriff Brown was going to be there to take the credit. With this Lieutenant Blake coming in to assist—probably some know-it-all who'd try to take over—Brown would have to keep on his toes. But if he played his cards right, he could turn this whole sorry mess to his advantage—maybe a promotion.

The sheriff looked around at the assembled press corps representing a good portion of Virginia's media and waited an extra few seconds, relishing the visions of promotion and exposure and higher office dancing in his eyes.

"Any questions?"

A dozen hands shot up into the air. The sheriff nodded at a very pretty woman in the second row.

"Tina Linsey, *Pittsburgh Times*," the woman said. "How was she killed?"

Brown waited for a second before answering, savoring their collective anticipation. They were hanging on his every word. The feeling was intoxicating.

"The Fredericksburg County coroner is still determining the cause of death," he said, already looking around to choose his next person, looking for someone from one of the bigger markets, D.C. or Philly. "We should have a time and cause of death soon. Preliminary evidence points to the victim being bound and gagged, and the cause of death was most likely strangulation. Beyond that, we are not prepared to give out any information."

The reporters scrambled to write it all down. His answer was far more graphic than it needed to be, but Brown was thinking more about his own exposure on TV than the feelings of the family and friends of the victim. Another nod of the sheriff's head, and a man from *The Washington Post* stood. Brown had asked one of the deputy's to find out which reporters were from which media outlets. Brown needed to make sure he called on the most important ones first—national papers, TV, etc.

"Was there any evidence of sexual assault?"

Brown gaped at the man, amazed at the callousness of his question.

"We don't have any information on that yet," he said quietly, frowning. Flashes went off around him as photographers grabbed the somber moment.

The *Post* reporter sat down, looking disappointed.

———

More questions were asked and answered, but Simon Jeffers wasn't paying attention. He was concentrating on not vomiting.

The assembled journalists scribbled down every word the sheriff said. The press were like rabid dogs, and the sheriff was handing out treats. No one seemed to be bothered in the least that they were talking about a murdered young woman.

"How was the victim found?" Jeffers heard, and it seemed like the room went silent. He'd been dreading the question and standing at the back of the platform, hoping that everyone had forgotten about him. Sheriff Brown turned to Jeffers and gestured him up to the podium. His heart pounded as he stepped forward, his legs of lead. He grasped the microphone like a drowning man thrown a life preserver.

Jeffers opened his mouth and slowly told his gruesome story again, his voice cracking as he started. He concentrated on getting through the story quickly, staring over the heads of the reporters. He concentrated on the windows and the parking lot full of news vans outside.

His hands sweated, his voice wavered. Even though he'd told the story a half-dozen times already, he rushed through it and left out crucial details, forcing him to go back and add them in later. He tried to ignore the reporters' eyes on him and finished, audibly sighing when he was done.

As soon as he finished, every hand in the room jumped into the air.

Jeffers didn't want to take any questions—all he wanted was to flee. But when he glanced at Brown for deliverance, the sheriff only nodded and gestured to the press. Jeffers might have imagined it, but it looked like the sheriff might have been wearing a slight smile.

He turned back to the assembled press of an entire state, flashes going off around him. After a second, he pointed at a lady near the front. His hand was shaking. He gripped the podium for support.

"Tina Linsey again," the woman said. "Did you say the girl looked like she was scared, like she was pointing at something?"

Jeffers nodded, thanking God it was an easy question. "Her hand was propped up on the wheel like it was pointing ahead. Her eyes and mouth were open. She looked scared to me," he said. Simon didn't mention the tongue. Brown had told him not to. That bit of information was being closely held.

Jeffers started to point at someone else when the woman from Pittsburgh shouted a follow-up question.

"Isn't it true that the victim's tongue had been cut out?"

The room fell deathly silent. All eyes were on Jeffers. The temperature in the room seemed to skyrocket.

"Ah, yes that's true, but we didn't have any—" he began to say, but suddenly felt hands on him. He was shoved away from the microphone by Sheriff Brown. He was pulled off the platform by a deputy, pushed down the aisle between the desks toward Sheriff Brown's office.

Simon didn't resist. He had to get away from the stares.

———

The reporters were in an uproar.

"Please, please, everybody, just calm down!" Sheriff Brown yelled from the podium as the reporters shouted questions at him. He raised both hands to calm them.

"Ladies! Gentlemen," he yelled again. "Please, may I have your attention? That information was to be held in strictest confidence." He'd decided to withhold it for two reasons: it was both a gruesome piece of information and a valuable one for when and if a suspect was ever charged. Law enforcement agencies routinely held back pieces of information to weed out false confessions.

Someone had talked, Brown was sure. His men had little experience in keeping secrets like this. One of his deputies had let the information slip into the wrong ear.

"Can you confirm it's true!" a reporter shouted.

"I'm disappointed to have it revealed to the public. But yes, I can confirm that detail," he said, quieting the room. The reporters were like animals, salivating for more meat.

He took two more questions before wrapping it up. "We will be ending the press conference now. Another one will be held tonight at approximately 6:00 p.m., or earlier, if we have new information," Brown said, leaving the podium amid a cacophony of shouted, indignant questions. Linsey, the reporter from Pittsburgh, smiled at him, which only pissed him off further.

Brown opened the door to his office, ready to start screaming at someone, and saw Simon Jeffers, on his knees beside the sheriff's desk. He was vomiting into a trash can. The sheriff quickly stepped in and closed the door before the reporters could see.

———

"...high winds and heavy rains have moved into the Middle Atlantic states as Hurricane Mandy continues its trek up the coast. Record rainfall amounts were reported overnight in several cities in Alabama, Georgia, and South Carolina. The Governor of South Carolina said today that crews were working to repair bridges and roads washed out by two days of flash floods in his state. Again, Hurricane Mandy still continues on its northerly path, the eye of the storm moving past Savannah, Georgia, at 1:00 p.m. today. Forecasters predict the storm will continue to move up the coast—"

David reached up and turned the radio down—they were repeating themselves. The hurricane was massive, and from what David could tell from the reports, it was only going to get worse. One expert had been on earlier, forecasting the storm path, but even the expert didn't sound too certain.

Maybe it was a sign that he was supposed to go back.

Part of him was worried about the folks in Liberty, like his aunt and Bethany and the folks at Big Video. But Aunt Gloria would be all right. Abe was looking out for her. Even if he was strange, Abe had her best interests at heart, David thought.

Maybe he should at least check in. Call his aunt the next time he gassed up.

And then there was Bethany. He glanced over at the passenger seat and saw the red binder. He still hadn't looked at it. But it sat where Bethany had sat so many times, heading to the movies or going to school or going into D.C. to see a concert. David thought about all the things they had done together, and all the things he had done recently to push her away.

The radio came back from commercial, and David turned it back up.

"Seventeen deaths in Florida and Georgia have been attributed to the storm. Officials at the National Hurricane Center in Coral Gables, Florida, said today that Hurricane Mandy is one of the most powerful hurricanes ever recorded, with sustained winds near the eye in the 160-mph range..."

There was a quiet knock on Julie's office door.

"Yes?" she said without looking up from her stack of books.

Chris Hanson pushed the door open with his foot because his hands were full. He brought in a thick stack of reports and set them on the corner of her desk.

"That's the result of your searches," he said, plopping down into a nice leather chair she'd "borrowed" from one of the abandoned offices on her floor. Her office was so small that the chair took up most of the usable room, but it made the office feel a little more official.

The first report had turned up over 1,500 unsolved cases in the past thirty years that had involved a missing digit. She had Chris run separate reports for each kind of extremity. Evidently the search engine somehow marked each file as it searched through the massive database, so second and third searches across the same material took far less time.

The "finger" list was 1,143 entries long, a headache just waiting for her. The "toe" list was much shorter. She decided to take them both home and work on them. It was a Tuesday night, and she had nothing to do until *NYPD Blue* came on, one of her favorite shows.

She heard somebody clear their throat and glanced up to see Chris staring at her from the chair.

"Oh, sorry, Chris. Just trying to decide how I'm going to tackle all of this," she said, smiling at him. "Thanks for running these."

"Well, at least it worked," he said. "The database search worked perfectly, flagging and eliminating the duplicates automatically. Anything else you get from these lists is a bonus, right?"

She was flipping through the finger listing and something on one of the pages jumped out at her. The fourth listing down on the page contained an interesting entry—"GRK." She asked Chris about it.

"Oh, I looked that up. That's a reference to a case that might have had some connection to the Green River Killer. A string of murders in the Seattle area in the '80s. They never caught the guy, as far as I know. But I thought Ted Bundy confessed to those before he died?"

"No, no. He was a consultant on the case," Julie said, remembering. "He didn't confess, but someone else did. This case here," she said, pointing at the sheet. "Is this one of them? It's got the code by it."

He glanced at the case summary and nodded. "Yeah. I didn't know that the Green River Killer was supposed to be one of your collector guys."

"Neither did I," she said, scanning the report. "Can you run another one..."

"No, no, no," he said, shaking his head and showing Julie his watch. "I'm off in half an hour."

"You can just start the search and leave," she said. "Then it'll be ready in the morning when I get here. A separate list of all the GRK cases, or cases where he's mentioned?"

She was being her most charming, and it really wasn't fair.

He finally shook his head and got up to leave. "Fine."

———

The red binder wasn't what David had expected.

Well, to be completely honest, David hadn't known what to expect.

Bored, he'd propped it open on the steering wheel and started flipping through it. It looked like a long letter of a dozen pages or so, with some pictures and other things thrown in by Bethany to remind him of their time together. All designed to make him feel guilty about leaving.

But there was more. It was like an entire history of their relationship, a chronicle of their time together.

There was a letter, but he wasn't sure if you could call something nearly 100 pages long a letter. It deserved a better word. And the pages of the letter were plastered with dozens of pictures and drawings, phone messages, ticket stubs, restaurant menus, and cards from birthdays and holidays. It was crazy how much work she'd put into this thing to show they'd cared for each other.

He couldn't really read the letter as he drove. Her handwriting had always been hard for him to decipher, even when he wasn't going eighty miles an hour. But he was able to pick out a few lines here and there between glances at the flat road in front of him. Instead of a pleading discourse, full of phrases like "Why did you leave?" as David had expected, this letter was more like a description of these important mementos and their significance to her.

It was a love letter to the good times that they'd had.

Here was a card he'd gotten her on Valentine's Day, only a couple of weeks after they'd started dating. It wasn't a romantic kind of card. They hadn't gotten to that point in their relationship yet. This card was a funny one that had made him laugh, something that was sorely lacking in his life before he'd met Bethany.

He'd never learned how to deal with people, and his aunt had been no help. Her only serious relationship was one with a half-empty bottle of Stoli. One of the girls he'd dated in high school had been interested in psychology, and she'd told him that he had bad luck with women, and people in general, because he always kept his emotions inside.

Well, it was time for a change. Trapped in Liberty, he'd never get past what happened to his family. Headed west to California, David was making a big change.

He closed the red binder and set it aside, but even as he was looking straight out the window, trying to keep his eyes on the road, he could still see the bright red cover out of the corner of his eye. It called to him, daring him read it this time. And not just glance at the pictures.

Tuesday afternoon and evening came and went.

Apparently, no one was concerned about Abe Foreman's and Gloria Thatcher's absence.

The only people who really questioned Gloria's absence were the folks at the new townhouse complex, where she was supposed to sign her lease on Tuesday morning. When she didn't show, they chalked it up to a missed appointment and called her house, leaving a message on the answering machine.

On Tuesday nights, usually, Abe and some of the other wealthy businessmen involved in the development and construction of the Liberty Place Mall would get together and informally discuss how the mall was doing. It was really just an excuse for this particular group of friends to meet at the mall's Ruby Tuesday and congratulate each other on their insight and forward thinking in investing in the mall when it was still just an open field and a set of sketches on an architect's wall. Each of the partners in the venture had already made back many times their original investments.

On this Tuesday night, the entire meal at Ruby Tuesday passed without Abe Foreman's smiling face appearing, apologizing for being late. He never missed one of their weekly get-togethers.

By the time the coffee and sticky buns came, the conversation had turned to Abe's absence. One man made quick calls on his new Motorola StarTAC folding cellular phone, the envy of everyone at the table, to Abe's home and work numbers. It was the first cellular flip phone any of them had seen, passing it around. But the calls proved unfruitful, and the man slipped his phone back into his pocket with a look of concern. One man made a comment that the only thing that could keep Abe away from the dinner table was a woman, and that launched a lengthy discussion on the importance of female companionship in every man's life.

After the dinner broke up, each man headed for home or the office, depending on their level of commitment to family or work. One of the men, on his route back to his office, happened to pass Gloria Thatcher's neighborhood, or things might've turned out differently.

As it was, the man was driving down her street and listening to classical music when he saw Abe's new car in the woman's driveway. He slowed and pulled in beside it, laughing to himself.

"That sneaky devil," he thought. Why else was his new car parked out in front of the single woman's house this late at night? Everyone knew that Abe Foreman worked closely with Gloria Thatcher, and lately he'd been trying to settle up her affairs and get her moved into a new townhouse. She was famous in this town, and everyone knew about her penchant for alcohol.

Apparently, Abe was giving the woman a little more "personal service" than he gave most of his clients.

Smiling, the man saw lights on in the house and decided to sneak up to a window. If only he'd brought a camera! Catching Abe in a compromising position, something embarrassing, would be great fun.

The man worked his way through some bushes, sidling up to the large picture window at the front of the house. He peeked in, hoping to see something interesting.

He did.

Abe was there, alright.

He was lying on the living room floor with broken pieces of a glass coffee table underneath and all around him. His head looked strangely flattened on one side and was surrounded by a large black stain. One big hunk of glass from the coffee table stuck rudely up through the meat of Abe's shoulder, the jagged point painted with dried blood.

The man looked in the front window for a full minute, his eyes taking in everything before he absently fished out his Motorola cellular phone and dialed. He couldn't take his eyes off the grisly scene. His dead friend, splayed across the broken table, legs bent in the wrong direction—

The 911 operator had to yell at him to get his attention.

The deputies took only a few minutes to arrive. Within an hour, things were starting to move very quickly indeed for the Liberty Sheriff's Department. They were already overtaxed with the investigation of Lisa Stevens' murder, and now they were called upon to investigate two more deaths. Three suspicious deaths in forty-eight hours, more than had occurred in the past fifteen years combined.

Abe Foreman had no relatives in the area, so the sheriff's office and county coroner were forced to get a positive photo ID from the individual who had originally discovered the body.

No one was able to contact Gloria Thatcher's next of kin, David Beaumont. A minor celebrity around town, every deputy knew who the boy was. Someone mentioned that the Beaumont boy had recently left town, moving to California. Could he have been responsible for these deaths?

A call to his last place of residence reached an answering machine. A deputy, sent to Beaumont's last known address, found a dirty apartment and another dead person—Beaumont's ex-roommate had apparently hung himself in the closet of the residence.

Four dead in two days.

The deputies tracked down Beaumont's last place of employment, talking to a man named Mel Rivers. He informed them of Beaumont's leaving town over the weekend. Rivers also mentioned David's ex-girlfriend was Bethany King, the same person who had reported Lisa

Stevens missing.

It was for that reason a squad car pulled up in front of Bethany's house just before midnight on Tuesday night. The Sheriff's Department needed her to identify Gloria Thatcher's body. The deputy knocked for several minutes before Bethany answered the door, her robe pulled tight around her, eyes streaked with tears.

CHAPTER 12
Wednesday, September 21

The Washington Post, the *Liberty Gazette,* and many other newspapers across the nation printed small stories about Lisa Stevens' grisly murder in their Wednesday morning editions, mostly because the AP wire service had picked up the story and spread it nationwide. A small-town girl found murdered in her home town would always be interesting news.

The Gannet people at *USA Today,* headquartered in Reston, Virginia, about 50 miles north of Liberty, took one look at the AP "flash story" and forwarded it down to the local department that oversaw the daily one-page summation of short pieces of local news for each state.

Every day, the "local" department sorted through hundreds of stories from each state and narrowed them down to four or five lines. A sensational murder almost always made it into the final copy.

Once written, the short blurb for "Virginia" was forwarded to the composition rooms via electronic computer link. The fact that the victim's tongue had been removed made the story even more likely to run—grisly, but very newsworthy.

One of the staff members of the local page mentioned to another staffer that it was two times in three days that they'd run a short blurb about a killing on the East Coast involving a missing body part. She'd remembered a short article in the Monday edition about a one-legged boy whose body had been found in a river in South Carolina.

The second staffer thought it was probably just a coincidence but suggested that the woman who'd noticed the connection mention it to their supervisor. The first staffer, blushing slightly, dismissed the notion, having only been with the paper for a few months.

The short two lines ran under a **Virginia—Liberty** banner. Most people who read *USA Today* don't read the local page, and if they did, just read about their own state. Only a few people who read the short summation paid it any attention.

Julie was back in her office early on Wednesday morning. She'd spent most of the evening reviewing every aspect of the "fingers" and "toes" reports, looking for possible connections or patterns.

The Green River Killer report had been waiting in the hallway outside her office when she arrived, left by a messenger at some point last night. It summarized every case connected to the GRK.

Chris had already checked in this morning and she had him printing out more reports, case summaries on any unsolved murders involving extremities from 1966 to 1996. She had a suspicion this was all going to come to nothing, but even if it did, it would show the higher-ups she could be a competent investigator. She wanted results, but that was beside the point. She needed to show Mike Wallace and Peter Turner, her still-unseen supervisor and head of the team, that she could get work done.

The first report, which included all extremities cases, had taken most of the night to run, the yellow sticky from Chris stated. The search parameters were printed on the first page, and the six-inch stack of computer paper would include all cases, solved or unsolved, that involved any removal of any extremities, pre- or post-mortem. She knew that the report would contain hundreds of cases that had nothing to do with her search, but she wanted a master printout to refer back to, just in case her search became too bogged down in the details.

She picked up the huge report, carried it out into the hallway and plopped it down on a skinny wooden table she'd "borrowed." The table creaked when she set the heavy stack of paper on it. She hoped it would hold.

The Green River Killer was the most famous unsolved string of serial murders in the nation. Hundreds of books had been written on the subject since the murders had abruptly started in the mid-1980s. She'd read a lot about the Killer in the last two days, but she couldn't imagine what it must be like to live in a town paralyzed with fear, scared to even go out, because a real monster was out there, wandering the streets. Monsters were supposed to be hiding under beds and lurking in dark closets or relegated to the safe pages of some Stephen King gore-fest.

But Julie was beginning to believe in the existence of monsters.

Not the hulking green kind, maw dripping with blood, of course. But the kind that lurked in the pages of the reports around her. There were monsters out there, real ones, preying on the innocent and the trusting, killing and maiming and torturing for the sheer enjoyment of it. And these monsters didn't look any different from regular people.

The printout was simply a list of the possible murders in the Seattle area from 1980 to 1985 that the Green River Killer was suspected to be involved with, but the details and garish quality of the murders left Julie shaken. So many women, killed over those short few years, some of them not found for months, their bodies rotting in shallow graves or under thick undergrowth. Some of them dumped rudely in the deep ditches near the Sea-Tac Airport, some of them had been raped—

Julie closed the report and stood, leaving her office. She needed a walk, needed to clear her head.

Outside, the weather was clear and sunny, brightening her mood. Hurricane Mandy, all over the news, would move into the D.C. area over the next few days, bringing days of heavy wind and rain.

Julie sat on a bench outside for a few minutes, clearing her mind, before she headed back in and made her way to the cafeteria and grab a soda or something.

It was just after 9:00 a.m. and the cafeteria was deserted. The breakfast rush had ended over an hour ago, and the cooks in the back wouldn't begin serving the lunch crowd until 11:00 a.m. The grills and steam tables and even the rotating toasters were shut down. Julie saw a man scrubbing one of the wide gray grills, removing egg and bacon grease. The only part of the cafeteria still open was one register and a table that held a selection of picked-over donuts, muffins, and bagels. The soda dispensers were still on, though, and Julie grabbed herself a blueberry muffin and a large Coke.

"Not too busy, huh?" she asked the lady at the open register.

The lady shook her head. "Always slow this time of day, but it makes up for the busy times. You have yourself a good day, okay?"

Julie thanked her and pocketed her change, then headed for the library. It was near the 7th Street entrance. A few minutes later, Julie walked back into her office and set her soda and muffin down, along with a hard-bound book from the bureau library. Many of the books, including this one, were classified and could not be removed from the building.

The hardcover book was actually the final bound report from the Green River Task Force and included pictures, sketches of the murder scenes, witness accounts, an FBI personality profile, and a chapter dedicated just to the killer's physical description. Julie sat back, propped her feet up on her desk, and began reading.

It remained one of the most notorious unsolved cases in U.S. history. The King County Police Department, where most of the murders had occurred, had struggled to solve the string of cases. Finally, they had formed the Green River Task Force in the early 1980s to investigate the killings. The Task Force shut down only last year, 1995, due to lack of budget. Only a few resources were still dedicated to the search, and a toll-free number was even included in the report, in case any members of law enforcement discovered new information about the murders.

Over the course of the investigation, a total of forty-nine unsolved murders had occurred in the Seattle/Tacoma Washington area over a stretch of about six years. Several other unrelated murders were investigated by the task force and solved by their exhaustive investigative work, but they were unsuccessful in even obtaining a full description of the killer who stalked and killed without retribution.

In most of the cases, prostitutes figured heavily in the tastes of the killer. A good percentage of the women found murdered were known prostitutes and worked the same area in Seattle, an area known as "The Strip." Because of the activities that these women were engaged in, it made it very difficult for the task force to investigate their murders. As body after body surfaced in murky rivers and small lakes or shallow graves near the Sea-Tac International Airport, the investigators became more and more frustrated. Several men were detained and questioned over the course of the investigation, but all were cleared.

Julie searched the book and pictures for clues, and eventually it paid off. In one report reproduced in black and white in the book, an original investigator wrote about a curious aspect of the case, one that had never been released to the public. In many of the murders attributed to the Green River Killer, there was some part of the victim's body missing.

Julie sat up a little straighter and continued reading. Keeping information from the public was a standard method used by police to keep attention-seeking weirdos from confessing to crimes. Several victims were missing parts of their fingers, most often the pinkie. Why the killer was collecting parts of his victims was not even considered— only the fact that the killer was tying all of the murders together for the cops.

She read the included FBI personality profile with interest. The most likely suspect in the murders, based on the information gathered so far in the case, would be a white male between the ages of twenty and forty, a heavy smoker and drinker. Exactly how they had come to these conclusions was not explained in the report, but Julie knew that there were whole offices at Quantico that specialized in this sort of psychological profiling. The report also suggested that the killer would be very intelligent, enjoyed the outdoors, and probably had some interest in perverted sexual acts.

Julie flipped through the back of the book, looking at the pictures of the twenty-nine known victims and the other twenty women who were killed around the same time and location but were not considered official victims.

Julie set the book and other files aside and pulled the green Cray printout toward her. All of the crimes in this report were connected to the Green River Killer in some way, and the cases where body parts were collected were highlighted. Julie narrowed the stack down to the twenty-nine killings mentioned in the book. She separated out those sheets, spreading them out on her desk and categorizing them by date and location.

All of the killings appeared to have taken place within a twenty-mile radius. Julie wondered if the killer was just toying with the cops. No one could kill repeatedly and never leave any clues. The investigators' frustration must have been monumental.

She sat back from the reports and thought about it. If this Green River Killer had come into the Seattle area in 1982, he must have come from somewhere. There was a break from 1987 to 1990. Barring the possibility that he'd died or was arrested on another charge, the killer must have somehow learned to control himself. Or the killer had left the area.

A chill ran down her back, thinking about the possibility, however small, that the maniac might still be out there.

1987 to 1990. Where had he gone? Had he moved on, or just taken a break? She walked around her desk and found the "fingers" report, a stack several inches thick, and opened it to 1986. She read each six-line case summary, eliminating those that didn't occur in the Seattle area or within a day's drive. Several of the same names from her GRK list also appeared here. She circled those cases that could've been carried out by the same person.

1987 held five cases from the Portland, Oregon, area, about 200 miles south of Seattle, and a couple of unsolved collection murders from the Yakima, Washington, area. All of the murders could have been carried out by the same person, and none of the dates of the victims' deaths, whether they be exact dates or coroner estimations, could eliminate them from all being done by the same person.

She needed a wall map of the Pacific Northwest and maybe another one of the United States. Logging into the building LAN, she requested help from the LAN administrator as to whom she could order these items from.

While she waited for a response, she started on 1988. There were no suspected Green River Killer slayings in the Seattle area that year—the last was February 1987, and no more until March of 1990. She continued through 1989 and circled forty-three killings that fit her basic parameters, but she couldn't see any type of pattern—all were extremities cases, but many could be eliminated by distance and time factors. She scanned for just those on the west coast but realized a chronological search like this could take months, and she just didn't have the patience.

But the Cray did.

Julie picked up her paperwork and headed downstairs.

Norma Jenkins directed her yellow school bus to a stop in front of the elementary school and dropped off the last of her kids. They filed off her bus, none of them looking at her. She sighed and put the bus in gear, driving around to the back of the school. On most days, between this last drop-off at 8:45 and the first pick-up run from the same school at 2:05, she parked behind the school with the town's three other buses and washed hers, spraying it down with soap and water. People had no idea how dirty a big yellow school bus could get, and it took almost daily washings to keep it clean.

After that, she'd usually get in her car, also parked at the school, and run errands or just head home until the afternoon runs. But today, as she pulled the bus up next to the others, she was interested in only one activity.

She wanted to read the papers.

She'd seen the paper's headlines today, and the murder of Lisa Stevens was the talk of the town. She'd heard a couple of moms discussing it at one of the stops as they pushed their kids aboard Norma's bus. The other three bus drivers had been talking about it this morning before they'd started the high school run. Most mornings, Norma didn't contribute to their little conversations, but this morning she had had a couple of questions. The other three members that made up the entire Liberty school bus driving squad had looked at her oddly, as if they'd gotten used to her silence and aloofness and were unsure how to deal with her sudden attempts at conversation.

The other three bus drivers were talking again as Norma pulled up. Jake was hosing mud off of his bus, the number 2, and Jess and Lynda were standing near him, chatting. Norma felt no need at all to join their little group, but she did wave and say hello before heading inside to the elementary school's empty cafeteria to scratch up a little snack and find a copy of the paper.

The *Liberty Gazette* wasn't a bastion of news-gathering might, but it usually did manage to report the local news. Today, as Norma munched on a bagel and read the paper, the story seemed thin, short on details and long on supposition. There were no direct interviews with any of the family members or the girl who'd originally reported Lisa Stevens missing. There was only a short blurb from the off-duty fireman who'd found the murdered girl.

For the first murder in Liberty in years, details were sketchy.

The sheriff's office was holding things close to the vest, Norma could tell. The only insight into the truly grisly details in the case had been the result of a question from some a journalist at yesterday's press conference. The exchange confirmed that the girl's tongue had been removed, a disturbing detail that Norma was sure the Liberty Sheriff's Department had wanted to keep under their hats.

But it was hard to keep sensational details of a case under wraps. She remembered the difficulty they'd had when Jasper Fines had been in town, and the lengths Sheriff Beaumont had gone to to keep the details of the slayings out of the public eye.

The sights and sounds of that night flooded her mind even as she resisted remembering. The evil man, standing over her and pretending to shoot her, then laughing. The feel of the cold wet asphalt as she listened as Jasper Fines shot Sheriff Beaumont. Crawling over and holding Beaumont's head, or what was left of it. The taillights of the car, driving away.

And the birds, following the lights into the night.

Her stomach turned over, and Norma set aside the rest of her bagel, suddenly not hungry.

The state police had found the abandoned police car south of Liberty, almost to where the Kings Dominion amusement park was now. Jasper Fines had killed three people in Liberty and then just vanished into the night.

She needed to focus on the present. Brown was obviously keeping stuff from the public about the Lisa Stevens murder, just as Beaumont had kept details out of the public eye. In all the deaths attributed to Jasper Fines, the Killer had taken a souvenir. And now there was someone else in Liberty, killing people and removing their body parts.

Her stomach rolled over again.

She put the questions out of her mind, trying to pretend that deep inside she wasn't still a deputy. She was just a bus driver now, one with a crooked nose and an ulcer-torn stomach. It was someone else's problem. Norma couldn't afford to worry about it. The stress could kill her. Literally.

———

"You think you've got something there, but I bet it's nothing." Chris Hanson looked at the report she was pointing at.

"I'm not saying I solved any crimes," she said, knowing he was right. But she couldn't help getting excited.

He looked at her. "What are the chances that you can have anything new to say about the guy when this task force up there in Seattle spent years and millions of dollars investigating the case?"

"Well, did he just stop?"

"I don't know," Chris said with a shrug. "Maybe he died. Maybe he got arrested. According to this, there have been no killings since 1990."

"In Seattle. That's my point," she said. "He moved on. The Green River Killer must've come from somewhere and, unless he was caught or killed, he must've gone somewhere after the killings stopped. Right?"

"Yeah, I guess so," Chris nodded, reluctant. "But what have you got here?" he asked, pointing at the reports and files she had strewn across an unused desk in the computer center for him to see. "You said the task force in Seattle connected him with twenty-nine cases. What else?"

"Nothing, Chris. That's what I want to use the Cray for—to search for other cases that fit the timespan and the details related to these crimes," she explained.

She grabbed the hardbound report on the Green River Killer and opened it to a photocopied map of Washington state. Each of the locations where the bodies had been found had been noted on the map, along with the date, and it was easy to see the pattern. "Mapping them like this helps group them chronologically and by region. There could be other murders in the surrounding states that could be attributed to him," she said, pointing at the map. "If he stayed with the same M.O., there might be other unsolved collector cases within a day's drive that never made it into the original investigation."

Chris thought about it for a moment, studying the map. After a second, he nodded. "That makes sense. Just don't get your hopes up."

"I know. I'm just using the Cray to sort the reports and display them."

"What parameters do you want?"

"I want a map. Do we have a big monitor we can hook up to display the Cray's output? It'll be easier than squinting at that little monitor," she said, pointing at the Cray's I/O room with its rows of keyboards and monitors. "I want to do something like the 'Dead' section does by plotting with colored dots over a full-color map."

He shook his head and headed off, returning after twenty minutes with a twenty-one-inch monitor. Setting it on a table just outside the I/O room, he hooked it up and attached a keyboard. He also pulled up two chairs to the newest Cray workstation.

"Okay, shoot."

They sat, and he began entering the parameters she'd jotted down in the margins of one of the reports. Chris hit ENTER and a detailed map of the Pacific Northwest popped up almost instantly. A numerical display in the lower right corner read "4:00."

"Four minutes? That quickly?"

He nodded. "It's not searching the whole database again, just the saved search we did on...digits. Wow, that was fast."

She looked at the screen. A red dot that just popped up near Billings, Montana. A tiny legend also appeared, designating the red dot as 1980. Three more appeared in Montana, Idaho, and Wyoming, and one more red dot appeared in California, north of Sacramento.

As they watched, green dots began appearing on the screen with ever-increasing speed—1981's cases. Most of them were centered around Seattle, the Green River Killer. But as Julie's hours of research last night and this morning had showed, five green dots appeared in the Portland, Oregon, area and two appeared in Yakima, Washington, southeast of Seattle.

"Those aren't GRK?"

She shook her head. "No. None of those were investigated by the Task Force. They were eliminated by distance."

The Cray moved on to 1982, noting those in blue and adding the year and color to the legend at the bottom. Most of those were centered around Seattle. 1983 and 1984 followed, labeled orange and purple, with much the same result, and then 1985 began popping up in yellow. They centered at first around Seattle, but soon stopped. Julie nervously watched the screen for several seconds, and then three yellow dots appeared in Portland in quick succession, followed by a couple in northern California and one in the Lake Tahoe area, on the Nevada/California border.

After several more seconds, the clock at the bottom of the monitor counted down to 0:00:00 and was replaced with a curt message: "Search completed."

They were silent for a moment before Chris asked the question that was on both of their minds.

"So, does this show—did he kill in Seattle and then move down here, down the coast?" he asked, pointing.

"I don't know. Some of these have to be erroneous. Surely—"

"If you discounted some of them, like this 1980 case in California and this 1986 case in Salt Lake City, there could be a pattern," Chris said, sitting back. "Either way, this kind of search really shows off the Cray. It took minutes to do what you spent all night on, right? And displayed them on a map."

"Can you get it to display the months without re-searching the whole database? Or draw a line connecting them all chronologically?"

Chris nodded and began typing. A few seconds later, the dots were joined by little numbers 1–12, corresponding with the month that the coroner had estimated the date of death. After the months were displayed, a thin white line connected all the dots chronologically, and the map looked like some kind of morbid connect-the-dots puzzle.

Chris was studying the screen, trying to see a pattern. "No, it can't be. This guy or a group of guys has been out there killing all this time, and all we had to do was type in a few lines on a computer and up pops a map of his travels? It's not possible." He sat back and crossed his arms.

Julie shook her head, pointing. "We are searching for very specific unsolved cases involving a particular kind of crime. And we've narrowed the search down to a location and time frame. But no, see, some of the killings took place at the same time far apart. They can't all be the same person. But mapped like this—it makes it easy to see a pattern. And these are just the collector cases involving fingers and toes. There could be others."

"I dunno. I guess it just seems too easy." Chris nodded, staring at the screen. "So, I guess the next thing to do is eliminate the other cases, right? How can we do that?"

She looked over at him and smiled. "For someone reluctant to help me, you're kinda getting into it."

"Let's just get to work," he said, smiling and pointing at her reports. "Tell me what to type."

––––––––

The cuts on her hands refused to bleed.

Sally, wearing her flowing wedding dress, continued to climb upward, struggling to make the summit of this mountain before the last of her strength abandoned her. She had cut her hands over and over, but there was no blood.

Her will was strong, buoyed by her strange encounter with that huge man from Greek legend.

She could see the squat building above her. Sisyphus had called it "the Temple of Zeus," but that was wrong. She recognized the building now. As she crested the summit, she could see the tall columns marching down either side of the building. But above each column, she could read the names of some of the United States along with dates in roman numerals.

It was the Lincoln Memorial.

Above the building, a huge group of disparate birds circled, swooping and diving slowly over the building.

She shook her head, then turned and looked back. The fog had followed her. She'd seen it again after she parted company with the big man. Now, the fog blanketed the entire valley and swirled up the mountain, climbing the slopes below her. The forest where she'd awakened was gone. Nothing existed but the top of this mountain, and the building, and an endless ocean of clouds.

Stairs led up into the memorial, and she climbed. Inside, the memorial was cold. And beyond the columns sat a huge and familiar figure, white of marble. The stony face of President Abraham Lincoln waited for her, silent.

She didn't know what to do. Sally looked at the president for a long time, waiting, but nothing happened. Turning, she saw the first tendrils of fog entering the flat area she'd just crossed.

"Do not worry. The fog cannot reach you here."

She turned to look for the source of the deep, booming voice. The granite visage of Lincoln was now looking down at her, his eyes clear and bright.

Sally gulped. "What did you say?"

She turned to see the

"The fog," President Lincoln said, and one marble arm came to life, breaking free of the carved stone armrest. Marble chunks crashed onto his white knees and the polished floor around his seat. "The fog only exists to...lead you to me."

She saw that, as he talked, the rock of his face seemed to split and then knit back together, stone healing itself in an instant.

"Where am I? Why am I here?" she asked. She felt small, talking to this seated giant.

"Here is where you choose, child." Lincoln looked at her. "You must decide whether you want to live or die."

She knew she didn't want to die, no more than the next person. But she was so tired. Her shoulder and hands and knees were screaming with pain. Somewhere during the climb, she'd realized her arms and chest were stitched with a hundred little punctures, each smarting like a bee sting. Small shards of glass, tiny slivers, protruded from some of the wounds.

A large part of her wanted nothing more than to sleep, even if it meant sleeping forever.

Her voice caught in her throat. "I climbed, didn't I? Didn't I already choose to live?"

"No," the huge voice answered, booming off the marble walls. "Fear is a strong motivator. But now you must choose." He looked at her for a long moment, his huge eyes never blinking. He brushed the broken stone from his lap as he waited for an answer.

"If I go out into the fog, I die?"

"Death is an easy choice," Lincoln said. "It takes courage to live, to accept the pain of life. If you choose life, there will be times when you will regret that choice. Many times."

Sally nodded. She didn't want to die; as much pain as she felt, at least it was something. She wanted to live, and she wanted to see Tommy, to tell him how she felt about him. She loved him. And there was something else important she was supposed to tell him. Something she couldn't remember.

"Choose now—go back to your life, or stay here and wait for the end."

This time, there was no hesitation.

"I want to live," she said, her words strong. Decisive.

The marble giant smiled, and the massive arm came up, dropping more pieces of broken stone around his throne-like chair. He pointed at the wall off to his right. There, etched in letters three feet high, were the immortal words of the Gettysburg address. Below the words, a glowing yellow rectangle appeared in the wall. The yellow lines widened, thickened, until they formed a doorway filled with bright yellow light that illuminated Lincoln and Sally and the cloud of dust drifting between them.

"Good luck," Lincoln answered quietly. When she looked back up at him he had returned to the stony form of her memory. The cracks and the marble pieces around his seat were gone. She smiled and walked into the light, pausing only for a brief second as the warm light washed over her. Then, without looking back, she stepped through.

———

Tommy was looking at her bandaged foot, wondering what kind of sick person would remove a person's toe. Had the killer kept it? The cop had been missing a toe as well. Sick.

Tommy felt her fingers move.

For a moment, he was sure he was simply dreaming. He kept imagining her moving, talking. He so desperately wanted her to wake up—

Her fingers moved again, and he was staring right at them when it happened. As tired as his eyes were, they could not deceive him.

Tommy jumped to his feet, almost falling over. He'd slept little in the days since they'd brought her in, and his feet barely held him as he stood and leaned over her.

"Honey, can you hear me?" He wanted to be hopeful, wanted everything to be back to the way it had been. And he wanted to apologize for causing this whole thing. If only they hadn't fought that night, and if she hadn't driven home—

A low moan escaped her lips, the most beautiful sound he'd ever heard.

Her legs shifted beneath the sheets, and one arm came suddenly alive, drifting up to her face to touch the bandages. Dozens of splinters of glass had been removed from her skin. Tommy could see the bruises around her wrist from the ropes that had held her. The man who had taken her...but his anger washed away.

He grabbed her hand, kissing it over and over.

Her eyes blinked and opened, dazed for a moment before slowly focusing on Tommy's face. He leaned closer and heard her murmur three words he didn't understand. She smiled, her hand dropping away. Her head turned as she drifted off again, this time back into a peaceful sleep.

Tommy screamed for the nurse, frantic that she might've come all the way back to him only to be lost again. He saw the slow rise and fall of her chest and relaxed. He leaned over to kiss her, and that was when the nurse and the policeman who'd been stationed outside her room burst in.

"She woke up. She talked! I swear!"

The nurse checked the monitors and instruments around Sally, confirming it.

"Yeah, she's sleeping now, a real sleep. She's got healthy alpha rhythms," she said, gesturing to one of the monitors. The nurse moved to Sally's bed and tucked the sheets in around her, touching her forehead and checking her color. The nurse turned and looked at the boy's face, and the concern there almost made her eyes tear up. "Don't worry, Tommy. Her stock just went through the roof."

The cop watched as the boy smiled. It would be nice to see a happy ending to this story. God knew if she recovered from her coma, it would be a lucky turn of events.

This young woman should have died out there on that lonely stretch of Florida road.

The young man turned and clearly wanted to hug someone, and the cop was simply the nearest target. Tommy embraced the surprised man, and the cop's expression moved through a quick range of emotions before smiling and patting the boy on his back with one big, beefy hand.

"That's okay, son. She's gonna be fine."

Tommy pulled away, wiping his eyes and apologizing, staring at his fiancé and watching the slow rise and fall of her chest.

"Yeah, she's sleeping okay now," he said, brushing the tears from his eyes with one hand. "She's gonna be okay. And when she's better, we'll have the wedding. She's already got the dress, you know?"

The cop nodded and started to turn away, but Tommy suddenly grabbed the cop's arm.

"When she woke up, she said something."

"She talked?"

The boy nodded. "But it didn't make any sense. Maybe she's so tired, she didn't know what she was saying."

The cop looked at Tommy, a young man he'd gotten to know fairly well over the past week. The policeman's assignment to the girl's room had been purely precautionary, just in case the wacko that had shot her in the shoulder and left her for dead came back to finish the job. He'd seen Tommy here every day, spending time in the hospital's chapel when he was chased from the girl's room. The boy was a good sort. He'd make a fine husband, if they could get through this whole mess and still end up together. And sane. But suddenly the cop was intrigued, his investigative senses sharpened after a week of dull hospital duty, guarding a girl that was probably in no physical danger other than her medical condition. If the girl had woken up and said "I love you, Tommy" or something like that, the boy wouldn't be discounting it so easily.

"What did she say, son?"

Tommy looked at the cop, hearing the sudden seriousness in his voice. "It didn't make any sense. She woke up, and looked at me, and it sounded like she said, 'Going to Liberty.' What does that mean?"

"I dunno," the cop replied, shrugging. "Probably nothing," he said, pulling a pad of paper from his back pocket to scribble down the mysterious words. "Look after her," he said, leaving the room and taking up his position in the hallway once again. On his next call in to the station, he'd would report on Sally's improved condition, and he would probably include these mysterious words, just in case.

To him, it sounded like she was babbling. Or maybe it was important.

David Beaumont made it all the way to Illinois before he could contain his curiosity no longer.

He'd driven all day through Indiana and the lower half of Illinois, looking for a place to stop for the night. He finally found an inexpensive hotel near the small town of O'Fallon, Illinois, just twenty miles short of St. Louis, and booked a room. Attached to the hotel, through a glass corridor, was a combination bar and restaurant where he could relax and get something to eat.

The news from the East Coast hadn't improved. The regular radio reports said the hurricane was moving slowly up the coast and was expected to make landfall again sometime tonight or in the morning. The reporters on the radio kept making the point that this would be the third time Mandy had made landfall—she'd already come ashore twice down in Florida.

David didn't know much more about weather than he had learned in school, but the way these guys were talking about it, this storm was one of the worst in a long time. There were reports of airports being shut down and roads and bridges being washed away by floods. It made David glad he left when he did—if the County Line Bridge east of Liberty ever washed out, it would cut off access to the highway. There'd be no way to get out of Liberty except for west, up through the Shenandoahs.

David kept remembering that strange dream of him and Bethany on a log raft, chased by a huge tidal wave. He'd been thinking about that crazy dream a lot today, driving through the flat country of southern Indiana and Illinois.

He checked himself into the hotel and took what was probably the best shower of his life. His shoulders ached from driving too long. After his shower, he toweled his hair off and put on fresh clothes, watching TV. The weather in North and South Carolina got top billing on CNN, with honorable mentions going to preparations for bad weather in D.C., Richmond, and Boston. Cities in the Carolinas were getting rain that was being measured in feet, not inches, and there was some scary footage of rising flood waters taking down a bridge in South Carolina.

Mandy was predicted to make landfall late tonight at someplace called Bogue Inlet, south of Cape Hatteras in North Carolina. The projected path showed the eye of the hurricane moving through eastern North Carolina and up into Virginia Beach, heading for Philadelphia. From what he could tell from the maps, the storm's eye would miss Liberty by less than a hundred miles.

Bethany's red book was in his bag, and he pulled it out and began leafing through it. She had spent a lot of time on it. He studied the pictures, the TV forgotten. She had chosen them carefully, smiling reminders of their trips up into the mountains or to Kings Dominion. There were souvenirs and receipts from their trips to D.C., and even a postcard from the American History Museum.

Had she bought a postcard that day? He tried to remember. They had walked hand in hand, eating lunch in the glass cafeteria at the Air and Space Museum before heading to American History. But he couldn't recall her buying anything during the visit.

He set the binder down and popped the rings apart, taking out the loose-leaf pages. All of the pictures and postcards were taped down, and he flipped over the page and examined it. David lifted up one corner of the Smithsonian postcard and it came loose from the paper. There was a date on the back of the postcard.

"9/12/96."

That was only a week and a half ago. The Monday he'd driven up into the mountains to think. That night he'd called Brian's house in California, talking to his crazy girlfriend.

He finally understood—she'd been planning this binder for a while, maybe since they broke up. She must have driven up to D.C. and collected these items, postcards and mementos. The menu from that great little Japanese restaurant in Georgetown, the site of one of their very first dates. Cards from the Smithsonian and the Washington Monument and the US Capitol building. All bought to fill out this binder.

David suddenly felt very stupid. Unworthy. Bethany clearly cared deeply for him, deeply enough to go to all of this trouble, reconstructing their relationship. She'd loved him, and he'd stepped on her heart.

He got up, disgusted with himself, and finished getting dressed, heading out to get some dinner. He walked to the hotel lobby and through the glassed-in walkway that connected the hotel with the bar and restaurant next door.

The restaurant was busy and the greeter, an older lady, stood with the clipboard in her hand, scribbling down names. David didn't want to wait and took a seat at the wide metal counter. He hated sitting at counters, but at least he could eat fast and get back to his room and catch some sleep.

"Can I get a menu?" he asked a waitress behind the counter as she went by, and she returned a moment later with one, handing it to him. He leafed through it, trying to decide what to get—dinner or breakfast. David almost always preferred breakfast.

"Coffee, hun?"

He looked up and saw an older lady waitress in front of him.

"Yeah, that sounds great." The cup of coffee helped him decide. Nothing went with coffee like breakfast food, and by the time he'd reached over to pick up a few packets of sugar, he knew what he was getting.

"Cream?" she asked.

"Yeah, a couple. Thanks." He poured them in and started mixing, expecting her to ask for his order. When a couple of seconds passed and she hadn't asked, he looked up to see that she was looking at him. It made him a little nervous, the way her eyes were taking all of him in. She smiled at him, setting the coffeepot down on a narrow, cork-lined shelf that ran around the inside of the lunch counter, a shelf that also held a collection of condiment bottles and drying water glasses.

"You're not from around here, are you, son?"

"Nope, just passing through," he said, shaking his head and reading her name tag. Doris. All he wanted was to eat and leave, not a lot of stupid questions. "Can you take my order, please?" he asked. The words came out sharper than he wanted.

She rolled her eyes and pulled out her order book, flipping it to the next blank check. "Sure, hun. What can I get you?"

He ordered, but the whole time, he could feel her eyes on him. When he looked up, she was still staring at him, even as her pen finished scribbling down the last of his order. His temper got the better of him.

"Did you need something else, Doris?"

She backed away from the counter and let out a little laugh, putting her hand to her chest. "My, you are in a testy mood, aren't you? Didn't your mother teach you better manners?"

He lowered his head a little, ashamed that he'd snapped like that. He was pissed about the weather and the red binder and he was taking it out on a nice lady, making an ass of himself. Standard operating procedure: pushing people away.

"My mother never taught me anything. She died, giving birth to me," he said, his voice considerably lower this time. He had no idea why he would tell a total stranger something like that, but the words were out before he realized what he was saying.

Doris stepped back up to the counter, patting David on one hand.

"I'm sorry, son. Nobody should have to grow up without a mother." She looked at his order slip again. "I'll be right back with your food."

She turned and hurried off. He could hear her in the back, telling the cooks to hurry with his food. It made him smile, hearing that nice lady doting over him even though he'd just been a jerk.

People were nice all over, if you really thought about it. Like Liberty. There were all kinds of nice people back there. Bethany, his roommate, old Mrs. Denners who ran the drugstore downtown. Great small-town folks who'd always been nice to him. And his aunt, even when she was in a poor mood and half in the bag, she was still family. As aggravating as she was, it was a hell of a lot better than having nobody.

Bethany.

Just the thought of her reminded him of the long, carefree afternoons they'd spent together at the video store, back when they had just been falling for each other. He remembered the playful banter that often accompanies the early stages of romance. Teasing around the edges, playful mocking. It seemed like a shame. It all added up to nothing.

But had it? They'd shared something real for a while. Their times together had been the best in his life. And Bethany had tried to help him, and he'd only pushed her away.

Other people had tried as well. What if the problem wasn't his job or Bethany or the Story or the ghost of his dead father? What if he was the problem?

"What's her name, honey?"

He looked up, surprised. His food had come, and he hadn't even noticed. And Doris had asked him a question.

"Who?" he asked.

Doris smiled and pointed at his food. "Must've been thinking about your girl. I brought you that food a while back, and you've been just staring at it. And in such an all-fired hurry to order, too! So, what's her name?"

"Bethany."

"Oh, that's a pretty name. Did you call her Bethany, or just Beth?"

"Bethany."

"Uh-huh," Doris said, looking at him carefully, her eyes studying him. "So why did you break up with her?"

He looked up, surprised.

"It's that obvious?"

She only nodded.

"I don't know. I guess I'm just so used to things going wrong for me, I figured we'd never last."

She nodded, not saying anything.

"Plus, I'm moving. Virginia to California. I broke up with her, but now I can't stop thinking about her." She seemed to understand. He felt like an idiot, opening up to this stranger, but she had kind eyes.

"I understand," she said. "My little sister was just like you, never lettin' herself be happy. Pretty soon she had nothing to live for at all," she said, her voice low. She shook her head as if she wanted to say more, but then she didn't. To David, it looked like she was trying to blink something out of her eyes. She smiled at him and walked away.

That was weird, he thought. She'd been happy and cheerful, and now she was suddenly sad. What had happened to her sister?

He dug into his breakfast. The omelet was amazing, and the coffee was a tonic for his soul.

After a few minutes, Doris came back over with her coffee and gave him a refill.

"Here you go. Sorry about that. Talking about Doreen makes me sad, even though it's been over a year."

David watched her carefully. "What happened to her?"

Doris started wiping the counter. "She gave up. Decided there was nothing worth living for. She was in high school and got dumped by a local guy she'd been dating. Vincent. That pretty much destroyed what was left of her self-confidence."

She looked at his questioning face and continued.

"Killed herself. Pills." Her eyes got distant.

"I'm sorry."

"She would have graduated from high school this past spring." She moved off to check on her other customers, leaving David to eat his omelet and toast.

Back in high school, he could've tried a lot harder. His Drafting 101 instructor told him he had real talent, and evidently the guy had been genuinely disappointed when David didn't sign up for any more of the architecture and drafting classes they offered. He told David that he had a knack for visualizing spaces and interiors. David was a whiz with maps, as well. But did that mean that he could've gone somewhere with it?

He thought about what Doris had said. What if he went on for the rest of his life always running away when things got too difficult?

It was the same with Bethany, with Liberty, with everything else in his life. The pictures in her book showed him how happy he had been. Now he was running away again. It was like getting drunk to avoid problems. David was beginning to see that his aunt's alcoholism wasn't too far from his own problems. They both ran away when things got rough. Maybe that's where he'd learned it.

He looked up and saw Doris standing down at the far end of the counter. She wasn't looking at him or talking to customers. Instead, she was looking at a guy. Actually, looking wasn't the right word. She was glaring at a big guy carrying two cardboard boxes of liquor. He walked around the counter and into the bar, a darker area off to one side of the restaurant. Over the door, a neon sign read "The Hole."

The man was ropey, muscular. As he passed Doris and headed for the bar, the man smiled and blew Doris a little kiss, his eyes fiery and strange. Even from his seat, David could see the man's smile wasn't meant to be friendly.

Doris didn't react—instead, she wandered back over and stood in front of David.

"Sorry, hun. I didn't mean to fly off the handle like that. It's just that I don't talk about Bird very much. When I saw you sittin' there, feeling sorry for yourself, you reminded me a lot of her."

He was confused. "Who's Bird?"

She smiled. "That's what we always called Doreen. She was always flitting around like a bird, diving out of one thing and into the next. I called her that one day when our family still lived down in Nashville. It just kinda stuck."

He remembered the black bird he saw in the Shenandoah Mountains, the one that flew around him and landed on his car. A little shiver worked up his spine.

"You okay?"

He nodded. "Just thinking about your sister. Why...why did she do it?"

Doris just shook her head. "She said there were things she regretted not doing with her life, things that she'd wanted to do but never got around to. But she lost hope after she got dumped by that pig. It was only a day or two after that she took the pills," she said, looking at the entrance to the bar.

"Is he the guy?"

"Yeah. I don't think he cared what happened with her, one way or the other," she said. "He's been a pig as long as anyone can remember. He's mixed up in all kinds of shady stuff. His whole family is. And he's married—got a pretty little wife. Uses her for a punching bag."

David nodded, not knowing what else to say.

"But it wasn't really about him, or his violent nature," she continued. "It was Doreen. She'd dropped out of high school, and she planned on going to beautician's college but never did. She kept puttin' it off. Afraid of failing, I guess. Afraid of starting, if truth be told."

David nodded, knowing exactly what she was talking about. He had been afraid that Bethany would eventually tire of him, so he'd ended it first. He was afraid to let himself be hurt. But the pictures in her book spoke so loudly about how she felt about him. Had his fear of happiness made that all impossible?

Maybe not. Maybe, if he went back right now—

"It's right over there, hun."

She pointed over his shoulder. He turned and saw two pay phones hanging on the wall.

"It's pretty obvious how much you miss her," she said from over his shoulder. "To tell the truth," Doris said, "she's probably thinking about you right now, too."

It was that last part, the part about Bethany thinking about him, that made him stand up and start fishing change out of his pocket.

"Here you go," she said, sliding two quarters across the counter.

The phone rang and rang, but she didn't get up from the couch. Bethany didn't want to talk to anyone, not now, not ever.

She'd spent the entire day on the couch in her sweats, mindlessly flipping the channels and wishing for a different life. She watched the weather, hoping the hurricane would come and destroy this town. Put her out of her misery.

The deputies came last night around midnight and woke her up and asked her to come with them. When the vehicle had stopped in front of David's old house, Bethany had no idea what was going on. For a moment, she was worried that David had returned and hadn't even called her. The house was surrounded by deputies and cars and yellow "CRIME SCENE" tape that flapped in the breeze.

When they led her into the busy crime scene, it had all changed into a horrible nightmare. Blood everywhere in the living room, broken glass among stacks of moving boxes. Deputies everywhere, dusting and taking pictures.

A deputy walked her into the garage, and there, in the car, was David's aunt, sitting upright. Dead. The smell was horrible. In her shock, the deputy asked her to identify the body. After Bethany nodded, saying "yes" to their questions, the deputies took her to Aunt Gloria's kitchen and interviewed her at length, mostly about her and David and their lives. She kept asking if David was okay, but no one knew anything. Just like with Lisa.

Finally, when the deputies had run out of questions, they brought her back home. She'd come inside, walking past the deputy now stationed outside her house, and crashed on the couch, not moving much since.

She'd tried to call her parents on the cruise ship again, but they reachable. The ship's concierge told Bethany they were off ship on some snowmobile trip out of Anchorage and wouldn't return until Friday or Saturday, depending on the weather.

Somehow she knew that the ringing phone wasn't them. Reporters again, most likely. They'd been calling all day, leaving messages. There was no one she wanted to talk to except her parents and David, and it surely wasn't either of them.

No one could help her. In the past twenty-four hours, Bethany's world had come crashing down around her. She'd reported Lisa missing on

Monday morning—had it been just the day before yesterday? It seemed like a hundred years ago. She'd talked to Lisa, asking about the toppings she would want on her pizza. It had seemed so important then.

The TV had nothing interesting to say, nothing new about Lisa or Gloria and Abe. The local TV station was offering continuous coverage of the story, adding the death of Bernie, David's roommate, to the mix. Bethany saw a clip of herself, walking into Gloria's house to make the identification.

The phone continued to ring, but she ignored it.

After six or eight rings, the phone fell silent, but as she reached for the remote, it began ringing again. She'd disconnected the machine. The last thing she needed right now was a tape full of "I'm sorry's" from people who weren't really sorry and would never understand exactly how she felt. The rest of the messages were from reporters or people at work or people. Other friends wanted to know if she'd heard from David, wanting to know if he knew what had happened to his aunt yet.

She'd been over there so many times when they'd visited his aunt. Bethany had talked to Gloria more than a few times in the months she'd been dating David. But on Sunday morning, when Bethany had dropped by to catch David on his way out of town, she'd barely acknowledged Aunt Gloria. And now the woman was dead.

Nobody seemed to know what was going on—not the deputies or Sheriff Brown, certainly. There was no news on David—apparently, the deputies were trying to track him down. News of the deaths had gotten out fast, and the TV reporters were already broadcasting the names of the victims and speculating about the causes of death, alternating that story with news about the approaching hurricane.

Mercifully, the phone finally fell silent. Bethany turned the TV back on and tried to lose herself in the show but ended up only staring at the screen.

After half a minute, she stood and walked into the kitchen with her blanket wrapped around her. She needed ice cream or something.

The phone rang loudly, making her jump. She ignored it, heading to the fridge.

The phone wailed at her to pick it up. The piercing sound was starting to give her a headache. She reached out and grabbed the phone to pick it up and hang it back up, but in her haste, her pinkie hit the CALL button. She rolled her eyes and reached to hit the END button when she heard a quiet voice on the other end.

"Bethany?"

She put the phone to her ear. It had sounded like David, but that was impossible.

"David?"

"Bethany, is that you?" It was David. His voice, somehow.

Bethany felt all of the strength leave her. Her legs buckled, suddenly unable to support her. She crumpled to the floor.

―――――――

"Bethany?" he yelled into the phone. Some of the customers turned to look at him. "Bethany, pick up the phone! What's wrong?"

Doris watched from the register, suddenly sure that things for the boy had taken a nasty turn. Maybe he'd be able to deal with it better than Bird had. She pulled the boy's change from the register and walked over and set it down next to his plate. She filled his empty coffee cup one more time and glanced at David before moving on to help her other customers. He seemed to be talking in normal tones now. She hoped for the best.

―――――――

He gripped the phone tightly. She said she'd fallen and hit her head, but his screams had brought her back around quickly.

"David, is that really you?" Her voice was soft, far away.

"Yeah, Bethany, it's me," David said. "I know you probably don't want to hear from me, but I just wanted to tell you what a fool I was. I've been thinking a lot about it. Maybe going to California is a bad idea. I think...maybe I'm just running away from my problems..."

He gripped the thick metal phone cord—one of those that keeps people from cutting off the handset and stealing it—and twisted it around his finger.

She was crying on the other end, confusing him. He'd expected a reaction, but maybe it was too late. Maybe she never wanted to talk to him again.

"Honey, you okay?"

"Yeah," she said, the tears coming faster. "It's just so good to hear your voice. And two days ago, I would've given anything to hear you say those things. But the problems we had just seem so small now, so easy to fix compared to..." she said, the tears slacking off.

"What? What happened, Bethany?" He leaned against the wall, shielding the phone with his body to hear her better.

"Oh, David, I can't believe it. It's just so horrible," she sputtered. Her words came out so fast that he could barely understand them. "Lisa is dead, murdered. They found her in her car. And your aunt is dead,

David. And Abe Foreman is dead."

He froze, unable to move.

"Bernie, too. The town is going crazy. The deputies are looking for you..."

A few minutes later, David stood with the phone in his hand, the conversation over. He'd promised to call her tomorrow, after he'd talked to the sheriff's office.

His aunt was dead, found by deputies on Tuesday night, dead in the garage of carbon monoxide poisoning. Bethany had been called in by the deputies to identify the body because David wasn't around.

Abe Foreman had been in the house too, dead, evidently having fallen from the balcony and smashing into the glass coffee table in the living room. How many times had he walked past that balcony outside his bedroom, thinking about what it would be like to fall over? And that glass coffee table. How many times had Aunt Gloria yelled at him for putting his feet up on it. She'd warned him to not get it dirty, even though David could point out a dozen white stains from the spilled vodka?

Lisa Stevens, Bethany's best friend, was dead, too. And not just dead—she'd been found murdered. Her body left in her car out by the mall. Naked and dead in that little Tercel of hers that she loved so much.

Bernie, too. Hung himself in the closet of their apartment. David's home until a few days ago.

It was all too much to process.

Bethany was in shock, too—he'd hardly recognized her voice. With him on his way to California and her parents gone on their cruise, she had no one to talk to. Lisa had been her best friend, her confidant, her only ear when he'd left her. And now she was dead.

Bethany had blamed herself, babbling on about how they were supposed to get together on Sunday night, because Bethany had been upset about David's leaving, and Lisa had never shown up. David suddenly felt like it was all his fault. If he hadn't left, Lisa wouldn't have been out that night.

She'd probably still be alive.

It was all too much. David stepped away from the phone and staggered over to his seat, oblivious to all the curious eyes on him.

The strange boy with the sad eyes sat back down at her counter, stunned. He grabbed the coffee cup with his change beside it and downed the entire cup in one huge gulp, ignoring the heat.

Doris walked back over, curious. Clearly, he'd had some kind of tiff with his girl, but now he looked shaken, like he'd seen a ghost.

She set the pot down and reached out, taking one of his hands in hers. She usually had a feeling about people, and this time she'd been right. Things for this boy were going very badly. From the look on his face, they'd just gone from bad to worse. Much worse.

"What happened?"

He looked up at her, but the words came slowly.

"I have...I have to go back. Right now," the boy said, shaking his head. "My aunt, she's...dead. Two nights ago. And Bethany's best friend is dead too. Murdered."

Wow, Doris thought. Sounded like the kid lived in an unlucky town.

She patted his hand. "Have some more coffee, and I'll heat this up and put it in a box, okay?" She filled up his cup, spilling a little as her shaking hand poured. "You leaving now?"

He nodded, staring ahead, deep in thought. "I need to get going."

"Hey, look at me," she said, waiting for him to look at her. "You're wiped out, son. I know you want to go now, but you're liable to wreck. My advice? Get a good night's sleep, eat some food, then leave in the morning. Early."

He looked at her and finally nodded. "Mind if I get that food to go? I want to eat in my room, watch the weather."

She nodded and whisked away the remains of his plate. Heading in the back, she heated it up and put it in a to-go box, along with some extra bread and a slice of pie.

As Doris cashed him out and bagged up his food, she glanced over at the kid. He was staring straight ahead, trying not to cry. Holding in his emotions. Eventually they would all come out. They always did.

He reminded her of Bird. She was always holding her tongue, never talking about things. Getting dumped by Vincent Luciano had sent her into a downward spiral that ended with a stomach full of pills.

Doris hoped things would turn out better for this kid.

She walked back over, handing him the bag of food. "I put some extra stuff in there. And a piece of pie."

"Thank you," he said, looking up at her. "And thanks for getting me to call. I don't want to even think about if I hadn't. I could've gotten all the way to California—"

She patted his hand. "Don't trouble yourself, son. Go eat, get some sleep, start fresh in the morning. You'll thank me."

He nodded and smiled.

———

David thanked the nice lady and left. He headed back to his room, thinking about how things can change so quickly in one's life. If he hadn't gone in there for dinner, or if he hadn't gotten Doris as his waitress, or if he'd waited for a table instead of sitting at the counter, he probably would've gone another day or two before he called Bethany, if he'd called her at all.

Bethany had said the deputies were looking for him. He was Gloria's only next of kin. But apparently, traveling across the country makes a person hard to find.

When David got back to his room, he called the Liberty Sheriff's Department. He talked to them as he packed, telling them when he'd left Liberty and explaining the circumstances of his trip west.

Once the deputy found out he had been out of town, they seemed to lose interest in him. David suddenly realized they had him on their list of suspects. It was suddenly obvious—four people were dead, all close acquaintances of his. But once they realized he'd been out of town, the questions got shorter. Finally, when he told them he was heading back, the deputy asked him to come in for a longer interview.

He hung up, frustrated. He wanted to leave, but the nice lady was right. He should probably get some rest and leave in the morning, but he couldn't imagine trying to sleep. There was too much going on for his mind to find any rest.

He needed to go. Now.

Coming back to his room from dinner, he'd seen it was clear outside, perfect for traveling. But a few minutes of the news back in his room revealed a different story—things were getting nasty all up and down the East Coast. The local weather guy in St. Louis couldn't seem to forecast anything with the hurricane messing up weather patterns all over the eastern half of the country.

He did some quick calculations as he finished packing: two days of driving, with a minimum of stops, would get him in around midnight on Friday. He'd be driving right into the storm, but there was no avoiding the weather. Things in Liberty were going into the crapper, and being 1,000 miles away only served to drive him on.

He took a quick shower—who knew when he'd get another one—and left the key in the room. Lugging his things out to his car, he noticed the wind was starting to pick up. He wondered if it was the far, outer fringes of the storm. No rain yet. But he should hurry.

The dark on-ramp carried him back onto the freeway, this time heading east.

CHAPTER 13
Thursday, September 22

Sheriff Brown's deputies were usually a laid-back bunch of guys. The sheriff ran a very loose ship, so to speak, and the deputies enjoyed very little oversight. He never really demanded much from the good old boys on his force except unquestioned loyalty and a closed-lip policy that made the Masons look like the Toastmasters.

But over the past forty-eight hours, things in Liberty had spiraled wildly out of control.

It had been two decades since this small-town police force was forced to deal with something like this. And this time, the sheriff was simply not up to the task. He'd badly botched his first press conference on Tuesday, and now members of his force were questioning themselves, their training, and their level of preparedness. There had been three more deaths in their town. Their ranks were stretched thin, as they worked to investigate the Stevens' murder and three other deaths. The media was calling for another press conference, something the sheriff was apparently dreading.

———

State Police Lieutenant Blake sat in the chair across from Sheriff Brown's desk, listening to the latest reports coming in from the deputies and keeping his opinions to himself. He had arrived from Richmond early on Wednesday afternoon and was trying to get a grasp on the situation—and trying to find anything to change his impression that this sheriff was a complete idiot.

So far, his initial impression was right on the money. Brown was in over his head.

Of course, four deaths in forty-eight hours would rattle anyone's cage. And it made Lieutenant Blake very nervous. Deaths like this weren't supposed to happen. Blake had never heard of a string of deaths like this in a small Virginia town. Richmond and the northern cities had their troubles, to be sure, but nothing like this.

The man that fell from the balcony, Abe something, had also suffered a massive trauma to the side of his head that could not be accounted for by the fall. Investigators found a broken jar, leading to the theory that the man was attacked upstairs, possibly by the woman, and fell to his death while trying to flee.

And the woman? Her wrists had been bound at some point and then the bindings removed, likely even before she'd gotten in the car. Had it been some kind of kinky sex thing gone wrong? Blake wasn't sure.

And that other kid, the roommate of the Beaumont boy. Hanging himself?

These deaths, all on top of the gruesome murder of Lisa Stevens.

But the fat man across the desk from Blake was woefully incompetent. Blake had seen this type before, the small-town sheriff ensconced in his own private kingdom, working the town's political figures to insure a lifetime position. Blake could feel the man grasping at straws, trying to conduct an investigation after years of organizational atrophy. Blake coming up from Richmond had started out as just a courtesy, but now he was ready to step in and take over the case. Officially, he had the authority to do so at any time, but the State Police usually avoided that—it didn't look good.

Even if he did take over, Blake was worried. The state police were spread thin already, with the hurricane. Many of their ranks were in the Virginia Beach area already, assisting in the coastal evacuation. If he needed help, he'd have to rely on this small-town police force. He could also request some FBI guys from the Richmond office. For the moment, Blake held his tongue as Sheriff Brown refused any outside help, stating that Lieutenant Blake was only there to "advise." But Blake wouldn't be surprised if, as soon as the weather passed, this sheriff's office was overrun by experts and officials from all over the state.

Norma Jenkins' stomach roiled in pain.

The report on the deaths of Abe Foreman and Gloria Thatcher was the lead story in the *Liberty Gazette* on Thursday morning, and the article affected Norma more than she thought possible. The deaths were reported on the news last night, but the newspaper article was longer and gave a lot more detail.

And Norma, an ex-cop, knew enough to read between the lines—the Liberty Sheriff's Department was taking it on the chin. They had no idea what was going on.

The deaths had occurred on Monday night but were not discovered until late on Tuesday evening, which explained why they weren't reported on the news until noon on Wednesday and hadn't made the paper until Thursday morning. But the deputies had all day Wednesday to work the case before the paper went to bed, and the few facts they had released to the press were very disturbing.

First, with even a casual reading of the report, it looked like the deaths were anything but accidental. Her stomach tightened at the thought. They were still being reported by the press as accidents. The bodies had been sent to Fredericksburg for autopsy, and the specifics of when and where and how Abe Foreman and Gloria Thatcher had died were conspicuously missing, replaced by conjecture and supposition on the part of the reporter covering the case.

Any beat cop, even in a town like Liberty, could take one look at a victim and have a pretty good idea what had killed them. And the third mysterious death, David Beaumont's roommate, wasn't helping. Norma was sure, by now, that the Sheriff's Department was on thin ice.

She'd seen it all before. Norma knew how the town would react.

Back before Jasper Fines had killed the best damn sheriff this town ever had, Liberty had worked itself up into a frenzy. Strangers were instant outcasts, shunned by the townspeople and, at the same time, watched very carefully for signs that they might be "the Killer." Townspeople locked their doors for the first time, or walked the streets with shotguns. Norma had seen the fear and confusion and the panic that could seize her town. If these new deaths turned out to be murders, Norma knew the panic would start again. It was no wonder the Liberty Sheriff's Department was keeping information from the press.

She was also sure Sheriff Brown would never be up to the challenge. People thought she'd left because of what happened to Beaumont. In reality, she had wanted to stick it out and make it a career, but she couldn't work for a witless bureaucrat like Jes Brown. He'd gotten Beaumont killed, and once he was in charge, he started insuring that he'd always have the job. Sucking up to the city council and looking the other way on the petty crimes of the rich and powerful. It had been enough to make Norma sick.

Norma's mind pondered these things as she went about her Thursday morning routine, which was identical to her Wednesday morning routine, and every other weekday, for that matter. She packed her lunch, drove to the school, climbed aboard her bus, and started her rounds. All along her route that morning, her passengers climbed up onto the bus, stopping to shake rainwater from their coats or stomp their boots. There were more parents at the bus stops, watching over their kids nervously.

She was distracted that morning, her passengers got away with a little more mischief than normal. Norma Jenkins was too deep in thought to pay much attention.

After the high school run was finished, she had a break of nearly an hour before she started the junior high and elementary school runs. She parked her bus and walked across the wet pavement and into the high school to use the phone.

Norma dialed the number from memory.

"Sheriff's department," the annoyed voice answered.

She cleared her throat. "Ah, yeah, is Deputy Frankin there?" Norma heard the rustling of some papers and then the voice came back on, utterly businesslike and devoid of human emotion. "No, she's not in today. Would you like to leave a message?" The voice sounded less than interested in the prospect.

"No, that's okay. Thank you," She hung up, dialing Joyce Frankin's home number.

"Hello?"

"Hi, Joyce, it's Norma," she said, trying to sound friendly. Norma rarely socialized, but she and Deputy Frankin had been friends for years, occasionally getting together. "Taking the day off, huh?"

Joyce answered, her voice thick. "Yeah, I'm not feeling too well. Too many late nights. How are you?"

"Oh, I'm okay. Hope you get better—that sounds like a nasty cold," she said. "Hey, I've got a question for you. A work-related one."

That was the cue that the friendly part of the conversation was over and the business part had begun. Norma had known Joyce for years, and they'd always felt comfortable talking shop. Two women in law enforcement could always find things to talk about, even if it was only to complain about how the men on the force treated them. Norma knew that Joyce couldn't and wouldn't tell her anything confidential, but Norma could usually glean a few interesting tidbits from whatever Joyce said—or didn't say.

"Sure. What's up?"

"I was reading about Abe Foreman and Gloria Thatcher. I'm betting they are homicides. Do I win any money?"

"What makes you think that?" Norma noted that it was not a denial in any way.

"Well, accidental deaths are rare enough, and double accidentals, the odds are like a million to one. You know that."

The other end was quiet for a moment. "Uh-huh."

"And there's nothing in the press release about method or time of death," Norma continued. "It sounds like they're still working that up. And if they're still working it, then the case would still be considered as foul play until that angle had been eliminated."

There was a chuckle from the other end, a low, nasally laugh.

"You should've stayed on the force, Norma. You're better than half the deputies, and you got all that from the press release."

The line was silent for a moment, and Norma knew Joyce was trying to figure out exactly how much she could say. Joyce didn't like Sheriff Brown any better than Norma did, but that didn't mean she could break confidentiality.

"Well, you're not far off," Joyce began, and Norma relaxed. "Abe Foreman took a twelve-foot swan dive off the balcony into a glass table."

"Tripped? How high was the railing?"

Joyce chuckled. "Thirty-six inches. Standard."

"Too high, probably."

"And Gloria Thatcher had rope burns around her wrists and ankles, indicating she'd been tied up prior to her death, but no rope was found."

"Uh-huh." Norma said, trying to file it all away in her head. It went without saying that this information was for Norma's use only—they were good friends, but if a word of what Joyce was saying ended up in the *Gazette*, she'd never talk to Norma again.

"How's the big man holding up?" Norma asked. "This must be a big change from covering up drug busts."

The sniff that followed Norma's question could've been cold-related, but Norma didn't think so. "He's doing okay," Joyce said. "He thinks it's a kinky sex-thing gone wrong. But that press conference on Tuesday was a joke. He looked like a horse in a burning barn."

Norma smiled at the reference. Joyce used it all the time.

"He was going to have them every day," Joyce continued. "Now he's changed his mind. Funny how getting embarrassed can do that. Now he wants to have some kind of a town meeting on Saturday or Sunday. I don't know if they can pull it all together by then."

Norma nodded. "Town meeting? That would be smart. It would calm folks down. Where?"

"Not sure yet," Joyce said after blowing her nose loudly. "Probably somewhere big, like the gym at the high school," Joyce answered. "If it happens, it will be on the news. He needs to do something—people are starting to freak out, Norma."

Just as she figured. "Yeah, I remember how that can happen."

"No, I'm serious," Joyce said. "They gave me crap about calling in sick. The department is short-handed."

"Is any of the press still around?"

Joyce grew quiet. "Most of the media has already left town after that press conference. Off to cover the storm. That was before the other three deaths."

"Are they coming back?"

"Not sure," Joyce said. "You better not be thinking of an anonymous tip, Norma," she said, her voice a deep growl. "That one lady from Pittsburgh has been digging around. Tina Linsey. You know how Brown loves attention? I don't think he likes the kind he's getting from her, even if she is cute. And anything you give them won't help—it'll just make things even crazier.

Norma had to admit—she had been pondering how an anonymous tip could ruin Brown's day.

"You read my mind, Joyce. But you're right—it wouldn't help. What about the Stevens girl?" Norma asked.

"Oh, that's a bad one. Strangulation, multiple sexual assaults, both pre- and post-mortem, and the missing parts..."

Norma gripped the phone, feeling her stomach clench.

"What? Her tongue, of course."

"Yeah, but that wasn't half of it," Joyce said quietly. "It was horrible. The thumb on the right hand was missing. The hand was propped up on the steering wheel like it was pointing at something. The tongue had been removed and placed inside her left hand, which was curled up into a fist in her lap."

"Oh, that's horrible," Norma said.

Murders in Liberty. Missing parts.

"The scene was way too gruesome to make it into the paper," Joyce continued. "Even some of the deputies were shocked at the brutality, Norma."

Norma finally found her voice. "Did they find the thumb...at the crime scene?"

"Nope, gone."

"Animals?"

"Clean cut. And the car door was closed."

Norma's mind raced with possibilities. It all sounded too familiar. Norma remembered Beaumont saying that murders where parts of the victim were taken were pretty rare. The guy had killed twice, each time taking pieces. Maybe these "collection" cases were more common now. Or maybe Fines had returned...

No, it was impossible.

"Norma, you there?"

She cleared her throat. "Yeah. I was just thinking about that poor girl and what her last hours must've been like." She was quiet for a moment, then continued. "Thatcher and Foreman, were they missing anything?"

Joyce was quiet a moment. "I really can't get into it. That information is being held really close."

Norma nodded, even though Joyce couldn't see her. "I understand."
Again, not a denial.

"Sheriff Brown is freaking out, Norma. Lieutenant Blake is getting
fidgety, like he's wanting to take over."

"What about the crime scene? Are they still processing it?"

"No, just guarding it. Why?" Joyce sounded suspicious.

Her stomach clenched. It knew what she was about to ask.

"I want to see it," Norma said. "I've got a really bad feeling about
this."

Joyce said nothing for a moment.

"I don't know, Norma. What do you want me to do, get out of bed and
let you into a sealed crime scene? So you can poke around? And what do
you expect to find, anyway?"

"I don't know," Norma said. "But I know something is going on,
something bad. I think looking at the scene might help. I worked the
other crime scenes twenty years ago. Maybe I can help. And if I find
anything, you can call it in. Take the credit."

"Norma, you're not a deputy any more." Joyce said. "You drive a
bus, for Christ's sake."

"I know."

"What could you contribute to the investigation that the rest of us are
missing?"

Norma could hear the anger in her voice, and probably some
frustration. Any member of law enforcement hated being second-
guessed, especially by civilians.

"Because I've been there before. I've investigated homicides, you
know. I know what to look for. And you just said that Brown has no idea
what he's doing, and Blake's still on the sidelines."

Joyce didn't say anything.

Norma dove into the silence. "I was on those cases with Beaumont,
Joyce. We almost caught the guy. I think I could help."

Norma heard a rustling of sheets and blankets. "Christ. Okay, but this
better not take long. I'm sick and don't feel like doing this. Meet me
over there in five minutes, and I'll get you in."

"Okay, see you there."

"And don't park too close."

Norma thanked her and hung up. Her mind was already starting to
discount the utterly crazy theory she'd come up with. Jasper Fines, or
whatever his name was, was most likely dead now, dead for many years.
Most criminals had a tendency to end up in jail or dead in a gutter. And
even if he were somehow still alive and free, why would he come back
here? What possible motivation could he have?

These thoughts and many others filled her mind as Norma drove to Gloria Thatcher's home. People died all the time, and people were killed. Maybe it was a copycat. Maybe Jasper Fines had ended up in prison and shared his story with the wrong set of ears, and the listener had come back to try his luck here, too.

Norma was sure the crime scene had been gone over carefully. The chances of her finding anything helpful were slim. But she wanted to do something. She wanted to help.

For the first time in a long time, the pain in her stomach dulled. But Norma did not notice—her mind was far too busy, pondering other things. Other courses of action, other memories from the past.

David Beaumont was driving east. It was early morning and the sun was blinding him.

He was cranky. The soda from this morning's McDonald's breakfast wasn't sitting well, and that, combined with the hundred other things going through his mind, made for a bad morning.

He had more Rush in and cranked to help him focus. Early Rush, "*Hemispheres*," filled with that relentless drumming from Neil Peart. He was listening to "Cygnus X-1" now, an eighteen-minute masterpiece. It was pounding in his head, keeping him focused. He was driving as fast as the weather permitted. He expected to be pulled over at any moment.

Bethany. He couldn't get the picture out of his head of her going down to his aunt's house to identify the body before it went to Fredericksburg for autopsy. Abe was dead, too. The chances of him falling over the balcony were pretty slim. It was a high railing. David knew it well.

And his aunt, dead from carbon monoxide poisoning? What had happened to her? Had she gotten drunk and fallen asleep in the car, starting it up but forgetting to open the garage door? She didn't even drive that much anymore. David knew her car could sit for weeks in that garage and never go anywhere. She'd called him regularly to fetch things for her, too lazy—or drunk—to drive.

The rope burns around his aunt's wrists didn't make any sense either. Just the idea sickened him. And why would the deputies ask if Aunt Gloria had ever tried to kill herself before? Was that their theory?

He squinted into the rising sun. It pounded through the windshield. He moved the visor again, trying to block it. Wasn't it supposed to be cloudy from the hurricane?

The driving was starting to get to him as he neared Dayton, Ohio.

The sun was in his eyes and the roads were busy, or maybe they just seemed busier because he was so tired. He tried to exit the highway and got confused, ending up on another one heading north. Finally, he saw an exit for some town named Cooper's Mill with a McDonald's next to the exit.

Relieved, he pulled off the road, finding an empty spot in the back of the McDonald's parking lot. Locking his doors, David sprawled out on his front seat for a couple of hours of shut-eye. Just a little sleep, he told himself, and then he'd grab another big soda and some food and be back on the road.

———

Norma pulled her car to a stop a few houses down from the Thatcher residence. As she parked, it started sprinkling. The weather report said it would start to rain heavily by Friday morning and then get really bad on Saturday.

The hurricane had slowed to a crawl—it had hit land this morning in North Carolina, and now the experts thought it would take several more days for the storm to move offshore. The school administrator mentioned this morning that they might have to close down school for a few days.

Joyce's little green car was already parked out front of Thatcher's house. Norma could see Joyce through the rain-streaked window—she was talking to a couple of uniformed deputies as they leaned on their patrol car in the Thatcher driveway. The deputies were wearing bright orange raincoats and easy to spot, even from halfway down the block.

After a few minutes, the two uniforms climbed into their cruiser and left, driving right past Norma's car. Norma ducked down as they passed, feeling like an idiot. After they left, Norma moved her car a little closer and got out, pulling her coat close around her as she walked over to where Joyce stood, waiting.

———

Joyce started to say something to her friend Norma but suddenly felt a sneeze coming on. She reached into her coat for another tissue.

"Hey," Norma said quietly as she walked up.

Joyce nodded. "They've gone to get donuts and coffee. You've got twenty minutes." Joyce's voice sounded odd, lower than normal. She held up a key. "I told them I had to pee."

Norma leaned in a little closer. "Okay. You sure you want to do this?"

The question was a simple one with a difficult answer. Joyce wasn't really risking her career on this, but it went without saying that bringing a civilian into a crime scene could get her in trouble, if the wrong people found out.

"Yeah," Joyce said, nodding at the house. "But let's get inside before someone sees you." She pulled out two pairs of rubber gloves and handed one set to Norma. The door was barred by yellow police tape, and Norma held it up and out of the way for Joyce to unlock the door.

The cause of death for Abe Foreman was immediately apparent as soon as you walked into the living room—massive blood loss. Joyce could see a huge dry lake all around the remains of the coffee table. Spatters and drops of blood decorated the walls and couch. Bloody streaks ran down the numerous brown boxes—apparently, Gloria Thatcher had been in the middle of moving.

Norma glanced up at the balcony, and Joyce knew what she was looking at. The high railing would be very hard to accidentally fall over.

Joyce cleared her throat. She felt like garbage.

"The garage is out here." She led Norma out through the kitchen past a small dining area to a door that led out to a small garage.

When they stepped out into the garage, Joyce imagined that she could smell the gas, even though carbon monoxide was such a deadly killer partly because of its odorless nature.

"The car was unlocked. Nothing out of the ordinary except for the garden hose jammed into the tailpipe, secured with rags," Joyce said, pointing with one gloved hand. "The other end was in the window of the door behind the passenger seat." Rain pounded on the roof of the garage, sounding deep and hollow. Joyce watched her friend's eyes as they took everything in. "The victim was in the front seat," Joyce continued. "Her hands and feet had been recently bound but there was no rope found anywhere in the house."

Norma nodded, looking up at the ceiling. Joyce glanced up, wondering what Norma was looking for. "If the guy inside killed her, how did he die?"

"One theory is that Foreman killed the woman, making it look like a suicide. He goes back inside and searches her room, then trips over the railing."

"Hmmm," Norma said.

"I know. It's lame. Plus he had a head wound. Brown thinks it was some kind of sex thing. She was tied up, the man tripped and died, and she killed herself out of shame."

"That's worse than the first one," Norma said. "Brown is reaching. He was never a good investigator, only good at working the system."

Joyce nodded. She knew where Norma's anger came from. Everyone in town knew the Story. "You still blame him for Beaumont's death," she asked, already knowing the answer.

"He's always been opportunistic," Norma said, avoiding the question.

Joyce nodded, not pressing the issue. It wouldn't do any good.

"Well, either way, she died in the car. That much was clear."

Norma nodded as they walked back to the living room, with its broken table and the dried blood. This was the room Joyce wanted her to look at. There was something off about it, something Joyce hadn't been able to put her finger on. But it would be best if Norma felt free to poke around. Joyce decided to make it easier for her. "I really do have to use the restroom. Back in a second."

Norma nodded and watched Joyce leave, heading farther back into the house.

Was it proper procedure to use the restroom at a crime scene? Norma didn't know, but she glanced at her watch. They would be leaving soon.

Norma took in the room, studying it from more than one angle, wandering around the other side of the broken table to stand by the large open window. She avoided the dark stain on the floor. There were several sealed boxes sitting around in short stacks, but on the floor next to one of the chairs was an open box filled with papers and letters. She glanced at the side of the box and was surprised to find the box was apparently full of Beaumont's original, handwritten case files. What were those doing here? Had they been given to his widow upon his death?

Norma squatted next to the box and flipped through the top few files with a pencil, not wanting to leave any prints. Suddenly, she realized that what she was looking for was right on top.

JASPER FINES, APRIL 1978

The file on the case that killed Beaumont was sitting right on top, a spot of dried blood on the cover. The box must've been open when Abe Foreman fell.

Norma heard the toilet flush and a door open, and in one swift and impulsive moment, Norma picked up the thick file from the box and stuffed it inside her jacket. She turned just in time to see Joyce come around the corner, and something else caught Norma's attention.

"Find something?" Joyce asked, pulling her jacket on.

Yeah, but nothing I can tell you about. Not nice to remove crime scene evidence, even if no one else would be interested in it.

Norma pointed at something else.

"That picture frame."

Joyce stepped around in front of the fireplace, something you could not see when you came into the house. You had to walk into the living room and turn around to see the fireplace and the mantle above it.

"Yeah. Who leaves an empty frame on a mantle like that?" Joyce picked it up with her gloved hands and flipped it over—the backing was barely attached and two of the little hinged pieces of metal had been moved aside. "She was moving. Or someone took a souvenir."

Norma shuddered, careful to hold the file inside her jacket.

"Maybe Gloria had already boxed the picture but left the frame. Though there are other pictures still in their frames."

All pictures of Beaumont and Grace and her sister Gloria. They looked so happy. Norma's stomach churned.

Joyce nodded. "No pictures of the boy. Strange? Maybe she already packed those."

Norma shrugged as she walked past Joyce and pulled the front door open, stepping out into the rain.

Jack slept in his room until 10:00 a.m. and then showered and went next door for a nice breakfast at Denny's. He read the paper and enjoyed his Grand Slam and coffee and wondered what he should do next.

He could tell the town was restless. The waitress acted skittish, and the other customers seemed preoccupied, deep in thought. The paper was full of conjecture but little actual information other than that the sheriff's office was now investigating the cases with assistance from State Police officials. To Jack, that sounded like they weren't really getting anywhere.

Surely the kid had heard by now. Which meant he was probably on his way back.

Jack smiled and pulled the picture from his pocket.

Beaumont had his arm around his wife's waist. The ocean behind the pair was wide and blue and calm, and they were smiling, happy.

beaumont

Jack didn't like to think about Beaumont being happy. He wanted to remember Beaumont as a quivering pile of fear sprawled on the wet pavement at Jack's feet.

But there was nothing but happiness and joy and hope for the future on the face of the man in the photo. Jack wanted to crumple it up and throw it away. Instead, he stuffed it back in his pocket and started on his pancakes.

The urge had been satiated Sunday and Monday, and it had been wonderful. But now it was Thursday, and he was getting restless again. Jack needed a plan, one that informed the town that their worst nightmare, the Killer from their Story, had returned. He needed to do something spectacular, something that would be remembered for years. Something that, as a side bonus, would kill a great number of Beaumont's precious townspeople.

Jack hated this town for what it represented to him—stability, happiness, acceptance. And he couldn't get Beaumont's smug, smiling face from the photo out of his mind. Beaumont had died "saving" this stupid town, managing to chase Jack off before he could kill any more people. But that was all about to change. Beaumont hadn't saved the townspeople. He'd only bought them a few extra years.

And now, Jack was here to collect on the longstanding debt.

———

Norma drove back to the school, the file on the seat next to her. She didn't like stealing, or breaking crime scene protocol, but it was necessary. Brown was an idiot, and in over his head. Norma had to help, whether Sheriff Brown liked it or not.

The rain was falling steadily now, and even though she knew it was supposed to go on for days, she just wished it would dry up. She wanted the sun to come out. Rain always reminded her of that night on the road. She'd held his head in her hands—

At the school, she climbed back into her bus and did her routes, her mind on the file in her car. As soon as her routes were over, she drove home in her car and carried the file inside. She made herself a warm cup of tea to settle her stomach. It was turning over like it was trying to escape.

Sitting down at her kitchen table, she opened the thick file. It was full of reports, photographs, and maps of the crime scenes. The top few pages, summing up the case and explaining how everything had turned out, were in a different handwriting, and Norma remembered that the temporary sheriff had filed those reports in the quiet days after Beaumont's death. Someone else must've boxed up the papers, along with his personal effects, and given them to his wife. These were his personal notes on the case, not the official case files, which were stored in a file room at the sheriff's office.

The folder was in reverse chronological order, starting at the bottom with the reports and coroner's findings on the first victim. Norma already knew most of the facts, but starting at the bottom, she read everything through to refresh her memory, in case there had been any details in the case she had not known about.

The little boy had been found by a landowner in a field north of town, where the Motel 6 and Denny's were now. The body, after it was identified, had been sent by ambulance over to Fredericksburg and examined. The details of the autopsy were gruesome and as disheartening as ever to Norma. When she got to the part about the boy's toe being missing, she simply nodded her head and continued. The other victim had been a town council member; the family man's murder kicked the investigation into high gear.

Beaumont had instituted a citywide curfew and instructed Norma and his other deputies to begin questioning outsiders and strangers in town, compiling a short list of names. One of the names was circled in bright red pen, "Jasper Fines," followed by a short interview of the man. Evidently he'd been stopped by one of the deputies near the drug store on Dale Street and had been asked some routine questions. The man had not acted strangely, the deputy's handwritten report said, so he was not detained.

Underneath, in bright red pen, and in the scrawl that Norma immediately recognized as Beaumont's, was a note. "Too bad—could've saved a lot of time!" She laughed out loud at his handwritten words, touching them gently with her fingers.

Next was a report on the famous stakeout at the Food Town. They had staked out the supermarket for three nights, finally catching a break. Deputy Norma Jenkins had been working undercover, dressed as a civilian, going in and out of the store all night. She'd been jumped by Jasper Fines, pulled behind a dumpster in the alley. It felt strange, reading about herself in third person in the report. It had happened so long ago, it was like she was reading about someone else. While she read, her hand drifted up to touch her bent nose.

Norma only skimmed the last section about that final night and the confrontation on the rainy highway—she already knew all of that. She looked only for new information, or things that others remembered differently.

She read the written remarks of the replacement sheriff: Beaumont had been, in his words, "crafty and clever and more than willing to stand up for what he believed in. He'd taken the necessary steps to make sure that no more killings would take place."

Strong words in support for Beaumont. Maybe that explained why he'd only served one term before being voted out in favor of Jes Brown.

It was all pretty much as she'd remembered it, and Beaumont's personal file wasn't too far off from the official record, only including his own personal observations.

She started over, reading the autopsy reports and the rest of the report again, searching for clues. She was about halfway through the report on the Food Town stakeout, reading every page carefully instead of just flipping through randomly like she had done before, when she tried to pull up the next page and found it was stuck to the page beneath.

She slid a finger between the pages and pulled easily, separating them. There was a small reddish stain up in the top left-hand corner of the second page. Norma saw a similar smudge of brownish red on the back of the previous sheet. She touched the substance gingerly and it flaked away. There was a faint coppery smell.

Blood.

Why was there blood in the report? Files like this were always kept away from any crime scene evidence. It wasn't possible this was from the original crimes.

Norma remembered seeing the spatters of blood around the room at Gloria's house where she had found the box. But the folder had been closed, hadn't it? Blood on the cover of the report she could understand, but inside? Had someone pulled it out to read it, someone else who had been at the crime scene?

Who would want to read about a string of murders that happened so long ago? It could've been one of the deputies investigating the crime scene, but Norma didn't think they would be interested in this ancient case.

Abe? Maybe. Abe surely already had all the information he needed on William Beaumont and his estate—why read a criminal case file? And it was probably Abe's blood, effectively eliminating him as the mysterious reader.

Maybe the aunt had glanced through the box and read through the file. But to account for the blood, she would have had to read it after Abe died. Why take the time?

It was almost as if someone had read it after the man had fallen, spattering blood everywhere, and the reader had flipped the pages with a bloody finger. But that didn't make sense either—who would read a report with a dead guy at their feet?

The deputies had listed the deaths as accidental and suicide, but Norma didn't buy it. No one with half a brain could believe that Abe had killed Gloria Thatcher.

Was there another person in that house the night of the murders?

What if it was Jasper Fines, back for another visit to his old haunting grounds? Or a copycat killer, seeking to emulate what Jasper had done so many years ago? Whoever it was, they had been interested in reading the file. If Abe and Gloria were killed by an intruder or a prowler, they would have fled immediately. Why wait around, reading and taking the chance of getting caught?

It was a ludicrous idea, one so completely "out there" she could probably be locked up just for mentioning it to anyone. Something straight out of "The X Files."

If Jasper Fines were back, or someone were copying him, their most obvious target would be the Beaumont family. The son was gone, and Beaumont's only other family was Gloria Thatcher. Had Abe just been in the wrong place?

Norma spent several hours more rereading the file, before she had to leave to make her afternoon runs. Later, as she was driving, the kids in her charge got away with more roughhousing than normal while Norma continued to ponder the case.

David woke and stretched. He glanced at his watch and cursed. Three hours! Christ!

He'd slept too long, sacked out in his car in the McDonald's parking lot. He was losing valuable time.

He opened his door and climbed out, his knees and back popping as he stood. The sleep had done him some good, and his head felt a little clearer.

Inside, he wanted breakfast, but it was too late. He ordered off the regular menu and grabbed his food, finding a table near a group of old people. He could've eaten in the car, but he wanted to think. He needed to clear his head.

While he ate, he listened to the group of old people chatting at the table next to his. They were enjoying their "senior" coffees and discussed politics and the local economy and other topics of the day. They were friendly, giving each other guff and arguing their points of view. It gave David pause—what was it like to have a group of friends like that? People you could debate anything with?

He went back to his food, scarfing it down. He needed his strength if he were going to drive through the night. His thoughts turned to her, seeing her and comforting her. She was a strong girl and more than capable of taking care of herself, but she needed him now.

How quickly had all his thoughts of going to California gone out the window? He couldn't think of anything else but her. David needed to grieve, too, but he hadn't really allowed himself to think about that.

He finished up and found a pay phone, checking in with Bethany and giving her a quick update on his progress. They only spoke for a few moments, but it made him feel better. She was okay. She started to share what had happened in Liberty in the last twenty-four hours, but he stopped her, telling her he'd be there soon. After saying their heartfelt good-byes, he hung up, refilled his large soda, and left, heading back out to his car.

A large black bird sat on the hood of a car a few spaces over from his Mazda, but David did not see it. He was thinking about the weather and Bethany and the shortest path back to Liberty, Virginia. The bird watched him start the car and drive away. It hopped over to the edge of the car's hood and stepped off, swooping up into the wide blue sky. It joined a flock of birds, a ragtag cloud of various species, as they circled slowly above the parking lot.

As a group, they turned, following the Mazda.

––––––––

Julie spent all day Thursday going through all the reports, and generating new ones, and she thought she'd begun to spot some patterns. She was working at her adopted desk in the computer center, downing cup after cup of bad coffee from the machine out in the hall. She split her attention between the latest computer printouts and the maps that Chris printed out.

He had gone home Wednesday night at around 7:00 p.m. and evidently was surprised to find her back at the reports at 6:00 this morning. He would've been even more surprised if he'd known that she'd only gone home to change clothes and grab some takeout.

The horrific Green River killings did seem to lead to other cases, if the times and dates and methods of death in each case were to be believed. Working chronologically, the Cray put together something no investigator could, finding another large group of similar murders in different parts of the Los Angeles area several years later, with a dozen or so murders in southern Washington, Oregon, and Northern California, linking the two.

And carefully working backward from the Green River killings and assuming the same method of operation in the killer, the Cray had found several score of murders across the country. It was almost impossible to believe, but she had the proof right there in front of her. If this was the work of one person, he was surely one of the most frightening and disturbing people to ever live.

"Okay, now what?" Chris asked over her shoulder, sounding tired.

Julie turned to look up at him and saw how red his eyes were. "I'm probably done with you for the day," she said, smiling. "Go home, see you tomorrow. This search that's running now should be it."

He nodded. "I have some other stuff to wrap up. I'll check in before I leave," for once not contradicting her. He must be getting tired. They were both running on coffee and adrenaline.

She studied the monitor. This new search had forty minutes left to run. It was prepping the data to display all the cases that fit Julie's parameters across the United States from 1966 to 1986.

As crazy as it was, somewhere along the line, she started to feel like they might actually be onto something here. The cases were all very similar, and investigators on each of them had made similar comments. If only the detectives had known about each other, they might've been able to track down a suspect. But interagency communication was difficult, and national clearinghouses of crimes and criminal records were recent phenomena.

She studied her printouts and was surprised to hear the computer beep at her—the forty minutes had passed in the blink of an eye. This sort of thing often happened to her—she got caught up, losing track of time while searching for the solution to a puzzle. And this puzzle was the most interesting one she'd ever tried to solve.

She slid the mouse out from under a pile of papers and clicked on the SEARCH RESULTS—GEOGRAPHIC DISPLAY box. The screen cleared, and a full-color map of the United States popped up, followed by a sprinkling of dots of many different colors. A legend at the bottom defined the years for each of the 21 colors.

Julie followed the loose pattern of colored dots back across the nation's midsection, moving into St. Louis and Chicago, then on to Indiana and Ohio and Pennsylvania. There were not as many dots as out west, and this information was consistent with a possible serial killer. They teach themselves the best ways to operate, and they grow in knowledge and experience, taking more lives as their confidence builds. There were also dots of the same colors that were far away from the other concentrations, and those cases could probably be eliminated.

She zoomed in on the East Coast and found several unsolved murders in the Pittsburgh area that followed the same pattern. She clicked again to scroll down the coast to show all of Virginia and was surprised. There were only three dots, colored the pink of 1978, all centered in a little town northwest of Fredericksburg, Virginia.

Julie reached over and grabbed her comprehensive printout, flipping through until she found Spring 1978. There were about forty-seven cases from all over the United States (this printout listed them chronologically), but only a few on the East Coast. She scanned for the mention of Virginia and found them.

Two collection murders and another death had occurred in a little town called Liberty, Virginia, in the spring of 1978. Local sheriff reports showed that in two cases, toes from the victim had been removed.

The first murder had been that of a young boy, and the investigating officer, a Sheriff William T. Beaumont, summed up the facts in his well-written report, clearly separating them from the speculation that inevitably works its way in. The crime scene investigation was thorough, especially considering that it had been done eighteen years ago and out in the sticks. The autopsy, carried out by a county coroner in Fredericksburg, determined the method of death as strangulation, and note the absence of the smallest toe on the boy's left foot. The coroner speculated that it might have been removed post-mortem by animals— the body had been dumped outside. Julie guessed that the coroner hadn't even entertained the idea of a "collector" back in those days.

A second killing occurred a few days later. By this time, the proactive sheriff had instituted extensive questioning of outsiders, roadblocks, and a dusk-to-dawn curfew. But it hadn't helped the second victim, a city councilman with a family and a successful business.

And one of his toes was also removed.

After that, Beaumont had set up a sting operation at a local supermarket in an attempt to catch the killer. The stakeout had worked, and the killer had barely escaped. One of the deputies, a woman posing as a shopper, had been grabbed and assaulted by the man—and had gotten a good look at him. On the next page appeared a black and white police sketch of a very scary looking man. His face was lined and aged, even though the reports said he couldn't have been older than twenty-five. Long scraggly black hair framed the face, and dark eyes glared back at her. The eyes were the worst part.

The rest of the file was in a different hand, surprising her. But it was because the third death in the case was that of Beaumont, the sheriff and lead investigator. A few nights later, Sheriff Beaumont had set up a roadblock, but the suspect had turned the tables, attacking the roadblock and killing Beaumont before escaping into the night.

Julie sat back from the computer screen, thinking.

She continued scanning the reports that followed the one for Liberty, working in chronological order through the late 1970s. In each case, some small part of the victim's body was missing. The sheriff in Liberty, Virginia, had come closer to catching this man than all the other big town police departments on the East Coast. If it was the same guy, he was a mean one, and very dangerous.

Chris returned to the computer center to find Julie hunched over her reports, a cold cup of coffee forgotten on the table beside her. She was staring at the monitor, which showed a map of the United States sprinkled with scores of colored dots. The legend at the bottom showed years from 1988 to 1996, each marked with a color.

"Any luck?"

She turned, looking tired. "Unless I'm crazy, it looks like with the parameters we were using, the same killer or killers has been working all over the country for at least twenty years."

"You're crazy," he said. Chris was carrying his coat and briefcase.

"I know," she nodded, her eyes bleary. "But the M.O.'s and dates match up. He started out in New England somewhere in the mid- '70s and is still out there, as far as I can tell."

"Look, I gotta go—"

"Just let me show this one thing," she said, turning and clicking on the screen a couple of times to bring up a map of the United States. The map's colored dots had been replaced with a full spectrum of colors, each marking a bar per year. Short blue bars covered the northern and Middle Atlantic states, green bars across the northern states to Seattle. Yellow bars, orange ones all down the coast to LA and across to Texas. Florida with a long red bar that stretched from Texas to Florida's Gulf Coast.

The colors were confusing, too much for him to follow. He leaned in closer. "What does all this mean?"

She pointed at the screen. "I think this guy has been traveling the country for over twenty years, killing. He came close a few times, but he never got caught. No one ever stopped him. He's been the Green River Killer and a dozen other aliases. And he's still out there, as far as I can tell."

"Don't get me wrong, but remember: we just supposed to be testing the database," he said.

"I know, I know," she said. "I can't believe it either. But I've been going over the cases for hours, and it all fits, as crazy as it sounds. No one figured it out because the cases were too spread out. They happened in towns all over the country, and there was no reason for the jurisdictions to communicate. The binding factor, the fact that the man was a collector, didn't get a lot of publicity in most of the cases, because it's just too gruesome."

She thought she was on to something. He didn't have the heart to tell her the whole thing was crazy. Instead, he just nodded.

"Oh, and I've got a picture of him."

On the screen, the colored map disappeared, and a black and white sketch of a man's face popped up.

"Ugh, he's an ugly sucker. Look, let's talk about this more in the morning—"

"He was almost caught in 1978, in a little town in Virginia. He got away, but they got a good description. They came closer to catching him than anyone, even the task force. Of course, the guy had just been starting out. The sheriff in the little town ended up getting killed for his trouble."

Chris thought about it. It might be possible. It was hard not to get caught up in her enthusiasm. "What are the chances this guy is still out there?"

She was looking down at his coat. "Sorry, Chris. I was supposed to let you go home by now. I guess I'm too caught up in this. I keep looking for holes in this data, but I can't find any."

"It's okay," he said, nodding. "Just remember, it's only an exercise."

She nodded. "The search algorithms we're using are doing a good job of sorting out the irrelevant cases, leaving nearly all positive returns that fit the parameters. And the sheer computing power of the Cray has reduced the search time by a factor of 10,000. A team of researchers would take two or three years to put all this together, and the Cray did it in under a week."

He nodded again, not answering.

"It's okay," she said, smiling. "Go. I've got a few more things to do—is it 7:30 already? Wallace has probably already left."

Chris' eyes widened. "Why do you want to talk to him?"

"Don't worry, Chris—I'm not going to embarrass myself," she said with a big grin. "I know it's a crazy theory. I just wanted to show him what the Cray came up with. See if he wants me to look into it further."

Chris exhaled. "Talk to him tomorrow. And go home-you need some rest."

The wind and pounding rain were adding hours to his drive. At 11:00 pm, David switched over from Rush's *Permanent Waves* to the radio to catch the latest news. The radio station wavered in and out of clarity, blocked by the mountains. He was in the hills of eastern Kentucky, and reception was iffy at best. He tuned the dial, trying to get the weather report back in.

"—Hurricane Mandy continues to move up the coast of North Carolina. High winds and heavy rains have caused severe damage in the Cape Hatteras region. Residents who ignored the National Guard's original evacuation orders are fleeing beach homes that are being destroyed by high tides and twelve-foot waves—"

The broadcast faded into static again as he passed between two large mountains. He fiddled with the radio but couldn't get the weather back.

It was late on Thursday night, and the car had been making strange, unhappy noises for about an hour now. David knew he was pushing it too hard. He'd topped off the oil and checked all the fluids at the last gas station, but the sounds coming from under the hood were wrong. He wondered if the car would even make it. Hell, he wasn't sure if he would make it. Parts of his body ached from sitting too long. He'd been driving for hours without a break. And the caffeine from the latest Big Gulp was fading.

The news came back suddenly, making him jump. "—and flash floods. The bridge linked several communities to the interstate. In other news, President Clinton and the First Family left for a week-long trip to California, and—"

David flicked the radio back to the Rush CD.

Suddenly, his head swam. He'd hit the leading edges of Mandy's outermost storms hours ago in southern Ohio, greatly cutting his top speed. The rain obscured David's already blurry vision, making it hard to see anything—or concentrate on the road. Maybe he should pull off, get a room somewhere in Kentucky.

During his last McDonald's break, David had spent a few minutes mapping out the fastest way back to Liberty. I-64 led through Kentucky and east into southern West Virginia. That was the way he'd traveled west, but going down through Richmond and back up didn't seem like a good idea. There were reports of massive traffic jams and multiple-car accidents as people fled the low-lying coastal regions, moving inland. He was planning to leave I-64 and take a shortcut through the Shenandoah Valley before crossing the mountains and heading down into Liberty from the higher country, avoiding the highway traffic fleeing the coast.

He cracked the window and cold, wet air played across his face, waking him. He reached for his last bottle of Jolt Cola in the passenger seat floorboard. If it couldn't keep him awake, nothing could. He wanted to drive straight through, but he was no good to Bethany if he ended up dead in a ditch.

CHAPTER 14
Friday, September 23

The door opened, and his secretary poked her head in. Mike Wallace nodded and pointed at the chair in front of his desk before going back to the call.

"Yes, sir, that's perfect," Wallace said. He was coordinating with the White House to assist with the storm evacuation. While he talked, his secretary held the door open and directed Agent Julie Noble, the young woman from the computer lab, into one of the chairs in front of his desk. She sat down and waited for him to finish.

"The storm's knocked out some of the communications to those stations," Wallace said into the phone. "But the backup systems are working for now. We're prepared to help. It sounds like the Cape Hatteras situation is the worst?" He listened for a few more moments, offered to help again, and then signed off the call.

"Sorry about that," he said to Julie, who sat up straighter. "The White House is worried about the North Carolina outer banks—those people are having a hell of a time."

She nodded. "Thanks for meeting me."

"So, what can I do for you?"

She cleared her throat, glancing at her notes nervously. "Well, sir, I wanted to let you know that we've tested the Cray, and I'm not sure what if anything I've got here, but the reports show a pattern..."

Mike interrupted her. "Ms. Noble, you were assigned to test the Cray. Did that go well?"

"Yes, sir," she said, nodding. "The Cray works perfectly. The search algorithms are fast and very good at weeding out items that don't meet the search criteria."

"Good," he nodded. "Anything else you might have found is gravy. Relax."

She breathed deeply for moment and smiled. "I guess I just wanted to prove I could do what you've asked me to do."

He nodded. Her assessment was good, and at the same time she wasn't kissing up. "So, the system works correctly?"

"Yes. The hardware and software work well together. Cray really knows what they're doing."

He'd heard similar reviews from other people familiar with the machine. Maybe that huge chunk out of their IT budget hadn't been wasted after all.

"Well, I hear that you've been burning the thing up. What have you been using to test it?"

She glanced at her reports and handed him a thin one marked "Chronological - Executive Summary." She also passed him a map of the Pacific Northwest, and he noticed a smattering of colored dots around the Seattle area, the dots marked for years in the early '80s. Something clicked in the back of his mind, and it reminded him of the infamous Green River Killer case, one of the worst unsolved crimes in FBI history.

Julie cleared her throat and began.

"I decided to use the search pattern we discussed, the one that involved cases with missing or removed body parts. We refined the search instructions and narrowed the results."

"Uh-huh," he grunted, looking at the sheets.

"I searched the cases and found that most of the Green River killings that occurred in Seattle in the early 1980s involved a 'collector,' something I had not known. Are you familiar with the case?"

Wallace was instantly disappointed. He had hoped she and the Cray might come up with something tangible, if only by accident. But just seeing mention of the Green River Killer at the start of her report confirmed that everything that followed would be a work of fiction. Hundreds of investigators had spent more than a decade trying to track down the most elusive serial killer in the history of the nation, and nothing had ever come of it.

He remembered the early 1980s, and the shame brought upon the FBI and law enforcement agencies all over the Pacific Northwest. Many investigators felt the killings ended because something had finally happened to the killer, but others, including Mike Wallace, felt that was only wishful thinking. Wallace had always thought the killer moved on, never getting caught. Sometimes, it still bothered him.

When he finally answered, his voice was sharp. Cold.

"Yes, I know the case. Very well, actually. I hope you're bringing all of this up for a good reason."

"Well, the search parameters were to look for a chronological and geographical list of unsolved 'collector' homicides," she said.

If she'd been put off by his reaction, she hid it well, Wallace noted. He nodded along, wondering where she was headed.

"The Green River killings may have only been a small part of them," she said, standing and walking around his desk, pointing at the color map of the United States she'd handed him. "From the data I've compiled, it looks like a 'collector' or series of collectors could have been wandering the United States for many years now. That map shows a listing of 376 unsolved 'collector' cases around the country from 1976 to present. Filtering out distances, I narrowed it down to 114 cases that could have been carried out by the same person. The colored dots show years, and as you can see, a pattern is readily apparent."

After a moment, she went and sat back down.

He scanned the map and the corresponding list on the report, trying to keep from smirking. It was what looked like a random scattering of colors, but as he studied them, the colored dots did slowly appear to form a pattern, almost like a loop. He needed to visually discount the grayed out, anomalous points of data, but a "pattern" of colors emerged, starting in New England in the early mid-'70s. The pattern went west to Seattle, south to LA, and then back east to Alabama. There were even a few dots marked "1996."

But what was he really looking at? The truth about the Green River Killer had never been released to the public because the investigators in the case were still holding that information back in case a serious suspect ever surfaced. Wallace remembered reading the reports coming out of task force in 1984 and '85, lengthy reports written by exhausted investigators using every method possible to stop the string of deaths.

The reports were always depressing—more killings, more deaths, no clues, and no suspects.

One of the leading theories surrounding the end of the Green River case was that the killer had simply moved away. Exhaustive work had gone into searching all over the country for other cases that matched the Seattle slayings, but few had turned up.

Julie's report showed many such cases, including five similar deaths in Oregon and three in Northern California in the years after the Green River killings ended. He remembered a mention of this in some of the later reports published by the Green River Task Force—some speculation followed that the killer had gone south to the San Francisco area, but there had never been enough evidence to corroborate that theory.

"These are all collector cases?"

She nodded. "Yes. The pattern is there, but the body part taken changed often. Toes and fingers, mostly," she said, making a face. "A few other parts."

"You searched for what, exactly?"

"We searched for all unsolved cases involving 'collection' of a body part, sir," she said. "There were many unrelated cases or cases that couldn't have been committed by the same person due to location. Those are in gray. We narrowed them down to a set of murders that could, theoretically, have all been committed by the same person. Those are in color."

He glanced up at her. "You sound nervous, Julie. Almost like you don't believe what you're looking at either."

"I don't," she admitted, nodding. "I know it sounds crazy. But I triple-checked everything, and it is correct. The data is right. I'm just not sure how much to believe."

He flipped to the first case report and began reading. Bangor, Maine, 1974. Victim was a young woman whose body was found dumped in a shallow ravine. Coroner's report mentioned that "the victim's thumb was not present," saying it had been removed prior to death and not by animals or scavengers.

Immediately, it sounded suspiciously like one of the Green River killings.

He flipped through five more short reports. Pennsylvania, New York, Ohio. More of the same, more pieces "collected." Cases where information was never shared between jurisdictions or states.

Mike reached forward and picked up his phone without taking his eyes off the report, buzzing his secretary. "June? Yes, cancel my 10:00, okay?" He grunted his thanks, hung up, and looked at Julie. "Give me a half hour to look through this stuff. Grab some breakfast."

She nodded and stood, leaving him to study the reports.

Rain pelted the windshield. The wipers were on high, flapping back and forth, futilely trying to keep the glass clear. Thick, black clouds blocked out the sun. At least it was daylight, David thought. It was easier to see.

He'd stopped overnight for a scant few hours of sleep, but now he was back on the road, the exhaustion wearing him down. David focused on thinking about Bethany, hoping that she was all right. He wanted to stop and call her, but didn't dare pull over, not even for a minute. Every time the car came to a rest, he felt the urge to sleep. And he needed to keep the car running—it was making those awful noises again. David knew that he was pushing it. After six days of almost constant use, the strain was starting to show. He dreaded seeing a whiff of smoke appear from beneath the hood or turning off the engine to gas up.

He willed the car to make it all the way back to Liberty. After that,

David didn't care. He would be happy to let the car expire in Bethany's driveway.

For now, he had the music cranked. Rush was helping keep him awake again. He'd been switching back and forth between Rush and Guns and Roses, mostly, wearing out the CD player. This one was *Roll the Bones*, one of Rush's later albums, with a song called "Dreamline." The song was about facing adversity and getting past it, getting on with life. It was what he was trying to do—go back to Liberty and face his problems instead of running away from them.

Maybe he'd end up in California anyway, but not because he was hiding out. Maybe she'd even come with him.

Geddy Lee, the lead singer for Rush, sang loudly about redemption. Between the high-pitched singing and the crazy drums and the manic guitar work, David was awake for now. He hoped he'd get another hour down the road before pulling off for breakfast and more coffee.

Twenty-nine minutes later, she was seated back in her chair in Mike Wallace's office, her stomach somewhat settled with a bagel and coffee. She was incredibly nervous—and she hadn't even gotten to her outlandish request yet.

"Ms. Noble, this is impressive," he said, gesturing at the map and stack of reports on his desk. "I had some of the other maps and reports brought up. The investigative approach you've followed has been very thorough, very professional."

"Yes, sir," she nodded. "I think that as crazy as it sounds, there might actually be something to all of this."

He nodded at her solemnly, as if admitting something he didn't really want to.

"Perhaps. I've decided to put a couple investigators on this, to look into your findings. I've also spoken to Chris Hanson, and he's willing to work with anyone we bring in on this. He'll run the Cray and you'll walk the others through your research."

Julie swallowed. She started to say something and then closed her mouth. He must be thinking there was something behind her report if he was assigning other agents to investigate it. Others would be looking at her reports and her maps, things she had produced over that past days, when all of this had been simply an academic exercise.

"Don't worry," he said, misunderstanding her silence. "I'm not taking you off of this. Even if it turns out to be nothing, we'll get more experience on the Cray."

She sat back, relaxing. "Thank you, sir. I'd like to stay involved, obviously."

"So, where should these investigators start?"

She thought about it for a second or two. "The original reports should be verified. Some of the "collector" data might be wrong, eliminating cases," she said, pausing for a moment before continuing.

"But, before that, I think someone should go down to Liberty, Virginia. This weekend or next week, at the latest. To interview one of the original investigators."

Mike Wallace looked up at her, surprised.

He'd read through the Liberty, Virginia cases—Ms. Noble had mentioned them several times, stating it was apparently the closest the 'collector' ever came to being caught. There was even a sketch of the suspect. He'd toyed with sending someone down there to interview some of the original investigators, especially after what he'd remembered reading in his *Daily Bulletin* yesterday morning, but that would have to wait.

They needed to take this slow, methodical. The Green River cases were the most important. The investigators would start with the original Green River Killer files from the task force, insuring they did indeed fit the 'collector' pattern Julie had come up with.

"You think that's where he was almost caught?"

Julie nodded. "Yes, sir. There and in Seattle, if it's really the same man. I also have a theory about Seattle—I think he trained an accomplice— but Liberty was the closest. They chased him, almost cornering him. And there's a witness—one that survived contact and lived."

He looked up, thinking. She was green, as green as they came. But she was excited, and he didn't want to crush her spirit. "You think someone should go down to Liberty? Any suggestions on who?" he asked with a smile.

"Well, I'd like to go, obviously. The original deputy's name is Norma Jenkins. And it would get me a bit of field experience. I'd just verify the facts, especially as it pertains to the 'collection' aspect of the case."

Mike Wallace thought about it. She was a new agent, trained to take care of herself, but nowhere near ready to manage an actual investigation. If the report in the Bulletin had no connection, then she was just doing a simple interview.

He leaned forward and handed her a copy of Thursday's *Daily Bulletin*, the daily internal FBI newsletter.

"Did you see this?"

Folded open to a photocopied article from Thursday's *USA Today*, it read:

Girl Found Murdered in Small Town

He watched her reaction as she read. A young woman had been murdered in Liberty, found on Tuesday morning. Investigators felt the murder was ritualistic in nature—some of the victim's body parts were missing.

He'd had June, his secretary, run down a copy of the article from yesterday.

She looked up at him. The look on her face made a chill race up his spine.

"It's a weird coincidence, right?" He asked. "I know what you're thinking. The possibility is intriguing but very unlikely, wouldn't you say?"

She nodded, agreeing. "But what possible motivation could he have for returning after so many years?"

"Right," Mike answered. "We can't send a case investigator down to question this woman directly, or officially. But if you want to go down, I'll approve it," he said, rolling the dice. It wasn't protocol, sending a green agent out on a two-decade old investigation. But she deserved the break. "You'll be on your own time, though."

"I'll go down tonight or tomorrow and talk to her."

"No need to do that," he said. "You can wait until the storm is over."

She nodded slowly, then looked at him. "Actually, sir, if you don't mind, I'd like to move forward on this. Immediately."

He smiled, not at all surprised by her enthusiasm. He knew her history at the academy. "Okay, but with the weather like it is, I doubt you'll be able to get through. And remember, this is just an interview. You're not an experienced field agent. If you're not careful, you could quickly get in over your head," he admonished.

"Yes, sir."

"You really shouldn't even take your firearm, but I don't like my agents wandering around unarmed," he said, smiling. "Also, take one of those new flip cell phones. If you find anything interesting, call it in."

"Yes, sir," she answered.

Everyone started somewhere; everyone had their first field interview. It might as well be on a case she understood well. He reached up and handed her a laminated card with two phone numbers on it.

"Those are our situation desk numbers. Anything happens, or you learn anything important, call. Those numbers are manned twenty-four hours a day, and the information is routed to the right people with top priority. You will assist whomever we send down. And don't get involved in their murder investigation—I'm sure they have their hands full."

"I understand, sir."

She nodded and left his office quickly. Wallace smiled—she was probably worried he was going to change his mind. He turned and looked out the window—it was raining again. The muted TV in the corner showed houses on the North Carolina coast flattened by the storm. With the weather as bad as it was, he doubted she'd even get out of D.C.

———

In a weird way, Jack was starting to like this town.

It reminded him of Salem, Maine, the town where he'd grown up. The similarities did not end with the size of the town or the nature of its people. Both towns reacted to deaths within their midst in much the same manner. First had come shock—the *Liberty Gazette* on Wednesday morning had echoed the town's surprise and disbelief at the gruesome murder of Lisa Stevens. The paper that day was short on details but promised to follow up on Thursday with more information, but Thursday's paper ended up filled with a sketchy account of Abe Foreman and Gloria Thatcher's deaths. They were two of the little town's better-known citizens. The other death, that of a local boy, was barely mentioned.

Friday's front page was mostly news on Lisa Steven's homicide investigation, along with updates on Gloria and Abe.

The paper also mentioned David Beaumont.

Apparently, he'd learned what had happened and called the Liberty Sheriff's Department for information on his aunt's death. He'd been traveling cross country but was now returning to Liberty! Could Jack have gotten a better break? The bait apparently worked.

The other big story was an announcement by the Liberty Sheriff's Department. A town meeting would be held Saturday night in the gymnasium of the high school. Any and all interested parties were invited to hear what was going on with the investigation.

Jack Terrington read the story with gusto as he enjoyed another breakfast at Denny's. It wasn't often that he got to read about himself or his exploits. Usually he was long gone before the news made it into the papers or onto TV, if it ever did.

Jack found a USA Today and was surprised to find a short article on the coed he'd killed in Florida. Apparently, she hadn't died—she'd been shot through the shoulder but recovered, unfortunately. His mood turned sour in an instant. Jack hated losing, and now he had to remove one from his tally, taking it back down to 200.

Gloria Thatcher had talked a lot, mostly in an attempt to convince Jack of her worth. The main reason David Beaumont had left was because of his father and the fame that surrounded defeating Jack. The pressure of living in his father's lengthy shadow had been too much for David. He'd come into some insurance money related to the sheriff's death and bailed as soon as he received the first payment.

Ironically, it sounded like David hated the sheriff almost as much as Jack did.

Jack looked forward to meeting the kid—they could chat about how much each of them hated the elder Beaumont. And when the conversation got boring, Jack would kill him. And retire.

break his leg first then shoot him just like the old man

His went back to the local paper—they had announced a town meeting Saturday evening at the high school to discuss the situation. "The high school gym will have ample seating for everyone, and all of the town's city council members, the mayor, and a member of the state police recently assigned to help the Liberty Sheriff's Department in their investigations will be attending."

seating for all of those liberty people in one location

Jack's mind thrilled with the possibilities. He wanted to add to the tally, and he wanted to go out in a blaze of glory before he retired.

Jack's mind conjured up pictures of fire and destruction.

———

The events of the past few days weighed heavily on her mind. Her stomach churned—the fire in her gut clouded her thinking. Lately, even the medications weren't helping.

Norma had called in sick this morning, something she rarely did. As a Liberty School District bus driver, she accrued sick leave but rarely used it. Her supervisor had been surprised to hear from Norma by the 5:00 a.m. call-in deadline. He would step in and drive the route for her.

She'd stayed up past midnight, reading the Jasper Fines case file again and comparing it with the articles in the most recent newspapers. She'd fallen asleep without taking her medication, and this morning she was paying for it.

Norma had taken her pills and tried to sleep, but around six she woke suddenly and ran to the bathroom, vomiting. And for the first time, she saw blood in the toilet. The doctors had warned her about the blood, either in her stool or when she vomited. But seeing it there in the toilet scared her. Ironically, her stomach felt better than it had in a week—probably all of the acid was gone for the moment.

The Jasper Fines case had almost killed her once. Maybe he'd already killed her—she'd just taken twenty years to die. Of course, it was her fault. She chose to pretend to be dead on that wet pavement that night, instead of helping her friend and mentor. Jasper might have killed her if she'd stood up to help, but at least she wouldn't have spent the last twenty years agonizing over that moment.

Norma took more medicine to replace what she'd thrown up. Giving up on sleeping, she made herself a bland breakfast of dry toast and cream of wheat. At her table, she flipped on the TV to watch the *Today Show*. The only story seemed to be the hurricane. It was still over North Carolina, moving slowly toward Virginia. People were out there dying, drowning. This world was a mess, and only getting worse with each passing day.

Norma tried to get her mind off the list she'd made last night.

It had all started out as an academic exercise. Norma had been pulling together her speculations on the similarities between the Jasper Fines case and the one going on right now. She'd jotted them down and set it aside, but the list had nagged her all night. After breakfast, she felt better. She cleaned up and risked another flare-up by picking up the list again.

In both cases, the victims were missing fingers. The coincidence could not be ignored. In both cases, the victims had either been lured somewhere and killed. Abe and Gloria, who were surely murdered, had been killed inside a large home and left for others to find days later. The killer would have to be strong to overpower Abe Foreman, so that probably meant a man. To be responsible for both sets of murders, he'd have to be in his late forties or early fifties.

And finally, there were the strange circumstances surrounding the gruesome death of Lisa Stevens. She worked at the same place as David Beaumont and was best friends with his girlfriend Bethany. She was found dead Nair the Mall, and Abe had been an investor in that project. And her body had been posed, pointing, with her removed tongue clenched in her other hand. Was it a warning or part of some bizarre ritual?

And Stevens had last been seen alive at the Food Town grocery store, the same location where Beaumont had set up his trap so many years ago. Norma touched her nose as she thought about the stakeout.

David Beaumont would be a target if he were still around. If Jasper

Fines was back, it made sense he would go after the relatives of Sheriff Beaumont.

Her stomach twisted, and she took a short break, chewing more antacid and watching a bit of TV. But the dumb show couldn't pull her mind away from the investigation. There was no way to prove that the killers were the same, no way to link the two together. And no one at the Liberty Sheriff's Department would listen to the ramblings of a sick ex-cop anyway.

She would give the file to the Beaumont boy when he got back—the papers were reporting that he was returning to town.

The phone rang, startling her.

"Hello?"

The phone connection crackled. Norma wondered if there were any phone lines down yet. Storms always took down trees in Liberty and up in the Shenandoah.

A voice came back to her, distant in the static.

"Yes, may I speak to Norma Jenkins, please?"

"You got her," Norma answered. Great, another bill collector. "Can I help you?"

There was another pause. "Hi, my name is Julie Noble, and I'm with the FBI. God, this static is horrible, isn't it?"

The FBI. A chill swept up Norma's arms, making her clench the handset of the phone. "Yeah, the weather's getting pretty bad out. Did you say you're with the FBI?"

"Yeah, I am. I'm up in D.C. You're aware of the Lisa Stevens case."

"Yes," Norma answered. "She was killed on Monday."

There was another long pause. "Sorry, but I can hardly hear you. Do you remember much about the murders you had there twenty years ago? They involved a suspect named Jasper Fines and occurred in—"

"1978. April. Yeah, I remember," Norma interrupted, her stomach flaring with sudden pain. Too many memories, piling up. "I think I know where you're going with your question, and I'll make it easy for you. Yes, there are many similarities between the cases."

There was quiet on the other end, stretching out to the point that Norma thought the connection had broken. "How did you know what I was going to ask?"

"I used to be in law enforcement," Norma said. "But I really can't speak about it—I have no idea who you are. You could be a reporter."

"I'm no reporter, I assure you," Julie said. "And if you don't mind me saying, you still sound like a cop. I'd like to come down and interview you. I can be there in the morning."

The pain in her gut flared again, but she ignored it. The woman was going to drive all the way down from D.C. in this weather to talk to her? "Yeah, but the weather is getting really bad. Are you sure you want to risk it?"

Maybe Norma wasn't the only one making connections.

"Yes, it's worth it," Julie said. "I'm packed, and I cleared it with my boss. I've got some interesting reports that you should see, and I think we could help each other out. I'll call you from the road, okay?"

"Okay," Norma answered, holding her belly. "And be careful."

"Will do."

Norma Jenkins hung up the phone and grabbed more antacids from her pocket and swallowed them dry, feeling them starting to dissolve in her throat. Her stomach felt like a hurricane, moving and churning. She could taste the coppery hint of blood in her mouth. Norma raced into the bathroom, barely making it to the toilet before her stomach heaved. She kneeled, heaving and spitting out blood and bile.

Finally, she stood and flushed, turning to the mirror. Blood spotted her face and stained her robe. Her sunken eyes and wayward hair made her look like an insane killer, streaked with the blood of her victims.

She cleaned up as best as she could, combing water through her hair with her fingers. The doctor said her body was tearing itself up from the inside, the corrosive acids leaking through two ragged holes in her stomach to eat away at the other organs. If the ulcers couldn't be contained, managed by medicine and a "calm" lifestyle, they could kill her.

And now she understood what he meant. This was the worst it had ever been. Norma felt weak in the knees and sat on the floor and hugging her arms around her legs. She felt light-headed and suddenly cold.

Things were only going to get worse. This FBI woman would be full of questions. The pain would only get worse until it consumed her. And, for the first time, Norma Jenkins didn't reject the idea outright. At least the chewing pain in her gut would be over, once and for all.

The policeman assigned to watch over Sally, the young woman recently awakened from a coma, had filed his case report on Wednesday evening. Her recovery was proceeding well, according to her doctors. For now, she was out of immediate danger. What had once been a gaping hole in her shoulder was now bandaged and healing, the bullet removed. And the medical staff was certain that few of the dozens of cuts from broken glass across her face, arms and chest would leave any scars.

At the end of his report, the policeman decided to include the three strange words she'd spoken during a brief moment of lucidity. The words didn't make any sense, and that intrigued him. It sounded like a location, but no one in the station had ever heard of a place named "Liberty." He'd included the word in the report for future reference.

The Florida division of the FBI was located in Tallahassee, the state capital, and a copy of the report filed on Sally was forwarded to their office on West Main Street, along with copies of every other report filed by every other police agency and office in the state. Most reports filed by the individual jurisdictions concerned petty crimes and were not reviewed; instead, they were boxed up and sent to a company in St. Louis that transferred the paper files to microfiche and computer data for storage and retrieval. All crimes in each state were eventually reviewed by the FBI, but most not for months.

Murder and attempted murder cases were the exception—these files were reviewed immediately by the FBI agents in each state office.

Sally's file was of great interest to the FBI because it had also involved the gruesome death of a law enforcement official, something no one ever liked to see. The FBI agent reviewing the file was personally pleased to hear that the coed victim was recovering. From the report, it sounded like the girl had a fiancé and a nice life ahead of her, fingers crossed.

The words "Going to Liberty" intrigued the agent. The girl fought her way out of a coma, and sees her fiancé for the first time since being nearly killed, and that's what she says? Those three random words? Why hadn't the first words been her fiancé's name, or something about her pain, or her injuries?

It did sound like the name of a place, so the FBI agent picked up the file and moved over to a desktop computer, one identical to hundreds of other desktop workstations in a hundred other FBI regional and state offices. The computer was linked to a central server in Washington, D.C., via a secure land line.

He tapped the keyboard to bring it out of the screen saver and typed in a command. He could hear the internal modem dialing up to connect with the FBI system in D.C. The screen beeped, and he chose "Location Database" from a menu, accessing a DVD-ROM database published yearly by the US Geological Survey that stored the names and locations of thousands of cities, towns, rivers, and other geographical features all over the word.

When the prompt appeared, he typed in the word "Liberty" and hit ENTER, waiting. Moments later, the green monitor displayed three towns in United States named Liberty—one in southern Maine, another in Virginia, southwest of D.C., and one in Alabama, east of Montgomery. Using the mouse, the agent pulled up maps for each.

There was nothing remarkable about any of the towns, all small and out of the way. He clicked out of the geographical files and searched for crimes in those towns. The young woman had been in the company of a maniac for at least forty-eight hours. Maybe she'd overheard something important.

There were no recent major crimes were reported in Liberty, Maine. A couple of recent arson fires had occurred in the Alabama location.

Liberty, Virginia, was different. The local authorities were investigating a recent murder. When the case officer saw the date of the murder, he stopped what he was doing and stared at it.

SEPTEMBER 18.

That was only five days *after* the Florida cop had been killed and Sally, the young coed, had been shot and left for dead.

After that, there had been three more unsolved deaths. Could there be some connection?

The agent was an experienced field investigator and had seen enough strange things to entertain the possibility. He turned, picked up the phone, and dialed the hotline for the FBI Situation Desk in Washington, D.C.

―――――――――

Three hours after leaving work, Julie Noble wasn't much closer to Liberty, Virginia.

She'd headed home to pack and left around noon, Julie was heading south. She took the beltway and then I-95, the main southbound artery out of D.C., as heavy rain fell from a dull, leaden sky.

The storm wasn't even here yet, and the rain had already caused several wrecks, backing up traffic. People in the D.C. area seemed to forget how to drive when there was any kind of weather. Last year, during a particularly nasty snow storm, she'd even seen abandoned cars by the side of major roads. It seemed some people would rather walk than drive in rain or snow.

After an hour of stop-and-go traffic, considered turning around—it was crazy, driving right into a hurricane. Instead, she exited the highway in Dumfries, thirty miles south of D.C., and sought refuge in a Bob Evans restaurant for a late breakfast and a several cups of coffee. The staff talked only of the weather—rivers and lakes were rising, and floodwaters were washing out roads in the southern part of Virginia. Whole sections of the Virginia coast were being evacuated.

Just after 3 p.m., Julie finished her coffee and her blueberry pancakes and headed back out into the rain. She walked to her Chevy Impala, a car she rarely drove. She nearly always took the Metro to work, and only used the car on the weekends. Julie pulled her jacket around her tighter—she'd decided to push on. Yes, the weather was bad, but what was going on in Liberty right now was important. And it was important that Julie be there. Maybe she could do some good.

Julie started up her car and then grabbed the phone the FBI had assigned her—it was one of the new Motorola StarTAC phones, the first flip-open cellular phone to come on the market. She made a call to the only hotel in Liberty and made a reservation—the woman on the line had been surprised to hear Julie was trekking to Liberty with the conditions as bad as they were.

When she was done, Julie pulled out of the parking lot and headed south.

The FBI Situation Desk filed the report from Florida along with the dozens of other reports that came in from all over the nation daily.

But the man assigned to the Desk at the FBI Headquarters building in Washington, D.C., was distracted by the weather outside. Yesterday, his wife and children had been involved in a minor traffic accident after she picked up their kids from school. He spent several hours talking to his wife, who was not injured, and dealing with the insurance company. Both of his children had minor injuries, and his thoughts were with them in the local hospital.

When his replacement arrived for the 4 p.m.–midnight shift, the exiting man only mentioned the most important items, including several weather-related incidents regarding agents and FBI offices in the south. He was too concerned about his wife and children to linger.

His less-experienced replacement reviewed the incoming Desk Reports and entered each into the computer, as was routine, but he saw nothing in them that was terribly important. He had not read the Friday edition of the FBI's Daily Bulletin until very late in his shift, and his tired mind did not make any kind of connection between the deaths in Liberty, Virginia, and words of a coma patient in Florida.

David was back on the water. The ocean stretched out as far as he could see in every direction. This time, he was alone on a small island.

A big wooden raft floated in the ocean fifty feet away. On it, David could see Bethany and Lisa and Bernie and his Aunt Gloria, along with a half-dozen other people he knew.

They were all frantically paddling away from a massive tidal wave that arched up over their raft. David yelled at them to paddle faster, but it wasn't helping. The wave and the hurricane behind it were almost upon them.

There were birds in the air all around the approaching wave, dipping and flapping and spinning in the air, nipping at the wall of water. It looked like they were trying to slow the wave. But it was impossible—the wave was just too powerful. One black bird broke away from the group and flew in David's direction. The huge black bird flew straight at him, screaming at him, putting out its razor-sharp talons. He ducked out of the way—

And woke up.

David blinked. He was in the wrong lane. A massive truck was bearing down on him. David swerved, his hands slick on the wheel. The truck zoomed by, huge and loud, missing his car by inches.

He sat up, panting, and slapped at his legs to wake himself up. He was in his car, driving through the rain. There was no tidal wave. Raspy unhappy sounds issued from beneath the hood.

David looked for any traffic and slowed the car, pulling over to the shoulder. His sweaty hands were shaking. He was pushing himself too hard and had fallen asleep at the wheel. He was tired, but he would be no good to Bethany if he wrecked.

The recurring dream was so odd—what did it mean? If that bird hadn't awakened him...

He shook his head and rolled down the window. Cold wind and spatters of rain invaded the warm car. He put his hands out the window and got them wet, then splashed his face. The cold rain was bracing.

It was starting to get dark. David was still on I-64, west of Waynesboro, Virginia. The highway began its slow climb up into the Shenandoah Mountains. At Charlottesville, he'd turn onto the back roads and then continue into Liberty.

"One, please."

The young girl looked up at him. She was set up to sell basketball game tickets at a table just inside the main doors of the high school. The hallway, lined with lockers, stretched away behind her table, and a paper banner that said, "Cream the Clams!!"

"Oh, sure," she said. He could tell she was momentarily taken aback by his appearance. "That'll be two dollars. I can't believe they're playing tonight. I figured they would cancel, right?"

"Me, too," he said. "I was hoping to catch a game."

Jack Terrington handed her a couple of wadded-up bills. Her eyes took in the scar on the palm of his hand.

"That looks like it must've hurt a lot."

you have no idea

He looked from her beautiful young face to his scarred palm, thinking back to that sunny day on his bike when he'd played with the fence and lost. The sun had been so warm, and the fence had been so close...

"Yeah," he smiled. "Broke a glass, a long time ago."

Jack took his ticket, heading in. He took a seat off to one side. While he watched the players warm up, he studied the interior of the gym.

The layout was familiar, one used by many high schools.

On the west wall, where he had come in, a large set of double doors led out into the hallway and the rest of the school. On the east wall, underneath one basketball hoop, doors led to locker rooms and showers. As he watched, members of the Liberty Fighting Bobcats and the visiting Fredericksburg Clams came out and began warming up.

The basketball court took up most of the space, the baskets suspended from large metal arms. The baskets could be ratcheted up out of the way by means of hand cranks on either end of the gym. Two huge sets of folding wooden bleachers on either side of the court took up the rest of the space.

The game started, and he relaxed, enjoying not having to be anywhere right now. He watched the game, picking out players to root for. Simple fun, like he used to have, back before the urge.

Halfway through the third quarter, Jack stood and stretched and headed out into the hallway. The girl and her table were gone. Jack was ostensibly looking for a bathroom, should anyone ask.

A left in the hallway would've taken him outside, so he headed right, moving north into the main part of the high school. The main office was to his left, under the "Clam" sign. To the right were two doors marked "Locker Rooms" and "Maintenance." He looked around, seeing no one, and tugged the maintenance door open.

A short hallway took him into what looked like a workroom with a messy desk in one corner. Jack found the boiler check-off sheet on the maintenance guy's desk. The man checked the boiler once every four hours during school days and twice a day on the weekends. He'd checked it twice today, once at noon and once around 6:00 p.m.

Two doors led out of the office/workroom. One was open and led to a room filled with pipes and hoses, probably something to do with the showers and locker rooms. The other door opened onto a set of metal stairs that led down under the gym. Jack smiled and climbed down them.

The high school's boiler room was beneath the gymnasium, nearly identical to one he'd visited once under a Los Angeles school. On one wall hung a calendar showing a naked woman with a huge pair of breasts, and Jack wondered if the principal knew the maintenance man had that hanging down here.

The boiler itself was a huge collection of pipes and tanks and collection ducts, all controlled by a small panel of lights and knobs near the center of the room. As he studied the controls, he could hear the pounding of the feet of basketball players just a few feet above him. The boiler was set for a PSI of around 250. A card taped above the main knob said the normal PSI output for heat production was around 200, but evidently the cold and wet weather outside had prompted them to bump it up a little. With the ball game tonight and the town meeting tomorrow, they needed to keep it warm.

He glanced around. The cops would be around tomorrow, maybe even guarding the hallways. And the janitor or maintenance guy would probably check the boiler at least twice before tomorrow's town meeting. Jack needed another way in.

He moved from the tangle of pipes and tanks and walked the perimeter of the underground room, looking. There were several windows on the walls, up by the ceiling, and any one of them would do. He unhinged the locking mechanism on several of them. With any luck, he could get in tomorrow night with no trouble.

Julie Noble pulled into the Motel 6 parking lot at just after 9:30 p.m., exhausted. There was a room waiting for her, and she took a very long and hot shower before unpacking her papers and clothes. She was tired and wanted some sleep, but during the drive down she'd done a lot of thinking, and she wanted to make some notes before she dozed off.

She had no reason to notice the large white van parked in the space next to her car. Julie didn't notice that the van looked bigger and older than most vans, or that dark curtains covered the back windows.

Julie also did not notice the birds in the trees around the hotel. Dozens of different species, fluttering and squawking at each other. At just after midnight, a large, black bird flew in from the west and settled onto one of the bare branches of a tree overlooking the parking lot. Some of the other birds nipped at the black bird, and it squawked on its branch, moving gingerly, favoring one leg.

———

David's vision was bleary, but his mind was clear. He slowed the car and turned into Bethany's driveway. The lights in her house were off, and he was sure she was not expecting him. But that was all right. He'd told her he was coming, and he'd gotten here as fast as he could.

The car wheezed to a stop, sputtering. Somewhere coming down out of the mountains, a thin trail of smoke had begun seeping from beneath the hood.

David got out, his legs feeling like rubber. He stumbled up the dark walk to her door. His back was killing him from sitting too long, but his heart was pounding. All he'd thought about for the last 48 hours was getting here in one piece.

He knocked on her door, and after a few long moments, lights came on inside, and the door opened. She was standing there in her robe, a robe he'd seen a hundred times before, but she looked smaller, thinner. When she saw him, she burst into tears and stepped out into the cold rain and threw her arms around him. They hugged as she sobbed into his shoulder, mumbling words he could not hear.

"It's okay," he told her. "I'm here. Let's go inside, okay?"

She pulled away from him, enough to look up at his face. "David, I'm so sorry about Gloria. She was your only family. When I saw her, I..."

"Don't think about it now," he said. "I'm...I'm just so sorry I left, that I walked away." The words hung between them for a long moment, the only other sound the hiss of rain falling onto the leaves and the ground around them. He remembered the mean things he'd said to her in the parking lot at work and wondered why he'd ever left in the first place.

She looked at him closely and then smiled, leaning up to kiss him. "You don't know how glad I am to see you," she said.

PART THREE:

LANDFALL

CHAPTER 15
Saturday, September 24

Tony Drayton, a desk officer for the FBI's Situation Desk in Washington, D.C., grabbed a cup of coffee before heading downstairs to relieve the late-shift guy. The coffee, from one of the machines in the break room, was hot but not very good. More like coffee flavored water, he thought. But this early in the morning, any coffee was better than none.

He carefully sipped it down from the rim so it would not spill as he made his way to the elevator, riding it down four floors. The "Room" was located in the sub-basement.

Tony liked to call the situation room "the Room," because it sounded a little more official, but it really wasn't necessary. The room was impressive enough, looking a lot like mission control at NASA, only on a smaller scale. The room was only about ninety square feet, but it was filled with a lot of sophisticated equipment and computers. Large television monitors covered one of the walls, each tuned to major networks, civilian news-gathering operations, or overseas broadcasts.

One of the sad facts of the '90s and the lower budgets for most of the country's intelligence-gathering operations was that with their resources stretched so thin by President Clinton and a voracious Congress, many times the civilian news agencies, such as CNN, broke important news before the FBI got wind of it through official channels. In natural disasters or the like, the workers in the FBI's situation room got most of their information the way the rest of the country did—by tuning in to Wolf Blitzer or another reporter.

Tony passed through security and entered the room, walking past other workers to make his way to the situation desk. The "desk" was actually several workstations, surrounded by chairs and covered with phone equipment and computers and monitors. It was one of the few places in the building that was manned twenty-four hours a day.

As Tony walked in, the midnight to 8:00 a.m. guy was gathering up his stuff. Tony had worked the late shift when he'd first come on board three years ago, and he remembered how long—and boring— the nights could get. He'd gotten a lot of reading done then, running through all the Tom Clancy books.

"Hey, quiet night?" he asked, joking. The room was hopping, he could tell. Every seat was taken.

The 12–8 guy was just a kid, a recent college graduate. He sported a huge shock of red hair.

"Yeah," the kid said. "All hurricane-related, really." He pointed at the others. "We staffed up this morning. A commuter plane crashed in Jersey, and other trouble up and down the coast. FAA people were working all night trying to keep the air traffic control systems up and running. How is it out there?"

Tony shook his head. "The rain is really starting to pick up. People in D.C. really don't know how to drive in the rain, do they?"

The kid shook his head. "Or the snow. The plane crash looks like weather. Some highways are closed, some bridges out in North Carolina. And a spate of bank robberies in Myrtle Beach—someone taking advantage of the evacuations."

Tony nodded. "Anything about when this is going to move out?"

The kid finished gathering his things. "I've been watching the NWS—they're doing updates every ten minutes." He reached for the mouse on its pad, pulling up a screen on the computer that showed a lengthy list of entries.

"Power and phone outages all along the East Coast," pointing at the screen. "Cellular One said the transmission stations in North Carolina weren't built to stand such high winds. Couple of towers down."

Tony nodded. "You can take off. Thanks."

The kid had been right, he thought as he sipped his coffee. Things were hopping. The story on the plane crash in Jersey had been pulled off the overnight feed from CNN. He forwarded the item to the appropriate people and deleted it from his list, as he did with the cell phone outages and several other items. It was always like this—the priority items got forwarded immediately, no matter what time of day or night. The more complicated incoming items needed to be sorted by a person with more experience such as Tony.

He scrolled through the inbox slowly, sorting and forwarding items until he reached the last item, a homicide report that had come in yesterday afternoon. He frowned—the report was from 3:30 on Friday. The 8–4 guy yesterday should have forwarded it on to the right people. It was the oldest message in the list. Tony double-clicked on it.

9/23 15:30–Homicide: From Florida State Office, Tallahassee. Agent Sims reported recovery from coma of Sally Townsend, victim of AH, in local hospital TALLAHASSEE COUNTY GENERAL. Subject is sole witness to H of State Police Officer Daniels, Tyrel (D) on 9/10. Subject woke briefly from coma and said 'Going to Liberty' to her fiancé. GeoSearch showed town of Liberty, VA, with recent H on 9/18. Sims felt there might be some kind of connection. Reference numbers 1853457, 1958439, and 5464325.

Tony wondered what it meant. He remembered reading in the *Daily Bulletin* a couple of weeks back about the cop killing and something about a college girl they'd found at the scene. Tony was pleased to hear the girl had recovered. But what did this part about "going to Liberty" mean?

Agent Sims had evidently found it curious enough to do a GeoSearch and locate the town in question, then run the crime records. An unsolved homicide in the same location from only a few days ago was interesting.

Tony searched the system to see if anyone else was already working on this before flagging it for review. He opened a new program that tracked every ongoing investigation and agent assignment within the bureau. The location of personnel was strictly confidential and called for a very high level of electronic security—he had to enter his login and password twice before the prompt came up.

Tony typed in "Liberty" and hit ENTER. After a few seconds, a message came up.

Liberty Search Result –9/23–Agent Julie Noble (in analyst capacity) to complete on-site interview with civilian Jenkins, Norma in relation to H of Lisa Stevens (5464325) of 9/18. Interview to occur in/near Liberty, VA, at subject's residence. Contact Mike Wallace, x4523.

Someone, an agent Tony had never heard of, had gone down yesterday to question someone in their local homicide case. It was the same day the message had come in. Had she been sent out because of the message, or was she already gone when it came in? The 8–4 guy yesterday might've forwarded the message and forgotten to delete it, which made the most sense, but Tony had to check.

He reached for his phone, trying the FBI Headquarters extension first and getting no answer. He listened to the message, which gave the man's home phone number. He dialed it and waited.

"Hello?"

"Good Morning. I'm looking for Mr. Wallace. This is Tony at the situation desk."

"I'm Mike Wallace."

"Go secure," Tony said, and after a second he heard the tell-tale rattle of the phone switching over to a secure line.

"Okay," Wallace answered.

"Good morning, sir. Badge?"

"4593-D."

"Thank you. Sorry to bother you at home, sir, but I have a report here you've probably already heard. I just need to confirm."

There was a pause on the other end, like he was reaching for a paper and pen. "Okay, shoot."

Tony read him the contents of the message, but he couldn't help but hear the sudden intake of breath from the man on the other end of the phone. Tony waited for a response.

"You say this came in yesterday afternoon?"

Tony nodded, a force of habit even though he knew the guy couldn't see him. "Yes, sir. Just before 4:00 p.m."

"So why am I just getting it now? I was there past 6:00 last night."

Tony swallowed. "Well, evidently the people working yesterday didn't see it."

Mike Wallace made a disgusted sound that Tony could easily hear. "I sent that agent out to do a routine interview, but now it appears that the situation might be more serious. Can you send me a copy of your Inbox entry and the number of that agent in Florida? I want to talk to him. And when this is all finished, I'll have a word with your supervisor about getting better people down there to work with you."

Tony thanked him and hung up, eager to send him the e-mail and be done with it. The man sounded pissed.

————

Mike Wallace, cursing under his breath, booted up his home computer and logged onto the secure FBI e-mail network, reading the message and shaking his head.

It could all mean nothing, of course. But the word Liberty was popping up more than he liked. Julie Noble's crazy theory had intrigued him, but he'd felt that it wouldn't go anywhere. She'd been eager to interview the Jenkins woman, and at least she'd get a little taste of fieldwork.

But this message from Florida threw things into a whole new light.

Assuming this killer was still out there, it was conceivable that he could've killed that cop in Florida. The cop and the young woman were both missing toes, and it fit Julie's pattern. And the girl had spent several unfortunate days in the killer's company. What if Julie's guy had mentioned the name of the town where he was headed? Why else would the coma patient's first words be the name of a town she'd probably never even heard of? The connections were starting to look more and more possible.

And there was the kid in South Carolina, the one with the missing leg. Another "collection" case, possibly. It was a straight shot up I-95 from Florida, right on the way to Liberty.

If the maniac had returned to Liberty, Julie was in trouble. Mike had some calls to make.

————

Julie slept in and showered, happy to have made it in last night to a warm room. Rain pounded the roof of the hotel. Yesterday's drive to Liberty had been harrowing. She congratulated herself again for deciding to come down Friday night instead of waiting until Saturday morning.

She ate a quick breakfast at the Denny's near the hotel and headed out. She found the Jenkins house with no trouble.

The house was small, and the woman who answered the door was small, too. To Julie, Norma Jenkins looked like she needed about two weeks off from life. The strange crookedness of her nose detracted from what might've otherwise been a pretty face.

Norma invited Julie in—after asking to see her identification—and went off to make tea. Julie could hear her bustling around in the kitchen, working up the boiling water and clinking cups together.

"Sugar?" Norma asked from the other room.

"Please." Julie opened her briefcase and started laying out her reports and maps on the coffee table. When Norma brought in the tea and sat down, she took her tea and sipped at it.

"Mmm, that's good. And it hits the spot," Julie said, nodding out the window.

"Yeah, it's pretty bad out there. Surprised you made it down." Norma's shoulders were hunched over, and as they made small talk, Norma's hands seemed always to be touching her stomach, as if she were pregnant.

Julie dove right in.

"I came down from D.C. to talk to you about what's happened here this week," Julie began. "But I'm more curious about 1978. You're one of the few remaining people I can talk to about that case. Can you give me any more information about the killer than what's in these files?" she said, sweeping her hand over the table between them.

"Not really," Norma said. "It's all in there." She leaned forward to pour herself another cup of tea. "I'm sorry you drove all the way down here."

Julie looked at her, curious.

"Why do you say that?"

Norma sighed. "Because it's in the past. Nothing can bring them back, or him."

"Sheriff Beaumont?"

Norma nodded silently.

"What if there's a connection—"

"It's impossible," Norma said, sitting back. "No one would believe it. And—"

"Miss Jenkins, I'm not dredging up all of this out of pure curiosity," Julie continued. "I'm not here in an official capacity related to the current murders."

"You're not?"

"No. I've been studying your files. I think I might have found a connection between them and a series of murders out west."

Norma looked up at her sharply, and her hand curled around her stomach again. Her file said she had ulcers, serious enough for her to quit the force. They must be acting up.

Julie set her cup down and handed Norma one of the colored maps. The title read "Chronological Crimes-National."

"These dots represent a series of murders in the Seattle Washington area in the early '80s," she said, pointing.

"The Green River Killer?"

"That's right," Julie said. "I'm working on a theory that the Green River Killer, responsible for those murders, also traveled the country, killing in other places. Many agencies and officers spent a lot of time and money trying to catch him, but they never did. And I think that your Jasper Fines was the same person."

Julie noticed that Norma seemed to shiver when she'd said his name.

"And these colors, they're the years?" Norma asked, pointing at the legend at the bottom. Her hand was shaky.

"Right."

Norma studied it. "What's the connection?"

"The 'collection' aspect. Victims with missing body parts."

Norma nodded.

"The Green River Killer followed the same M.O. as your killer did," Julie continued. "Parts were missing, also. I think that he might be a special type of serial killer, the kind we call a 'collector.'"

Norma nodded.

"The FBI has recently gotten access to a new computer system, one capable of processing vast amounts of raw data," Julie said. "I used it to search for 'collector' cases of unsolved nationwide murders. Eventually the computer and I sorted out the unrelated cases, and that's what brought me here. Jasper Fines, or whoever he was, might be the same person as the one in Seattle. And in St. Louis and a dozen other places. If so, he would be the most prolific serial killer in history."

Julie wasn't sure exactly what kind of response she'd expected, but she was not prepared for what came.

Norma burst into tears.

Julie, caught off guard, watched as Norma cried loudly, hitching her shoulders. After a moment, Norma got up and ran for the back of the house. Julie heard the unmistakable sounds of someone throwing up.

Norma came back, apologizing.

"I can't believe it. I just can't."

Julie shook her head. "It's just a theory, Ms. Jenkins. It's probably not true."

"Norma. Call me Norma."

They talked for the next two hours, each telling the other about their experiences and intuitions about the Jasper Fines case. Norma opened up to her, and Julie learned a lot of information that had not made it into the original files, writing it all down in her notes. But none of it changed her opinion about the identity of the killer.

She learned that Sheriff Beaumont had been a very smart man and, from the way she talked about him, one Norma deeply respected. Norma recounted the whole Story again, especially the last night out there on I-95. When Norma got to the part about holding Beaumont's head in her lap, Julie started to understand why the woman was so upset. He had died in her arms. And that guilt had wracked her body every day since.

Julie told Norma about the string of unsolved murders that seemed to follow the same M.O. Norma nodded and pored over the reports, asking tough, insightful questions. She sounded like a cop.

And Julie noticed something else. Since she'd told Norma that the killer might've gone on to kill many more people, Norma had grown even quieter. Julie realized that Norma might think she was partly to blame for the death of hundreds of people. It was not an easy thing to hear.

"So, what do you think?" Julie asked her, refilling her tea and sitting back to sip it. Rain clattered on the roof.

Norma was slow to respond, still staring at the reports. Julie could not imagine how the woman might feel, especially if this all turned out to be true. If she had killed Jasper Fines that night so long ago, how many people would still be alive?

"Well, you make a good argument. It could be the same person, traveling the country for decades, chopping up people, but I've got one more question. If he's never been caught, where is he now? Retired?"

Julie looked at Norma carefully and saw that, in her mind, Norma already had an answer to her question. They'd avoided all of this earlier, discussing only the historical facts of the different cases.

"Maybe. Though I've read that people like this don't quit or give up their obsessions voluntarily. He can't stop doing this. It's a compulsion."

"Dead?"

"Maybe," Julie said. "But what about his trophies? Someone would have found a basement full of body parts."

Norma only nodded.

"He could've been picked up on a lesser charge and be doing time," Julie said. "Or he might have died of natural causes or been killed. They say people who live in a violent world have a better chance of dying in a violent way."

"Or...could he still be out there?"

"I know what you're thinking," Julie shook her head, sitting back. "It's unlikely. You've had a recent murder here, but thinking he's involved is two steps past crazy. I mean, why would he come back here after all these years?"

"Actually, three murders. And another mysterious death. All connected to Sheriff Beaumont's son."

"What?"

Norma stood and excused herself for a moment, leaving the room. When she came back, she was holding an old brown folder and a piece of paper. She sat down and handed the file to Julie, who took it gingerly.

"Three murders, you said?"

"That is Beaumont's original case file," Norma said, ignoring Julie's question. "I've spent the past couple of days reading through it. There are a lot of similarities to what's going on right here, right now, in Liberty."

Julie carefully flipped through it. She had seen computerized scans of the official case file on her computer screen back in D.C., but these pages were different. This looked like the sheriff's personal notes. It contained new information in handwritten notes, which she read with interest.

"This isn't the official case file," Norma said. "It's Beaumont's personal notes on a copy of the file. He kept them in his personal papers."

Julie nodded, reading. There were brown stains on some of the pages. "What are these?"

"I'm not sure," Norma said, shaking her head. "To me it looks like blood. I stole the folder from the Thatcher/Foreman crime scene."

Julie looked at her. "What?"

"Gloria Thatcher and Abe Foreman died. I got a friend to let me in the crime scene. I think they were murdered, probably by the same person who killed Lisa Stevens."

"Why do you think that?"

"Lisa Stevens was killed on Sunday night and found on Tuesday morning. On Monday night, Thatcher and Foreman died mysteriously. The talk around town is homicide, but the deaths are still being officially listed as accidental. Sheriff Brown is taking his time on the investigation. Do you know who they were?"

Julie shook her head, confused. The names didn't sound familiar, and she hadn't heard about any other deaths in Liberty.

"I didn't think so. Their bodies were found at her home. Gloria was Sheriff Beaumont's sister-in-law. When Beaumont's wife died in childbirth, Gloria raised Beaumont's son, David."

More odd connections in a case that seemed to be filled with them. "That's strange. The other victim?"

"Abe Foreman, one of the town's leading attorneys. He oversaw the distribution of Beaumont's will after his death, set up the trust fund for David. He helped Gloria manage her accounts. She was a drunk, spent away a lot of the money intended for David before Abe stepped in. Gloria was in the process of moving to a new place. Abe was helping her make the arrangements."

"How did they die? Why do you think they were murdered?"

"Abe fell over a railing, and Gloria died in her car in the garage. Carbon monoxide. But there was evidence her hands were bound at some point."

Julie sat back, thinking. Why would Jasper Fines come back?

"I know what you're thinking," Norma said, smiling. "I don't know why. Maybe that's not important. The important thing is that he is back."

"But why, after all these years?"

Norma shrugged. "I don't know. But the coincidences keep piling up."

Julie nodded. "Revenge? Beaumont's long gone. Fines came close to being caught here, but that had to happen all over the nation, right? He was probably in a lot of scrapes."

Norma picked up a piece of paper and handed it over—she'd made a list of similarities between the current cases and those from 1978. Julie smiled. Once a cop, always a cop. There were several connections that Julie and she had already discussed. Under each victim, both in '78 and the more recent ones, there was something missing from each of the victims, including Sheriff Beaumont. Next to his name, Norma had written "Star."

"What does this mean?"

"In all cases, something was removed," Norma said. "But there wasn't time with Beaumont—Fines had to flee. The only thing missing at the crime scene was William's shield, a six-pointed star that read 'Liberty Sheriff's Department.'"

"The symbol of Beaumont's power, his office," Julie said.

"Right," Norma agreed. "The perfect trophy." She took two more antacids.

"That's eight, just since I got here. The ulcer?"

"No, I just love to pop these gritty, chalky things," Norma said, suddenly angry. "They're as good as candy. That news you gave me? Being responsible for the death of dozens of innocent people? Really made my day."

"I'm sorry," Julie said. "That wasn't—"

"I think I'll take myself out for Mexican tonight," Norma spat. "Something spicy, really celebrate. Go out with a bang, right?"

Julie didn't answer for a moment.

"Can't they operate or something?"

Norma sat, defeated. "My doctors have tried everything. Two surgeries, but they only delayed things. There's nothing else they can do except recommend I stay calm. Avoiding excitement, things like that."

Julie turned to look out the window as a strong gust of wind rattled the glass. Outside, water was backing up in the gutters. Norma looked as well, one arm in its natural position, curled around her stomach. She wore a strange expression on her face, one that Julie couldn't read.

"Hate to break it to you, but this town is anything but dull."

Norma nodded, her thoughts far away. "Oh, and that other death? Bernie something. Hung himself."

Julie nodded, confused. "Who's he?"

"David Beaumont left town a week ago, heading to California. Bernie was his roommate. And Stevens was David's girlfriend's best friend."

Julie shook her head and stood, gathering her files and reports. "I have to inform the local police that I'm conducting an investigation in their jurisdiction. It's professional courtesy."

"Good luck with that. Jes Brown, the sheriff, doesn't like anyone near his territory. He's like a dog with a bone-no sharing."

Julie flipped open her cell phone and tapped some digits, waiting for the call to go through, but nothing happened. "Hmm, that's strange."

Norma looked up at her, pulled from her thoughts. "What?"

"Well, I tried to call D.C., but I'm not getting anything." Julie tried again with the same result—no connection.

"Maybe the weather's messing it up?" Norma offered.

Julie nodded. "Yeah. Can I use your phone real quick?"

Norma pointed to the kitchen. "Help yourself. Calling for backup?" she asked, a wry look on her face. Outside, another strong gust of wind battered rain against the window.

"I do need to call in what we've talked about," Julie agreed. "And tell them that I'm going to go talk to the local authorities. But you're right—it would be a good idea to get a more experienced agent out here. I've never done a field investigation."

Julie walked into the kitchen and picked up the phone and started dialing, but a recording came on. The voice said phone service outside of the local calling area was temporarily unavailable. She went back in the living room.

Norma looked up. "Trouble?"

"Yeah," Julie said, sitting down heavily. "The land lines are down, too. Looks like I'm on my own for a while."

"You think it's a good idea to involve the sheriff's department?" Norma asked, her implication obvious. "In my experience, they're a bunch of idiots."

Julie shrugged. "It's procedure. Technically, I should have informed them before interviewing you."

Norma stood, pulling on a jacket. "Okay."

Julie nodded, surprised that the woman would want to become further involved.

Outside, Norma held an umbrella over Julie as she carried the reports out to her car, and then they both climbed in and began the drive to the sheriff's department. The rain grew in strength, falling like a curtain of water, darkening the sky. The gutters were full of dirty water, racing into the sewers.

Mike Wallace had more information now, but it didn't make him feel any better.

He'd talked to Chris Hanson, the Cray liaison. Wallace asked him to review the report from Florida. After a few minutes, Hanson called back to say that the cop's death and mutilation was consistent with Julie's killer's pattern. They agreed that the fact that the only witness to the cop's death had repeated the name of the town was a coincidence too large to be ignored.

Next, Wallace called Agent Sims in Florida. The cop and girl were both indeed missing body parts—before fleeing the scene, the killer had removed one toe from each victim. Wallace thanked Sims and hung up, thinking. Now what? Somewhere in the middle of all of this speculation and evidence and innuendo was the truth.

What if the Green River Killer had moved on? It would explain why he'd never been caught. Wallace grappled with the possibility. On the tiny chance any of this were true, then the greatest serial killer in history was loose and still killing, as recently as a few days ago. And no one knew except a bunch of small-town cops and a rookie FBI agent with no field experience.

Wallace knew in his gut that Julie would need backup. He thought about it for a few more minutes and then decided that if he were going to make a mistake in this case, it was better to make a mistake on the side of caution. No one could fault him.

Wallace called his supervisor to fill him in on the situation, but he got the machine. Due to the nature of the case, he left a cryptic message for Darren Paynod to call him back as quickly as possible. There was no way Wallace could explain what was going on to Darren's answering machine. That went against everything he'd always been taught about secrecy. Hopefully, Paynod would return the call soon. Until then, Wallace was calling the shots.

Next, he called the closest FBI office to Liberty, the state office in Richmond. He talked to the highest-ranking agent on the premises. It was a Saturday and the office was lightly staffed, with most of them out assisting local law enforcement as they reacted to the hurricane. Wallace explained as much of the situation as he could, and the Richmond agent offered to drive up to Liberty once the storm was through. He also mentioned that the Virginia State Police had already assigned a lieutenant to assist local law enforcement in the Stevens case. Wallace agreed that an experienced FBI agent was needed in Liberty and officially requested it. He also passed along the case file numbers for them to download and study. Wallace warned them to be careful.

After those calls were made, Wallace felt a little better. Things were working, the wheels were in motion. But the final three calls he made that morning only left him more frustrated with the situation.

His call to Julie's borrowed cellular phone came up with a "cannot connect" recording. His next call, to the phone company, informed him that they had no idea of how long it would take to repair the phone lines. His final call, to the number listed in Julie's report for Norma Jenkins, also came back as "cannot connect."

Mike Wallace hung up again. Experienced agents were on the way, but not until Sunday at the earliest. He couldn't contact Julie to pass along any of the new information. Or to tell her to be careful.

At the station, a group consisting of Sheriff Brown, Lieutenant Blake, Agent Noble, and Norma Jenkins, met in a private conference room. Sheriff Brown took the chair at the head of the table, of course, and settled his considerable bulk into it.

Lieutenant Blake was surprised to find out that an FBI agent was in town. Blake was even more surprised to hear that she was investigating something that had happened eighteen years ago. Blake had assumed she was up from Richmond to take over the Stevens case, or to "assist" with the Thatcher/Foreman investigation. Maybe someone at the federal level had grown tired of waiting for Blake to step in.

Sheriff Brown took the news as expected: he was immediately furious.

Agent Noble only got three minutes into her theory about connections between the current killings and those from 1978 before Brown started laughing.

"Whoa, little lady," Brown said. Blake thought he looked like Santa when he laughed. The man was so portly, he should have elves working for him. "You say the guy is back, the guy that killed Beaumont?" He looked at Norma Jenkins with disgust. "And you're in on this, too? Jasper Fines, back from the grave? Better call out the dogs."

Blake noticed that Norma Jenkins didn't look at Sheriff Brown, only nodding in response to the question. She clearly hated the man. Lieutenant Blake knew nothing about her, but her revulsion of this man was written on her face.

The FBI agent spoke up again.

"Yes, and my supervisor in D.C. felt the connection was important, too. Enough to send me down here to interview Ms. Jenkins. In light of your four recent deaths, I think it's something that needs to be investigated."

Blake kept quiet. It all sounded a little far-fetched to him. He hated to side with the piece of blubber sitting and the end of the table, but really? What were the chances this famous killer from out west would still be following the same pattern twenty years later? The pretty FBI agent had an interesting theory, but Blake would've bet his career that the criminal was long dead, taking a dirt nap. The connections with these recent deaths were simply horrible coincidences.

Brown was talking again, picking apart the agent's theory, and Blake noticed that while this was all going on, the Jenkins woman just sat and watched everything, taking it all in. She was a sponge. She had the eyes of an investigator, and she was obviously dismissing most of what

Brown was saying. That right there got her points in Lieutenant Blake's book.

"And just because the Stevens girl was missing her tongue, you just assume this is the same guy? And then you get in your car and come all the way down here from 'Deeee Ceeee' to enlighten us yokels?" Brown was in his element, berating someone.

"There are connections—" the agent began, but Brown cut her off.

"Who do you think I am, Sheriff Andy Taylor? This isn't Mayberry, dear," Brown said, shaking his head and rolling his eyes at Blake, who looked away. No reason to give the guy any more support. Brown looked back at the FBI agent. "I don't need you coming into *my* town and telling me what to do."

"Her murder was ritualistic in nature and involved the removal of body parts. In the FBI, we call that a pattern," Noble said, saying the last word very slowly as if talking to a child. Blake could see her temper was getting the best of her, the sure sign of a rookie. But it was fun to watch someone skewer Sheriff Brown. He had it coming.

Brown was flabbergasted, his face working in an angry grimace. To Blake, it looked like he might just burst.

"You don't think we know how to conduct an investigation out here in 'the sticks'?" He stood up and looked down at her. "How long have you been an agent, girl?"

Agent Noble stood, too, staring right back at the man. "I graduated from the FBI Academy in Quantico with top scores, and I was good enough to be assigned to headquarters. How long is none of your business," she said, her voice rising.

"Just what I thought—a couple of months," Brown nodded. "Still wet behind the ears."

"No," Agent Noble said, holding her ground. Blake was starting to like her.

"Tell you what," Brown said. "Why don't you come back after you've got something serious to talk about, okay? I have work to do and murders to investigate."

"I can assist, sir," Julie said.

Brown waved one beefy hand over the colorful reports spread out on the table. "I don't have time to listen to rookie agents or bus drivers or their crazy fantasies about ghosts." He stormed out, slamming the door.

Blake watched as Agent Noble looked at the Jenkins woman and sat down, speechless. He stood and walked around the table, picking up one of the maps and looking at it thoughtfully.

"You have an interesting theory there, agent," he said. "If there is one thing I've learned in law enforcement, it's that nothing is too wild to

be true." He smiled and lowered his voice. "Between you and me, this
case is not going to be under local jurisdiction much longer. Tomorrow,
Monday at the latest, we'll be taking over. I'm just waiting to hear back
from Richmond. Stick around a day or two, and you and I and some of
the state boys can sit down and discuss this again."

Lieutenant Blake said goodbye and left. For now, he was a glorified
babysitter, but it wouldn't be for too much longer. He left to find Sheriff
Brown, hoping the big guy hadn't done anything stupid in the last three
minutes.

Julie and Norma took their papers and left, running to Julie's car to
avoid getting too wet. All the way out to the car, Norma reminded Julie
that she'd thought it was a bad idea from the start.

"Yeah, well, I had to try. That guy isn't that smart, I take it?" Julie
asked, shaking her head. "He let a lot of things slip, like he thinks
Foreman and Thatcher were murdered."

"What?"

"Brown said, 'I have murders to investigate.' Plural."

Norma smiled. "He's an idiot. He got Beaumont killed."

Julie looked at her. "Are you serious?"

Norma nodded again. "Yeah, and I'll tell you the story on the way.
We have to go somewhere."

"Where?"

"Just drive."

David and Bethany shared a peaceful, quiet night together. Even
though he was exhausted, they talked into the early morning hours,
him sharing stories about his aunt and his years growing up with her.
Bethany talking about Lisa. David learned things about Lisa that he
hadn't known. They talked and cried and even laughed a little. When
Bethany finally dozed off in her chair in the living room around 4:00 in
the morning, David moved her to the couch, lay down next to her, and
covered them both with a blanket.

They woke together in the morning. Those few minutes quietly
talking, lying next to each other, were the happiest moments either of
them had had in weeks.

David took a much-needed shower while Bethany whipped up a
quick breakfast. Over pancakes, they discussed what else had happened

in the small town in the few days since David had left.

When they were done, David called the sheriff's office to let them know of his return. Ten minutes later, two deputies arrived to collect David. They drove him through the streets of Liberty, passing high water in some places, on their return to the station.

David was led into a conference room, past the stares of deputies in the station. His interview was conducted by Sheriff Brown, accompanied by Lieutenant Blake from the state police and several of Brown's deputies. Brown asked him a bunch of questions but refused to answer any of David's.

Sheriff Brown's questions proved only one thing to David—no one knew why his aunt and Abe Foreman were dead. Instead, Brown and another deputy asked several questions about Abe and "shady dealings." They also wondered if anyone had it out for his aunt, or if Abe and his aunt were romantically involved. Questions that David had no answers for.

Blake was the only one to ask David about his connection to Lisa Stevens, and David quickly got the impression that the lieutenant was the smartest investigator in the room. Maybe the only investigator in the room. Contrary to the half-baked questions posed by the sheriff's department, Blake's questions revolved around David's connection to the victims. Blake seemed to think that David could be next to be targeted—an idea that scared David.

The only other smart person in the room seemed to be a lady deputy with a cold. She asked good, insightful questions when the fat sheriff wasn't cutting her off or talking over her. At one point, Sheriff Brown made a rude joke about female deputies. David couldn't believe the sheriff would do that, especially in front of Blake or civilians.

After the interrogation, David asked to see the crime scene. There was also a natural curiosity in him. He'd spent so many years in that house—he needed to see it.

It took a while to make it across town—a fallen tree had shut down part of Main. When David and the deputies arrived at his old home, there was still yellow police tape strung up across the doors and windows. It was probably intended to keep away the curious, but the yellow tape only made the home stand out like a sore thumb.

The deputies let David in—he no longer had a key. The blood in the living room took him by surprise. A huge pool of blackish-red stained the living room carpet. The shattered fragments of his aunt's glass coffee table slumped in the middle of the room, shards glittering in the hazy light from the window.

His aunt never allowed him to put his feet up on the table. She was always worried his shoes might mess it up. Now it lay in a hundred pieces, its four metal legs lying at crazy angles in a circle of dried-up blood.

The couch and chairs and walls were spattered with drops of blood, some running in streaks. It looked like a horror movie. Stacks of boxes stood around the dark stain like silent witnesses, their tops sealed with glossy brown tape. Sealed by his aunt, no less, and now she was—

"You need a minute?" one deputy asked, standing in the foyer.

David turned.

"Uh, yeah. My aunt...they found her in the garage?"

The other deputy nodded. "They aired it out, so it's safe. We'll wait in the car. Take as long as you need. Lock the door when you leave." They left, closing the front door behind them.

David walked into the kitchen, looking around. The place was a mess, though he had no idea how much of that was his aunt and how much was the deputies and people who had followed. It was a crime scene. What had the deputies taken? David realized that the house and everything in it was probably his now, and he started tearing up. It was all too much to think about.

He wandered out through the open door into the garage. His aunt's car was parked in there, a car she'd never let him drive. He walked slowly around it. Lieutenant Blake said she died of carbon monoxide poisoning. To David, the car and garage looked normal—everything related to the suicide had apparently been removed by Brown's men. There was no indication that his aunt had died here. It was just a garage, empty and cold. Rain water leaked in under the garage door, and he could hear the wind gusting outside. It seemed like a lonely place to die.

He shook his head and left, heading to the front door but stopping. He glanced back into the living room, focusing on the big dark stain. He walked back into the living room and climbed the stairs up to the second-floor landing, finding scratches and scrapes on the railing where Abe must've fallen. Why scratches? Had he caught himself, maybe tried to pull himself up before falling? David had tripped against the railing a dozen times but he had never fallen over, or even come close to it. The railing was too high to just fall over.

Looking down, David saw the stacks of boxes around the living room. Behind one stack, he saw a box sitting on the carpet by itself, back in a corner and hidden from view from the rest of the living room. The lid stood open.

He went downstairs and walked around to the box, pulling it over to look at it. The flaps stood open. It was the box of his father's personal files, the box he'd longed to explore on the day he'd told his aunt he was leaving. There were drops of blood staining the open flaps of the box, and David touched them gingerly with his fingers. Abe's blood. What was the box doing open? Had it been open before? There wasn't any tape on it, so maybe it hadn't been sealed yet. The box was open when Abe fell...

On a sudden impulse, he decided to take the box with him. He lugged it outside and locked the door, then jogged to the car. David held his jacket over the box to keep it dry and climbed in the back.

"You guys mind me taking this box? It's a bunch of my papers from school," he lied, covering up the wording on the side with one arm.

One of the deputies looked at the other and shrugged his shoulders. "Naw, the investigation is over. Technically, all of that stuff is yours, anyway. Where are we dropping you?"

He gave them Bethany's address and sat back. Wind gusted through the trees. Rain fell hard on the windshield as the car navigated the wet streets of Liberty. When they pulled up in front of her house, there was a car in the driveway David didn't recognize. Probably a friend of Bethany's.

He got out and thanked the deputies and headed to the door, dreaded finding out who was there. David didn't have the energy to deal with anyone right now. Coming from his aunt's house, he felt numb, tired. All he wanted to do was sit down and have a beer and go through his father's papers. Maybe something in there would give him some insight about his father and what he'd been like.

Bethany opened the door and smiled when she saw it was him, tears in her eyes. He stepped to her, concerned, and set the box down before hugging her.

"You okay?"

She nodded, wiping her eyes. "Yeah, I'm fine. Come in."

He picked up the box and followed her into the living room. There were two women there he didn't recognize. They stood to greet him, and he set his box down. The coffee table was covered with reports and maps of the United States.

"David," Bethany began, "this is Norma Jenkins. You know her—she was a deputy for your father. School bus driver."

David stepped over and shook her hand, recognizing her. He'd seen her around town. And, of course, she was part of the Story.

"You worked with my father."

The woman nodded. She looked like she was in pain.

"Yes," she said. "He was a good man, David."

David nodded, not knowing what to say. "Um, thanks." He looked at her broken nose, another part of the Story.

"After he...died, I didn't want to be in law enforcement anymore," she said, sitting down. Her arms curled around her stomach in a strange way that made her look pregnant.

Bethany pointed out the other woman, but there was no need. David would have to be blind to miss her. She was tall and beautiful and exuded an air of confidence.

"This is Agent Julie Noble. She's with the FBI."

"FBI?" David asked, confused, shaking her hand.

"Hi, David. Nice to meet you."

He sat down. "Are you here about Lisa? Or my aunt?"

Agent Noble sat, smiling. "Let's just say I'm here to investigate a few things. I came to town to talk to Norma."

David nodded, looking at Norma and back to Agent Noble.

"Afterward, we talked to your local law enforcement authorities," Agent Noble continued. "Did they interview you yet?"

"They asked me a lot of questions," he said, sitting back. "I get the feeling they're confused. Brown thinks Abe was stealing money or something. One guy, Blake, from out of town, seemed smart."

Norma spoke up. "Sheriff Brown's an idiot."

David smiled. "Yup."

"They want to talk to you, David," Bethany said. "Norma and Agent Noble, here. They have a theory—"

"We tried your apartment first, in case you went back there," Norma said. "Sorry about your roommate."

David nodded. "Thanks."

"After, we called Bethany here," Norma said. "Asked if we could speak to both of you."

"David, some horrible things have been happening, obviously," Agent Noble began. "I have developed a theory that might explain it all. Norma and I discussed it. And if our theory is true, you could be in a lot of danger."

Suddenly, David grew worried, a sense of self-preservation kicking in. "What do you mean?"

"Well, these murders—you knew all of the victims," Norma said.

David laughed. "You think Aunt Gloria and Abe were murdered? That's not what the deputies said."

Norma shook her head. "Something else is going on here. And yes, I think they were killed. Agent Noble has been researching the case," Norma said. "It may be that we are dealing with something horrible here, something that's coming for you."

David looked at Julie. "I'm in danger?"

"They are all related to you."

"Not Lisa."

"True," Norma said. "Could just be a coincidence. She was last seen at the Food Town," she said, touching her nose.

"They're here to help you, David," Bethany said." She looked at the women and pointed at the maps on the table. "Explain it all. Start again, from the beginning. They started explaining it to me while you were gone."

Agent Noble looked at David. "Okay, you know the last case of your father's career?"

David nodded, leaning forward. "Of course, I've heard the Story. Too many times. I doubt there is anything new you could tell me. My father the hero, the Killer," David said, sarcasm creeping into his voice.

"That's not how it happened," Norma started to say, but he cut her off.

"I don't want to hear it again," David said. "I never want to hear it again. It's like a bad movie I've seen too many times. Big shootout, parents die, kid grows up alone. You're going to tell me what a hero my father was, right?"

They were quiet for a moment. David could feel the waves of anger coming off of him.

"Yes, your father was a hero," Norma said quietly.

"Yup," David said. "And then he left. Died saving this stupid town."

"But he didn't leave you to grow up alone, David," Norma said. "He was killed."

"I know."

"He didn't have any choice about that," Norma said. "A Killer came to our town, and your father stood up to him. Died because of it. If that doesn't make your father a hero, I don't know what would."

David looked at her, not sure of what to say.

"And your mother didn't abandon you, either—she died giving you life," Norma continued. "I knew them both. They wanted to see you grow up."

He remembered suddenly that this woman had known his parents. Aunt Gloria had never talked about them, but this woman didn't seem to have any trouble. And, even though she hadn't been a deputy in a long time, her voice still held a commanding quality. David looked at her and nodded.

"He was a good man, your father, and a very good sheriff," she continued. "He was the only person who could've caught Jasper Fines," the name acid in her mouth. "And, thanks to Agent Noble, we now think he came closer to catching him than anyone ever did. Before or since."

Norma looked at Agent Noble for a moment.

"Go ahead," Agent Noble said to Norma. "You start."

"Okay," Norma said, turning back to David. "First, the Story you have heard is close, but it's not the truth. After the initial homicide of the little boy, your father figured that the killer had to be someone from out of town..."

David listened to the Story again. But this version, as told by Norma Jenkins, was different, more detailed. She told the Story as only someone who had been there and seen everything could tell it.

For the first time, the Story sounded real and alive.

He listened as she spoke about his father's intelligent search for the criminal, and how he'd coordinated the response. She talked about how his father had set up the searches and the roadblocks on that final night of his life. The plan probably would've worked, too, if it hadn't been for Deputy Jes Brown and his incompetence. Jes had instructed the dog handlers to make much more noise than normal, tipping their hand. Jasper Fines, or whatever his name was, had evidently figured out he was being driven and circled around the roadblock, shooting several deputies from the cover of trees. In the end, the man had stood over David's wounded father, sprawled and helpless on the road, and killed him, laughing the whole time.

A rage welled up inside of David, deep and murky. Rage at the Killer and Deputy Brown.

Norma went on, telling how Jasper Fines had taken the sheriff's star from where it had been pinned to his chest. When Norma got to this part of the Story, she had to stop and collect herself. It ended with the squad car driving off, the twin taillights like demon eyes in the darkness.

David's father died in this woman's arms. And, by the end of the telling, Norma was crying, as was Bethany beside him, holding his hand.

He knew he should feel like crying as well, but he felt nothing but deep, fiery anger. And, somehow, David's opinion of his father had shifted. Over the last half hour, he'd learned more about his father than in all the previous tellings of the Story.

David sat for a moment, and they all looked at him. Finally, he spoke up. "I guess 'thank you' would be in order. I'd heard it so many times, I assumed I knew the truth."

"He was a good man, David," Norma smiled, wiping tears from her eyes. "And he did a lot of other things besides being a great sheriff. He loved to talk about you and your mother. He had plans for your family. One of the last things he talked about was how he was going to take you and your mother on a trip as soon as you were old enough."

He nodded. He couldn't help but hear the admiration in Norma's voice. Could his father really engender this kind of loyalty in someone 20 years later?

"Go on," David said.

"He was talking about you in the car that night," Norma said. "He never got a chance to tell you, but I know that he loved you and your mother very much."

David looked at her.

"And he never left you, David," Norma continued. "He was taken."

Hearing that sent him over the edge. He stood suddenly and walked into the kitchen, not wanting anyone to see. The words—they were just words, right? He wasn't any different from hearing them, and yet, the words had affected him so deeply that he hadn't even seen it coming. It was like a punch to the gut. To hear that his father had loved him so much, even before he was born. To hear that his parents were overjoyed with anticipation at David's birth...it was too much to take in. He'd hated them for so long for leaving him...

After a few minutes alone, Bethany came in and put her arms around him.

"It's okay, David. He loved you, and you've always known that, somewhere in your heart. You've pushed it away, just like you've pushed everyone else away."

She stood with her arms around him as he sobbed on her shoulder. And he didn't care if it was wrong or stupid—for the first time in a long time, David cried. And it felt good.

Norma and Julie sat in the living room, wondering what to do or say next. The young woman, Bethany, was in the other room, comforting David Beaumont.

Julie tried her flip cell phone again, but now none of her calls were connecting.

Norma flipped on the TV and changed stations to The Weather Channel. The bands of rain were getting stronger. Mandy had slowed to a crawl, and the protracted hours over land were causing widespread flooding. The eye of the storm was over Virginia Beach. Video played of frantic motorists fleeing the path of the storm, intermixed with clips of roads and bridges being washed out. Julie started to change the channel when Norma yelled to drop the remote.

"...county officials said that the bridge will take weeks to repair. Until that time, Anne County residents will have to travel some thirty miles north to the nearest crossing. Another bridge, connecting Cape View and Bay Charles..."

"What?" Julie asked Norma.

"That bridge you crossed coming into town? Near the mall? That was the County Line Bridge. It's the only connection Liberty has to the east and the freeway. That video—the bridge was getting hit by trees and high waters, and then it collapsed into the river." She was quiet for a moment before continuing. "Only way out of town now is west, up into the Shenandoahs."

"So, what are you saying? We're trapped?"

Norma nodded. "If you get through on that fancy cellular phone of yours, tell them we're cut off from the highway."

Their conversation ended when David and Bethany came back into the room. Norma told them about the bridge.

"That's the way I came, down from the mountains. I was just trying to avoid any traffic. Crazy to think that bridge is gone now." He turned to Norma. "So, why did you tell me all of that?" David asked. "What good could it do to bring all of that up now?"

Norma glanced at Julie, then back at David. She could feel his curiosity radiating in the air. "Well, like I said earlier, we have a theory. It could explain the deaths in Liberty. And if we're right, there is a very dangerous man in town."

David sat down on the couch with Bethany, taking her hand. "What kind of danger?"

Norma sat back and pointed to Julie. "This is her part to tell."

Agent Noble spoke up. "Let me start from the beginning. I'm new with the FBI. They brought me in to test a new computer system. I tracked crimes of a particular type of murderer, someone who takes trophies from the crime scene."

"They're called 'collectors,'" Norma added.

Julie nodded. "We searched for crimes where something was missing, including parts of the victim. The results were very interesting..."

Julie talked for nearly an hour, stopping to point at her maps and charts or to flip through her reports. They interrupted her occasionally and asked for clarification, and Norma watched as these two civilians listened to the tale. It was interesting—civilians reacted very differently to parts of the story. Norma could tell they grasped the importance of the consistent M.O. They asked smart questions about different collection methods, and listened as Julie talked about the multiple searches and narrowing the data down to a list of homicides that could've been committed by one person because of their physical location and proximity to other homicides that fit the same pattern.

Norma ignored the pain that rumbled in her gut, excusing herself more than once to sneak off to the bathroom. It was all so much, knowing that she might have caught the Killer and failed. All those people dead in the years since...she coughed up blood, spitting it into the sink. Norma cleaned herself, hoping the others wouldn't notice.

Returning to the living room, Norma watched David closely as he digested the different steps of the investigation. The kid had his father's eyes, and she watched them drink in the reports and maps, following up with smart questions. He even found a few minor discrepancies, pointing them out. Norma smiled—he was so much like his father. Norma had heard the "slacker" rumors, but now she had reason to discount them. He was a clever young man, making connections on his own and adding refinements to Julie's theory.

"I can't believe this could be the same guy," David said, studying the national map of Jasper Fines' activities. "Someone would have caught him by now."

"Not necessarily," Julie answered, launching into a discussion of the Green River Killer and how he operated in a specific area for a long time without being apprehended. "They had a dedicated task force searching for him in a limited area."

He nodded as she continued, discussing the more recent deaths. Agent Noble covered the murders in the Los Angeles area, then those in the Southwest and Texas, ending with the murder in Florida of the policeman and the attempted murder of the young college student. Thankfully, Norma thought, the girl had not died. She was now in a coma in a Florida hospital, with law enforcement eager to speak to her if she recovered. Julie also mentioned a young man in South Carolina that might have been another victim.

When they got to Lisa Stevens, Norma spoke up. She knew the most about the case and recounted what she knew. Julie added in a few details from the official coroner's report, which Norma had not seen. It all added up to Lisa being killed by a collector.

"It sounds the same," Bethany said quietly. Norma and Julie took pains to not be too graphic, but Norma could see the muscles in Bethany's face working as she struggled not to cry.

"I agree," Julie added. "The crimes are very similar."

"So, what makes you think Aunt Gloria and Abe were victims of the same person?" David asked.

"I have a friend on the Liberty sheriff's office," Norma said. "She said that the deaths are being investigated as homicides," Norma said, glancing at Julie. "Parts of...your aunt and Abe Foreman were not found at the scene."

"It's so disgusting," Bethany added. "How can people..."

She trailed off, and no one answered. No one knew what to say.

Julie cleared her throat. "But it all fits. Either your 'Jasper Fines' is back, or someone else is copying his particular method. What we don't have is a motivation for his—"

"I read everything the papers have said on my aunt's death before I was interviewed," David interrupted. "The deputies never even hinted that they might have been murdered."

"They are investigating links between the four deaths," Norma said. "Don't forget, Bernie died as well."

David nodded, not saying anything.

Norma looked at him. "Did they ask if Abe was in any kind of financial trouble, or were the two of them dating?"

David nodded. "Yeah. Seemed like they were trying to piece things together. But Lieutenant Blake kept asking about my connections to the victims."

"We explained our theory to them," Julie said, pointing at the maps and reports. "Blake was the only one who took us seriously."

Norma watched the conversation, chewing on an antacid, and decided it was time for the final piece. "David, I see you grabbed that box of your father's files from your aunt's house. I think we have absolute proof that Jasper Fines is here. That he killed Gloria and Abe. Probably Lisa as well."

He looked up sharply. "What?"

Norma nodded. "Julie, hand that file to David."

Julie handed David an old-looking brown file that had been sitting off to the side. David took it and looked it over.

"I saw the box of files and wanted to read some of them, maybe get a better idea of what happened to my father, so I took it." He looked up at Norma.

"I know. I saw the box, too, when I walked through the crime scene. And that file, your father's notes on the Fines case, was on top."

David opened the folder and began looking through the pages. Norma wondered if the kid recognized his own father's handwriting. Probably not.

"You took the folder?" Bethany asked. "Isn't that theft?"

Norma shrugged. "Technically, it's obstructing. But someone has to conduct an actual investigation."

Julie nodded grimly. "David, flip to page 34, where your father is writing about the Food Town stakeout."

David flipped through the file, stopping to read his father's handwriting. Norma watched him read the report and touch the red stain at the top corner of the page. He flipped back a page—the sheets stuck together momentarily.

"Bethany, look."

She touched it. "Gross. Dried blood. Abe?"

"Yeah," he nodded. He looked up at Julie and Norma.

"It doesn't look that old," Bethany said.

David looked at her strangely. "How would you know?"

"Remember my junior year? I worked at that Western Sizzlin' out by the mall. I did salads, but we talked to the cooks a lot. I know what dried blood looks like. The butcher paper they used was always covered with that stuff. Dark brown. Starts out red and gets darker the older it is. That's not that old," Bethany said, nodding at the smear of reddish-brown on the page.

"So, could this blood be really old and just preserved, because it was packed in the files?"

Bethany chewed on one lip. "Maybe, but I don't think so. Blood dries, and the drier it gets, the darker. And it had to be fresh to make the pages stick together, if it did," she said, pointing at the report and looking at Norma, who was nodding.

"When I read through the file, those pages and a few others were stuck together," Norma said.

He nodded, and Norma saw it—his analytical mind, running through the possibilities. Just like William used to do. She knew he was thinking 'how would fresh blood get into his father's files?' and 'there was blood around his aunt's living room' and 'the box had been hidden back behind another stack of boxes.'

David looked up at her. "The way the boxes were arranged, there was no way the blood could get on the file. Or in it. It would've only been on the cover. Was the file on top of the box when you saw it?"

Norma nodded. Smart kid, smart like his father. "Right on top, like someone had just set it down."

"Was it sitting open to this page?"

Norma shook her head, enjoying watching him put it together. "No, closed. Other pages had stains, too. And a few smudges, like fingerprints."

"Why would anyone want to read this file?" David asked aloud, flipping through the pages. He couldn't even imagine how the blood had gotten in the file, dried and flaky in one corner.

No one answered.

"It had to be one of the deputies investigating the scene," David said. "Curious enough to pick up the case file and flip through it, getting blood stains on some of the pages."

"Maybe," Julie said. "It's one theory. Or whoever killed Abe and Gloria could have read it."

"Why wait around?" David asked, not believing it. "If you just killed two people, you would need to leave as quickly as possible."

"Maybe," Norma said. "Maybe you would flee, or maybe, if you had lots of experience with this type of thing, you would draw it out, make it last. What if someone sat down and relaxed and read that file while the victims died?"

David didn't want to think about his aunt suffering.

"And what if someone was particularly interested in that file, as opposed to all the other files in that box?" Norma looked at David and Bethany. "What's special about that case?"

David nodded. "Fines would want to read this."

"Exactly."

David shook his head and handed the file to Bethany, who thumbed through it. "It's just too...I can't even fathom it. Even if it was true, why would he come back?"

Agent Noble spoke up. "I'm not sure. My theory is that your father came close to catching him, maybe closer than anyone else. Maybe it bothered him—all these years. He drifted back this way and ended up here. Maybe he didn't even realize it until he got here."

Norma leaned forward. "David, he sought out your aunt. And possibly your roommate. You're in serious danger."

David glanced out the window. The wind was picking up again, and the rain that had been falling since last night was now coming down at a weird angle, slapping against the panes of glass. They had left the TV on during the discussion, muting the sound, and he'd seen intermittent satellite pictures of the hurricane. The worst of it was coming through the area tonight and tomorrow, the eye moving a hundred miles to the east. What would that mean for Liberty? They were already cut off from the highway?

He turned back to Norma and Agent Noble. "So, you think this guy is back, and he's looking for me. He read the file for insight into the case and my father's techniques."

The FBI agent nodded.

"And he killed my aunt, maybe out of revenge, or maybe he's using my aunt's death as bait to get me to return," David said.

"Yeah," Norma said. "Fines can't kill your father again, but maybe you would make a worthy substitute in his mind."

"I'm no cop," David said. "I don't know anything about catching criminals. I've never even held a gun," David said, exasperated. He didn't like this one little bit. He stood, pacing as he talked. "So, why don't the deputies believe you? I mean, it's common knowledge that Brown is an idiot, but your theories are strong enough to at least be considered. If it's all true, shouldn't someone be looking into it?"

Julie agreed. "My boss is assigning more experienced agents. And Blake assured me that he would be taking over the case soon. He'll aggressively pursue our inquiry when he takes control of the investigation on Monday morning. —"

"No, that's not good enough," David said, and the room grew quiet. "We have to get out there and do something. If this guy is running around, he needs to be stopped. We should go talk to Brown again, or at least warn people, right?"

He looked over at the box of his dad's paperwork that he'd brought with him and wondered what else was in it. There were files on his other cases. If there was someone out there that wanted him dead, it wouldn't take long for him to find David.

"There's that town meeting tonight," Bethany said. "The sheriff will be answering questions."

He shared his thoughts with Bethany and Norma and Julie, and then they discussed what had to happen next. He also saw Norma take more antacid. He knew her ulcer was bad, but not that bad.

"Well, the bridge being washed out has altered my plans," the FBI agent said. "I tried to call for backup, but the phones aren't working."

"I want to read all these files," David said, pointing at the coffee table. "And I'd like to study the maps some more, if that's okay. Norma, you said earlier that we were pressed for time—what did you mean?"

"Well, I wanted to drive around and look for him," Norma said, looking slightly embarrassed. "I know it sounds silly, but I feel like I know this guy. And it's not that big of a town—there are only so many places he can be. I wanted us, Julie and me, to show his picture around, too."

"That's a good idea," the agent added. "I can ask at the hotel. We probably know this guy the best."

"I was thinking we might be able to guess where he was, or what he might be up to." Norma looked outside and saw that it was starting to get dark. "The town meeting is in three hours."

"Maybe Fines doesn't know I'm back yet."

"Could be," Norma said. "Although you were interviewed. Word will get out."

"But he set out the bait. With my aunt," David said quietly, looking at Agent Noble. "If I show up at the meeting, maybe he'll make a move. Come after me. And then you can catch him, right?"

Julie nodded. "Yes, we can. With the other deputies in town, and Norma making an identification—yes, it's possible."

"Possible?" David raised his voice. "Possible?"

Agent Noble shook her head. "It's the best we can hope for."

David nodded, sitting back down. It wasn't that reassuring.

————

Norma wasn't sure what to do next. She was talking to Julie about the meeting tonight, and Bethany was asking about getting a deputy to guard her and David. All Norma wanted to do was get into Agent Noble's car and drive around. Norma knew what he looked like, or at least what he had looked like. If she could spot him on the streets—

"Okay, it's three now," David said, speaking up and setting the file down. "Let me go through my father's files. There might be something else in there that could help."

Julie nodded, listening.

"Norma, why don't you and Agent Noble drive around a little, check out his old haunts," David said. "Not sure if it will do any good, but it will give me time to study. Bethany, maybe you could grab us all an early dinner before we go to this town meeting thing?"

Bethany nodded. "I can do that. I need to go see Lisa's parents, too."

David looked at them all. "If the deputies won't listen to us in their office, maybe they will listen in a more 'public' setting. Does that work for everyone?"

He looked around and Bethany was giving him a funny look. "What?"

She smiled at him. "Oh, nothing. It just sounds like you're in charge."

Norma nodded, keeping her opinion to herself. The voice was even the same. Doling out assignments, leading by explaining what he needed from each person instead of barking orders. The resemblance was uncanny.

"Sounds good," Julie said, glancing at her watch. "I like that—confront them. Brown will stammer and look like an idiot. Then Blake can step in and take over. We could meet with them after, go over our theories again in more depth."

David nodded. "Yeah, but that's not why I'm doing this. If the deputies won't investigate this, we'll have to. You and Norma have already gone a long way toward figuring out what's going on."

Julie nodded, agreeing, and jingled her keys. "Good luck with the reports, David. The reports on the Green River killings are the most comprehensive," she said, pointing. Norma had already been through all of those. "We'll be back around five—I might try calling from other areas of town, see if I can get through. Norma, let's roll."

Norma got up and they said their goodbyes and followed Julie out.

"You know this is hopeless, right?" she asked the FBI agent.

"Hey," Julie said. "At least we're doing something."

David took his time going through his father's file on Jasper Fines. The case read as he'd expected, and there were few surprises. David's father had taken a bullet in the leg during the stakeout, a detail he must've forgotten.

Reading, David felt a growing sense of pride for his father. He finally understood why the town seemed to hold him in such high regard.

After he finished the Fines case, David spent a solid hour studying Agent Noble's maps and files. He sketched out his own version of the national map, making his own notes. It was hard to ignore the connections in the case, especially when you saw how so many "incidents" could have been carried out by the same person. And he studied the sketch of Fines, letting the image burn into his memory. He'd seen it before, of course, but never really studied it. Not like today.

Just before 5:00 p.m., David heard a car pull up in the driveway and sat up, his back stiff. All that time driving in the car, topped with reading for hours. And only a few days ago, he'd been on his way to California. It seemed like a lifetime ago when he was sitting there at that counter with a cup of coffee in his hands, debating about whether or not he should even call Bethany.

He heard Julie and Norma talking loudly as they came in.

"Any luck?" he asked them.

"No, nothing," they said, shaking the rain from their clothes. "But the weather's getting worse. They've put up roadblocks on a few flooded streets."

Bethany came in as well, carrying Chinese food. "They were the only place open. Hope that works," she said.

"Looks great," he said. David stood and helped her set everything out on the kitchen counters, and everyone helped themselves before sitting around the dining room table, scooting the files over to make room.

"Agent Noble, that map of yours is very interesting," David said when she sat down.

"Julie, please," she said. "It took a while to narrow it down to those cases. And I'm sure we missed some."

Bethany sat next to David. "Figure anything out?"

"Well, for one thing, my dad was smart," David said. "Once he put up the curfew, no more civilians got hurt. The coroner said he'd never seen anything like it—torture..."

"That's enough," Bethany said. "I'm trying to eat."

Agent Noble nodded. "Remember, the term 'serial killer' hadn't even been invented yet. Only a true psychopath could have committed the crimes I tracked."

The conversation continued, four people sitting around the table, eating and discussing the cases and David's father. And somewhere along the line, David realized he was enjoying himself. The subject matter was dark, of course, but he'd never really sat around a table just talking. The experience was strange and golden, something to be savored. When Bethany reminded them that they needed to leave for the town meeting, David was disappointed to see their group break up.

———

The town meeting was being held in the high school gymnasium, the only place in town large enough to hold the expected 250 to 300 people. Wooden folding bleachers stretched along both walls of the gym, pulled open for the meeting and providing seating for those who didn't want to sit in the rapidly-filling rows of folding chairs set out on the basketball court. A wooden platform and podium were set up on the eastern side of gym, away from the doors.

The few members of the press who had elected to stay in town during the storm were grouped in the front row of the floor seats or off to one side, setting up cameras and grabbing people at random for interviews. Tina Linsey from the Pittsburgh paper was among them, trying to interview one of the officers guarding the podium.

Seated nearby were members of the city council and other town officials not important enough to be seated on the raised platform. The rest of the seats were rapidly filling with local townsfolk. The low babble of excited conversation filled the large room.

The place was filling fast, something David would not have expected. The weather outside was bad and getting worse, and that should've kept most folks away. Evidently a lot of people in town were concerned enough to venture out in the storm.

David and the others were seated in the stands on the north side of the gym, a place he hadn't visited since his high school graduation. David was thinking about his father—he'd spent the last few hours in his father's world, going over his files and getting to know the mysterious figure that had left such a giant hole in his life. While sheriff, David's father had reassured the people, calming them with assurances that the killer would be caught, that the reign of terror would be ended. But tonight, people were on edge. Sheriff Brown evidently failed to inspire that kind of trust in the townsfolk.

"How many people do you think are here?" he asked.

Bethany scanned the crowd, one hand casually resting on David's knee. "Oh, 250, 275, I'd say." Julie and Norma sat in the row in front of them, chatting discretely.

"How would you know?" he asked good-naturedly.

She smiled. "Last year the Bobcats made it into the playoffs, remember? I went to one of the games, and it was about this full. They had a 'guess the attendance' contest. I remember it was a little under 300."

David nodded, looking at the large Fighting Bobcats seal painted on the parquet wooden surface in the middle of the gym. It was now hard to see, covered with rows of folding chairs.

She looked at him. "You still nervous?"

"Yeah, I mean, it's a long shot, right?" He shrugged. "What are the chances the guy would come back after so many years? People are going to laugh me out of here."

She thought about it. "Maybe you should've just called the sheriff up and suggested it straight to him, instead of getting up in front of all these people."

He shook his head. "No, he won't listen to me, just like he didn't listen to Norma or Agent Noble. He laughed at them. And look at the way they treated you when you went in to report Lisa missing. They did nothing to make you feel any better," he said, looking at her. "No, I have to do it in public, where everyone can hear. I don't care if people think I'm stupid—it's just too important."

His words came out with a degree of defiance. Hours poring through his father's files and the reports that Julie had brought with her from D.C. had told David two very valuable things: Jasper Fines had been very clever, and his methods were nearly identical to the person who was now terrorizing Liberty citizens.

Five feet beneath the Fighting Bobcats seal, Jack Terrington loosened the last bolt. It was very warm standing next to the boiler, which was cranking out hot water and pushing it though hundreds of feet of pipes, trying to warm the school and gymnasium against the cold rain and winds outside. Jack's face and arms were covered with dust and streaked with sweat.

come on come on

The huge bolt finally spun loose, and Jack glanced around to make sure no one had come down the stairs. Jack removed the gauge housing, exposing the back of the apparatus and the metal wire connected to the gauge's pointer. Gingerly, he plucked the wire off of the gauge and immediately the needle spun to read 0 PSI. Any fool could hear the dull roar of the boiler and see the gauge shouldn't have read zero, so Jack spun the needle around to 250 PSI--normal pressure and well out of the danger zone of 600 PSI--and bent the needle back to make it stick.

Checking to make sure the gauge still read 250, Jack slapped the gauge housing back into place, replacing the transparent cover, and screwed a couple of the thick bolts back into place to hold it.

Wiping his hands on an old rag, Jack made his way over to the boiler pressure controls and turned the knob up to its sticking point. The boiler was now at maximum. Pulling the plastic knob, he wrenched it free from the control panel. Now all that stuck up from the panel was a thin metal rod—if anybody managed to figure out the boiler was going to go, there was no way they could turn it down without pliers or the knob, which Jack slipped into his pocket for safekeeping. It would make a great addition to his collection—the knob that controlled the boiler that blew, killing so many people in a small town in Virginia. Just the thought made him smile.

Even in the time it took him to pocket the plastic knob, the boiler rumbled louder, the pressure growing steadily. Yet the gauge still read a serene 250 PSI.

perfect

Jack left, grabbing the topless calendar on the way out and heading back up the stairs to the maintenance office.

————

"Any luck?"

Julie shook her head, the frustration obvious on her face. "Nope. I guess all the lines are down now."

Norma nodded, agreeing. She knew next to nothing about cellular phones. Only a few people in Liberty had them, and certainly nobody that Norma knew. But as with any new technology, she figured they were finicky.

"Who are you trying to get?"

Julie looked at her and shrugged. "I'm not supposed to say, but I was calling the Situation Desk at headquarters. Any time an agent is out in the field and needs help, they're supposed to call the Desk. I need to contact my boss and let him know what's happening here. And what's going on with the sheriff and his investigation," she said, nodding at the podium.

Norma turned and looked. Jes Brown was walking up to the microphone, and most of the sheriff's office was on the podium with him. "At least Blake seems smart," Norma said, nodding at the man sitting behind the sheriff, his uniform out of place among those of the locals. Joyce, Norma's deputy friend, was there too, near the row of press. One reporter was asking Joyce a question, but the deputy was shaking her head like she didn't want to answer.

––––––––

The bleachers on either side of the gym were filling up fast as the meeting began. Most of the attendees were families, a mom and dad and two or three kids, all bundled up against the rain and wind outside. David could imagine the whole parking lot outside overrun with minivans, and he wondered what it would've been like if he'd grown up with a set of parents. These families seemed happy, even in the face of such troubling events. They had people to talk to, people they could rely on.

David saw some of the city council talking to a group of town officials, a very animated discussion with hands waving and fingers pointing in the general direction of the podium.

And David saw lots of deputies, milling around and scanning the crowd, probably looking for people they didn't recognize. It was assumed that Lisa's killer was a stranger from out of town, and David had gotten some idea of how people reacted to a killer in their midst through reading his father's notes. Outsiders and strangers still evoked the same visceral reaction.

David continued to scan the crowd, recognizing many people. The lady who cut his hair at the Hair Cuttery, the one with the bad breath and the never-ending questions about his love life and the accent he couldn't understand half of the time. There were kids he knew from school—kids who'd always hung out smoking behind the auto shop and were now grown up and working in gas stations. A few people said "hi" to him, recognizing the town's most famous orphan.

David saw lots of faces he knew, and he studied the ones he did not know closely.

––––––––

Jack stood by the gym doorway, looking in at the assembled crowd. He felt electricity in the air, an aliveness in his body that he could hardly contain. In his pocket, his hand toyed with the boiler knob, turning it over and over in his scarred palm.

Jack had planned to leave the boiler room the same way he'd come in, through one of the small exterior windows, but he hadn't been able to resist the urge to see the faces of the people he was about to kill. These people were already dead—they just didn't know it yet. And he was used to watching the faces of people as they died. That wouldn't be an option here, so this would have to suffice.

count them quick how many are there

Jack was able to pick two or three people he recognized. The current sheriff, of course. A few of his deputies, the old lady from the library who had helped him with his "research."

Beaumont had given his life to protect this little piece-of-shit town, but Jack was going to do something about it. The Beaumont kid was probably all the way to California by now, not coming back no matter what kind of bad news he got from this town. Maybe the kid hated this town almost as much as Jack did. But maybe Jack would run into little David Beaumont someday out in Los Angeles. They could chat and get coffee, and then Jack could finish off the Beaumont family in grand style.

time to go clock is ticking

Jack savored the moment. These people were all going to die soon, and at his hand. It would be Jack's greatest triumph, blowing this town off the map. Too bad there was no way—

It was her. It had to be. Jack stared at the woman sitting on the wooden bleachers next to a very attractive brunette. He'd broken the cop's nose, and this woman's nose took a strange twist near the end, long healed but still ugly. She'd kneed him in the crotch, but a couple of nights later he'd shot her and then killed her boss. She'd quit the force, and now she drove a school bus, the librarian had told Jack. She suffered from horrible, debilitating ulcers.

Oh well, lady, your pain is about to end, he thought. Blaze of glory and all that. The cute girl next to her would die soon, too. Too bad I can't hook up with that hot little number before this place goes up. Oh, the sacrifices Jack made. A little laugh escaped his lips as he started to turn and leave, already aware that he was staying too long—

And he saw Beaumont.

It was him, out of uniform and looking fit and happy. It had to be him. The chin, the face. But the man was dead, and this version of him looked younger, skinnier. The face was the same, though. David Beaumont.

... there he is

He had come back, after all. The kid was sitting in the bleachers next to a pretty girl, right behind the deputy with the broken nose. The pictures at Gloria's house were old—this kid was grown. The spitting image of a younger Beaumont.

Jack couldn't stop staring—he had half a mind to stroll in there and climb the bleachers and strangle the brat with his bare hands, right in front of all those people. They'd be dead soon anyway.

Damn, Jack cursed under his breath. He'd wanted to catch the kid and kill him slowly—dying with rest of the town was too quick an ending.

———

David was looking out the windows at the storm when he saw the black bird.

It was impossible, of course, because the winds were howling outside, and the rain was coming down again in thick sheets. But there it was, hovering outside the steamed windows on the opposite side of the gym. It was flapping its wings like crazy to stay in one place.

There were others, too, more birds of different types, eagles and crows and even a seagull, flapping in the gusting wind. They bobbed in front of the windows and dropped out of sight. How could they fly in that wind? It had been hard for David to keep his car on the road on the way over here.

The black bird seemed to be looking right at David.

And then all the birds were gone, blown away by one huge gust of wind. Gone, as if they had never even been there in the first place.

David stared at the windows. Strange birds. Owls and crows and seagulls—he'd seen a black bird like that up at the rest stop pullout when he'd been trying to decide if he should leave Liberty. And then there'd been that lady at the coffee shop with the sister who was nicknamed Bird. Birds everywhere, crazy birds ducking and spinning and looking in the window, looking at him. Weird, he thought, glancing at the doors to the outside, wondering if he could see the birds through the front doors.

Some guy was staring at him.

A chill rushed over David's body. Craggy, worn face, deep, piercing blue eyes. The hair and beard and mustache unkempt, making the man look more like a homeless person than a concerned citizen. David had never seen that man's face around town.

And he was looking right at David, angry.

David thought, for a second, that the old man looked like the police sketch of Jasper Fines. Older, tired, but similar.

David turned and nudged Bethany. "Bethany, look at that guy by the door, staring at us."

She turned and looked. "Where?"

David turned to point out the man, but he was gone.

Jack left in a hurry. The kid had spotted him, and for one long glorious moment their eyes had met. There was some kind of connection between them. Too bad they didn't have time to meet for real.

Jack walked across the rain-swept parking lot toward his van. The wind was blowing so hard that it threatened to blow him off his feet.

Jack needed to find a place to watch. After, he would collect his stuff from the hotel and leave this town forever—though he'd need to keep an ear out for the final number of dead. Jack needed to add them to his tally. By then, Jack would have put the ghost of Beaumont to rest.

"Please, everyone, let's settle down," Sheriff Brown said into the microphone. It took a minute, but the crowd quieted. "Okay, folks, we all know why we are here. Some pretty bad things have happened recently, and we're here tonight to talk about them. First we're going to tell you what we're doing, and then we'll take all your questions."

Sheriff Brown launched into his speech. And even with all the talk of protection and safety and public good, to David it still sounded like a campaign speech. The sheriff was running for reelection, apparently. He announced deputies would begin around-the-clock patrols and other measures to catch whoever killed Lisa Stevens.

He spoke for several minutes about Lisa, talking about what a lovely girl she was, and David saw some of the people in the crowd nodding, like they were at church listening to a sermon. He wasn't buying any of it. There was no mention of Abe Foreman and Gloria Thatcher or their mysterious deaths.

During the speech, David glanced back at the door several times, but the man who looked like Jasper Fines never reappeared.

Brown prattled on and on without really saying anything of value. He promised to keep the town safe and to catch the perpetrators. Some of the crowd seemed bored with his speech, growing restless and taking off their coats in the warm gym.

After the sheriff was done, Lieutenant Blake stood and spoke for just a couple of minutes on the progress of the investigation into Lisa's death. David saw that the sheriff and his deputies didn't seem to pay any attention to Blake as he spoke. Instead, they were talking amongst themselves.

Suddenly, David had had enough—he wanted some answers.

He stood suddenly. "What about my aunt?" he shouted, making Bethany jump. She grabbed at his legs, but he ignored her.

Every eye in the place turned to him. At first it was scary, but as the moment drew out, it felt almost comfortable. Everyone was looking at him, sure, but he'd asked a good question.

Sheriff Brown stood as Lieutenant Blake backed away from the microphone.

"You want to know what happened to your aunt?" he asked, his voice carrying like a tent preacher. "Your aunt's death is going to be ruled a suicide. Abe Foreman's death looks like an unfortunate accident." The crowd murmured.

"I know that's what you say here in front of all of these people," David shouted. He could project as well. "But why did you ask me so many questions when I was at the station? So many questions about her life and her relationship with Abe Foreman, like you were investigating a homicide instead of an accident?" His voice had lost its nervous tremble.

The sheriff smiled. "We were only trying to understand why your aunt might have wanted to commit suicide."

"She didn't."

The crowd murmured louder. He stood firm, staring at the sheriff.

"Oh, no?" Brown asked, smiling. "You know something that the entire Liberty Sheriff's Department, in cooperation with the Virginia State Police, doesn't?"

"All I know is that there are too many questions surrounding her death, and Abe's," David said loudly, warming to the argument. "Why were there burns on her wrists like she'd been tied up? Why were there scratches on the banister where Abe fell, like he'd tried to grab hold and keep from falling? My aunt didn't have any reason to kill herself." He paused for a moment, glancing around, then continued. "Whenever my aunt wanted to escape, she'd just pour herself a drink, or two, or ten. Everyone knew that. So why kill herself—and if she did, how did Abe Foreman die? Trying to learn how to fly?"

"None of that's important," Brown said, dismissing him and the low ripple of laughter. "She might've finally run out of liquor, for all we know. She might've changed her mind after starting the car. We don't know. But we do know that she killed herself."

The crowd murmured louder—the fact that she killed herself had been widely publicized, but the manner in which she accomplished it had not. Few people knew it was carbon monoxide, the standard closed-garage suffocation.

"I lived in that house for years," David shouted. "I never came close to falling over that railing."

"Maybe you're just more coordinated," The sheriff continued. "Who do you think killed your aunt? Maybe O.J. did it?"

Nervous laughter from the crowd, and David blushed, then recomposed himself. "No, I think they were killed by the same person who killed Lisa Stevens."

That sent the crowd talking. No more murmuring for a while, but actual conversations. It took the sheriff a minute of waving his arms to quiet the crowd. "Oh? And how did you make that leap of deductive reasoning, might I ask?"

"Because someone went through my father's files at my aunt's house. While my aunt was dying, someone rifled through his papers, leaving blood on them. IN them. I think it was the same guy who killed my aunt, and Abe Foreman, and Lisa Stevens. The same man that killed my father."

Silence.

No one knew what to make of it. It was so sudden, and outlandish, and unthinkable—to think Jasper Fines had returned was off the reservation for most of the people in the gym.

First came a low bout of giggling, followed by a swell of laughter. Suddenly, the whole idea struck the crowd as funny, and the nervous laughter grew until David thought he was going to fall over from embarrassment.

They might've been laughing at the crazy idea of his, or they might've just been laughing to let off some steam. There had been precious little to laugh about in Liberty over the past week. Either way, they were laughing. At him.

David started to shout, yelling for everyone around him to shut up. He waved his arms, his voice held a power that quieted them, a voice full of honesty and authority. At that moment, the older citizens were reminded of another voice, another Beaumont, one long dead.

The crowd quieted, all except for the sheriff up on the dais, who continued laughing, holding himself and chuckling like a department store Santa Claus. After a moment, he stopped too, and stared at David, a look of sheer pleasure on his face.

"I know what you all are thinking," David shouted over the dying laughter. "I've looked into it. Back in 1978, the victims were missing parts of their bodies, and so was Lisa Stevens. She was missing her thumb, and her tongue was cut out."

At this, he heard Bethany beside him begin to cry, but he couldn't stop, not now. Not while he had the crowd's attention.

"How many murders have we had?" David asked. "Five in ten years, and now three in two days? Four, if Bernie was killed. I think that Jasper Fines is back, or whatever his name is. He killed Lisa the same way he killed those people back in 1978."

Everyone was listening, but their faces were confused. Scared.

"And then he killed my aunt and Abe," David continued. "And while they were dying, he looked through my father's records and read the file on his case all those years ago." He waved his father's file. "I found dried blood inside this file—do you know what that means? Someone read this file after Abe was killed. There was blood everywhere. The reader got some of Abe's blood on his hands and smeared it when he was turning the pages of these files!"

David's own blood was boiling. It felt like a hundred degrees in the gym. In the heat of the moment, his imagination took over. It almost looked like the windows were beginning to sweat moisture. "With me is Norma Jenkins, one of my father's deputies. You all know her—she was there, and she agrees with me. And this is FBI Agent Julie Nolan. She came all the way down here from D.C.—in the storm—to investigate the connections."

"Right, I understand, son," the sheriff answered in a very caring, understanding voice, a voice that might've sounded caring and understanding if it had come out of someone else's mouth. Here, it just sounded condescending. "You lost a father and an aunt, and it makes sense to you that they somehow be connected. But I'm sorry to say that it's just not possible. The man that killed your father is probably long dead, and your aunt killed herself, possibly after seeing the accident that had befallen her lover, Abe Foreman."

Another murmur went through the room. David started to say something, but the sheriff put up his hand.

"Let me speak, son—you had your chance. We already discussed these wild theories with Miss Jenkins and Agent Nolan, and I dare say that the FBI needs to be a little more selective about whom they send out to investigate things. Perhaps you should be an FBI agent for more than a week before they let you out to play," Brown said, clearly enjoying himself.

David started to say something, but Brown plowed ahead.

"One way or another, you need to leave this to the experts, son,"

Sheriff Brown said. "We're having this meeting to calm people down, not stir them up. Please leave and take your 'friends' with you."

It was deadly silent, and David knew that he had lost. There was no way he could argue his case in front of all of these 'understanding' eyes, eyes that only saw his pain and wouldn't listen to his reasoning. He reached down and grabbed his coat and the files and started down the creaky wooden steps of the bleachers. After a moment, he heard creaking behind him as Bethany and the others followed. There were no other sounds in the room except for the heavy rumbling of machinery beneath the floor. In the silence, it sounded impossibly loud, rattling and clanking.

David got to the bottom of the wooden steps and hopped down onto the parquet floor of the gym, weaving between the rows of folding chairs and making his way out into the hallway, Bethany steps behind. He walked across the hallway and leaned against the brick wall of the hallway, sinking slowly to the floor, his heart pounding.

Bethany kneeled beside him, but it didn't help—he was just too humiliated to even feel her warm arms around him. It was all for nothing; no one would listen. They didn't want to see that the killer was back, and this time there was no legendary sheriff to save them. This town was in serious trouble, with a pandering, politicking sheriff at the helm and a brainless group of half-witted deputies following his every word—and no one with an ounce of leadership in his body except for that Blake guy, and he wasn't standing up to the fat man.

Bethany leaned over him. "Don't worry, David. It's okay—"

"No, it's not okay," David said. "Don't you see? This bastard could be back here, and no one cares. I feel like I'm going crazy!"

A low rumble issued from beneath the floor of the school, a low rattle of pipes and hoses, as Agent Noble and Norma came out and over to where David was sitting against the wall.

David saw a man came out of the gym from the doors behind Norma and for a moment thought he was coming out to talk to David, maybe to chastise him for his stupid ideas. Instead, the man walked over to the main doors leading outside, pulling one open. He stood in the doorway for a long moment, enjoying the fresh air. His face was very red. The cool blast of rainy air felt good.

Julie noticed, too, turning around to look at the man as he stood in the doorway for a moment before letting the door close and heading back inside the gym. She was quiet as Norma and Bethany talked to David, asking him what they were going to do now. Norma was suggesting they drive around town some more, searching, but he wasn't listening. When Julie turned around, David was looking at her seriously.

"You know," he started, talking to the group but looking at Julie, "before the meeting started, I thought I saw him. Fines, standing out in the hallway, staring at me from this doorway. The more I think about it, the more I think it could've been him."

The others fell silent.

"You saw him?" Bethany asked. He hadn't told Bethany his suspicion before, only pointing him out. Julie and Norma looked at each other, Norma running a hand through her hair. Her forehead was dotted with beads of sweat.

"But why?" Norma asked. "Why come here tonight? Beaumont is gone, his wife and sister-in-law are gone, and you're supposed to be out of town, on your way to California. Few people know you're back. Everyone connected to your family is gone—who else is there to hate? Or did he come back for some other reason? Maybe he left something here, or followed someone, or was planning to abduct someone from here?"

David glanced at Julie again, but she was looking at the front doors still, a curious look on her face. "I don't know. Maybe it wasn't him."

"It was him," Julie said, still looking at the doors that led outside. "But what is his motivation? He killed your aunt, and presumably he thought you were gone. Maybe he thought killing her would draw you back. But that was Monday night. Why is he still here unless he's waiting for you? Have there been other murders here in town that we don't know about yet? If he can't kill all of the Beaumonts, what's the next best thing?"

Norma shook her head, and Bethany wore a look of confusion on her face, but David knew where Julie was going.

"There has to be some other target."

"Right," Julie said, nodding. "More victims."

Bethany stepped back, pulling off her jacket and slinging it over her shoulder. "Can we get a breath of fresh air? I'm sweating bullets."

Something clicked in David's head and he hopped to his feet. "My father loved this town, loved the people. Gave his life to protect them."

"Right," Julie repeated. "And how could Fines hurt this town?"

"That's easy. Kill as many people as he can before he gets caught," Bethany answered.

Another low groan issued from beneath the wooden floor, this time louder and longer, like an angry beast trapped beneath the floorboards. Julie stopped the question she had started and listened, trying to localize the sound. She stepped to the doorway leading into the gym and listened as the sound died away.

David watched her. "And the easiest way to kill a lot of people is to do it all at once," he said, a shiver racing through his body. He understood the look on Julie's face. "In a central location. With lots of people are gathered."

Julie nodded. "Right. You saw him here tonight, and it feels like a hundred degrees in here. And half the town is in that gym right now."

He looked at Julie. "The boiler?"

Julie nodded again. "It would explain the sounds. Fines could have been here to mess with the boiler and looked in to get an idea of how many people were here. He's a collector, so he couldn't help but look at his victims, maybe even try to get a quick count. He saw you and was pleasantly surprised—you are his last Beaumont. Both his goals would be achieved at the same time."

"Oh shit," Bethany said.

"Yeah." David agreed.

"So, what do we do?" Norma asked, her voice suddenly high, nervous. "Get everyone out of there? Is there time?"

"I don't know," Julie said, shaking her head. "There's no way to tell when it will go, unless someone goes down and checks the boiler itself."

Norma nodded, starting off. "I'll go—I've been down there before. Julie, go back in there and use your badge and clear everyone out. Tell them there's a bomb. Even if we're wrong, at least the sheriff's touchy-feely session will be canceled." She walked to a door marked "Maintenance" and pulled it open.

"I'll go down with you, Norma." David said.

"Okay," Julie said, walking toward the gym, getting out her badge. "Bethany, you stick with me. Everyone, meet outside at the car when we're done."

Bethany turned to David. "Be careful. I'm not losing you again," she said, kissing him. He nodded and smiled, then chased after Norma.

Julie swallowed, nervous, and walked back into the gym, ignoring the murmurs that grew as she walked right up onto the podium. She began talking to the sheriff, who was in the middle of addressing the crowd again.

The crowd heard a muffled "What the hell..." and nothing more as the sheriff and the FBI agent talked, one of his beefy hands covering the microphone. Her voice was powerful and carried to the first few rows; listeners heard words like "explosion" and "responsibility" and "catastrophe," but the sheriff continued to shake his head. Finally, she simply pushed her way around him and took the microphone.

A younger woman—some of the townsfolk recognized as Bethany

King—stepped up to the podium and stood next to the FBI agent, as if lending her credibility.

"Your attention, everyone. My name is Julie Noble, and I am with the FBI. Everyone must exit these premises. Immediately."

Her words were forceful and full of menace, even delivered as calmly as they were, and after only a moment or two, most of the audience stood and began climbing down from the wooden bleachers. After a few moments, a small traffic jam appeared at the main doors out of the gym, and she stepped up again, preparing to say something else.

Sheriff Brown stepped up and pushed her away from the microphone.

"Now everyone, please be assured that nothing is wrong. Anyone who wants to leave may feel free to do so, but I can assure you that everything is fine. My deputies have inspected this building."

At this, some of the people by the doors stopped and turned back around, filing back toward their seats. Julie was horrified to see that many of them were families. Why would the sheriff of this town want to put them in such danger? Didn't he care about their safety?

Julie looked at Bethany, but she only shrugged her shoulders, unsure, her eyes nervously eyeing the doors. It was obvious that Bethany wanted nothing more than to leave. Another moan rattled the floor beneath them.

A rash thought went through Julie's mind, and she quickly slipped the gun from her holster and stepped up next to the sheriff, jamming it between his thick ribs but shielding it in a way that no one else could see. He let out a little grunt of surprise, glancing down at the hard hunk of metal in his side, and then up into her eyes.

"Tell them all to leave," she hissed. "Now."

He shook his head, amused. "Little lady, you've just bitten off a world of hurt. I don't care if you're with the FBI, the NRA, or the NFL, you're gonna wish you hadn't done that."

He slowly stepped toward the microphone, leaning over to say the words she wanted to hear. He began speaking but was drowned out by a huge, moaning sound that issued from beneath the floor, directly under the painted Fighting Bobcat in the center of the basketball court.

Norma knew her way around the basement, David could see. How she knew her way around she didn't say, but he could tell she'd been down here before. She'd worked for the school system for years. A narrow staircase led down from the janitor's locker room into the basement and boiler room. He followed her down the stairs, feeling the air temperature skyrocket as they approached the boiler.

"Damn, it's running hot." Norma said, coughing again and wiping sweat from her forehead as they walked into the boiler room.

Steam cloaked most of the machinery in the room, and the noise was deafening. David wondered how much longer it could hold. He didn't know anything about boilers, but the concept was pretty straightforward. Water heated in the big tank and piped out to the school to heat things. Too much boiling water would overtax the tank and cause an explosion.

A big one.

"Now what?" David asked, leaning against one big pipe and yelping as the searing metal burned his hand. He shouted a long string of curses and shook his hand, already seeing the skin on his right palm starting to redden and pucker from the burn. "Damn it!" he shouted, shaking his hand and looking around for something to wrap his hand in. The last thing he needed was a big scar on his palm.

Norma ignored him. "This way," she said, heading off into the steam. David followed her, mad at himself for being so clumsy. She paused to cough loudly, hacking up something and spitting it out. She found the boiler controls and looked them over.

"The boiler pressure gauge is reading a normal 250 PSI, well beneath the red zone of 600 PSI. But it's not supposed to sound like that," she said, pointing at the roaring pipes overhead. She tapped the gauge on the faceplate, but the needle didn't move—it seemed stuck.

David had found a rag stuffed into a crevice near the boiler gauge. The rag was oily and dirty, but it would have to do. He wrapped his hand tightly and made a fist, and it felt a little better.

"Help me find the controls to shut off the boiler."

They looked around and he saw a large circular area in the middle of the control panel marked "Pressure control."

"That looks like it, but there's no knob to twist or turn," David said. "It's just a little metal pole sticking up about an inch and a half."

Norma grabbed it. "He's screwed with the gauge to make it look like the boiler was just running normal, not working its way up to explode. And taken the knob," Norma told David, who simply nodded. The man was a planner, David would give him that. Fines wouldn't want anybody messing up his plans. "Look around for pliers or a toolbox," Norma continued, grabbing his shoulder. "Maybe we can still shut this thing off."

———

A rumbling moan shook the entire gym. To Julie, it sounded like it was coming from beneath them, straight up from hell.

She didn't see the sheriff make his move—he was surprisingly fast for such a large man. He turned and grabbed at Julie's gun, pushing it away. He succeeded in grabbing her wrist and twisting. Involuntarily, the muscles in her hand clenched, squeezing the trigger.

A shot rang out, whizzing across the gym and shattering a window high above the bleachers on the south side of the gym. Rain and wind began coming in the ragged hole. The crowd erupted in a panic, screaming. Chairs fell over and people fled for the exits, pushing others from behind. People raced down the wooden bleachers and ran for the narrow doors, already jammed with people trying to leave.

Julie wrestled with the sheriff, desperate to keep the gun from going off again. This sheriff was a maniac. She managed to overpower him before she was rudely grabbed from behind by two deputies. One stripped the gun from her hands and pocketed it while the other deputy pushed her off the stage. She was airborne for a moment, flailing, and then crashed painfully into several vacant folding chairs, landing on her back and side.

In the commotion, Bethany fell on the podium. By the time she could stand, Julie had been pushed from the stage, falling awkwardly into some chairs. Another hellish moan issued from beneath the floor.

The sheriff had made his way down from the podium and was talking to the mayor and some of the city council members, who were visibly upset. He was using his best ass-kissing voice to soothe them, telling them that there was nothing to be concerned about. Most of the council members looked like they wanted to run, but they trusted this portly man. They stood in a circle arguing, their feet covering the Fighting Bobcats symbol in the middle of the floor.

Bethany looked at the main exit—it was crammed with people clawing at each other. The two deputies were still on the podium, their guns drawn and pointed at Julie, who was climbing awkwardly to her feet.

"You need to go help them!" Bethany screamed.

One of the deputies looked at her, pointing. He looked at the doors and cursed.

"Watch the FBI agent," he said to his fellow deputy. "I'm gonna go help."

Bethany waited until the other deputy looked back at Julie and then stepped up quickly, swinging a folding chair, knocking him to the podium floor. Julie grabbed his gun from the stage, along with her own from his waist.

"You okay?" Bethany asked.

"Yeah," Julie said, grimacing. "My back is killing me. I hit those chairs wrong. Let's get out of here," she said, passing the sheriff and his group, but Bethany grabbed her arm. The ground rumbled so loudly beneath their feet that it was no longer a question of if the boiler would blow, but when.

"No way we're getting out that way," Bethany said, pulling her in the opposite direction. "The girls locker room has an exit."

Bethany ran, and Julie followed. Inside, the locker room smelled of old towels and sweat and mildew. Piles of dirty towels were strewn on wooden benches.

"This way." Bethany yelled, leading her to a pair of doors marked "Tennis Courts." Other people were following them now, including Lieutenant Blake. Bethany let go of her and stopped, and Julie slammed into her. A heavy metal chain looped around both doors, joining at a heavy looking padlock.

"The door is chained," Bethany said, turning to Julie. "We're trapped."

––––––––

There were no tools anywhere, no way to slow the boiler's angry howl. Norma was still at the boiler controls, trying to turn the knob with her bare hands, but it was no use.

"Nothing," David shouted from the other side of the room. The boiler moaned above her.

She shook her head, her hands falling away from the control panel. Her fingers were bloody. "It's no good. I can't get a grip on it without the knob."

David looked around. "The other control knobs? You could take one of those off—"

"Already tried," she said. "None of them work."

She nodded, cursing Jasper Fines under her breath. He'd beaten her eighteen years ago, and he was doing it again now.

"Norma, you tried. We gotta go."

She looked at the controls again, desperate, but there was nothing to be done. She nodded and followed David as he ran for the stairs. They were about halfway up when the whine started behind them, low at first and slowly increasing in pitch.

It was as if the boiler were screaming at them to get out. Now.

––––––––

Bethany's eyes were wide, the frantic need to escape written across her face. Julie knew they couldn't go back.

There were too many people between them and the doors, and the boiler could go at any moment. No, Julie had to get them out...

"Step back. Quick!"

Julie raised the deputy's gun and shot at the padlock, the chain and the door, hoping to hit something and hoping the ricochet didn't kill anyone.

The first bullet punched through the door, but the second one hit the padlock dead on and split it open. Julie leapt up and tugged the chains away and threw the doors open.

Cold air and lashing rain blasted her, the howling wind threatening to push the door closed again. She held the door open for Bethany and a dozen other people before letting the door go and stumbled across the rain-covered tennis court.

"This way!" Bethany shouted. "Over here!" She was running across the tennis courts to the far fence. Julie chased her, running awkwardly. Her back was screaming, but she corralled a half-dozen people toward the fence.

She heard the doors open behind her and turns to see more people were exiting the doors.

Julie caught up with Bethany, who was waiting on the other side of the tennis courts.

"I need to get around front," Julie said. "I need to clear those doors if I can."

Bethany nodded. "This way."

Julie followed her out through the tennis court exit and ran around to the front of the school. Scores of frantic townspeople were streaming out of the main doors and into the rain, running for the parking lot and the field beyond. The rain pounded the pavement around them, louder than the screams of the fleeing people.

She tried to get a count, but not nearly enough people had made it out. There were too many people still inside, as far as she could figure.

"Bethany, stay back—I'm going to try and clear the main doors," she said, turning for the front of the school when a loud, rough groan issued from the gym. It sounded as if the walls and the floor and the ceiling of the gym were straining, buckling, striving to contain something that would not be contained. A high-pitched whine accompanied the deafening moan, and as the squeal whined higher and higher, Julie knew what would happen next.

She turned, grabbed Bethany's hand, and sprinted away from the exit.

Jack sipped his Hardees coffee and waited. It was getting later, but he hardly noticed the time or the lackluster coffee. He'd forgotten the cinnamon raisin biscuits he'd bought. He only stared down the hill at the collection of buildings and lights and cars below.

lots of cars lots of people

The van was parked on a hill a mile north of the high school, overlooking the town. He'd been lucky to find such a vantage point. Now he could just sit back, relax, and watch the show. It was going to be just like the fireworks they used to shoot off in Salem at the Harvest Festival every September. And when it was over, he'd go straight to his hotel and pack and leave in the morning.

The coffee wasn't great, but the entertainment would make up for it.

David was out into the main hallway first, bursting out of the janitor's room. Norma was right behind him, her stomach twisting in horrible knots of pain. People were milling around the doors into the gym, jamming the doors to get out. Norma heard David shout at them to leave, shouting that the boiler was going to blow. Some listened, and some looked at him like he'd grown a second head.

Norma saw three children cowering in the corner, scared. To Norma, it looked like they were waiting for their parents, who were probably still trapped inside the gym. She could see the doors crammed with people trying to get out.

Norma considered for a moment shouting after David but then thought better of it. If he made it out, that would be good. She'd let his father down, and Norma owed the Beaumont family. She wasn't going to let David die, too.

She stopped and grabbed the smallest kid around the waist, hoisting him up, asking him where his parents were and shouting at the other two kids that they had to get out now. They seemed stunned, not sure if they should listen to this stranger but also confused by the noise and the situation around them. She used her best bus driver/cop voice, and that got them moving, along with some of the adults.

"GET OUT OF THE SCHOOL!!" She screamed. For a moment, the pain her belly lessened. She scooped up the middle one as well and grabbed the thirds' shirt with the same hand in which she carried the smallest boy, shoving them toward the door.

They made it outside into the pouring rain and were running down the front steps of the high school when it happened.

Below, the boiling steam filled the last empty spaces inside the sizable metal tank.

Water strained the metal, stretching it. Finally, the metal could hold the fervent water's energy no longer. The pipes below the massive metal tank blew first, shooting boiling water from the bottom of the tank like rocket engines.

The boiler exploded with the force of a bomb.

The massive boiler itself, weighing nearly four hundred pounds, leapt six feet straight up into the air, crashing into the ceiling above it. The myriad connections between the boiler's pipes and the gas main used to heat the water were severed as well, adding more explosive energy to the conflagration.

Anyone still trapped in the gymnasium had a front-row seat to madness. The floor buckled up from below, the ferocious visage of the Liberty Fighting Bobcat leaping upward as if it had come to life. Wood tiles and flooring burst up into the air as the school's boiler leapt out of the floor. In an instant, the room was filled with boiling water and a wave of fire and shards of metal and flooring. People were thrown high into the air as the roof of the gymnasium was destroyed. One man was skewered with a jagged piece of the wooden floor, stumbling away and falling. The outer walls of the gym peeled away, bricks and metal girders and bodies thrown high in the air.

Julie and Bethany and David and Norma and at least a hundred other people outside heard the explosion and collectively felt something like a huge warm hand slam them to the ground. Julie and Bethany were almost to the parking lot. David was crossing the grass near the large oak that stood in front of the school. A huge noise that sounded like a combination of screams and thunder roared behind them.

The next few seconds were filled with a deep rumbling sound as the whole world vibrated around them, shaking the ground. The force of the explosion threw Norma, and she landed next to the small child she was carrying, shielding him from the blast with her body.

When the sound finally died, David rolled over and looked.

The gym was gone, blown in a hundred different directions. Large pieces of the roof crashed to the ground around the gym, falling with the rain. One of the metal basketball hoops had embedded itself into the wet ground not ten feet from him. The bare oak had been slapped over, its naked roots reaching for unfamiliar dark sky. Heavy bricks littered every surface. He didn't see Bethany, or Norma, who had been right behind him. Some people had made it out behind him—he could see them on the ground between him and what was left of the school. There were some kids struggling to their feet just outside the doors, but he didn't see Norma.

David staggered to his feet and was starting back toward the school when the gas main blew, throwing him to the ground again. A massive, roiling ball of flame and gas boiled up into the air, flash-evaporating all the rain puddles for a hundred yards around the school and bathing everything in a blast of hot air, searing those still inside or too close to the building. David lay on the wet ground and covered himself against the blast.

Julie and Bethany were not so close. They didn't feel as much of the heat as David. After the boiler explosion, they ran, making it to the parking lot and crouching down behind a car. Julie had guessed that the gas main would go soon after the boiler went, and she had pulled Bethany most of the way to the car. Julie's back screamed in pain.

Bethany cried his name, over and over, yelling at the sky. She begged Julie to let her go so she could go look for him, but Julie wouldn't. Julie knew that David Beaumont was probably dead now. Even if he and Norma Jenkins had somehow managed to make it out before the boiler went, they wouldn't be able to find each other in the mass confusion. There were hundreds of injured. Scores of dead.

When the gas main exploded and sent up a massive fireball, Bethany tried to dart around the car and back toward the school, but Julie held her fast. It would probably be safe in a minute or two, but there was no need to let one more person die. After the sound quieted, she finally let Bethany go, and the girl jumped up and ran off.

In the parking lot and on the grassy approach to what was left of the school, people wandered and shambled through the howling rain. They all looked dazed, as if shock was setting in. Julie reached for her cellular phone to call 911 but realized it wasn't in her pocket; she must've dropped it somewhere in the chaos.

Julie staggered to her feet slowly and looked at the school. The gym was gone. The roof vanished as if by magic. Two walls were gone, and the one next to the school was slumped over, collapsed onto the main entrance. That was bad. Anybody trying to get out at the last minute, like David Beaumont and Norma Jenkins, would've been crushed. Flames flickered up from the blackened remains of the gym, and a massive cloud of black smoke hung over all. The falling rain, combined with the flames and the smoke, made the scene look like hell on earth.

The mayor, the sheriff, the city council and most of the town's deputies had been in that gym. Most of them had still been inside when she'd bolted through the doors to the locker room. Had any of them made it out? Who was in charge?

There was also the fact that Liberty only had one hospital, not nearly enough capacity to handle the sheer numbers of injured people she could see just from where she was standing. The field was littered with bodies, some moving around, others ominously still. This community didn't have the personnel for the major rescue mission that would be necessary to extricate any living people from the wreckage of the school. And what about the Liberty Fire Department, an all-volunteer force? How many of them had been inside? How many were left, and how fast could they respond?

She heard crying, and then shouting. One woman was screaming, on her knees and facing what was left of the school. People were starting to panic. Already, there had been several wrecks in the school's parking lot and grassy areas as people frantically tried to flee. Julie took a series of long, deep breaths and organized her thinking, ignoring the pain in her back. She heard, off in the distance, the first wailing of sirens.

Jack hadn't expected it to be that big. The first explosion had rocked the van, shaking him and making him almost spill his coffee, catching him by surprise. The second explosion was accompanied by a billowing mushroom of fire boiling up into the sky. It must've been the gas main going, something he hadn't even anticipated.

He reached around behind his seat and felt around, pulling out a pair of binoculars. Holding them up to his eyes, he scanned the wreckage below. Even though it was dark, the flames and fires lit the area. The rest was obscured by billowing smoke and the heavy rain falling between him and the school. He could see a few people had gotten out. They crawled around on the grass near the school or hid behind cars in the parking lot, and it looked like some of them were getting into wrecks trying to get out of the lot.

The carnage was beautiful. Beaumont's precious town was gone, and all the people he'd tried so hard to protect years ago were now smoking pieces of meat sprawled on wet grass.

He put the binoculars down and started up the van, rubbing his hands together in front of the vents, feeling the warm air flowing out. There had been around 250 people inside that gym, and maybe half of them had gotten out. That made his tally go up by at least 125, making his new total 325 or 350. He'd have to wait and watch the papers for a final count. This would surely be a national story.

Sadly, there was a chance the whole thing might get blamed on the storm—bad weather, boiler running too hot, tragic accident. But he would know.

Jack Terrington shook his head, delirious with joy. This town would dry up and blow away, fading off the face of the Earth. People might move in and rebuild, but they would be new people, new faces. Beaumont's people were all gone, dead. Jack smiled and turned his van toward the Motel 6. He would collect his things and leave this town behind him forever. There would be years of happiness and contentment for him in California. Reaping from the weak, taking what he wanted, slowly adding to his tally. He could retire, finally settle in one place. And no more dreams of this place or its people would trouble him. It was clear from the smoking evidence around him. Jack had won.

David stumbled toward the school, looking for Bethany. She *had* to have made it out, didn't she?

He stepped over the bodies of people he knew, all wearing faces he recognized, and he prayed that she wasn't one of them. Some of them were moaning or holding themselves, and he tried to help them, but he didn't stop long. He had to find her.

He'd already found Norma, dead. The little kid next to her body had been spared the brunt of the explosion. David had picked the child up and brushed him off and sent him on his way. David had closed Norma's eyes and covered her, wishing there had been more time for them to talk. He'd only really known her for a few hours, but he missed her already. And the kid would never know her, the person who saved his life.

There were so many people he *didn't* see, so many faces he'd seen inside the gym that weren't here now. The mayor, the city council, even the sheriff—not a sign of any of them. Had they gotten out? Were they somewhere else? Panic welled up inside of him—did anyone he knew make it out alive?

In the sky above the wreckage, David saw a dozen birds floating in the rain. They seemed to be circling the school, somehow managing it in the gusting winds and heavy rain. Why were they—were they carrion birds, drawn to the field of dead?

David suddenly heard his name being called out.

He turned and there she was, staggering toward him. Bethany's hair was a mess, and her face was smudged with soot and dirt, and she was the most beautiful thing he had ever seen in his life. He ran to her, holding her tight and never wanting to let go. Ever.

Julie finally found a deputy in the grass. He had escaped the initial explosion only to be knocked unconscious by the gas main going, apparently. She'd slapped him until he'd come around. Her back was still hurting, but seeing the dozens of injured and dead around her helped her ignore the pain.

The deputy, dazed, listened as she identified herself and told him that in the absence of an organized police response, she was taking charge of the scene and would need his help. They'd walked to his car and climbed inside, and over the initial disbelief of the dispatcher, Julie began giving orders.

First, firemen and paramedics had to be directed to the scene. Her first "order" was to get all of the emergency services units onto the same radio frequency, so she only had to say things once instead of four or five times. All five squads of the town's volunteer fire department arrived and began putting out the fire. Others pulled the injured from the smoking ruins of the school. Civilians began helping, too, assisting the firemen and taking direction from anyone in a fireman's hat.

Within minutes the fire was doused and smoldering, and the firemen and paramedics turned their full attention to helping the wounded. The local EMTs and rescue crews worked to triage patients and transport them to the local hospital and other local medical facilities. One EMT called in a group of construction workers to assist in digging people from the wreckage of the school entrance.

Julie contacted the local hospital to assess how much they could handle. The woman manning the emergency room's radio quickly estimated exactly how many wounded they would be able to help, and Julie advised her to have every medical staff member of the hospital paged or called. Unfortunately, a lot of those people were probably dead now, victims of the explosion.

A triage protocol was established at Liberty Hospital to sort the incoming injured and categorize them by priority. It hardly mattered, though—there weren't enough beds, or doctors, to help them all. Some of them would die waiting for surgery. It was a county hospital, but not a big one and not one designed to help a hundred seriously injured patients all at the same time.

An ER nurse also called the other three local medical facilities, small clinics located in strip malls scattered around town, and began coordinating medical services with them. Normally, in cases like this, small towns were able to rely on the hospitals in neighboring areas for assistance, but the storm and the flooded-out bridge eliminated that option. Rains and flooding had also shut down many of the roads in and out of town, and paramedic units from other towns could not get through to help them.

Liberty Hospital also contacted the largest regional hospital for help, but Fredericksburg General had its own issues: they had lost power and were running on backup generators. Winds and heavy rain had knocked out power to much of the city and grounded their helicopter. Virginia state authorities were contacted—some of the land lines were still operational—but they too wouldn't be much help until the storm cleared the area. They were spread too thin, already, with Virginia Beach getting so much damage from the hurricane.

Julie also asked anyone she talked with to contact her boss in D.C. or the Richmond FBI office and request backup, but she didn't think that would happen anytime soon. There were too many people hurt or dying to worry about the investigation right now.

A half-hour later, Julie sat in a sheriff's cruiser, exhausted. Others were helping now. The injured were being transported for medical care, and several of the town's deputies had reappeared, along with Lieutenant Blake. He'd escaped the gym by following her out through the tennis courts. Those courts were now being used to as a makeshift morgue, the bodies lined up on the wet green surface. Too many bodies.

Blake climbed in the car, taking the driver's seat. A large bird, standing on the hood of the car, took flight and disappeared. "You did well, especially for someone without any formal training in emergency response."

She nodded, tired. David and Bethany were okay and leaning against the hood of the cruiser, talking. David told them about Norma, and Julie was deeply saddened by the news, even though she'd only met the woman this morning. She looked over at Blake, handing him the radio.

"Thanks, but it shouldn't have happened at all. We were pretty sure Fines was back. The sheriff thought I was wrong, and now a lot of people are dead."

Blake nodded soberly, taking the radio and hanging it back on its hook on the dashboard. "Yeah, it looks he wanted to get as many as he could. I only wish I could get some of my boys in here so we could catch this guy." Blake leaned over, looking at her. "You did everything you could. Remember that."

She nodded again, this time feeling a little better. "Well, one way or another, this town is going to be cleaning up for a long time."

She looked out at the rain as it came down around them, falling on the injured and the dead. Fines had killed all over the country and they didn't even know his real name. Tonight he'd killed upwards of another hundred people, and they were no closer to catching him. She wondered if he would ever be caught.

If he were half as smart as she thought he was, the guy was long gone.

———

Jack collected his things from the hotel room at the Motel 6 and stowed them in his van. He had a small collection of new items and put them into their places with quiet contemplation. The knob from the boiler, the flyer of his face from the library. The coffee cup he'd been drinking from when the school went up. It all went onto the shelf above his small fridge, a place of high honor, where he also kept his victim's jewelry collection and the police badges and stars he'd collected.

He had finally won. The ghost of Beaumont was dead. The kid was dead, and half this town with him.

glorious fire and death

As he was driving off of the hotel property, he thought about the quiet years ahead of him in LA. Getting there might be tricky at first. The front desk clerk said most of the roads were out and gave Jack alternate directions out of town. The County Line Bridge had been washed out, so Jack couldn't leave the way he'd come into town, which disappointed him. He'd wanted one more look at that mall east of town.

In the aftermath of the explosion, his heart was warmed with an expansive feeling of omnipotence, as if nothing could go wrong ever again. He'd defeated a memory that had plagued him for years, and now things were perfect. He hadn't felt this good since he'd walked up that roadside hill so many years ago, gunning down the deputies as they scattered before him.

He felt like a god.

On a whim, Jack decided to take one last look at the carnage before leaving town. He'd like a piece of the wreckage. And he couldn't resist one last look at his greatest triumph.

———

"Let's go," David said, exhausted.

Bethany pulled away from him and looked up into his eyes. "Don't you think we should stay and help?"

David looked around. The fire was out, and he saw the cars and the firemen and the paramedics were fighting the rain and the wind to collect the injured and move the dead to a second temporary morgue set up in the Methodist Church across the street from the school. He could see Julie and Blake inside one of the patrol cars, coordinating the rescue efforts and directing the incoming paramedics and firemen to the places where they could be most useful. They had everything under control, or at least as much as anyone could control a disastrous situation like this.

He looked back at Bethany and saw the concern for all of these innocents in her clear eyes. Impossible as it seemed, he felt even more love for her. "No, we've done everything we can. Leave it to the professionals. Julie and Blake are coordinating things now, and I should get you in out of this rain."

She nodded, looking at him. "You sure that's it?"

"Actually, I'd like to drop you off at your house and drive around and look for him," David said, shrugging. "I know he did this, and he's probably still in town, but he'll be leaving soon. He thinks I'm dead. He thinks we're all dead. I know what he looks like, and I know he's been here for at least a week. I want to try the motel, describe him to the people working there. Maybe someone will remember him."

He turned and watched as volunteers carried a woman past them on a stretcher to a waiting ambulance. One of her legs was gone. "And if I can find him, I can call in law enforcement, whoever's left. Or Julie. They could finally catch this bastard."

She nodded, not saying anything, and they headed off toward his car. The curb was submerged in several inches of water that raced for the sewer drain. Looking back on it now, it was lucky they parked on the street—if they'd been in the main parking lot, it would've taken hours to get out.

———

Jack Terrington turned onto the main street that ran parallel to the school, a street packed with cars. Half of the car windows had been broken by flying bricks, which also littered the street. Farther down, by the entrance to the parking lot, several ambulances and squad cars blocked traffic.

Jack was busy staring at the high school—or what was left of it. The gym was gone. The walls and roof were blown in every direction. Where it had stood was only an empty shell, twisted pieces of metal and wooden bleachers intermixed with thousands of bricks

such glorious destruction

from the gym's facade. Wooden bleachers pointed at the rainy sky with broken wooden "fingers." Bricks littered the road in front of him. Jack was amazed by the sheer power of the explosion. It had been more powerful than he anticipated, but that was fine. The more people that died, the better. The sheriff, the city council, that state police lieutenant from Richmond, and all of those townspeople that Beaumont had died to save

lots of them dead maybe two hundred

were all gone. And the kid, too—that was the best part. Creepy how much he looked like his old man. There for a minute, Jack thought the sheriff had come back from the grave. Jack couldn't have planned it better if he'd spent years setting this up. Everything had gone off perfectly, and now, this town would never forget him. He had finally won.

Jack was busy staring at the smoking ruins of the school. He didn't see the two people walking in the middle of the wet street, hand in hand, until it was almost too late.

He kicked the brakes, skidding to a stop on the wet pavement, and eyed them. They must've been spectators who'd come to see the carnage— they couldn't be survivors of what had taken place at the school. They turned around and looked at him, and Jack's mouth dropped open.

It was David Beaumont.

no

Their eyes locked for a moment. Jack felt electricity in the air. They were face to face. He ignored the rain falling between them and the ticking of the van's engine. All Jack could see and hear was the face of David Beaumont and the rushing of blood in his ears as his heart beat crazily.

David stared back, seemingly ignorant of all around him. Out of the corner of his eye, Jack saw the girl next to him—it was the same girl from inside the gym. The boy recognized him.

Jack thought he saw the boy's face curl up slightly. To Jack, it almost looked like a smile.

no no kill him kill them both

Jack floored it.

The girl screamed, and the boy saw the van coming and pushed her out of the way. Jack felt the front grill of the van strike the boy hard, throwing him backward. He landed roughly on one side and slid on the wet pavement before coming to a stop, grasping at his right leg and curling up in pain.

Jack's mind raced as he popped the door open and climbed down, the rain and wind curling around him. There were people and cops all around—he couldn't kill the boy here, as much as he wanted to.

Jack walked to the front of the van and crazily, even in the heavy rain, he could clearly hear the clinking of the short metal chains on his rattlesnake-skin boots

clinking just like before clinking in the rain

as he walked over to the Beaumont boy. There were the headlights behind Jack, and the rain was coming down, and the kid on the ground looked so much like his father that for one crazy second Jack was sure he was back on that interstate eighteen years ago, standing over Beaumont in the rain and he reached for his gun

you can't kill him here

but no, he was here, and it was now. Jack's gun was in the van. The boy was holding his leg like it was broken, but Jack saw no blood or anything. And it was the same leg, the right one, where Jack had shot his father. It was all so strange. But he didn't want the boy dead.

Not yet.

David Beaumont started to get up from the wet road but felt a weight on his chest, pinning him to the pavement. He saw an odd-looking boot, snakeskin, wet with rain. A man smiled down at him, a man he recognized.

The man he knew only as Jasper Fines.

"Well, boy, I have to give you credit—you are one resilient son of a bitch."

David looked up at the man.

"But your father was a tough bastard, and I got him, too."

David couldn't breathe. The boot was pushing on his chest.

"Just like I'm going to kill you." Fines glanced around, but no one was paying them any attention yet. "God, this is so familiar! Too bad you're not wearing a star."

The man pointed at the star on his chest. Before David could get a good look at it, Fines lifted his foot off David and kicked him hard in the ribs. David squeaked and rolled onto one side, holding his chest.

When he rolled back over, David turned and saw the man was dragging Bethany roughly across the wet road, shoving her inside an old white van that had been idling nearby. She slapped at him a couple of times until he punched her hard in the stomach. David watched as Fines pushed her inside and then got in and pulled away, waving casually at David.

David lay helpless on the rainy wet pavement. The last thing he saw before the van disappeared into the darkness was twin red taillights, fading into the night like the eyes of a demon.

———————

"Any sign of David Beaumont and his girl?"

Julie looked up—it was Lieutenant Blake again. She was resting against the side of one of the ambulances.

"No, they were taking off."

He nodded. "One of the deputies wants to talk to them," he said, sitting next to her. "You okay?"

She shook her head. "No, not really. I can't believe Fines got away with it."

"Don't worry," Blake said. "If he's around here, someone will catch him. I have faith."

"No one's caught him. Not in twenty years. This is the closest anyone's gotten in a long time," she said, glancing up at the destroyed building and the field of dead that surrounded them. "And now he's gone. Again."

———————

The pain was excruciating. His leg was broken, either from getting hit by the van or the fall afterward. It didn't really matter. Shivers and bolts of hot pain shot up his leg every time he pressed down on the gas, and he could feel bones grinding inside him. It was like his leg had been emptied out and filled with sharp knives, each cutting and scraping at the others.

Each movement brought a renewed torrent of pain.

David tried to ignore it while he drove.

He'd gotten to his car and found the keys and managed to climb up inside. The passenger side window had been shattered, and he'd found a brick from the school in front seat.

The streets of Liberty were covered with several inches of water, sluicing off into the gutters and sewers, spilling over into vacant lots and ditches. There was just too much water for the system to handle, and the water was backing up, filling the streets and flooding low-lying areas. The baseball field between the gym and Highway 132 was a muddy lake, second base a square island in the water. Trees and power lines brought down by the hurricane-force winds littered the streets and lawns of the town. The power lines hissed and sparked and probably would have caught fire had it not been for the torrent of water falling from the sky in thick, angled sheets.

David thought he knew which way the van went, but he couldn't be sure. The Mazda chuffed and groaned as he popped the gearshift and coasted to a stop at the red light. He cursed and wished again that they'd taken Bethany's car, but she hadn't felt like driving. Julie and Norma had driven in Julie's car. And now Norma was dead.

He shook his head and concentrated. David was at the main turn for the school on the road that bordered the western edge of the campus. There was the Methodist Church directly in front of him at the junction— paramedics were setting up a makeshift morgue. David remembered back in high school he had visited the church once during a bomb threat called into the school. Anybody who had been on the southern side of the school had been evacuated to this church, a quick walk over the baseball field and across Highway 132.

Here, the road made a T. David could either go east, out toward the interstate and the mall and out of town, or west into town. He could not see far enough in either direction to see the van, so he had to guess. East meant the mall and the County Line bridge, out by the freeway where Jasper Fines had killed David's father. West was heading toward town and the supermarket and other locations where Fines had abducted people.

David didn't know. He'd read his father's files and handwritten notes, along with Julie's FBI psych profile. He'd also read about the other cases that Julie thought his father had been involved with, and David tried to remember everything the cases had described.

Three cars ahead of him, the light turned green.

Which way? If Julie were right, the guy would want a confrontation with David to settle this whole thing, once and for all. If the guy had wanted David dead, he could've just run over him with the van or shot him there in the street. There was enough confusion to cover it, and there would've been plenty of time for the man to get away. So why hit him and grab Bethany and run?

Bait. Bethany was bait, just like killing Aunt Gloria had been bait to get him to come back to Liberty. Fines wanted David to follow. Fines wanted a confrontation.

So, where was the signal? If Fines wanted him to follow, he would have left David a sign. Fines would make sure things happened exactly as he wanted. The cars started rolling, and he lifted his foot off the brake and pressed gingerly down on the gas. Pain shot up his leg like a bolt of hot lightening. The car rolled forward.

East? West? David glanced in each direction. West, toward town, he saw nothing but another EMT van racing toward the school.

To the east, in the direction of the mall, David saw a car off in the ditch. It had extensive damage—it looked like it had been pushed off the road. When he rolled into the intersection, he turned east. David passed the wrecked car in the ditch, up to its hood in brackish water. The driver's door was smashed—the car had been run off the road.

Highway 132 took him past a few subdivisions and out of town. David had to drive slowly—branches littered the road. As he passed out of town, there were more branches and deep water for David to get around and through. Near the mall, a felled tree blocked one whole lane of Highway 132.

His car sputtered, making more angry sounds and threatening to die. Why had they driven his car to the school? It was on its last legs. He gave it more gas, ignoring the pain to keep the engine turning over. Please, just get me to the mall, David thought. After that, I'll put you out of your misery.

All the speeding up and slowing down was killing his leg. Every time he pushed down on the gas, the bones in his leg ground together, wracking his entire right side with spasms of pain. Blood matted his right pant leg, sticking to his skin and the fabric of his jeans and the seat. He tried to push with the ankle instead of pushing down with the leg, but that hurt just as much.

David didn't have time to tell Julie or have a paramedic look at his leg. He'd hobbled to his car and drove off, and now nobody knew where he was. The killer was loose again and roaming the town, circling like a shark in dark waters. And David was the only one who knew. In the mass confusion at the school, no one would miss David or Bethany for several hours or bother to look for them. Even Julie had her hands full, coordinating the town's rescue efforts. She also probably assumed Fines would leave after the explosion. She had no idea it was coming down to a one-on-one confrontation.

No, it was all up to him, a kid with no weapons or training.

The pain was a roar in his head, and visions of sleep, long and quiet and restful, beckoned. It felt like a thick fog had settled around the edges of his vision, a welcoming blanket of relaxing sleep. It would feel so good to sleep right now, to pull over and stretch out on the front seat. He was so tired from the long drive back and all the talking and thinking.

All he wanted was for the pain to wash him away...

David jerked upright, cursing loudly at himself.

No, no sleep for him, not for a while. And he certainly didn't need to pass out and drive his car off into a ditch.

He cranked down the window a little and a blast of cold air and stinging rain struck him, rejuvenating him. He held a hand out the window, getting it wet, then slapped at his face with it. David couldn't pass out. Not now.

He had to at least get to the mall and see if that was where it would happen. If Fines wasn't at the mall, he'd be at the closed bridge that led to the highway. Or Fines had gone in the other direction and it was all over—David didn't think he had it in him to continue the chase across town.

David had guessed Jasper Fines would want to recreate the whole shoot-out, based on the psych profile. He would want to relive the moment. It was possible Fines could have taken Bethany back to his hotel room, assuming he was staying in a hotel, but someone might see him dragging her around. As on edge as this town was, someone might interfere.

No, Jasper would want some quiet, out-of-the-way place for them. Surely he was planning on killing them both, and with a penchant for torture and long, lingering deaths, Jasper would want his privacy.

The mall made sense, too. It was built on some of the ground Jasper had traversed on his way to gunning down Sheriff Beaumont. It was familiar territory. Fines was making this up as he went, but he would want everything to be just right. And the mall was a large enclosed space, in out of the weather.

After what seemed like an eternity of pain, David finally pulled into the Liberty Place Mall parking lot and almost passed out. As it was, after he coasted the car to a stop near one of the entrances, he used the parking brake to stop the car. It hurt too much to use the real brakes.

He laid his head back, trying to ignore the waves of pain washing through him. It had been impossible to imagine at the time, but the pain had gotten much worse since—pushing down on the gas felt like pushing an exposed wound into a bed of hot nails. The pain was huge and red and blinding, like a bubbling volcano, with lava streaking down his leg and pooling around him. Crazily, his mind reminded him of the volcano he'd made, with the lava coming out the top.

He sat up and looked at his leg. Blood soaked the pant leg all the way down his thigh and calf. This pain felt like a living thing, itching and scraping at him. He tipped his head back and screamed at the ceiling of his car. The pain didn't go away, not by any means, but it did seem to back off a bit, like a monster retreating back into the shadows of a dark closet. It was still there, though, and it would be back.

No one could help him. He had no way to contact the sheriff's department—and even if he could, they were all helping at the high school. He couldn't count on them for help, not for a while. Thinking about Bethany in trouble helped him get past his own pain. It cleared his head a little, giving him the clarity to look around and think.

The parking lot around the car was a lake. There was not a sign of life in any direction except for the hazy glow of the yellow halogen lamps as they fought to illuminate the lot even as rain fell through their pale cones of projected light. There were no cars or vans anywhere to be seen. The wind buffeted the side of his car, and he saw the empty branches of trees whipping furiously back and forth.

Where was the van?

The entrance to the mall was lit up, a hazy square of light in the darkness. It occurred to David that there might be a night watchman. It wasn't a huge mall like Potomac Mills or Springfield Mall up north in the suburbs of D.C., but it was the biggest mall in the area and needed to be guarded twenty-four hours a day. And the guard had to have a gun.

As much as he dreaded the idea, David started up the car again and tried to press down on the clutch with his left foot and quickly move it to the gas, but the Mazda shuddered and died before he could give it any gas. He would have to use both legs.

He started the car again, gingerly pushing down on the gas with his right leg, and runners of heat and fire shot up his leg. The engine caught and turned over, and he quickly popped it into first and slowly began looping around the mall's entrances, giving the engine just enough gas to keep it from dying.

David knew the mall had something like twelve entrances, all of which he'd been in a dozen times, but tonight, in the darkness and the rain and the confusion, the Liberty Place Mall looked alien, strange, and foreign. The Mazda slowly worked its way around the mall. David didn't want to shift the car into second, so the car moved with maddening slowness as he searched for the van. He prayed that Fines was here. David couldn't imagine driving back out there on 132 again. Too much shifting, too much pain.

Finally, he saw something.

Hecht's, one of the main anchor stores for the Liberty Place Mall, was located on the west end of the mall, closest to town. The large clothing and household goods store had three entrances, and one of them was covered by a wide overhang.

Parked next to the curb in front of the entrance was a white van.

David coasted to a stop behind it and looked at the double doors that led into the mall. So now what? Go inside? Walking seemed impossible. The pain from sitting and driving had been terrible, so how would it feel to walk? He had no idea, but it wasn't helping just sitting here in the car. He had to do something. He was here, and he was going to finish this, one way or another. No more quitting.

David popped open his door and climbed out.

The first hesitant steps felt like fiery brands. The broken bone above his knee screamed, and when he gingerly put any weight on the leg, it seemed to bend awkwardly just above the knee. But, amazingly, it held. The pain was like the sea washing over him, a red tide of agony. He leaned back onto his good leg and took another step, slamming his door behind him.

Each step was a concert of agony. He stumbled to the van and leaned on the back doors, trying them. Maybe there would be something useful inside. But the doors were locked.

He sucked in his breath and stumbled to the mall. With each step, he was better able to ignore the pain. David concentrated on Bethany, on her face, on where she might be. By the time he made his way under the awning by the doors, he was moving better.

Large double glass doors led into the mall. Near the doors he saw footprints: two sets, one made by a set of small shoes and the others made by a pair of heavy boots like the kind Fines had been wearing. The footprints were staggered and confusing. Although David had absolutely no experience with reading tracks, even he could tell it looked like Bethany was fighting him.

Fear welled up inside him. Fines was luring him into a trap and was going to kill him, just as surely as he had killed his father. Fines knew all the angles, had everything all figured out even as he invented the scenario. He was waiting inside somewhere, using Bethany for bait, waiting for David. But David was determined to find her. Even if it meant giving his own life up to the monster, he would get Bethany out.

For a moment, he wished he were someone else's kid. If he had grown up in a normal family with normal parents, everything would be different. But he was David Beaumont, and nothing could ever change that.

David reached up and slowly pulled the doors open. They were unlocked, and a warm blast of air greeted him as he limped inside.

He didn't turn around, so David did not see the first of the birds arrive, flapping in from the darkness of the storm to land on the concrete and on the van and on the hood of David's car. A few pecked at the windows of the van, trying to get in. Others landed on the wet concrete and on the shiny pavement outside the awning. A flash of lightning illuminated the dozens of birds as they arrived in groups. As their numbers grew, the birds nipped and squawked at each other nervously.

And waited.

———————

Hecht's and J.C. Penney, the two main anchor stores, were located on either end of the L-shaped mall. In the middle of the mall was a six-screen theater complex, the first multi-screen theater in the area. It showed the latest movies during the week and older movies and classics on Saturday mornings. Below the movie theaters was a sunken food court, the only area of the mall that had two floors. Hanging above the food court was a huge American flag to go along with the patriotic theme of the mall.

The rest of the mall was taken up by the usual assortment of shops and restaurants. The stores leaned toward the tastes and preferences of the many women who shopped there. There were women's clothing and shoe stores, each with witty names like "Gene's Jeans" or "Fun Two Go." There were greeting card stores and men's clothing stores and a drugstore, a couple of sporting goods stores, video and music stores, and book stores, each selling their particular wares and turning a profit. Almost every single lease was signed, and there were only two vacancies in the fifty-six-store mall. The builders were pleased to see that the mall was a success, both financially and as a thriving boost to the economy of Liberty and the surrounding communities.

David stepped into the Hecht's department store. The first thing he noticed was how quiet it was. When he'd visited the mall before, it would be ringing with life, the sounds of people and registers and machines and equipment running. All he could hear now was a low buzzing from the lights above, and he looked up. They were all on. Was that right? Maybe the night guard kept them on to see intruders. But all of the lights? Wouldn't it be just as good to leave a few on and save some money on electricity?

He hobbled on, the pain a constant roar in his head, like he was standing under a waterfall of pain, feeling it cascade over him. He passed a rack of umbrellas near the door and saw in among them a walking stick carved from dark wood. It was shaped like a cane with a curve at the end. He grabbed it and tried putting some of his weight on it, and it worked better than he'd hoped. The stick curled right up under his arm like a crutch, and he was able to hobble along much better. He didn't have to put as much weight on his leg, allowing the pain to back off a bit.

David started toward the main part of the mall. He was at the Hecht's entrance leading out into the mall proper when he saw the body. It was lying in a massive pool of blood, face down, and for one horrible moment he thought it was Bethany. But it was too big. It seemed to be wearing a uniform of some sort.

The man was lying face down, his arms and legs splayed out. David hobbled over to him, leaning down to roll him over. It was an older man wearing a security guard's uniform, and David could see the massive hole in his chest. Next to the body was a large "201" drawn in blood on the tile floor of the mall. So Fines was keeping count? It made sense. He was a collector, so he'd be obsessed with tracking his kills. It was a much bigger number than Julie had estimated. Did the "201" include the number of dead back at the school?

And Jasper was armed. But how had he gotten in here in the first place, and dragging Bethany, too? Or maybe he'd used her to lure the guard outside or something, or gotten him to unlock the doors...

The keys.

Fines probably wanted access to all the stores. David saw no keys on the guard's belt, and he checked both pockets, avoiding the blood as much as he could. No keys. It was safe to assume that Jasper had them. He could be hiding anywhere. But what was his plan? Would he hurt Bethany? Or had he already killed her?

No, couldn't think about that. David had to keep moving. Fines would use Bethany as bait, and that meant keeping her alive. For now.

He rolled the guard back over onto his front and saw that he had a pair of handcuffs attached to the back of his belt. They were covered with blood, but David worked them loose from the leather belt and cleaned them off on the guard's pant leg before slipping them into his pocket. He stood painfully and moved on.

The mall was lit up brightly, like every light in the place was on. Did that mean Fines had turned them on? David had no idea.

On this end of the mall, just outside the Hecht's, there was a small grassy, park-like area of water features and a fountain, spurting water up into the air and crashing down with a quiet roar.

David was no expert, but he was pretty sure the fountains should be turned off at night—it just made sense to not leave those things running. Jasper must have turned them on. But why? A distraction or something more?

David continued through the mall, stopping to look at a directory. He had no idea where the lights and fountains would be controlled from. Probably a security or maintenance room, where these controls were located. Maybe there were cameras—

Thinking about the maintenance area made him remember the basement of the high school. Had that been tonight? It seemed like weeks ago. Norma digging at the controls, her fingers bloody, trying to stop the boiler from exploding. He and Bethany had driven to the school in his dilapidated, filthy car. Julie and Norma had come separately, and once they were together, they'd talked while he nervously planned what he would say in the town meeting. David had been carrying his father's file on Jasper Fines, now lost in the gym explosion. Norma was gone now, too.

He glanced at his watch and saw that it was only 11:00 p.m.

Slowly, he made his way through the mall. He'd seen on the directory that the security office was on the J.C. Penney end, next to the bathrooms, across from the anchor store and the large fountain and gazebo at that end of the mall.

David walked around a large, potted tree. In front of him, on the tiled floor, he saw a long streak of fresh blood, scarlet against the white floor. His stomach tightened as he followed it.

It stretched from one side of the mall to the other, impossible to miss, leading to the closed entrance of a store, a woman's clothing store called 357. The lights in the store were on, but the gate was rolled down. The bars of the gate were wide enough to see through, and as David followed the trail of blood, he saw someone on the carpet just inside the gate.

It was Bethany.

She was alive, and sitting up, but bleeding from a serious wound in her stomach. One arm curled around her stomach, holding a shirt against her to slow the bleeding. It looked bad. Her other hand was handcuffed to the base of a large rack of clothes. A mannequin lay at a crazy angle next to the door, shoved out of the way, so David could see into the store better. This whole thing was being planned down to the smallest detail.

"Bethany?"

She moved, and he let out his breath, not even realizing he'd been holding it. Bethany looked up and saw him and burst into tears. For a moment he was confused, and then he realized that she was happy to see him. He grabbed the bars and reached in for her, but his arms weren't nearly long enough.

"Honey, what did he do to you?"

She moved the hand on her stomach gingerly while keeping the shirt's pressure on and laughed. David wondered if the pain was getting to her. "David, he cut me. Across the stomach. It hurts. He said that it would bleed a lot."

Her voice sounded different, higher than normal. It had a singsong quality. Pain was powerful, mind-numbing. Confusing.

"He said you would come," she continued. "He called me '202,' like I was a number. He also said that his 'numbers were off' because of the school." She shivered and let go of the bloody shirt to pull her jacket a little tighter around her. "He kept calling you by your name. Said you were following us and that he needed to talk to you. What does he mean?"

David shook his head. This was bad. She was losing a lot of blood. He looked up and grabbed the metal bars of the cage and shook them, pulling savagely up on them, but the gate would not budge.

"Bethany, what else did he say? Did he say where he was going? I need to get the keys, so I can let you out."

Bethany's head came up, and she looked at him as if noticing him for the first time. "David. You came...he said you would come." she said, and blood dribbled out of her lips. It was almost more than he could bear, seeing the woman he loved in so much pain.

"Bethany, you have to stay awake. Keep the pressure on." If she passed out, she would die attached to that metal rack of clothes, chained like a gutted animal. "Which way did Fines go?"

She smiled again, and her teeth were stained red. "His name's not Fines; it's Jack. Jack Terrington. He told me to tell you. He said it was important. And he said you two had to have a talk...what are you going to talk about?"

"We're going to get you a doctor. Which way did he go?"

She glanced in the direction of the theaters and the food court, farther down the mall. "He said you guys were going to see a movie. An action movie, with a gunfight at the end."

David simply nodded his head. He told her he loved her and turned to go, but she called him back.

"David," she said, her voice suddenly clear and strong. Her eyes were momentarily clear. "David," she continued, "it hurts. Please hurry." He felt a chill run through him. She was doing her best, but it wasn't going to be enough.

"I will," he said, and stood and hobbled away. Leaving her like that, in such pain, bleeding to death on the carpet of some stupid clothing store, was the hardest thing he'd ever done.

———————

Jack was waiting, rubbing his chest. The girl was quick and had caught him by surprise, kicking him hard right in his chest. It felt like she'd bruised a rib. All the young girls must be doing soccer from birth nowadays. It made his breathing heavy and painful, and he had angrily cut her to teach her a lesson.

It wasn't supposed to be like that. Jack was going to use her to bring the boy to him, but he'd cut her too much. She was bleeding more than he needed and he couldn't drag her along. The boy was coming

he is almost here

and so Jack had locked her in that store. Now, there was no way the boy could save her without confronting Jack.

Jack reveled in the irony of the situation. Before, Sheriff Beaumont had set a trap to end Jack's short-lived career. But that trap failed. Now, here, on some of the same ground from that night eighteen years ago, Jack was setting a trap and baiting it to catch the last Beaumont.

Jack regretted at first that the boy wasn't killed in the explosion at the school, but the more he thought about it, this was better. Take the kid on one on one. Savor it. An epic showdown, a matching of wits between a professional killer, one who'd spent his life learning and perfecting the art of taking lives, up against a kid with no experience. At first it didn't sound like a very fair fight, but Jack knew better. The Beaumonts were crafty. The girl had told Jack how David had figured out the boiler was going to blow. He'd rescued a bunch of the idiots from this town. The Beaumont boy was smart

or lucky lucky like you

and Jack knew it. If Jack were going to win this last fight, he would have to be on his toes. The kid was young and inexperienced, but he was clever, just like his father.

Maybe it was in the blood.

David limped down the mall, trying to put the bleeding vision of Bethany out of his mind. He knew she was back there, hurting, but he reminded himself that the only way to save her was to confront Jack and get the keys. He had to get her to a doctor. If that meant killing the man, so be it. David didn't think of himself as a violent person, but he would do whatever was necessary to save her.

There was a Rush song to that effect, a song he had sung along with a hundred times, singing the words without really thinking about them. The song was "Lock and Key", and it was about how we all have a demon, a monster trapped just beneath our skins. The right—or wrong—situation can unleash that Killer Instinct, letting it out to kill.

Anyone, put in the right situation, could become a killer.

For some, the instinct might be much nearer the surface than in others, but we all have it. And when pushed to a certain point, anyone, an army general or even Mother Teresa, would push back, calling upon those instincts that they kept locked up to defend themselves. Or those they loved. David felt like he'd crossed that line. Or been pushed over it, more accurately. He saw nothing except doing whatever it took to save Bethany. Killing was fine. And if David died to save her, that was fine, too.

He reached the middle of the mall and hobbled up to the railing that overlooked the food court below, leaning against it and breathing heavily. His entire leg was throbbing now, and he imagined that if he looked down at it he would be able to see it pulsating with fire and pain. He shook his head, trying to concentrate on the situation at hand.

There were a dozen food shops in the sunken area below him. The middle of the food court was taken up by scores of plastic chairs and tables arranged around a large reproduction of Independence Hall in Philadelphia. A diorama of the Continental Congress, where the Declaration of Independence had been signed, stood directly in the center of the food court, and in the top of the clock tower was a large copy of the Liberty Bell. Chimes rang on the hour, filling the food court with sound.

Off to his left, on the same floor as David, was the entrance to the Cine-Six Theaters. Above the entrance was a large marquee listing the names of the movies currently playing and their show times. Opposite this on his right were a large arcade and a music store, both closed, and in front of them were escalators that led down into the food court.

He started toward the theaters, hobbling around the balcony, and as he approached the theater he saw that one of the doors was propped open. Bethany said this is where Jack was headed, and David walked inside, cautious.

The inside of the theater's lobby was trashed. Posters were torn from the walls, the ticket stand was shoved over, spilling torn tickets all over the dark carpet, and the concession stand was ransacked. Popcorn was flung everywhere, blanketing the counter and carpet of the lobby like huge yellow flakes of snow. Cash registers and soda dispensers were shoved over, their broken pieces lying scattered. Even the back-lit pricing signs over the concession stand were smashed, and little letters stood at strange angles on the counter below.

David could hear music and voices coming from somewhere behind these walls, like the theater was open and showing movies. But why would he smash the concession stand? Why make such a mess? It was almost like he wanted David to come in here and see his handiwork, almost like a diversion...

David caught movement out of the corner of his eye and turned to look in that direction, but it was in that moment that his leg betrayed him. It was probably the sudden twisting movement. His leg buckled and collapsed, sending him crashing to the ground.

He heard what sounded like the muffled bark of a big dog from the darkened area in front of him. At the same moment, the tinkle of shattering glass from behind him. David saw movement behind the ticket stand. He rolled painfully and stood—behind him, in the framed poster of a new movie on the wall, a small, smoking hole.

Jack was shooting at him. David had never been shot at before. His first reaction was to run.

He used the wooden stick to prop himself up and limped out of the theater's lobby as quickly as he could. He hobbled away, feeling like he had a huge target on his back. He made it outside and around one corner and then stopped.

It was fine to go up against the guy and try to take him out if they were equals. But Jack had a gun and the element of surprise and David had only his stick. It would be a quick, unexciting match. David would walk in and demand the keys. Jack would shoot him. David would die. Roll credits.

No, they had to be on more even terms if David was going to make it out of this alive. And David couldn't kid himself: he wanted Jack dead. It was a comforting thought, an idea full of power. Maybe David could win. Maybe he could have a real life, a life with Bethany, a future. But if any of that were going to happen, he had to survive.

There was a sporting goods store on the other side of the theater, down in the opposite direction from where he came in. David had been in there a hundred times. Maybe Jack had gotten his gun there, or maybe he'd brought it along. Either way, if it were open, David could get a gun, too. He started toward it when he heard shouting from inside the theater.

"Hey boy! What are you doing out there? Aren't you gonna come get me?" Jack laughed, his voice loud and strong. "She'll die soon. That was a lot of blood. She'll bleed out. I know—I've seen a lot of them. I bet she's in a lot of pain. I didn't think a pretty little girl like that could bleed so much!"

David suddenly envied him. The guy wasn't injured. He had a gun or two and lots of experience doing this kind of thing, stalking and taunting and killing. It was obvious who was more prepared going into this fight.

David summoned his strength, not wanting to sound hurt. "How am I supposed to face you, Jack? You've got a gun, and me, I've got nothing but..."

Pain suddenly shot through his leg. The words trailed off in a painful gasp.

"Not doing so good, huh, kid?" Jack laughed. "You need a cast. Just like your old man! I'll tell you what. Let me kill you now, quick and painless, and I'll let the girl go. Or I could just kill you and take her with me. She is awful pretty."

David didn't want that, and he didn't want to think about it. But he knew what Jack was doing—baiting him, trying to make him madder, to get him to do something stupid.

The problem with Jack's plan is that David didn't care if he died. The pain was too much to bear—all the cared about was saving Bethany. He had to get her out, get her away from this madman. It wasn't her fault at all. This was between David and Jack—and his father, the always-present silent partner in this crazy dance of his.

"I don't think so," David shouted, standing again. "Is that what you want? You want me dead?"

"Yeah, kid. Nothing personal. Your dad was clever, and it got him killed. And now you should be dead too, blown up in that school," Jack said.

"Sorry to disappoint you," David said, working his way toward the sporting goods store.

"It's fine. I am the Angel of Death, and I have come for you. Don't you know that?"

Great. Crazy as a loon.

"Jack, why don't you just leave? Why all the killing? You beat my father, killed him. And a lot of other people. Why did you come back?"

It was quiet for a half-minute, long enough to think that maybe no answer was coming. David kept moving, sliding along the railing. David thought maybe Jack was circling around, but finally his voice emerged from the theater lobby.

"I don't know, kid. Your dad was good, and he came real close to getting me. Too close. And all these years, it's bugged me."

Julie had been right, David thought.

"Pretty soon I'm going to kill you and your girl," Jack shouted. "And then I can get on with my life."

Several sharp gunshots rang out in quick succession, shattering glass and tearing holes in the walls just outside the theater. One of them zinged off something metal inside the theater lobby and smacked into the wall next to David, punching a good-sized hole in the fiberboard.

Time to make himself scarce.

David hobbled away from the theater's entrance, off toward the other end of the mall. The bullets continued haphazardly for a few more minutes, and then they faded off. He could hear Jack talking again, but he was too far away to hear what the guy was saying. Or care, really.

David worked his way down the mall, trying to hurry. The leg was on fire. By the time he made it to the entrance of Dan's Sporting Goods Store, he was gasping in pain. David wondered how long it would be before secondary symptoms started to set in. He was feeling tired, his mouth thick and cottony. Shock would kick in next.

The sporting goods store stood open, its gate pulled up. All the lights inside were on. David saw a phone on the store's counter and hobbled over to it, leaning his stick on the wall. There was a dial tone, and he dialed the sheriff's office.

"Liberty Sheriff's Department, please hold."

"Wait, don't put me on hold. I need to report a murder." David said, hoping to get their attention.

It worked. "Hold on. Let me get my supervisor." There was a momentary silence as the phone was handed over, and then someone else came on. "Okay, sir. I'm Deputy Stewart. Are you reporting a homicide?"

"Yes," David answered. "My name is David Beaumont, and I am calling from Dan's Sporting Goods Store at Liberty Place Mall. A security guard has been killed, and a man named Jack Terrington did it. He stabbed my girlfriend, and now he's holed up inside the theater, shooting at me."

There was nothing but silence on the other end.

"Can you hear me? My name is David Beaumont. My dad used to be the sheriff."

"Look, kid, we don't have time for jokes."

"I'm not kidding," David said, angry. "You have to get some people out here!" David had a bad feeling about this. But he needed help, "backup" like they called it in the movies.

"Kid, we're very busy tonight," the deputy said. "In case you haven't heard, there was an explosion—"

"THIS is the guy that did it," David yelled. "

"We don't have time for pranks, son," the man replied. "If you don't hang up, we're going to arrest you for interfering with official—"

"Yes, that's fine," David yelled. "Damn it, come and arrest me. I'm at the mall, shooting up the place. Just send deputies to the mall. And make sure they're armed!" He slammed the phone down on the counter and left it there—he could hear voices, trying to talk to him.

He couldn't count on them—he'd have to do this himself. No one else would get here in time to save Bethany.

He looked up at the guns on the wall, hanging in racks behind the counter along with boxes of ammunition.

David knew nothing about guns, only what he'd seen in the movies and on TV, but he did know that for his situation, he needed one or two guns. Small ones that held clips of ten or twelve shots. The more the better—he had no idea if he was a good shot or not, so quantity would have to win out over quality. He also didn't want to reload.

He looked down into the gun case, which doubled as a counter, and found handguns more to his liking. There were small, snub-nosed pistols, larger revolvers, and small automatics that would accept clips in the hand grip—that was what he needed.

The sliding metal doors on the back of the counter were locked and he looked around for the keys for a moment but didn't see them. Screw it. He pulled one of the larger rifles down from the unlocked gun rack behind the counter and, using the butt, shattered the glass top of the case. Well, if there were any silent alarms in this store that hadn't already been tripped, they were going off now. Maybe the deputies would take him seriously now.

David also knew nothing about ammunition, so he inspected the gun he was holding and the box it came in until he found the markings that identified it as a 9 millimeter. He grabbed two boxes of matching cartridges off of the wall behind the counter and set them down on the next counter, the glass unbroken. He opened the box and fed the bullets into each clip, making sure they were pointing in the right direction. He found three other empty magazines designed to fit the guns and loaded those with bullets as well, then pocketed the guns, the extra magazines, and two handfuls of extra bullets. You couldn't be too careful.

It occurred to David how crazy this whole thing was. Here he was, a normal guy, loading guns with ammo, so he could go out there and face a madman down and save his girlfriend.

After he finished, David decided to do the same thing with a third gun, a smaller one that took the same ammunition. He loaded it and leaned over and rolled up the ragged pant leg of his injured leg, sticking the little gun in his bloody sock.

And he was supposed to kill a serial killer—Jack was probably getting a kick out of this, too, waiting for David to come back, so they could... wait a second. This is exactly what Jack Terrington wanted David to do, right? Jack left the gate up, knowing that David would go for a gun. Maybe that's why Jack had shot at him before at the theaters—he wasn't shooting at him; he was trying to scare him. And now David was here, getting loaded up, doing exactly what Jack wanted.

Jack wanted David to be armed. Jack wanted another gunfight. Never mind that David was hurt and Jack was a cold-blooded killer. Jack still wanted his dramatic showdown, the last ten minutes of a movie.

But what else could David do? He wasn't an action hero. If he were, he would come up with some clever solution. But all he could think about was Bethany, bleeding to death. Waiting for him to come back. The last thing she'd think about, before she died, was that he'd let her down. He'd failed her—

No. He shook his head. Jack wanted a gunfight, but David had to be unpredictable if he had any chance of winning.

He needed to mix things up, take charge of the situation? Yeah, that sounded good. But how?

David figured that Jack was coming for him by now. David had taken too long, and Jack didn't seem like a patient man. He would show up and say something cute. David would come out and they'd both draw and David would die.

He glanced out the front of the store but saw nothing. How long would Jack wait before he came for David? Not long , but maybe long enough.

He grabbed two boxes of ammunition under one arm, then grabbed his walking stick and moved painfully down the first aisle of merchandise, searching for inspiration.

———————

Where the hell was that kid? Jack was growing impatient. The kid had gone off in the direction of the gun store but still hadn't returned. That was the beauty of Jack's plan—the kid would feel the power of a gun or two

gunfight

in his hands and come for Jack in a futile attempt to get the keys and free his girl. It wasn't like the kid would walk away, not with his girl dying back there. He was trapped.

Jack was still in the lobby of the theater, expecting the kid to be back at any moment. He wanted to draw the kid into one of the theaters and shoot it out there. Before the kid had gotten here, Jack had gone up to each of the projection rooms and started the movies, remembering how to work the projector from that summer he'd worked in a theater. He started four different movies. By the time these movies were finished running, it would all be over. The whole thing would be confusing for the kid, with overlapping dialogue and sounds. Throw the kid off and maybe make him screw up

he's not that smart he's just a kid

or something cool like that. And wasn't that the way epics were supposed to end, anyway? With a really cool scene at the end where the two powers face off?

But the kid hadn't returned and Jack grew tired of waiting. The girl was dying—what was the kid waiting for?

Finally, Jack made his way across the lobby and out of the theater, looking for the kid. There was a slim chance he was trying to get one up on him, waiting for him to come out. But no one was there. Jack shook his head and, trying to ignore the pain in his ribs, started down the mall in the direction of the gun store.

David found a few things he could use and a backpack to carry them in. When he was done, he moved out of the gun store, watching. He didn't see Jack yet, and he needed to get farther down the mall toward J.C. Penney if his rudimentary plan were going to work.

Using his new, lightweight metal walking pole, he hurried to the closest trash receptacle and lifted the top off. It was metal and half-filled with trash. David tossed seven or eight small cardboard boxes from the backpack into the small pile of trash. They fell with solid thunks. He pulled a long piece of string out and laid it over the edge of the trash can, leaving half of it dangling outside the can. He zipped up his backpack and pulled a lighter from his pocket and lit the fuse. The string caught and slowly began burning as he replaced the lid, leaving it at an angle and limping quickly away.

There were another fifteen or twenty stores on either side of the mall past the gun store before the mall widened out into a large plaza, signifying this end of the mall. The entrance to J.C. Penney took up the entire western wall. The rest of the space was taken up by a wide, park-like grassy area surrounding a tall fountain.

More stores angled out from both sides of J.C. Penney, circling the fountain that cascaded water down over a large pile of multicolored stones, creating the effect of an indoor waterfall. The water sprayed up into the air and ran down the faces of the large stones, collecting at the bottom. From there the water ran down a stream and a short series of rapids for about twenty or thirty yards before emptying into a large collection pond a good distance from the waterfall.

On either side of the stream and the rapids, a grassy area was designed to look like an outdoor park, with fake grass, a number of bushes, and several trees. One tree was large enough to scrape the expansive glass ceiling forty feet above the water.

Near the waterfall, a white gazebo stood on one of the flat areas next to the wide stream, and the brook made for a romantic setting, or at least as romantic as one could find inside a mall. David had even heard of one or two couples getting married here, cheesy as it sounded. He might not know a lot about what was romantic or not, but getting married in a mall didn't sound like something you would want to tell your grandkids about.

Near where David stood, the stream dropped into the shallow collection pond, where pumps recirculated the water back up to the waterfall. The pond at this end, farthest away from J.C. Penney, was about twelve or fifteen feet across and maybe two feet deep. The bottom was covered with dark stones, making it appear much deeper than it really was. Plants and shrubs surrounded the pond and water lilies and other aquatic plants dotted the surface with green.

Around the walls, couches and chairs were arranged in small seating areas for tired shoppers. And above it all, the expansive glass ceiling was crossed with metal struts painted dark green. Through the roof, he could see the rain blowing in sheets against the glass. The storm still raged outside, but in here it was quiet, and for a moment, peaceful. After a moment, David hobbled up onto the grass and followed the short trail of flat stones to the gazebo. He had work to do.

―――――――――

The sporting goods store was empty.

Jack checked each aisle slowly, expecting to find the kid cowering in a hole or maybe concealed inside one of the tents they had set up in there, waiting to take a potshot at him. Jack found nothing. The kid wasn't in here or back toward the theater, which meant he had gone further—

Gunshots clattered out in the mall, firing off in quick succession, a deafening hail of bullets. Jack dove behind a stack of boxes to get out of the way of the gunfire. The metal popping continued—a lot of bullets, more than Jack would've expected. Jack peered out from behind the boxes but didn't see the kid. Sounded like he had loaded at least four guns and was firing them all now, trying to catch him on a ricochet.

"Hey, David! What are you going to do, shoot me!?"

Maybe the kid was hoping to pin him in the store and make him surrender the keys. But that wasn't going to happen.

Jack pulled revolvers from his coat. He had three, the old one from the Liberty Sheriff's Department and two newer models, a total of eighteen shots without reloading. He could've picked up a smaller automatic that carried more rounds and would be lighter and faster, but he was used to these guns. He liked the way they felt in his hands. They had traveled with him, crossing a hundred rivers and a thousand counties, his ever-faithful companions.

They would see him through.

He yelled again, taunting the kid, but there was no answer. Jack edged out from behind the stack of boxes, expecting more gunfire. And he was right: more gunshots, another long burst of them. Jack dove back behind his cover, feeling the ribs in his chest hurt as he landed on his stomach. He answered the bullets with a few of his own, hoping to maybe catch the kid gawking.

this is stupid it's taking too long

Jack waited another few minutes, calling to the kid and baiting him while he reloaded. Finally, Jack slipped toward the front of the store, peeking around the boxes and displayed merchandise, half expecting to see the kid come down one of the aisles, looking for him.

Instead, he saw a pall of smoke rising up from one of the trashcans out in the mall. A wispy layer of smoke covered the whole area, and as Jack stood and carefully walked toward it, he saw several dozen holes in the sides of the metal trashcan. The floor and the benches and planters around the trashcan were pitted and fragmented, and there was one big ragged hole in the plastic bench next to the trashcan.

He tipped the lid off and peered down inside, finally understanding. It had been a small fire

that is funny he got you good with that one

with several boxes of ammo thrown in. This kid was smart. Or maybe had just seen a lot of TV.

Some small part of Jack's mind suddenly wondered if this whole thing was such a good idea. He had come back to this little town to face his ghosts, to face the memory of a ghost

better than you smarter than you

And not get killed by a lucky shot. The kid was presenting Jack with several interesting problems. Chief among them was how to kill him quickly and painfully, while still making the whole thing interesting.

But it was good to see that the kid had a little spunk left in him, even with that broken leg. Jack had been worried that he would just roll over and die. Jack kept walking, heading off toward J.C. Penney.

David stood up from his painting in the gazebo. He heard the gunshots from back by the gun store. Jack was coming, he was sure. David was surprised the fuse had taken so long to burn.

He bent over painfully and finished up, standing back to look at his work. It would have to do. The coat was propped up and ready. David grabbed the backpack and his walking pole and worked his way down the steps and over to get behind the largest tree to wait.

Hopefully the maniac wouldn't notice the long wire cord stretching across the concourse. It ended at the large water collection pond below the rapids. The far end of the wire was plugged into an electrical outlet. When David had thrown the bare ends of the wire into the pond, he was amazed to see the bluish-white sheet of electricity skitter across the surface. He'd wondered if it would work or just short out the system, but the blue haze remained, and he could smell the odor of ozone burning.

As David checked his guns again, he saw movement down the mall, past another group of trees and bushes and the big collection pond. He ducked back behind the largest tree and waited, peeking carefully around the trunk, his guns ready. Part of him felt like Rambo, but the rest of him wanted to run. Run and hide.

Jack came out, wary, slowly crossing the concourse and edging along the store fronts, trying not to expose too much of himself. He had two guns out, one in each hand, and he looked ready for action. But David had picked a good spot and had a good view of Jack's approach.

Outside, the rain continued to fall heavily on the glass ceiling above.

Jack rounded the tree-lined pond and spotted the gazebo. To David, it didn't look like he'd been down to this end of the mall yet. Jack was looking around at everything cautiously, carefully. That might give David a much-needed advantage—he'd been here a hundred times.

Jack crept up to where he had a good view of the gazebo and spotted what he was looking for. He pointed his gun. Two quick THUMPS coughed out of the gun, and David saw the heavy winter coat he had propped up in the gazebo shred in two places and fall over, making almost no sound.

That wouldn't fool anyone.

But Jack was curious. He slowly approached the gazebo. He had to cross the little stream to get to it, and as he put his guns out to each side to balance as he crossed on the little rocks in the middle of the stream, David opened fire. The sound was impossibly loud, much louder than David had expected, and the guns bucked in his hands.

Surprised, Jack slipped on the wet rocks and fell. David didn't know if the man had been hit or surprised or was just trying to hide; David was far more concerned with the guns in his hands. He aimed and fired with each, alternating, and by the time he'd fired four or five times with each, he was better able to judge the recoil and aim. The first few shots had bucked the guns in his hands and gone almost straight up in the air, shattering some of the large panes of the glass ceiling.

David aimed and fired six or eight shots from each in the direction of the gazebo and the stream's rock crossing. He was too far away to really worry about hitting his mark—he was just trying to shake Jack up. And he desperately needed practice.

When his guns were empty, David dropped down behind the tree and started to pull the magazines from the butt of each gun to reload. The gun barrels were very hot, and he yelped from surprise when he grabbed the first one, burning himself. It was the same hand where he'd burned his palm on the hot pipes of the high school boiler. Now, it looked like the skin was going to scar.

It only took him a couple of seconds to reload, something that he had guessed would take much longer. He felt incredibly vulnerable as he reloaded, but he didn't dare take his eyes off the guns until he was finished. He only had one chance and he had to do this right.

It was raining inside the mall now. While David was reloading, several large panes of glass screeched and fell in, crashing to the grass below. Sheets of heavy and cold rain followed.

The fierce wind raging outside tugged and pulled at the metal fasteners and strips that held the remaining glass panels, tearing at the other panes of glass. Some panels moved, pieces of them breaking away, as the wind lifted them up and away into the dark storm. The hole in the glass roof grew, and rain rushed down on the grass and on the waterfall and on the gazebo, sluicing off its wooden roof and pattering to the grass below, running through the grass and swelling the fake stream into a real one.

With the rain, a smattering of birds flapped into the mall, probably to escape the torrent outside. David glanced at the birds as he reloaded and saw that several of them landed on the gazebo. Others flitted off into the rest of the mall.

When he was done reloading, David looked around. In the time it had taken David to reload, Jack had climbed out of the stream. Jack had easily guessed which direction the bullets had come from and backed away from David. Jack circled around to the gazebo and climbed up inside it, getting out of the rain, and was starting to stomp his wet boots on the wooden floor of the gazebo when he stopped.

Now he was just standing there, staring at the floor between his boots.

———

Jack was looking down at his resume.

A thousand questions raced through his mind as his eyes tried to grasp the enormity of what he was looking at. But how could anyone know any of this, least of all this kid? How could anyone have figured all of it out? Jack had been so careful. He had been so quiet and cunning, always sure to move on before it got too dangerous. Even if someone had figured some of it out, how did this kid know?

But it was all there. Right at his feet, painted in black and white and red.

On the white-washed wooden floor of the gazebo, the kid had painted a rough outline of the United States. And the interior of the painting was dotted with dozens, scores of small red dots of paint. The outline had been done in black paint, but the red dots were more carefully placed, with meticulous accurateness.

It was all there, and it was almost too much for Jack to believe.

There were six red dots in what had to be Liberty, Virginia, plus a big splotch of paint, probably to represent the conflagration at the school.

There was a smattering of other dots up and down the Eastern Seaboard. Philly, Boston, up to Maine. More dots scattered across the plain states. Chicago, St. Louis, Denver. A thick knot of the blood-colored dots in the Seattle Area, a tight grouping of fifty or sixty. More sprinkled down the coast to San Francisco.

Los Angeles was a constellation of red pinpricks, another dozen or so dots packed tightly together in southern California.

Phoenix. Austin. Florida. Scattered all over the rest of the crudely drawn map were a few dozen more dots, seemingly sprinkled randomly.

But Jack knew better—he remembered them all. He remembered the little blonde girl in Minneapolis.

she had cried the whole time

He remembered the twins just north of Albuquerque.

remember how they had each begged him to let the other go each willing to die to spare the other

He remembered the years in Seattle when the cops and the FBI had chased the Green River Killer until Jack had grown tired of the whole game and walked away. He remembered training his helpers and that the men kept it going after Jack left, following in his footsteps.

Jack remembered the happy years in Los Angeles, when he did whatever he wanted and nobody cared. He had taken and taken until it felt, for a short time anyway, that he would never need to kill again.

He remembered the little boy here in Liberty.

dropped the kid in that lonely muddy field

raining raining inside the mall

He remembered the mother in Casper, Wyoming, who had pleaded with him to just kill her and let the little kid go.

you made her watch while the boy died and then you killed her too

Jack stood in the small white gazebo, the rain falling around him, and remembered them all. They were all here, a grisly family reunion. And he had thought they were the only ones who knew. He'd kept them in his van even after he'd left the rest of them behind.

But now this map was a glaring reminder of his past. No, not a reminder of his past. It was his entire past, laid out naked on the floor of this gazebo.

there is just no way for this kid to know everything

Forcing himself to turn away from the map, he roughly grabbed the thick coat he'd shot. Jack tossed it out of the gazebo, but not before his eyes caught something—the stream he'd fallen into had turned a red.

A horrendous color of blackish red. His eyes tracked up the stream to the waterfall, and it looked like a huge cauldron of blood, spewing up

a fountain of blood

into the air and crashing to the rocks below.

It was crazy.

It looked like when you cut someone's carotid artery, and the blood sprayed eagerly into the open air. The fountain pumped blood into the air

a volcano of blood

where it hung for a moment, glittering in the lights like scarlet diamonds before crashing back down to join the clear rain falling from the sky. A river of blood, spewing out of this fountain and washing down past the gazebo and into the pond.

blood blood a whole river of it

Jack staggered down the steps of the gazebo and over to the water, his mind temporarily not in control of his legs. A river of blood, the life force he'd spent a lifetime spilling. It all made sense somehow—the map, the river. It was like this really was the end. He would be free of everything that had come before, and he could start again. Coming back here had been a good idea.

He was thinking about dipping his hand in the river of blood and never saw the boy step from behind the tree.

The shot caught Jack from behind in the shoulder, spinning him around and knocking him down.

David was only twenty feet away, propped on the metal walking stick, both guns out. He was behind a tree, but it didn't matter—the guy was out of it, confused by the crude map David had painted on the floor of the gazebo. Confused by the leftover paint David had dumped into the fountain.

David knew how sick this guy was. Learning about it had sickened him, all the blood and mutilated bodies and missing parts. It was horrific, but now he was glad he'd studied all the maps and files. He'd always been excellent with maps, something related to his interest in drafting and architecture, so remembering the spots on the map was easy. And they weren't really that accurate—close enough to shock, close enough to throw the guy off. That was the distraction David had needed.

More birds flew into the mall, escaping the storm. The roof of the gazebo was nearly covered with birds. Dozens, scores more were flapping around loudly inside the mall, squawking and cawing.

The bullet had caught Jack from behind, high in the shoulder, and even at that distance it was like a hard punch, spinning him around and knocking him down. He was near the stream, about ten feet from where the stream emptied over a small waterfall, downhill from the gazebo. He rolled into the stream, face up, half of his body submerged in the water.

David wasn't sure what to do next.

The guy was down, but he wasn't dead. Shoot him again?

Could he just walk up and shoot the guy?

He thought so. If it meant saving Bethany. She was back there on the floor of that clothing store, her body surrounded by a dark, spreading pool of her own blood.

And this guy, this Jack Terrington—sounded like a made-up name to David—had killed his father and his aunt and a lot of other people. Dozens, maybe hundreds. He didn't deserve to live.

No, he wouldn't have a problem with killing the guy. Jack had pushed David over his line. David just wanted his old life back. Nothing more, nothing less.

The rain fell heavily around David as he hobbled up to the edge of the stream and pointed one of the guns at the man's face.

Jack looked up at him and smiled.

"I hid the keys, kid. Somewhere in the mall," he said. Water and blood bubbled from his mouth. "You kill me, and you'll never find them in time to save her."

This hadn't been part of the plan. He had expected the guy to fake getting hurt, but he could see the man's blood welling out of his shoulder and joining the stream of crimson already in the water. Couldn't fake that. But hiding the keys—was he just trying to buy some more time?

"You think you're pretty clever, don't you," Jack shouted at David to be heard over the roaring wind of the storm above and the birds squawking around them. Jack propped himself up on one arm. "But you gotta tell me, how'd you know about all of that? Nobody could know all of that," Jack asked, nodding at the gazebo.

David glanced away for a moment, but that was all it took. As soon as his eyes were off of Jack, the man's hand came up out of the water, pointed the revolver at the boy, and pulled the trigger.

Jack shot David in his broken leg.

David collapsed to the ground, screaming.

It was as if his injuries before had been nothing—the leg screamed and burned as if were dipped in lava. David heard someone screaming and realized it was him. He rolled to the side and tried to get a handle on the pain, but it was just too much. It was like a hurricane whipping around him, the screaming pain keening in his ears. He couldn't think, he couldn't see, all he could do was hear the roaring in his mind.

In a moment the pain went from bad to worse. Jack stood over him and a second bullet tore into his leg, shredding most of the bone above his knee. The pain washed over David again like a tidal wave of jagged edges. His leg was like a separate entity now, an appendage made solely of burning fire, yet still attached to him.

Some part of his mind began to shut down. Another noticed calmly that his leg rested on the bloody grass at a crazy angle, an angle the bones were never designed to make. A fog surrounded his mind, but he pushed back, trying to stay present. He ignored the waves of pain running through him and concentrated on the rain falling onto his face. The rain falling on him. And he thought about the birds in the mall, fighting for any flat surface, flitting around inside the mall.

The water was cold. After a moment, the pain retreated to a different part of him. He didn't understand, but he welcomed it. He propped one elbow underneath him, then the other, shoving himself painfully into a sitting position. Some other part of his mind was in control now. He saw the rain and the birds on the gazebo and the man before him and the volcano of blood—it was all so clear. The pain had somehow trapped behind a hastily erected mental wall. David thought he could keep his mind clear, if only for a few more moments.

Jack couldn't believe it.

He'd shot the kid twice, both in his broken leg. The more pain
washing over him like the ocean
the better. He should have passed out by now. But now the kid was sitting up, rising up from his prone position like a ghost. Jack saw that the kid's pain had gone away.

"What are you doing, kid?"
he's not hurting why isn't he hurting
As Jack raised the gun and pointed it at the boy's face to finish the job, he cursed under his breath. This kid was tough. Jack had wanted to draw this out a little longer, make it more interesting, but the kid was starting to annoy him. Faking Jack out with that map
all those people he had killed all that spilt blood all those trophies
had been smart. Jack glanced at the gazebo and saw several birds standing on the scrawled map of the country, picking at the wet paint. One of them scratched at the map and, when the bird's beak came up,

Jack saw that the tip of it was red with paint.

David cleared his throat, spitting blood and rainwater from his mouth. "Before you shoot me. Ask. Ask your question."

The kid was sitting up now, a hand touching his right leg gingerly, pressing, trying to slow the blood that pumped from the two ragged holes high on the thigh.

A part of Jack's mind offered that if the boy didn't get that bleeding stopped soon, he might die. Another part of Jack's mind told the first part to shut up, you idiot, of course he's going to die. He's going to die from a bullet to the brain in about four seconds.

question what question

But how had the kid known about all the murders over the years? Was that the question? Jack didn't think that was what the kid meant. It seemed bigger than that, more important.

was there something here that he was missing

Behind the kid, Jack saw a group of dark birds flit in front of the volcano, the fountain of blood splashing down into the river behind them. More birds gathered on the grass near the gazebo. Another bird splashed into the red river.

He lowered the gun just a little.

"What question do you want me to ask you?" Jack asked impatiently. Time was running out. "I don't know what you're talking about." Jack waited for an answer, but nothing came. The kid was just stalling. Jack raised the gun, his finger on the trigger.

David laughed. It sounded so strange.

"All these years," David asked, smiling. "All these years. You don't want your answer?"

Both of the boy's hands were on his right leg now, one by the knee and one lower. It looked like he was trying to turn the leg around to the correct angle—now, it was just flopped over on its side. The boy pushed up on the knee, rolling the leg over to match the vertical position of the other leg, and the right foot now pointed straight up. That had to hurt, but the kid didn't even seem to notice—he was just staring at Jack and blinking the rain out of his eyes.

"What?" Now Jack was frustrated.

the kid is stalling can't you see that

David leaned forward, and one hand touched his bloody pant leg at the ankle.

"I thought all of this killing was for a reason. All those years, crossing the country and killing people. Torturing them, taking parts of them with you. And never getting caught. Was it all for a reason?"

Jack didn't know.

"Were you just wandering around, looking for meaning? Weren't you looking for something? Searching...for the answer to some important question?"

The boy leaned forward a little more and his hands stopped moving. He was looking up at Jack and, impossibly, the kid was smiling.

"Don't you wonder if I hated my father as much as you did?" the boy asked. "You came all the way back here because you hated him so much. Don't you want to know if I hated him, too? He abandoned me, right?"

Jack nodded, the gun
i hated him so much
in his hand dipping again. Yeah, he had always been looking for some meaning in what he did—he had covered the entire country trying to find his place, to find out why he did what he did. But Jack was past all that—he understood that he was simply here to weed out the weakest. He was the Angel of Death. Jack was a gardener, pruning, making mankind stronger and better.

A bird darted between them, then flitted away.

As for wondering if the kid had hated his father as much as Jack did? Well, that question was about to be moot.

"Actually, I loved the guy." David said, smiling. "Though I never met him. Thanks to you."

The kid's pant leg wrinkled up a little as his hand moved on it
that is strange
and as Jack lifted the gun to shoot the kid in the face and end all of this stupid talking, the kid's pant leg seemed to explode outward, the fabric shredding instantly.

In the same moment, something hard smacked Jack squarely in the middle of his chest, something wet and heavy. His breathing became almost impossible. His chest felt weird, light, and at the same time his arms felt like thick blocks of lead, too heavy to lift. The gun felt like it weighed a ton, and he let it go, the gun dropping away and falling to the wet ground between his boots.

this is wrong this is wrong
Jack looked down and could see his heart.

There was a gaping hole in his chest, and the leather jacket and the shirt he had been wearing were gone and now there was just this blackened hole in the middle of his chest. He saw the points of some of his ribs, and he could see the glistening muscle of his heart, fist-sized and dark, as it pumped away.

blood my blood my blood my blood
Blood ran out of the hole in him. He lifted his concrete arms and used

both hands to try and hold himself in. There were things he recognized, parts of him that he had seen in so many other people.

Jack stumbled backward, away from the kid. There was so much blood. All he wanted to do was to try and back away from the pain. It hurt so much.

Finally, for the first time, Jack understood what real pain felt like.

David shouted as Jack backed away.

"My father was a hero."

His words barely registered with Jack, but some part of his mind heard them and hated them. Beaumont had been a chump—he had beaten the old man. But Jack had no time to think about ancient history—he was too busy backing away, trying to hold himself in. There was so much of him trying to get out, so many things that he never wanted to see—

One of his rattlesnake-skin boots caught the edge of the concrete retaining wall surrounding the pond. Jack tipped over backward, a victim of his own momentum, falling into the lake of blood-colored water.

Smoke and steam erupted from the surface of the water. The lights in the mall flickered from a surge of power. From where David was laying, still trying to work the gun out of his sock, he could see sparks and flashes of light. Electricity from the wire sparked over the surface of the pond and the man who had fallen into the water.

The barrel of the small gun he'd tucked into his sock burned against the inside of his calf. He finally worked the gun free and lay back on the soft, wet grass. In a moment, the world swam around him and David passed out.

Something landed on his chest.

David came to. He realized there was something on him, some small thing walking around on his chest. David came out of a hazy fog, blinking his eyes. The rain fell on and around him, the storm still raging above. He blinked the water away and looked down at his chest.

There was a bird on him.

It was on his chest. There was almost no weight to the bird, but David could feel it anyway, moving around and looking at him, one eye and then the other. Its feet and claws felt strange.

David sat up slowly, painfully. The bird hopped off him, down onto the muddy grass, turning to look at him. It looked like the same black bird from the mountain turnout, but he couldn't tell for sure—birds all looked the same to him. But this one seemed to be favoring one leg, just like the bird up in the Shenandoahs had done.

But it couldn't be the same bird—that was impossible.

David looked slowly around. He was surrounded by birds.

They covered the roof of the gazebo and sat perched on the mall benches and trash receptacles. The grass and trees were covered, and he saw more coming in through the hole in the ceiling, coming in with the falling rain. Outside, the storm raged. They came in groups and floated down to settle on the grass and the trees and the tiled floor of the mall.

David sat up, and at that the birds quieted. Scores of them, two hundred, maybe three hundred—he couldn't tell. They littered the ground around him, all keeping a distance except for the black bird that had hopped about five feet away and stopped.

Now, it was staring at him, watching him.

He smelled something horrible, like something left cooking on the stove too long. He hadn't noticed it because of the birds. David struggled to sit up, then painfully removed his belt. The leg was still oozing. He ignored the birds and tied it tight around the top of his thigh. David hoped it would slow the bleeding. He took off his jacket and wrapped it around his thigh, his jacket quickly turning a bright burgundy color.

Finally, he tried moving, crawling painfully toward the steaming collection pool. On the grass around him, the birds quietly parted to make a path to let him through. A few nipped at him. He struggled across the muddy grass, pushing and pulling and dragging his leg.

When he finally got to the pool, he pulled himself up and peeked over the edge, careful not to touch the water. Jack Terrington was there, floating on the steaming surface. The water looked like a lake of blood. The red water moved around him. Smoke came off the man, stinking of overcooked meat. He looked dead.

David crawled over to the electrical wire, pulling it out of the water. He yanked hard on it to pull the plug at the other end from the outlet, which sparked and caught fire as he yanked the cord loose. In moments, a small river of flames was running up the wall toward the ceiling, racing up one of the patriotic banners that decorated the wall.

David didn't care. Right now, he was only worried about one thing— retrieving the body. He needed the keys, praying that Jack had lied and kept them on him.

David leaned on the edge of the collection pond, the birds already there making a wide hole for him. He looped the wire into a crude circle and painfully threw it. On the fourth try, he caught one of Jack's upturned boots and pulled, tugging the body over the edge of the pool. David wondered what was drawing the birds here. What did they want?

He got a hand on Jack and pulled him to the edge.

The body was still warm. David expected the man to come alive at any moment. If this were a movie, Jack would sit up and grab David and laugh and pull him into the brackish bloody water with him, drowning them both.

But the body just floated there, moving gently on the surface. And the keys were in Jack's pocket. To the end, the man was a liar. When David pulled them out, he exhaled a deep breath that he hadn't even realized he had been holding. If the keys hadn't been there, or if Jack had really hidden them like he said, Bethany was dead. It would still be a miracle if he could still save her in the condition he was in.

As David dug in the man's pocket, something else pricked his finger. A sheriff's star. On the front of it David could read, in very faded letters, the words "Liberty Sheriff's Department."

His father's star.

David remembered Norma crying as she had told that part of the story. She was dead now, just like his father. As the rain fell heavy through the broken ceiling onto David and the collection pond and the flock of birds, he looked down at the rusty old star, feeling the dulled edges and running his finger along the words. David turned and looked at the body, floating on the steaming red water, and pushed it away, sending it floating back into the middle of the water.

David pinned the rusty, precious star to the front of his own shirt and smiled.

He glanced up at the birds. They were perched on the metal strips and the broken angles of glass ceiling above the collection pond, ignoring the wind that raged outside. There were gulls and crows and ravens and sparrows, robins and blackbirds and pigeons. A large vulture flapped in from outside and settled near the fountain. The top of the gazebo was full of black birds, and more pecked at the wet grass around the stream. The map of Jack's travels inside the gazebo was covered by the dark shape of a murder of crows.

Quickly the sound of them grew to a shrieking symphony. The ragged hole above was lined with them, all manner of winged creatures. They jockeyed for position on the edge of the collection pond, nipping at each other. Their shrieking grew so loud that it matched and finally surpassed the howling of the storm outside.

He had no idea what was happening. Birds didn't congregate with different species, did they? He didn't know. The sound was deafening, scratching and squawking and cawing, and along with the wind and the rain falling around him, David started to wonder if this whole thing were some kind of crazy dream.

David crawled across the smooth tile of the mall floor— he'd tried to use the metal walking stick, but his leg was just too far gone. It could not hold any weight any more—the bones were jelly. He couldn't stand, much less hobble along with a crutch. He dragged the leg behind him, leaving a long streak of blood on the white tile.

The fire from the outlet was spreading now, catching other banners and licking at the ceiling. One banner fell into a seating area, setting fire to a couch. He thought the rain would put the fire out, but maybe the whole mall would burn. He needed to hurry.

David glanced back at the birds, but he didn't have time to be curious—he had to get to Bethany. It was creepy, the way they had all stood around quietly, looking at him. They seemed to be waiting for something, maybe for him to leave. Were they just trying to get out of the hurricane, or was there more to it than that?

But what did the birds want?

He crawled his way along the stores, turning the corner and leaving the birds and Jack behind. He was thinking about Bethany. He moved as quickly as he could, exhausted and hurting, fueled only by willpower. Finally, David saw the gun store. He struggled inside, remembering they had first aid kits. Maybe he could find a tourniquet.

Around the steaming collection pond, the birds settled, watching. They stood quietly where they could find space. With unblinking, coal-black eyes, the gathered flock stared at the floating body in the middle of the brackish, scarlet water.

When the boy was gone, one black bird stepped off the roof of the gazebo and flapped toward the body.

The other birds grew quiet.

They watched with small eyes as the black bird circled once, twice, and then carefully landed on the shiny metal tip of one upturned rattlesnake-skin boot. The bird's head bobbed back and forth as it regarded the floating man, looking at the legs and the outstretched arms and the gaping hole in the man's chest. The bird cawed quietly and hopped gingerly up the leg and onto the chest. The bird appeared to be lame, favoring one leg. Looking into the hole, the black bird chirped loudly and hopped up onto the man's shoulder.

The black bird glanced at the other birds and then turned to the man's face, regarding it with one eye and then the other, its head bobbing back and forth. A long moment passed, and suddenly there came loud, impatient cries from the other birds. They cried at the black bird, cawing loudly as the rain fell around them.

The black bird hopped gingerly up onto the man's cheek, issuing a loud, angry shriek. It looked back and forth, back and forth, then leaned over, plucking out one of the man's eyes.

The other birds squawked and cawed and shrieked their approval. A horrible cacophony sounded, an avian chorus of mournful and joyous cries, each distinct and yet all coming together in a haunting symphony. A score of other birds jumped into the air, eager to join the feast. Eager to collect their own piece of this carrion.

Above and around them, the sound of so many birds in the enclosed space was deafening. Their cries carried up into the night sky, out of the broken ceiling, and joined the fierce howling of the storm.

David was out of the sporting goods store, doing slightly better. He had wrapped his leg with a real bandage and swallowed a handful of aspirin and the deputies were on the way. He'd called, told them he was hurt very badly and that he had just killed someone and that part of the mall was on fire. He'd not given his name. David didn't know which part had worked, but the dispatcher took it seriously and said deputies and a paramedic were on the way.

He pushed himself along with both hands, his bottom and legs straddling the skateboard he'd found. He probably looked like an idiot, but David made his way quickly down the mall, rounding the railing by the theaters and reaching the clothes store in a matter of minutes.

He looked in and called to her, but she wasn't moving. She was on her side, and it looked like the bleeding had stopped. She had lost an awful lot, obvious from the pool around her and bloody shirt tucked against her belly. David called to her, shouting, but there was no response.

He fumbled with the keys, but there were so many. Each store had a key, plus there were keys to all of the maintenance rooms and the security office and the doors to the outside.

He tried to calm his mind. David studied the lock, finding the name of the company who had made it, narrowing down the number of possible keys. The fifth key from that company he tried slid into the lock with a satisfying 'click,' and he turned the key and pulled the padlock off. He grabbed onto the chain curtain and pulled up, unlatching it from the floor and sending it up into the recessed ceiling.

He dropped the keys and fell off the skateboard and moved over to her, ignoring the blood around her. He took her face into his hands, and shouted at her for a response, but nothing came. He tried to feel at her neck for a pulse, but his heart was beating so fast, he couldn't tell if the frantic pulsing was his or hers.

David shook her gingerly, trying to get a response, but there was nothing. He started to cry. It wasn't something he even noticed, but the tears were suddenly there, and he looked down at her face and leaned over and kissed her. Her lips felt cool and lifeless. He began to pull away when he felt the flutter of her eyelashes against his cheek. Her eyes were blinking, trying to focus on him. He felt her hands move weakly beside him.

"David," she said, her voice almost too quiet to hear. "You came back. I didn't think you would..." She looked up at him. In the distance, he heard the sounds of sirens and breaking glass.

"Of course I came back," he said to her, his tears gone. "I'm not going anywhere."

EPILOGUE:

AFTERMATH

EPILOGUE

David Beaumont nervously straightened his tie, watching the door.

He was in his best suit. Actually, it was his only suit, new and stiff. And the tie didn't look right—he'd tied it three times before it had looked halfway decent.

He had to consciously keep his hands from working through his hair to flatten it and make it look better—there was so much gel in it, his hair felt like a helmet.

He saw the waiter and flagged him over.

"I'm going to run to the restroom. If she comes in, just seat her, okay?"

The waiter nodded, smiling.

David got up carefully and walked slowly to the restroom, his hands straightening the front lapels of his jacket. The limp was still there, but it was getting better. The scar on his palm was there as well, clearly visible. The doctors said both the limp and the scar would be permanent.

He finished in the bathroom and washed his hands, careful not to splash any water on his pants—nothing looked worse than water spots on your pants. He checked his hair and his tie and washed his face again, wondering if she'd arrived. He headed back to his table, his hand nervously toying with the small black box in his pocket.

David walked back over to his little table for two and sat down. She wasn't here yet. He wanted to eat some of the fresh bread the waiter had brought, but the table looked so nice he didn't want to mess it up. And he didn't want to get any crumbs on him.

He was waiting for Bethany in one of the nicer restaurants in Liberty. It had opened in the months after the explosion at the high school. Some people who had come to town to help with the cleanup efforts had relished the small-town atmosphere of Liberty and decided to stay, opening this quiet French restaurant. So far, it had been very successful.

David was nervous, trying to think of other things besides this dinner and what he was going to say. He'd worked out the words, but he didn't want to come off sounding canned. He tried not to think about it—he needed a distraction.

The explosion and fire at the school, and the subsequent fire at the mall, had been the biggest events to happen in this town in a long time—well, for eighteen years. Just as the fire trucks returned from extinguishing the high school fire, they were called to the mall. More than a third of the mall burned before they managed to put it out.

The group of mall developers, the same men that Abe Foreman used to have dinner with every Tuesday night, decided to rebuild that portion of the mall and, because of the unique opportunity, actually expand it. New spaces for more stores were added, and the theaters expanded from six screens to twelve. Construction was nearly complete, and, with summer approaching rapidly, the developers were racing to fill all of the stores with occupants and businesses. The mall would end up being almost twice as large as it had been.

David glanced at the door, waiting. David had arranged for a limo to pick her up at Big Video and More after her shift and drive her and two of her friends around town. First, they were going to a hair salon that also did manicures and facials, and then to one of the nice dress shops in downtown Liberty. He'd left instructions—and his credit card—with the owner to catch Bethany as soon as she came in and set her up with a beautiful dress and accessories.

David had asked the owner to steer Bethany toward something formal, something in black.

He looked at his watch—it was 8:15. He'd asked the lady at the dress store to get Bethany out of there and back into the limo by 8:00. Bethany should be on her way—

No, not going to get nervous.

He thought about some of the people he'd met last fall. David missed Norma, regretting that he hadn't gotten a chance to talk to her more. She'd died saving those children. The new sheriff posthumously awarded her a medal and plaque, bringing the little kids she saved up onto the stage and letting them thank her.

David and most of the town had attended the memorial service, held at the school two weeks after the explosion. He hadn't seen a dry eye in the library—the only other place in town besides the destroyed gym where they could get this many people together at once—when the smallest boy had quietly thanked Norma Jenkins for saving him and his brothers.

FBI Special Agent Julie Noble, her back still in a brace from her fall, had gotten up and spoken a few nice words about Norma, relating stories from the one and only day she had known her. After that, David had gotten up and made a few more comments. The audience had applauded when he stood and hobbled to the podium, his right leg encased in a huge cast that made him feel like he was lugging around a tree trunk.

The memorial service was his idea, and after what happened last fall, people seemed to be listening to him a lot more.

Agent Noble also related how Norma and David and Bethany had assisted in her investigation. There were a few referential comments on the ex-Sheriff Brown, but Julie did not ponder on him. Most of the town wouldn't even speak his name any more, as hated as he was. He was blamed for ignoring too many clues and facts, blamed for too many deaths. Aside from Jack Terrington, of course, Brown would probably go down as the most hated man in this town's history.

Jack Terrington—now there was a name David would like to forget. Julie and the rest of the FBI were still poring through the mountain of evidence recovered from the inside of his van. That story had been the talk of the nation for almost a whole week last fall. The name "Van of Death" was coined and instantly stuck. The FBI removed the van to their compound in Quantico, Virginia, and were still culling information and clues from its contents. So far, over one hundred outstanding homicide cases nationwide had been solved based on information collected from inside the van. It seemed like more cases were being solved every day. All across the country, there were stories of closure for families who had lived with the knowledge that their loved ones' murders were unsolved. The FBI had made a point of personally visiting each family when the identity of the victim was conclusively determined from the evidence collected from inside the van. It turned out that Jack's penchant for saving parts of his victims had, in a way, helped give the victims' families closure and peace.

Jack Terrington surely would've hated that idea.

Agent Noble received a commendation for her efforts in the Green River Killer case, as it was now known nationwide. She was still working the case, wrapping up more unsolved murders, and would soon lead a team of computer experts to use the bureau's sophisticated computer systems to track down more criminals.

Hurricane Mandy went down in the record books as one of the strongest hurricanes to make landfall in a long time. There was a lot of damage up and down the East Coast, but thankfully not many lives were lost. It sounded like the experts were busy adjusting their prediction programs for the next season. They didn't want to be surprised again.

David glanced at his watch again. He took out the box and checked it. He opened it and made sure the ring was centered and facing up. It looked nice. He'd recruited a couple of Bethany's friends to help him pick it out, swearing them to secrecy. He knew nothing about engagement rings, but Bethany's friends had loved it, making weird noises when the salesman mentioned the price. David had bought it without hesitation.

He clapped the box shut and put it away, checking his watch again.

———————

The waiter stood near the front door, watching the limo as it pulled up. When it stopped, he saw the chauffeur hop out and open the door for a very pretty brunette. Bethany King was wearing a lovely burgundy dress and carrying a matching bag. Two other young women waved and smile from the limo but didn't get out.

Everyone in town knew the story. Everyone knew what happened last fall. The story of David Beaumont and Jack Terrington and the others had reached mythic proportions.

First came the explosion at the school, with David and his friends trying to save as many people as possible before it exploded, killing the mayor and the sheriff and most of the city council. The explosion and fire at the school had made a profound impact on the town, and many locals had lost family members. But the people of Liberty were recovering. New people were moving in, and with them came renewed energy and raised spirits.

What happened at the mall was also legend, with the girlfriend kidnapped and used as bait. David driving with a broken leg, the epic gunfight with the storm raging outside, the map of murders on the floor of the gazebo. The electrocution and death of the Killer—it all sounded too crazy to be believed. It made for a great story, and most of it had been printed in a series of full-page stories in *USA Today* in December. They even managed to get most of the facts straight. There were full-color pictures of the mall and the school and of David and the killer and even one of David's long-dead father.

The waiter had heard that the boy would always have a limp, but he seemed to be walking just fine tonight. David was healing, and Bethany had surgery and recovered. The waiter even heard that, with the city council nearly wiped out at the school, David was considering running for city council. People seemed in favor of the idea, agreeing that Liberty needed some fresh blood running things.

The waiter was happy for David and Bethany. They had gone through enough. And now, it looked like they might have a happy ending to the tragic tale, and the waiter might have a small role to play in the story, too.

The brunette smiled at the chauffeur, waved at her friends, and headed inside. The waiter stepped around the greeter's stand to hold the door open for her.

"Good evening, Miss King."

She smiled at his usage of her name, and her eyes looked like they were on fire. "Hi." She nervously straightened the front of her dress. He motioned to her. "Please follow me."

———

David was glancing at his watch again and didn't see her come in. He heard murmuring and looked up to see what the commotion was about. The other diners in the restaurant were turning to look at something.

She was wearing a beautiful burgundy gown that fell all the way to the floor. She looked lovely, and the restaurant patrons commented and talked amongst themselves. They all recognized her.

Bethany seemed embarrassed by the commotion, and as soon as she saw David she hurried over to his table. David stood and pulled the chair out for her as she approached, but she leaned in and kissed him on the cheek before thanking him and sitting down.

"You look beautiful," he said, sitting down.

She smiled and set her purse on the table. "They were very nice to me at Victoria's. The girls loved all the attention. And at the dress store, the owner herself came out and helped me try on things. They let me have my pick. Thank you for that. And the limo was awesome, too. What's this all about?"

David smiled too. "Well, I thought you deserved a new dress and a nice dinner. Why, did you have other plans?"

She laughed and smacked his hand. "No, I didn't have plans. Nice suit, by the way."

He was nervous, but not as nervous as he'd expected to be. The waiter came with water and took their drink order. "Thanks. Actually, I wanted to ask you something."

Bethany shifted a little in her chair, facing him.

He swallowed.

"Well," he said, toying with the box in his jacket pocket. "I have been thinking a lot about things lately. I mean, I think you and I make a good team, and a great couple. And with the way things are going, and you and I being so happy, I think that we should...I was thinking that we might..."

He glanced up at her and she was grinning.

"What?" he asked, a little sheepishly.

Bethany took his hand in hers.

"You never ramble like this unless you're nervous," she said. "And your face is so red you might burst. Just slow down and ask me your question."

He nodded, taking a sip of water to compose himself.

"Okay. Bethany, I love you," he said. "I've loved you for so long that I can't remember a time when I didn't love you. And after all the craziness from last fall, I don't want to lose you. Ever."

He stood and took the box out of his pocket, handing it to her. She took it as he moved the chair out of the way. As she opened the box, he gingerly knelt down next to her, being careful with the leg. She was looking at the ring, and when she looked down at him, her eyes sparkling with joy.

David Beaumont smiled at her. Suddenly, he wasn't nervous at all. In fact, he felt perfectly calm.

"Bethany, will you marry me?"

Slowly, she smiled.

"Yes, David. Yes."

ABOUT THE AUTHOR

Greg Enslen has published seven mysteries and thrillers, including the Amazon bestsellers "A Field of Red" and "The Ghost of Blackwood Lane." His four-book "Frank Harper Mysteries" series has received critical acclaim. He also writes original screenplays and has published twenty other titles, including in-depth binge guides for popular TV shows such as "Game of Thrones" and "Mr. Robot." His books are available from major retailers and on his **Amazon Author Page** at http://bit.ly/geauthor.

Greg lives in southern Ohio with his wife, three children, five dogs and an indeterminate number of cats. His interests include travel, reading, film and television, and yelling at various sports franchises. Greg enjoys writing late at night, after everyone else has finally trudged off to bed and the house is quiet. For more information, visit his website at **gregenslen.com** or check out his **Facebook fan page** at http://www.facebook.com/gregenslenswriting.

BOOKS BY GREG ENSLEN

Greg has written and published twenty-six books. Most titles available from Amazon, other major book retailers, and on Kindle:

Frank Harper Mysteries
A Field of Red
Black Ice
White Lines
Yellow Jacket
Welcome to Cooper's Mill (free companion guide, available exclusively at gregenslen.com)

Fiction
Black Bird
The Ghost of Blackwood Lane
The 9/11 Machine

Guide Series
A Field Guide to Facebook
"A Viewer's Guide to Suits," Season 1
"A Viewer's Guide to Suits," Season 2
"A Viewer's Guide to Suits," Season 3
"Game of Thrones: A Binge Guide" for Season 1
"Game of Thrones: A Binge Guide" for Season 2
"Game of Thrones: A Binge Guide" for Season 3
"Game of Thrones: A Binge Guide" for Season 4
"Game of Thrones: A Binge Guide" for Season 5
"Game of Thrones: A Binge Guide" for Season 6
"Game of Thrones: A Binge Guide" for Season 7
"Mr. Robot: A Binge Guide" for Season 1
"Mr. Robot: A Binge Guide" for Season 2
"Mr. Robot: A Binge Guide" for Season 3

Newspaper Column Collections
"Tipp Talk" 2010 Newspaper Column Collection
"Tipp Talk" 2011 Newspaper Column Collection
"Tipp Talk" 2012 Newspaper Column Collection
"Tipp Talk" 2013 Newspaper Column Collection

CAN I ASK A FAVOR?

Thank you for reading this book—I hope you enjoyed it! If you did, I'd really appreciate it if you could take a few minutes to post a short review on Amazon. Reviews of this book on Amazon, Goodreads, or Facebook help new readers find out about my books.

To leave an Amazon review, use the following link: **http://bit.ly/geauthor**. Select the book you'd like to review, scroll down to the "Customer Reviews" area, and then click on the button that reads "Write a customer review." And feel free to be honest in your review—I love feedback, good or bad, and the total number of Amazon reviews affects how Amazon lists book titles. Every review helps increase the "social buzz" of the book, and I truly appreciate it.

While you're at it, you might want to join my newsletter, where I highlight upcoming title releases, discounts, beta opportunities and appearances. You can sign up at **www.gregenslen.com/newsletter**. My monthly newsletter isn't spammy, and I promise not to sell or share your information. Thank you for your support!

— Greg Enslen

www.ingramcontent.com/pod-product-compliance
Lightning Source LLC
Chambersburg PA
CBHW020509260626
47156CB00006B/1936